THE DRESSMAKER'S SECRET

Lorna Cook is the author of the Kindle #1 bestseller *The Forgotten Village*. It was her debut novel and the recipient of the Romantic Novelists' Association Joan Hessayon Award for New Writers as well a the winner of the Katie Fforde Debut Romantic Novel of the Year Award. Lorna lives in coastal South East England with her husband, daughters and a Staffy named Socks.

The Dressmaker's Secret

LORNA COOK

Published by AVON
A division of HarperCollins*Publishers*
1 London Bridge Street
London SE1 9GF

www.harpercollins.co.uk

HarperCollins*Publishers*
1st Floor, Watermarque Building, Ringsend Road
Dublin 4, Ireland

A Paperback Original 2022
1

First published in Great Britain by HarperCollins*Publishers* 2022

A catalogue copy of this book is available from the British Library.

ISBN: 978-0-00-837909-4

This novel is entirely a work of fiction. The names, characters
and incidents portrayed in it are the work of the author's imagination.
Any resemblance to actual persons, living or dead, events or
localities is entirely coincidental.

Typeset in Sabon by Palimpsest Book Production Limited,
Falkirk, Stirlingshire
Printed and bound in the UK using 100% Renewable Electricity
at CPI Group (UK) Ltd

MIX
Paper from
responsible sources
FSC™ C007454

This book is produced from independently certified FSC™
paper to ensure responsible forest management.

For more information visit: www.harpercollins.co.uk/green

For Natalie:
Godmother, organiser of fun, high priestess
of generosity and Champagne, best friend for life.

Prologue

The Ritz, Paris, 1944

The Resistance fighters pulled her from her rooms, ordering her into the street. She went screaming, begging them to leave her alone. 'I haven't done anything wrong.' But it was no use. The ornate suite of rooms with its soft carpets, Chinese screens and high ceilings had once represented sanctuary. But over the last few weeks the hotel had been her prison as she kept herself hidden from the outside world. After weeks of fighting, the Resistance had won and she'd known they would come for her.

What awaited her now didn't bear thinking about. She'd seen it with her own eyes, the head shaving that awaited *les collaborateurs horizontales* – horizontal collaborators. A name brandished against women who'd remained in France, done whatever they'd had to in order to survive – but never the men. Oh no. Never the men who'd collaborated willingly with the army, never the men who'd been complicit with the new regime, traded black market goods with the invading enemy. Never them.

It was women like her who were paying the price for a romance that shouldn't have been. For a friendly pair of arms, a safety net, in that long mountain fall towards despair and loneliness. Yes, the women were the ones subject to the pent-up aggression of a nation brought to its knees and now desperate to recover, desperate to punish. Parisians – sickened by the suffering they had felt, the Resistance they had been a part of, the arrests by the Gestapo they'd been subjected to, the deportations to concentration camps their friends and family had endured, the executions of fellow Resistance fighters outside the city as the gunshots of firing squads rang through the air.

This was the moment they had been waiting for, the payoff.

Now she was being arrested. Now it was her turn.

After all these years, when she had so very nearly got away with it, she was being arrested for everything she'd done in the war.

And everything she hadn't.

There was only one real choice to make. She would go with them.

And then she would deny everything.

Chapter 1

The Ritz Paris Auction, Paris, 2018

'We start the bidding at . . .'

The floor-to-ceiling white screen behind the auctioneer lit up, showing the conversion from euros to pounds, dollars and a host of other currencies the moment a new sum was announced.

The auctioneer's hammer fell repeatedly down as lot after lot sold for astronomical sums, revealing the wealth of the few hundred people buying up pieces of furniture from the long-awaited Ritz Paris hotel auction.

Hundreds of thousands of euros were being exchanged for antique beds once slept in by Maria Callas and bar stools once sat on by Ernest Hemingway. Even the first bathtub installed in the opulent hotel was being sold. It made for quite a collection of items, which was exactly why Chloé was here: the eclectic history, the old-fashioned glamour being stripped from the hotel piece by piece and held up for the admiration of buyers from around the world.

'The next item is the sign from Bar Hemingway. Lot number 2905.'

The lure of the opulence surrounding the items was too

good even for Chloé's boho sensibilities to ignore. When else would she find herself in Paris at exactly the same time as an auction such as this? The broadsheet newspapers had been reporting on the sale for weeks, giving snippets of information about items that were going under the hammer and how much they were expected to fetch. From what Chloé could see so far the newspapers had been wrong, as bids far exceeded asking prices.

Chloé followed along with the fast proceedings, her mind whirring as the numbers of euros escalated. Around her – seated, watching eagerly – were people from a variety of walks of life. Middle-aged women elegantly dressed, elderly men in brightly coloured suits, and young men and women in skinny jeans and tees were caught up in the rush and excitement of it all, just like her. She'd hankered after something small, something trinket-sized because it would have been a historic item to treasure forever; something with a story attached. But even more than that, something purchased today would have been the perfect gift for her grandmother, back in England: a reminder of Paris, a reminder of her youth.

While Chloé didn't know too much about how her grandmother Adèle had lived during the war, she did know that she had once lived in the opulence of the Ritz, during some of the darkest days of the war. When some of the glitter of the hotel had faded just a little, thanks to the Germans and their need to conquer Europe. And that was – Chloé knew – putting it mildly.

Maybe she could afford something such as a pen or a tablecloth? Chloé flicked through the catalogue as she sat in the ornate auction room off the Champs-Élysées in vain hope that something small and trifling might be available to purchase. But even sets of soft monogrammed towels, robes and slippers in the signature Ritz rose pink were expected to fetch in excess of five hundred euros. Compared to everything else in the catalogue, that was cheap.

She was glad she hadn't told her grandmother she was coming to the auction. Chloé had intended to surprise her with a small but meaningful keepsake but had to acknowledge anything that looked desirable was going for far too much money, even for Chloé. And she knew her grandmother would only chastise her if she bought something outlandish. Her grandmother was downsizing to a warden-controlled flat; she could hardly present her with an antique dressing table. No, it was clearly meant to be. She was only supposed to be an observer, not a participant. It was the story of her life. That and her belief in fate.

Holding a lot of faith in fate had never really paid off but nonetheless Chloé had persevered with this concept throughout much of her adult life. *It was meant to be*, had been her stock phrase. Until recently. But now she was only a few months away from forty and surely by now the idea that *it was meant to be* should have rung true. But so far nothing about Chloé's life was as it was meant to have been.

What was the life that Chloé actually wanted? She'd always harboured a dream of living in Paris which, with her extensive CV and her French language skills, would have been the most obvious option. And so, twenty-one years after she'd originally intended, Chloé decided to do something different. She was going to do something more fitting with the concept of a gap year, a dust-herself-down year. She'd accepted the low-pressure offer to work in her friend's vintage boutique for the summer in Paris.

It really did feel like the very thing she needed in her life, a summer of easy calm, compared to what she'd just been through, while surrounded by vintage clothes; earning money, eating delicious French food and drinking good wine, possibly learning to cook. Perhaps not all of these things were in line with what the eighteen-year-old version of herself had expected from a gap year, but the late-thirties Chloé had new standards, new dreams and that was how it was going to be, because she was meant to be here. Just as her grandmother had been surrounded by these items in her youth, Chloé was meant to pause among things her grandmother would have touched as she walked to the suite of rooms she inhabited during the occupation.

Maybe the chair being auctioned right now was something Adèle actually had in her room, along with that gold carriage clock or one of those bedside tables positioned along the wall, waiting to be lifted onto the stage to be shown off under the glare of the auction house spotlight. She watched with interest as the asking prices escalated – buyers raised paddles a fraction in the air to indicate financial interest in the item before it finally sold. This was a different kind of wealth to what she'd been used to with her ex husband, Rob. This wealth was fast and furious.

But it didn't matter because Chloé was out of that now. She couldn't look back to a relationship that had never been right. She could only look forward. As if to punctuate this, she sat up straight suddenly, shifting in her chair and garnering the attention of a man at the far end of the row. Her sudden move forced him to lean forward, glancing past the two people sat in between them and in her direction. The auctioneer, now busy selling a Louis-the-Sixteenth-style dog bed, acknowledged the man and his accidental move of his paddle, which stilled both Chloé and the man who'd just given her such a curious stare. She watched his eyes, sudden shock registering over his face that he'd broken the first rule of auctions: don't attract the auctioneer's attention unless you actually want to buy something. He sat back, ever so slowly and Chloé smothered a smile as he purposefully turned statue-like.

And then the auction moved on to what Chloé had been most interested in, items from the Coco Chanel suite – not only because Chanel was the grande dame of Parisian fashion but because back in the war the Chanel suite was where her grandmother had lived, as lady's maid to the indomitable woman herself.

The excitement was palpable. Around her, people fidgeted in their seats, sat up straighter as if intending to bid. The sale of items from the Chanel suite was what she had come to see and it was clearly what others had come to see too. She wasn't going to bid, but she sat up, inching forward in her chair.

'Originally decorated by the designer herself . . .' the auctioneer started, cutting through Chloé's thoughts.

As the bidding got underway, ardent Chanel fans were buying and preparing to scatter the collection around the world to their various homes.

'Ladies and gentlemen, we draw your attention to lot number 3221, the Louis-the-Fifteenth-style chair and desk from the Coco Chanel suite.'

Chloé looked towards the contrasting dark wood desk and pale chair.

It surprised Chloé that although it was opulent, the furniture being sold was soulless and she watched gilded item after item go for swathes of euros before it occurred to her that it was a good job this was all too lavish to sit in a warden-controlled flat in Richmond because her grandmother might not actually have wanted *anything* from the suite, after all. That perhaps a reminder of where she had lived during the Occupation, some of Paris's darkest days, might not be quite the suitable gift for a ninety-seven-year-old woman.

Perhaps Chloé was overthinking it but she was pulled from her reverie as the bidding hit outrageous figures. The numbers on the screen climbed higher and higher. Bids arrived by telephone – auction staff raised their hands to agree to the amounts, paddles in the audience raised in quick succession. Chloé couldn't keep up with the numbers being agreed to until the figure reached a climactic $223,860.

'That's three hundred times its estimate,' the woman next to her said in wide-eyed amusement. Shocked laughs and a hurricane of applause rang throughout the room and Chloé couldn't help but join in. 'The lure of Chanel,' she mused to the woman next to her who nodded in agreement.

The lots moved on and the bids increased rapidly for a pair of Louis-the-Fifteenth-style Chesterfield chairs in green fabric. Seeing it all, she realised these items probably meant nothing to her grandmother after all this time, even if she had lived among the opulence. And strangely, there was something consoling about that, something that told her it was OK to stand up when a few others did, intent on leaving at the pause in proceedings as the next lots were announced and the auction of Chanel's items came to an end.

She went out into the foyer where the auction house had created a series of 'rooms', taking pieces of furniture and staging them to resemble the various near-infamous hotel suites. She stood by the Windsor suite, named after the abdicated King Edward VIII and Wallis Simpson who'd been regular visitors before the war, and took in its grand duck egg blue and gold opulence; very eighteenth century, very French.

Beside her, a male voice said in French, 'Did you bid on anything?'

Chloé looked at the early forty-something dark-haired man who was dressed in a beautiful deep blue suit complete with red pocket square. He was elegant, the epitome of Parisian effortlessness. But there was something about the faint hint of stubble on his face that indicated he'd shaved late last night and then hadn't bothered again this morning. There was an air of elegant yet faintly dishevelled handsomeness.

'No,' she said, taking him in. 'Far too expensive for me. Did you?'

'*Non*, but in a rare lapse of concentration I almost found

myself the proud owner of a dog bed that the Duke of Windsor's dog may once have slept in.'

She stifled a laugh, and adopted a serious look. 'It was a very beautiful bed for a dog.'

'It should be for two thousand and six hundred euros.'

'Good God, is that what it went for?'

He laughed to himself, looked at the staged room in front of them. 'Beautiful furnishings,' he said.

'Yes, lovely,' Chloé said while thinking they were actually a bit gaudy. She could see why the Ritz had since undergone a refurbishment.

They moved on naturally to the next 'room' – the staged Chanel suite. The auction staff were moving around, returning a few items that had just been displayed in the auction room and would remain displayed here until the close of day. Would her grandmother have once touched any of the items in here? The lacquered cabinets, heavy draped blush-pink curtains, gold clocks and Chinese rugs did nothing for her and she certainly wasn't missing the opportunity to bid for something on the off-chance her grandmother had once touched it or might recognise it. The items felt more as if they belonged in a museum than in real life.

And besides, what was her grandmother really to Chanel? Just the hired help. Chloé may have glamorised the story to friends over the years as she'd grown more interested in fashion, 'Oh yes, my gran worked for Coco Chanel; she even lived with her during the war,' but the reality of her day-to-day existence was probably more mundane than Chloé wished to believe.

She realised the man was looking at her as she debated this.

'You don't like the Chanel suite?' he asked. 'Surely the room the famous Chanel waved her magic wand across is the most exciting one of the entire collection?'

Chloé laughed at his clipped attempt at humour. 'I thought it would be. But actually, I think I'm a little disappointed. I'm not sure what I was expecting. It's very nice but very OTT.'

'OTT?' he queried.

'Over the top.'

'It's the Ritz,' he said by way of explanation.

'I just can't envisage my granny living like this. The way she lived through her life, I mean . . . she lived well but this is just not her.'

He stared at her. 'Chanel was your grandmother?'

'No no, my grandmother lived with Chanel. During the war.'

He narrowed his eyes. 'In the Ritz?'

'Yes,' Chloé said. 'Obviously not in the suite itself. Well, I'm guessing not but I don't really have a clue. Some people are funny when talking about the war and my gran is one of those people. But working for her, she'd have seen these things, touched these things and I just . . . wanted to see them for myself. Especially laid out like this, just as my gran would have seen the room when she worked for Chanel.'

He looked at her curiously and Chloé felt the need to ramble on. 'I thought it might help me to understand her in some way; understand a time of her life I don't know anything about, bring me a bit closer to her. But . . . I'm not really sure it has.'

'But has it made you feel more distant from her?' he asked.

'No,' Chloé replied thoughtfully. 'No, not that.'

'Then no real damage has been done,' he said.

She smiled. 'That's true.'

'I'm Etienne, by the way,' he said.

'Chloé,' she said and shook his outstretched hand.

People were emerging from the auction room during a lull in proceedings.

'I think they have stopped for a break,' Etienne said. 'Are you going back in afterwards?'

'No. I think I've seen enough. Are you?'

He looked around thoughtfully and shook his head. 'I have been here all day. I could use a good coffee.'

'Coffee sounds good,' she said without thinking. And then she realised she'd implied she should go with him.

'I know a very good café with outside seats,' he said after a beat. 'It would be a shame not to take advantage of the sunshine. Would you . . . like to accompany me?'

This wasn't what she'd intended at all. Chloé looked at her watch, stalling for time. Should she go? Should she be this spontaneous? Surely that's what this time in Paris was for? New things; living differently, spontaneously. She had dinner with a friend who lived in the city to look forward to but that wasn't until much later. Until then she had time to kill and coffee wasn't a bad idea. Neither was the idea of making a new friend.

They walked side by side, talking about the weather, which Etienne said was a distinctly British way for her to have started a discussion.

'It was you who mentioned the sunshine first,' Chloé protested.

'This is true.' He laughed. 'So . . . tell me how did your grandmother come to live in the Ritz with Coco Chanel. Was she French or English like you?'

'French,' she said as they moved only a little way down the wide Champs-Élysées, bustling with people, cars and red sightseeing buses; and coffee shops with tourists spilling into the street. Then through a carefully chosen side street, where the roads grew narrow, the trees giving welcome shade against the bright sun and a small patch of grass offering something in the way of a park.

'But in all honesty,' Chloé continued, 'I'm not completely sure how she ended up there. It was a very strange time,

11

and the way my mum explained it, some people just don't feel comfortable talking about the war. My gran is one of those people, which is a shame really because . . . she's ninety-seven and that generation aren't going to be around much longer.'

Etienne nodded in sympathy. 'Stories will inevitably be lost.' They emerged to find a modern-looking outside coffee bar with low black and white tables and chairs. It was frequented not by tourists but by well-heeled Parisians enjoying five minutes out from the office.

'But,' Chloé continued, 'some stories don't want to be told and I'm surmising that it was too painful a time for my gran to speak about now. England wasn't occupied by the Nazis so the stories I'm used to hearing in snippets of British history – such as what happened in the Blitz – won't reflect what my grandmother went through, here in Paris under Nazi rule. It would be completely different.'

Chloé sat down and waited for her new acquaintance to say something. But he didn't for a while. He seemed so at ease with himself as he sat opposite her. He pulled sunglasses from his inside jacket pocket and put them on. Chloé hadn't brought hers and she felt at a disadvantage. His eyes were shielded and he was able to see completely into hers. He appeared to be looking at her, appraising her, and as she ordered a café au lait from the young waiter she doubted her French accent even more when Etienne ordered the same in much neater French than she possessed. The waiter responded to him differently, more fluidly and Chloé understood that no matter how fluently you spoke a language, the natives always knew you weren't one of them.

'You are right, of course,' he said eventually. 'What your grandmother went through in Paris, would be incredibly different compared to what happened in, say, London during the war. But what your grandmother went through would

12

also probably be very different to what ordinary Parisians went through.'

'What do you mean?'

'She lived in finery in the Ritz, with Chanel *non*? I don't think too many people lived through the Occupation in such a way.'

'Do you mean . . . it couldn't have been that bad?' Chloé asked. She wasn't sure if she was annoyed or not by his suggestion. She had no idea how her gran lived, not enough to defend a position. And Chloé wasn't sure she actually had a position to defend, yet.

'What do you know about Coco Chanel?' Etienne asked.

'A fair amount, I think. I studied her at college, in part. I found her quite intriguing, especially because of the connection to my gran. I know she had lots of lovers but never married. I know she and her sister were orphaned and that Chanel ended up living in an orphanage and I remember reading something about her affair with the Duke of . . . damn, I've forgotten.'

'Westminster,' Etienne said.

'That's it. Westminster. There's a rumour that all the lampposts in Westminster have interlocking C's on them in tribute to Chanel and it was because he had them put there. Although actually it's meant to stand for City Council, which is a bit more boring, I suppose.'

'I didn't know that,' Etienne said. 'I must look next time I'm in London.'

Chloé continued. 'I know she lived at the Ritz during the war even though she had an apartment across the road above her boutique. And I know that my gran was her sort of lady's maid, I guess you would call it. But my gran would never really talk about Chanel or the war years much so I only really know what I studied in brief about Chanel's early life and her rise to greatness. I must admit I haven't taken it much further than that. Life gets in the way, I suppose. Why?' Chloé prompted. 'What do you know?'

'You see,' Etienne inched forward. 'I am completely different to you. I know very little about her early life and quite a lot about her life in the war. I know that a few years of Chanel's life were almost . . .' he paused and then seemed to opt for almost clipped sentences '. . . white-washed from French history. There was nothing about this period of her life in the history books, until very recently. It benefited her and France to forget. And little by little details have emerged of her life during the war. Files have been released. And what she did slowly emerges.'

'Files? What she did?' Chloé asked. 'I didn't think she *did* anything during the war. I didn't think French women enduring the Occupation could *do* anything much.'

Etienne shrugged as their coffee arrived and a car went past hooting its horn at a tourist not looking in the right direction as they crossed the road.

'You seem quite interested in her,' Chloé pointed out when the noise of the car had died down. 'Why?'

He nodded. 'I am. For so many reasons.'

She narrowed her eyes to avoid the glare of the sun.

'This auction made me curious,' he continued quickly. 'I came to . . . see.'

'See what?'

He leant back. 'Everything. In Chanel's suite there used to be a great artwork on the wall. Nobody knew how long it had been there, but most importantly no one knew where it came from.'

Chloé waited for him to continue.

'When the Ritz closed in 2012 to stocktake ready for auction and refurbishment, hanging in Coco Chanel's suite was the most magnificent picture. A lost masterpiece, by Charles Le Brun from 1647. Colourful, vibrant, dubbed *The Sacrifice of Polyxena* but its provenance was unknown. I wanted to see the suite laid out at the auction. To many it was theatre but to me I just needed . . . to see.'

14

He looked as if he was grasping for something deep in the recesses of his mind but couldn't quite get there. Chloé waited as he fetched the sentence he'd been trying to say. 'I just wanted to get a feel for the room and the woman who had once been in possession of the Charles Le Brun. Does that make sense?'

'Yes. A bit like how I wanted to see it to feel the connection to my gran.'

'Yes,' he agreed. 'Sort of. I think. There has been . . . speculation about where lost art from the war actually went. Some destroyed; some lost.'

'By lost you mean . . . stolen?' Chloé clarified.

Etienne shrugged. 'Not always. But mostly. No one can prove where the Charles Le Brun came from but it took my interest over to a side of the war that is only recently coming to be spoken about in real detail. People who were once good citizens had made free with other people's belongings.'

'Other people's belongings?' Chloé asked.

But Etienne's reply was simply a nod of the head.

'Where is it now?' Chloé asked. 'This Charles Le Brun. Is it being auctioned here?'

'Non,' Etienne said, finishing his coffee. 'It was recognised as a great master, removed immediately from proceedings and now hangs in the Metropolitan Museum of Art in New York. I saw it when I was last in New York. It's stunning, vivid. But I wanted to see the room where it had hung for all those years and I could never afford to sleep in the suite itself, so I came today. In my opinion it didn't really work with the rest of the furnishings she had curated so meticulously. An odd choice, which I feel reinforces my point.'

'And so you think Chanel once had a piece of *stolen* art in her suite?'

'I think someone stole it and gifted it to her. Or maybe

she bought it when she shouldn't have, not caring enough to discover where it came from. There was a lot of that . . . stolen art, looted art. Looted from prominent Jewish families. Not just art. But antiques, furniture, their entire homes in some cases. Have you seen the Rothschild mansion in the Bois de Boulogne?'

Chloé shook her head.

'Not many people have or even know it's there. Stolen from the family during the war. It still stands, covered in graffiti, completely obliterated internally. Not even the Rothschilds wanted it back in the end.'

Chloé's mouth fell open but she didn't speak.

Etienne continued. 'Maybe Coco Chanel took the Charles Le Brun as blood money. Maybe not. After all, it never appeared on any inventory of purchases as part of any decoration that the Ritz carried out. And yet, the colours are so bright, so vivid and the picture is a strange choice for a woman whose rooms were decorated so ornately in the Chinese style.'

'Perhaps she hung on to it, thinking it might be worth something one day,' Chloé suggested.

Etienne agreed. 'And at the end of the war when people started looking closely at those who were tied in with the Nazis . . . perhaps that was not the time to move a painting, perhaps it was best to just walk away, leave it behind, pretend it had nothing to do with her.'

The waiter brought the bill and Etienne beat Chloé to leaving a fistful of coins on the silver tray.

'Thank you,' she said as he paid.

'My pleasure.'

'You think Chanel was tied in with the Nazis?' Chloé asked. 'Not quite as squeaky clean as my grandmother made out then.'

'That is an interesting way to put it,' he said. 'Your grandmother said Chanel was . . .' he paused and then repeated her words with a smile '. . . squeaky clean?'

'Well I—' Chloé thought. Actually, her grandmother had never said what Chanel had been like as an employer or as a person. She had only ever given Chloé the barest of facts. That Chanel was already famous, rich, living very well in the Ritz, that she herself had lived alongside her, worked with her, that Chanel had employed her because she said she saw a lot of herself in her and that if it hadn't been for Coco Chanel, Chloé's poverty-stricken grandmother would probably have been living on the streets. But as a person . . . these facts had implied Chanel had been benevolent and kind. But Chloé's grandmother had never actually said this. And as for what happened during the war, Chloé was forced to admit she didn't know.

'The concept of Chanel being entirely innocent during the war, surprises me,' Etienne said. 'She was a collaborator and I mean that in the truest sense of the word.' He delivered this line so without preamble that it took Chloé a few seconds to acknowledge what he'd said.

Slowly she raised both eyebrows in surprise. 'What?'

He gave her a knowing look.

'She was a collaborator?' Chloé queried, wondering why her grandmother would have spent her days in such close proximity to someone like that. Perhaps the truth of it wasn't as bad as Etienne was making out. 'How much of a collaborator?' she asked.

Etienne looked at her. 'In the Second World War, Coco Chanel was a Nazi agent.'

Chapter 2

Chloé's mouth fell open and Etienne shrugged at her reaction. 'Clearly, this isn't as common a fact as I imagined it was.'

Chloé found her voice. 'She can't have been. My grandmother wouldn't have worked for her if she'd been a Nazi agent.'

Etienne stayed diplomatically quiet.

Chloé's mind whirred. Would her grandmother have worked for her if she'd known this? Silently she sipped her coffee, allowing her mind to run through what she knew about her grandmother. She was a good woman, a kind woman. No anti-Semitic tendencies – of that Chloé was sure. She had only sympathy for oppressed people. She donated money to charity when she saw the plight of starving children in India and had been especially fond of a charity that gave sanitary products to teenage girls in Third World nations. She'd cried when she'd seen the advert shown on TV. She wasn't racist. Not even close. She wouldn't have been a Nazi sympathiser. She would have resisted, surely?

'Why do you know all this? How do you know Chanel was a Nazi?' Chloé asked, leaning forward. 'I need proof.'

Etienne removed his sunglasses, scanned the table and

cleaned his shades with the napkin that accompanied his coffee. It was a strangely disorganised gesture for a man who looked so put together. 'I have researched because there are elements of my own family history linked to Chanel. And so because there are elements of yours linked to her . . . so should you,' he suggested casually. 'It is an indisputable fact that she was a Nazi agent. She even had a code name: Westminster. It was supposed to be funny; a nod to her affair with one of the most well-connected men in Britain.'

Chloé stared at Etienne and he continued, 'And a string of letters and numbers represent her agent number,' he said dismissively. 'But I admit I don't remember what they are.'

With this one conversation, everything Chloé thought about her beloved grandmother had been turned completely on its head. Her grandmother worked for a fashion designer turned Nazi agent in wartime Paris. This couldn't be true. If it was true, how involved had her grandmother been in all of it? She looked into her coffee cup and sipped the remaining liquid before replacing the cup into its saucer. Around them office workers came and went, someone nudged their table as they tried to squeeze past to their own.

'How do you know this? How do *I not* know this?'

'Files are coming to light only now. They have been . . . well hidden.'

'Well hidden?'

He nodded knowingly.

'I . . . I don't know what to make of this,' Chloé said.

'I am sorry,' Etienne said, seeing her reaction to his news. 'I have upset you.'

'No, you've not upset me,' Chloé said truthfully. 'Confused me, but not upset me.'

'Good. After all, I've not told you that your grandmother was a Nazi.'

'No,' Chloé said slowly. 'Just implied it.'

'Actually, I have relayed to you a neatly forgotten piece of history about one of the world's most famous women. I honestly did not mean to imply your grandmother was complicit in anything . . . untoward.'

'Untoward?' Chloé repeated, noting how Etienne appeared to be backtracking on his salacious argument. 'Is that what we call collaborating with Nazis?'

He sighed and apologised again.

'It's all right,' Chloé said, standing to leave. 'Really. Thank you very much for the coffee. And the information. You've given me a lot to think about.'

But Etienne missed her tone as he stood also and held out his card in a gesture almost as abrupt as Chloé's eager departure from the café. 'How long are you in Paris for?' he asked.

Chloé paused. 'This summer at least, possibly a year. I'm having a gap year,' she replied, unsure why she'd said that. She reached out automatically to take his card. 'Part of it spent working at my friend's shop.'

He nodded thoughtfully. And then: 'What is a gap year?'

'Never mind,' Chloé said feeling the heat flaming her cheeks.

She barely had the chance to glance at his card before he gestured to it saying, 'Please stop by.'

She pocketed his card in her bag without looking at it. 'Thank you,' she said. 'It was nice to meet you.' It had been a long time since she'd been out for coffee with a man who either wasn't a work colleague or Rob.

As she crossed the road she glanced back in his direction and noticed he was watching her, a look of something resembling shame or dismay on his face. Or maybe that's just what Chloé wanted to see.

'And then he told you Gran worked for a Nazi?' Chloé's younger sister Ava almost shouted down the phone as Chloé sat in her rental apartment, looking out of the Juliet balcony and over the rooftops. She'd chosen this apartment in the seventh arrondissement because of the photograph showing the view from the bathroom. If Chloé fancied, she could run a bubble bath, open the door to the balcony and gaze out at the Eiffel Tower while Paris moved busily in the streets below. She'd barely needed to look at the other photos. That was the one that clinched it. But as it turned out the rest of the apartment had been bright, airy and with tiny balconies off both sitting room doors. The listing of the sixth-floor attic-style apartment had described it as bijou. Chloé would have described it as tiny.

'No, he didn't exactly say Granny was a Nazi,' Chloé said honestly. Now she'd had time to think about it she might have overreacted by standing up and leaving so abruptly after Etienne had imparted news she just hadn't wanted to hear.

'That's outrageous,' Ava said in a tone that implied she was about to embark on a small rant. 'And you'd only just met him? Who does that?'

Chloé wasn't sure if Ava was talking about Etienne's news that their granny may have been a collaborator, or Chloé herself for going for coffee with a man she'd just met, which was distinctly un-Chloé-like. She thought she'd better not ask her sister to clarify which.

When Chloé had returned to the apartment the very first thing she'd done, after opening the balcony doors and sighing that deep sigh at the view that she always emitted every time she looked out since she'd arrived a few weeks earlier, was head straight for her laptop's web browser and look up what Etienne had told her. He had, of course, been correct. Chloé knew he would be. Although it was only a hunch, he didn't look like the kind of man who went around making things up for ten minutes of chat with strangers.

Chloé had looked up images of Chanel's Ritz suite from

21

years gone by, and when she zoomed in on pictures taken from certain angles, there was the painting Etienne had told her about, taking pride of place on a drawing room wall. It was quite startling now she thought about it. She'd looked up information about the picture dubbed *The Sacrifice of Polyxena*, about how no one knew where it had come from, how there was no record of it having ever entered the Ritz as part of their inventory, or as part of Chanel's for that matter. And this had intrigued many art critics, each of them with their own theory about how it entered the hotel and when. Reuniting lost art with descendants of Jewish families from whom items were stolen remained as important now – if not more important – as it had been directly after the war, and many critics had enjoyed speculating about its provenance.

And then Chloé had moved on and had searched for her grandmother's name but there was very little online about her, just a few mentions in biographical pieces that Chanel had once had a lady's maid called Adèle Fabron. And that was it. Chloé ran her finger over her grandmother's name on the screen and smiled. And that was where the information ended about Adèle. Whatever Adèle had done or hadn't done during the war, she wasn't a part of written history.

But there was so much more about Chanel during the Occupation that Chloé grew quite weary of reading it. None of it was pleasant, most of it was vague and accusatory and she closed the laptop lid after reading confirmation of what Etienne had said, that Coco Chanel was an active agent of the Abwehr – a Nazi intelligence organisation, that her code name was Westminster and that her agent number had been F-7124.

And before she'd had a chance to process any of what she'd just read and how it related to her grandmother Adèle, her sister had chosen that moment to call.

'What do you think?' Ava had questioned when Chloé had relayed all the information.

'I'm not sure,' Chloé replied. 'I don't think it means anything. Granny just wasn't that kind of person – isn't that kind of person. And she was just some sort of hired help no?'

'Yes, that's what I thought. I mean, I know we play it up a bit but she really was just some sort of domestic staff, surely.'

The girls were silent for a moment until Ava asked, 'When did you last pop in to see Granny?'

'The week before I left to come to Paris. When did you?'

'Weeks ago. I'm definitely overdue. She's not going to live forever.'

'Ava!'

'Chloé, she's ninety-seven.'

'And fit as a fiddle with a mind as sharp as anything.'

'If that was true,' Ava said, 'do you think she'd have needed to have gone into a warden-controlled flat?'

'It's warden-controlled, not an actual care home. She still looks after herself and takes herself off to the communal lounge to play bingo with her little gang.'

'She goes on a Zimmer frame though,' Ava said for what Chloé felt was no reason at all.

'That's because she's ninety-seven,' Chloé retorted.

'My point is,' Ava clarified, 'we should be spending more time with her, not less. How often are you coming back to London?'

'I've only just got here,' Chloé pointed out and then she relented. 'But the Eurostar means I can be there whenever I'm needed.' There was no need for her to return to London. Ava was being dramatic but she didn't want to engage her in an unnecessary argument and so she left it there.

Ava changed the subject. 'So what else have you found out about Chanel and Granny?'

23

'Enough about Chanel and it's not the most delightful reading. There's some very one-sided arguments about her on the internet, very accusing, but there's nothing about Granny other than as a footnote in Chanel's life.'

'Well there you go then,' Ava said.

On the street below the balcony a couple were arguing in rapid-fire French and Chloé walked out and looked down as the streetlights glowed. In the time it had taken Chloé to notice the sun was already setting over Paris, the couple had finished arguing and were already locked in an embrace. Part of Chloé hankered for that level of passion that she'd never had with Rob, part of her didn't. 'Ah Paris,' she murmured.

'What?' Ava asked from over two hundred miles away in West London.

'Perhaps,' Chloé focused on the call, 'if she really was a footnote in Chanel's life, that's why we never heard much about the war years from Granny.'

'Strange though . . .' Ava started. 'She must have known Chanel had a chequered past. And yet . . . chose not to say.'

'Upstairs, downstairs,' Chloé reasoned. 'Not her place to say anything derogatory about her employer.'

'I'm not sure,' Ava said. 'I wonder if we should ask her when one of us next sees her.'

Chloé raised an eyebrow at her sister's words. She wasn't sure how she felt about that. 'What would we say? Hey, Gran, good to see you – shall I flick the kettle on? Oh, by the way, we've just been researching Chanel and found out she was a Nazi. Were you one too?'

At the other end of the phone, Ava snorted. 'Well I wouldn't phrase it like that, obviously. I'll think about how to phrase it. I'm not able to get up there for a few weeks yet and it's not something you can ask down the phone is it really?'

'Not really,' Chloé agreed. 'I've got to go. I'm out for dinner with a friend and I need to wallow in the bath with some flickering candles and jazz playing in the background and pretend I'm really French.'

'Chloé?' Ava asked.

'Mmm?'

'Granny must have known. Would you have stuck around to work for someone who was a Nazi?' Ava asked.

'No. I don't think I could have done. But what if she had no choice? What if it was more complicated than we could ever know?'

Chapter 3

Paris, Summer 1941

Adèle stood in the balcony of her employer's suite in the Ritz and watched the movements of grey-green-uniformed men in the cobbled square of the Place Vendôme below. The happiness on the faces of the Wehrmacht soldiers as they went about their newfound, easy life was grating enough to make Adèle's teeth grind together as they passed the tall grey column and Napoléon's statue sitting proudly at the top. These soldiers were enjoying themselves in the city but none of them were looking up at the sights in front of them. Her fists clenched by her sides, Adèle thought her anger over their arrival would have abated by now, a year after their invasion, but with every passing day it just grew stronger. She would never get used to this.

She remembered that first week they'd arrived, the shock of finding out the Nazis had crossed the 'impenetrable' Maginot line, with its solid line of concrete fortifications. But instead of ramming their way through, the Germans had chosen the weaker fortified Ardennes forest and simply worked their way round and into France that way. And then came the mass evacuations, long lines of French refugees including those from the capital city as Parisians felt the bite of Hitler snapping at their heels. Paris had failed to concede to the Germans and had found itself on one side of a dividing line, becoming part of the Occupied zone. And now it was paying for this with staunch Occupation.

Out in the Place Vendôme, rain started falling and Adèle watched it gently patter against the balcony edge. The snapping sound of the swastika flying in the breeze over the Ritz, just above her, was drowned out by the rain. There had been a time when she had looked out of another balcony on the other side of Paris and watched the city of light become covered in ash. Particles flew through the air, landing on everything – a layer of dusty, fragmented film clinging to her hair as she'd watched in horrified awe. At first she'd thought it was snowing, in the middle of summer, and then she had felt her stomach tighten, believing the entire city must be on fire.

But it had been paper – more paper than she'd probably ever seen in her life being incinerated across civil administration courtyards throughout all of Paris. What remained of the government had been burning all the files before the Germans arrived to get hold of them. What they'd have done with them was beyond Adèle. But then when was there ever sanity in wartime? She had thought that was the end and if she had listened hard enough she could have heard the German panzer tanks as they'd entered the city and stormed through the Champs-Élysées. Everything they said would happen had, including the unthinkable: Paris had fallen to the Nazis.

Falling was a theme of Adèle's life. She remembered the day she had fallen into the path of the indomitable Coco Chanel; the way everything happened for a reason. Or so she thought. She had been on rue Cambon, newly arrived in the most beautiful city on earth. She thought it then and she still thought it now, even though now it was immersed in Nazi officers enjoying the finery that Paris under pressure of Occupation had to offer. But back then, only a few years ago, it had been everything she had known it would be.

She had left the orphanage at St Nazaire behind with skills taught to her by teachers who knew girls needed to make their own way in the world. She could type fast with few mistakes and take dictation, could keep ledgers, was highly organised and eager. Too eager, the brush of youthfulness and inexperience evident in every part of her, what she wore, how she greeted people, even the way she walked. She had thought her skill set would be enough to secure her employment as a clerk or secretary but as she visited agency after agency to be told her lack of experience put her far down the list when it came to the opportunity to be sent out for gainful employment, her hope had faded as quickly as the December light in which she'd arrived.

But outside the Chanel boutique on rue Cambon, the glow from within had entranced her. The light sparkling from the bottles of Chanel No 5 fragrance lining the window, casting a dance hall glow and turning the rain-soaked cobbles glistening and bright, the white awning draped high over the doorway as if it were a bride's veil. She'd stood outside and debated where she would sleep that night, where she would eat and what she'd be able to buy with her few remaining coins. With the shops already closing for the day, Adèle's grand plan to better herself, change her life through gainful employment in France's capital city, was dying in the night air.

Until an argument had broken out and a woman had run out of the shop and straight into Adèle sending both of them flying. Adèle's small suitcase, with her few precious possessions of a life left behind, clattered to the ground.

The woman didn't look at all sorry that she'd done it and, almost as if Adèle was not there, turned to look back at the shop as if it was the source of all her dismay. 'I did not want to be her assistant anymore anyway,' the woman had cried to no one in particular as she adjusted her hat and strode off purposefully, without a backward glance at the mayhem she'd left behind.

It took Adèle a moment to react, to squash that seed of doubt that momentarily planted in her mind that she shouldn't enter that shop, that she shouldn't put herself in the path of someone who had elicited that sort of reaction from an employee. But there was something spurring Adèle onward inside the shop, something spurring her to beg an audience with the owner, telling her that her timing was fortuitous because Adèle could do all the things necessary to be an assistant and hadn't somebody inside this building just that very moment lost one? The thing that had spurred Adèle on was hunger and the fact she never wanted to know starvation again.

'Come, Adèle,' Coco Chanel snapped her fingers. Adèle turned from watching the Wehrmacht soldiers from her position at the balcony and re-entered the suite in the Ritz.

Chanel looked stern. 'You have unpacked my things?'

'Yes, Mademoiselle,' Adèle agreed. 'Everything is as it should be. Just as you like it.'

'Good. I will have Champagne sent up before dinner.' Mademoiselle reached up to the mantelpiece where her cigarette case sat next to her lucky emblem, an ornament of a lion. 'Quicker, Adèle. I do not pay you to dally.'

Adèle hurried across the Chinese rug, rang for Champagne to be brought up and no longer blinked in rapid disbelief at the indulgent extravagance of her employer at a time such as this. Under Mademoiselle's employment Adèle had known nothing but luxurious surroundings even if her actual pay would never be enough to afford anything like this, no matter how much she saved. But she bore witness to glamour, extravagance and every now and again drops of finery made their way to Adèle in the form of small gifts that Mademoiselle no longer wanted.

Europe had been ready for war for months, if not years, and she and Mademoiselle Chanel had sat and discussed her strategy. At first it was to escape the Nazis, head to the south and sit out the war in her house in Roquebrune on the French Riviera. The war would affect them all in one way or another, had been Mademoiselle's suggestion. 'We may as well enjoy ourselves in the balmy climate in the process.' It was a case of when, not if the Germans came. And when they did, Mademoiselle and Adèle would be ready.

Mademoiselle had closed her atelier and Adèle had the sad task of seeing the dressmakers and milliners leave the building for the last time in God knew how long. 'War is not the time for fashion,' Mademoiselle had declared. And Adèle believed that after three years her role as an assistant to such a woman must be coming to an end; that she too would be forced to pack up and leave as the war reached them. And the fear of hunger and unemployment in a time of war, a time of enemy Occupation would be upon her.

Adèle had given the seamstresses words of encouragement, condolence. But what had confused Adèle was that they had given her the same, almost as if they had felt sorry for her, keeping her job with Mademoiselle Chanel. But it was surprise and relief intermingling together that prevailed in Adèle's mind. Mademoiselle needed at least one person to rely on to carry out the day-to-day tasks.

Adèle had a small box room across the hall from Mademoiselle's suite at the Ritz and a small desk in Mademoiselle's private office at the top of the atelier around the corner where she carried out her daily tasks. She was on hand to assist her employer at any hour of the day and night and happy to do so. Adèle had once been part of a small household staff that included a chauffeur and a maid but they had fled the moment the rumour of the invading force became a reality. And while it was only a few metres from the atelier and apartment at rue Cambon, Mademoiselle Chanel – on arrival from a brief flit to the South of France for safety – changed her mind as swiftly as she'd made it. She'd suggested the return to Paris; that they would enter the lion's den and decamp to the Hotel Ritz for the duration of the war where she'd been living throughout the Thirties. As her assistant, Adèle would be expected to continue accompanying her.

Adèle had failed to see the attraction of sitting out the war under the watchful gaze of the Nazis. But she had agreed to stay on under such an arrangement. After all, what else would Adèle do in the war? No one was hiring an assistant in this climate, and if unemployed she would surely starve in these uncertain times.

Madame Ritz had acquiesced to Mademoiselle Chanel's return to the hotel. But the Nazis also had to agree to having her in their midst. As they had taken over the hotel, it was up to them who lived alongside them – who could be trusted. Everything was up to them now. Famous names such as Coco Chanel and the Dubonnet family staying in the hotel at the same time only bolstered Nazi propaganda.

In a moment of care and concern for her young charge, Mademoiselle had placated Adèle's concerns. 'We must look after ourselves,' she'd said. 'We are women, alone in this city, with no one to protect us, but us. We must rely on ourselves for our own survival.'

'But, Mademoiselle, we are going to be living among them. We are going to be living in the same hotel as senior Nazis – you heard what Madame Ritz told us. We could not be closer to the Nazis if we tried.'

'Exactly, Adèle. Exactly. But you do not need to worry. After all, you will not be doing anything to give the Nazis cause for concern, will you?'

Chapter 4

Adèle took dinner in her small side room across from Mademoiselle Chanel's suite. The rooms were to be their home again for at least the next few months, maybe even years. For Mademoiselle it was like coming home. But for Adèle, she was reminded she'd never had a real home as she trudged towards her old servant's room. Who knew how long the Nazis would remain in residence before setting their sights on greater prizes than Paris? Where would it stop? London? Beyond? She heard her employer sashay out of the front door of her suite of rooms and along the corridor, heading down to her table in the dining room. Adèle did not know how Mademoiselle did it. How she could enter a dining room full of Nazi officials and mix among them with confidence?

Adèle wasn't schooled enough in the ways of the world, the ways of men, or even the ways of women. Mademoiselle Chanel was nothing like Adèle. Mademoiselle was so much older for one thing, experienced in all manners of life from what Adèle could glean. Mademoiselle never quite revealed how old she was at each passing birthday, only hinted enigmatically. With her dark raven hair and pearl-white teeth, Adèle had placed her somewhere between fifty and sixty and even then she might not be anywhere near correct.

Before Adèle's mother had died she told a young Adèle that: 'It is having children mixed with poverty that makes a woman look old before her time,' and that was why Adèle's mother herself had looked so old whilst actually being so young. She had still been so young when she'd passed away, before Adèle's father had left his wife with a young daughter to look after and no income with which to do it.

But all this was before; before her mother had died, before Adèle had been sent to an orphanage. It was this information, gleaned from Adèle by a barely interested Coco Chanel the day they met when Adèle had dared to enter the boutique to seek a job that had made the older woman blink, pause and after a moment's hesitation offer Adèle the job. Right there and then.

It had been enough to make Adèle feel eternally grateful to Mademoiselle, even when her employer did things Adèle did not entirely approve of.

Despite having many lovers, Mademoiselle had never married, never borne children and deep down, Adèle thought there was a faint trickle of motherly affection emanating from Chanel towards her. But it could disappear as swiftly as it had arrived and with the snapping click of her fingers and a sharp word, they were employer and employee once again. The ups and downs were plentiful when working and living in the environs of such a woman.

So far Adèle had trusted her, liked h er almost. But as Adèle folded her employer's immaculate day clothes, readying them for steaming, even she had to acknowledge the madness of living in a hotel predominantly inhabited by Nazis.

As she climbed into bed Adèle opened her black Chinese lacquered box in which she kept her most treasured possessions. The box had been a gift from Mademoiselle on Adèle's last birthday. She had decanted her treasures from the inner pouch of her card suitcase where she'd kept them for so long and moved them into their finer surroundings. She touched the sepia photograph of herself as a child with her mother. Her mother was sat, posed, unsmiling. Over the years Adèle had come to know this photograph was not a true likeness of her mother for she had always smiled as often as she could. With the passing years Adèle had known her mother's tendency to smile was to protect her young daughter, keep Adèle unworried by the mounting pressures of a life rendered impossible by lack of money. In the only photograph she had, her mother looked sallow, the lines around her eyes prominent, her hair prematurely streaked with silver strands, the skin around her eyes dark from exhausted sleep.

Adèle touched her own dark hair, blinked her own dark eyes, which she knew weren't lined around the edges or tired from lack of sleep. How only a few years had changed Adèle's fate, had brought her here. She had been handed such luck. How different it was to her mother's path.

The box contained further emblems of an existence she was so far removed from now: a pebble from the beach of St Nazaire, her home town, taken before she'd left as a memento; a rag doll she'd managed to keep safe throughout her remaining years in the orphanage; a small cross on the chain given to her on her baptism – the clasp of the chain long since broken, kept safely now inside the lined box. The items all looked so small inside the oversized box and Adèle closed it, placing it back on the shelf above her bed, under-neath her small skylight, and then thanked the world and Mademoiselle Chanel for having handed her this opportunity to survive. And then Adèle fell into a fitful sleep, not knowing what the next few days, months, years would bring.

While downstairs her employer dined with Nazis.

*

The next morning, Adèle opened the newspaper and read what could only possibly pass for Nazi propaganda.

Hitler Solidifies Presence in the Baltic States

Lithuania, Latvia and Estonia welcome Herr Hitler as troops enter and free the Baltics from the Soviet Union.

Adèle didn't know what to believe. 'Invading to *free* the Baltics?' she questioned.

There was nothing about how the war was faring in other parts of the world. Was the news censored already? What news of the exiled French government in London?

But underneath the article her eye was caught by news from the nearby American Hospital. A blood drive, now considered urgent. She had never given blood before. It had never occurred to her to do so. She only had to run an errand at the bank and, as she didn't consider herself particularly faint-hearted, she could tack on a visit to donate blood. She gathered her hat and gas mask, walked through the wide cobbled streets to the Metro station, producing her ticket to be clipped as she descended to the platform.

She sidestepped more Wehrmacht officers than she could count above ground and underneath Paris's streets the story was the same. Officers looked overjoyed to be riding Paris's famous Metro, taking them off to see the sights they had perhaps only been privileged enough to see at the cinema. She had no sympathy for their cause, but she smiled at them when they smiled at her because she had not been bred to be impolite. She could understand their excitement at the city. That same excitement had been hers when she'd arrived. She still felt that anticipation all these years later, that love for Paris: its cafés and wide spanning streets, the pale stone architecture, the Eiffel Tower that had made her gasp when she'd first set her eyes on it, the Seine slicing through the city, dividing it and uniting it at the same time.

After her visit to the bank, she rode the Metro and disembarked at Pont de Neuilly, walking through the streets towards the hospital. The Kommandantur, the Nazi civil administration, had set itself up in the building across the road from the hospital and Adèle forced herself to look away from it. She didn't want the ugly reminder of how she and other Parisians were being bullied and dominated from within those very walls.

The hospital's red brick and white stone façade curved around the long drive and Adèle walked through the hospital's double doors and stepped inside, expecting to find a queue to join or at least a German sentry or two standing guard as they did at every other building of importance. But it was a sign of American neutrality that there were no German sentries standing guard, ready to question her innocent motives in being there. Equally there was no queue to donate blood and so Adèle continued in past a draped US flag on one side of the entrance hall and an empty flag post, where Adèle assumed perhaps until recently a French Tricolore flag would have been. She hadn't seen a Tricolore since the Germans arrived and had made it law that the French flag could no longer be displayed. Neither could citizens sing the *Marseillaise*. Every French flag that she had been so used to seeing in the city had long since been removed, their flagpoles either bare or replaced with swastikas. There was even a swastika on top of the Eiffel Tower, a daily reminder of how high the Nazis had risen.

Adèle walked to the reception desk where a doctor was standing, holding a clipboard and notes, looking down at them. There was no administrator and Adèle stood awkwardly, wondering where to go in order to donate blood.

The doctor looked up from his notes, cast his eyes over her briefly and then glanced around to see where his colleague had gone.

'I should think the secretary will be back soon.' He spoke to her in her native tongue but with an accent she couldn't place.

'I'm happy to wait,' Adèle replied as she adjusted her hat and smoothed down her red pencil skirt.

He nodded and continued with his notes. Adèle took him in: his dark hair and his dark eyes trimmed with thick black eyelashes caught her attention and unashamedly she watched as he blinked, his lashes lowering and raising, almost hypnotically. It served to occupy her in the stillness of the reception area with only the two of them in the vast entranceway.

Suddenly, he looked up at her again. Perhaps he'd sensed he was being watched. Adèle looked away, embarrassed she'd been caught intently watching him.

'Perhaps I can help?' he asked.

'Perhaps you can point me in the right direction to give blood.'

He paused. 'The blood drive was yesterday.'

'But I read it in the newspaper this morning,' she said determinedly.

The doctor smiled. 'Did you read it in yesterday's newspaper this morning?' he joked.

Adèle thought. She had just picked it up from the table. Perhaps the housekeeper had left it out. Perhaps Mademoiselle had left it out. Either way, no one had placed it in the kindling basket for the fireplace.

'Possibly,' she admitted. She felt silly now, heat rising up her face. 'I'm so sorry,' she apologised, 'for wasting your time.'

'You've not wasted my time,' he said, putting his notes down. 'You've wasted yours though.'

'Yes,' she said. 'But it's all right.' She turned to leave.

'Wait,' he said. 'Not so fast.'

Adèle turned back to him.

'If you want to donate blood—' he looked at his watch '—then I've got a few minutes. If I'm honest we'll take everything we can get our hands on.'

She nodded, smiled. 'Yes please. If you have time? I am here and I would like to.'

He looked down at the clipboard, finished writing something, placed it on the desk for the administrator to see and turned to Adèle. 'Shall we?'

She nodded. 'I'm so sorry if I'm putting you out.'

'You are absolutely not putting me out,' he replied as they walked the corridor. He pushed a button for the lift and they waited patiently. Adèle watched the cables run above them as the metal lift ascended and as it arrived he dragged open the cage door in front of them.

He led her through another long corridor when they stepped out of the lift towards a small consulting room with a couple of chairs, surgical equipment, cupboards and a long metal hospital bed pushed under the window. 'Take a seat,' he said and gestured to the bed. He lifted the back of the bed up so Adèle was able to sit upright. 'Remove your jacket and roll up your shirtsleeve,' he ordered and she thought he was rather officious all of a sudden. His bedside manner had disappeared the very moment he'd arrived bedside.

He gathered the implements needed from cupboards – tubing and long needles – and asked her to wait a moment while he left the room. He then returned with the glass bottle in which her blood donation would be stored. He was carrying two. 'We've run out in here,' he explained.

She watched as he swabbed the crook of her arm and then suggested she look away.

'I don't faint at the sight of blood, if that's what you're worried about.'

38

He raised his eyebrows. 'No . . .' he said after he'd inserted the needle, watching her reaction carefully. 'You don't look the type.'

He watched her while the blood trickled slowly through the tube and into the bottle.

'What do you mean?' she asked but not unkindly.

'You look like you're made of stern stuff,' he explained.

'I am,' she said and then under her breath, 'I have had to be.'

'Me too,' he said equally quietly and the two shared a small smile before he quickly moved on with the task in hand.

When she was finished, he pulled paperwork out and told her to rest for a moment while he filled in a form with her name and details.

'Adèle Fabron,' she told him and he wrote it down and then apologised that he'd not introduced himself.

'Doctor Dixon,' he said.

'Dixon? That's not a very French name.'

'No it's not. I'm not French. I'm an American.'

That explained his strange accent that had been almost, but not quite masked, underneath his perfect French.

'I could not tell,' she said.

Doctor Dixon smiled. 'I'll take that as a compliment.'

'You should. Your French is excellent.' The moment she said it she regretted it. 'I'm sorry, I didn't mean to sound condescending.'

'You say sorry a lot,' he said. 'There's really no need. Wait until you really offend someone and then apologise. That's my golden rule.'

'Is it?'

'One of them anyway,' he said and they looked at each other before he broke eye contact first, a hint of a smile creeping across his features as he filled in her information on a form. Then he began tidying.

Adèle noticed he'd left the second, clean glass bottle and the needle out and hadn't put it inside a cupboard. She glanced at it curiously. 'You're taking someone else's blood after?' she enquired. 'Even though the blood drive was yesterday?' she teased.

'Yes,' he said. 'Mine.'

She was half-impressed by this but chose not to comment as she rolled the sleeve of her blouse back down and did up the tiny pearl button on the cuff.

Perhaps it was because she made no comment that he said, 'I give blood as regularly as I feel able to these days.'

'Why?' she asked slowly.

He sighed. 'How long have you got?' he asked with a laugh.

'All day actually,' she replied as she swung her legs round on the bed in the most ladylike way possible in order to sit properly, picked up her red jacket from behind her and put it on. It was one of her favourites as it nipped in gently at the waist, defining her figure.

'Well,' he sat back in his chair. 'We don't know how bad it's going to get, do we?' he said tentatively.

'The Nazis are here,' she offered. 'The worst has already happened.'

'I don't think so. I think the worst is yet to come.'

She watched him, waiting for more.

'The Brits could bomb us, for one thing.'

'But we're friends with them,' Adèle pointed out.

'Sure. But the Nazis aren't. And the Brits will want to drive them back. They'll want to bomb the factories nearby so they can't produce weapons for Hitler or aircraft bits for Hermann Göring.'

'And with bombing comes casualties,' Adèle said, understanding.

'And fatalities,' he said sadly. 'I can't help the dead. But I can help the injured,' he said nodding towards the blood-letting apparatus. 'But I can't worry about the things I can't fix. I can only worry about the things I can.'

'Is that another golden rule?' she asked.

'Something like that.' He laughed. 'My time here's limited,' he offered. 'I can only do what I can do.'

'Limited?'

'Being American my days are numbered here. The chances of being allowed to stay here are slim to none if my lot join the war, even though I'm officially under the directorship of the International Red Cross and so is the hospital now. That's why we don't have to be full to the rafters with Krauts.'

'That's unkind terminology,' she chastised.

'I call them worse things,' he said darkly.

'Not to their faces I hope,' Adèle teased.

'No. I'm not that stupid.'

'You don't seem stupid at all,' she said thoughtfully.

He smiled and then his face took on a serious expression. 'They're spilling blood everywhere and I'm doing what I can to counteract that. One pint at a time. And so I'll take your blood. And be very grateful for it. And if you want to come again in a few months . . .'

'You'll happily stick a needle into me again?'

'Exactly.' He laughed again and took her hand in his to help her from the hospital bed. She looked at his hand briefly before he unclasped it.

He pulled at the collar of his shirt. 'The nurses usually do this,' he said indicating the blood-banking paraphernalia. 'And I know I'm supposed to give you something to eat and a drink. If you're not too wobbly, my office is upstairs. We'll take the elevator and I'll find you a madeleine or two to nibble on.'

'A madeleine? With real butter?'

'A parting gift from a very well-off American patient.'

'That was kind of them,' Adèle said as they walked the corridor and took the lift up a floor.

'It was.' He said it in such a soft way it made Adèle want to ask more. But instead she opted for: 'Did you extract a pint of blood from them as well?'

He laughed. 'No. Damn it. I should have done though.'

When they reached his office door he opened it ajar and a nurse came running towards him from the direction they'd just come. 'Doctor Dixon!' the nurse called, 'Doctor Dixon!' Adèle turned towards the nurse.

'Please,' the nurse begged him. 'Don't go in there.'

Adèle turned away from the woman who approached crying out in rapid French and looked inside his office through the slim crack in the doorway. Adèle blinked, once, then twice as she processed what was inside. And then the door slammed closed so fast she couldn't be sure she was correct in her assumption as to what she'd just been looking at.

'The floor has just been bleached,' the nurse said. 'After the spillage you had earlier. The smell is too strong for you to step inside.'

'Of course,' Doctor Dixon replied, his hand firmly on the door handle. 'I forgot about that. Nurse, would you please find something a little sugary for Mademoiselle Fabron to eat and a tisane, perhaps. She's just donated blood for us.'

'Come this way, please,' the nurse instructed and waited for Adèle to obey orders.

Adèle glanced at the frosted glass on Doctor Dixon's door as if she'd be able to see clearly through it, which of course she couldn't.

'Thank you for taking the time to donate today,' he said in genuine tones.

She held out her hand to shake his. 'It was my pleasure.'

He faltered before removing his hand from the door handle and grasping hers gently once again. Before she accompanied the nurse, she gave him a slim smile as if to silently tell him that she would not report him to the authorities. Because she had seen exactly what was inside his office before he'd slammed the door. And she knew what it was because she'd seen it on the newsreels at the cinema – back before the Germans had arrived and replaced real news with propaganda. And if the Nazis found out what Doctor Dixon had in his office they would have no hesitation in sending him to his death by firing squad.

Chapter 5

'Ah there you are, Adèle,' Mademoiselle said one afternoon as Adèle arrived carrying a diary, which she used to help plan Mademoiselle's social engagements. 'And with the diary too, clever girl.'

In truth, Adèle was pleased to be carrying out such an administrative task even if it was only social planning. With the maids having both now left and there only being the part-time housekeeper and herself employed now, Adèle had been finding herself taking over the more menial tasks, such as dusting the horrifying accumulation of dust on the ferns and potted plants or worse – being bored stiff with nothing to do and waiting around.

'Tomorrow, cross through whatever is in the agenda for dinner. I have new plans.'

'Tomorrow evening it's dinner and cards with Madame Ritz.'

'Non,' Chanel said. 'Non. Strike a line through it and please send my apologies.'

Adèle unscrewed the lid from the fountain pen and was poised to write the new information in. But none was forthcoming.

'Mademoiselle? What should I put instead?'

'What's that? Oh do not write anything.'

'As you wish,' Adèle replied. 'What will you be wearing?'

'The pale silk. I have already selected it,' she said with a girlish smile. 'Have it pressed please.'

Adèle entered Chanel's large bedroom, dotted with ornate hangings and oversized antique furniture, to retrieve the flattering gossamer dress and to organise for it to be gently pressed.

'Oh and Adèle?' her mistress called.

Adèle carried the dress, draped delicately over her arm and waited for further instruction. 'Please ask the sommelier to select a bottle of Château Latour Premier Cru. I think . . . 1929 and ask for it to be sent to my rooms tomorrow at midnight precisely.'

The younger woman frowned and then straightened the frown out as quickly as it had appeared. 'Of course, Mademoiselle.'

'Thank you,' Chanel said, almost as an afterthought as she moved to the window to look out over Place Vendôme. The tall window was thrown open wide so her brown hair bustled in the wind. She lit a cigarette and leant back against the doorframe so she could see and be seen.

It had only been a few months since the Nazis had entered Paris, bringing with them fear and so much change. Her position was secure, in as much as it could be, and she found herself working for an employer who kept them on the right side of Nazi law. How easy it could be to tumble towards the wrong side with just one fatal move. Adèle had too many moments when she wasn't busy these days. And in one of these moments she reflected on how her role had changed since those heady days of organising secret appointments between Chanel and her various lovers; travel to and from the boutiques in Deauville, Biarritz; travel to Venice where she'd see Chanel off on her holidays onboard friends' yachts; the frenzied travel Adèle would carry out by rail back towards whichever port Chanel was headed for. It would not have done for her to travel with her mistress onboard a yacht. These jaunts with friends were Mademoiselle's private time.

Frenetic. If there was one word she could use to summarise her role in the few short years since she'd begun working with Chanel until this very year, it would be frenetic. She missed it. She missed all of it – that pace of work: ensuring models arrived on time; running up and down the floor-to-ceiling mirrored atelier stairs snatching accessories that had been forgotten in the run-up to a show where high-profile Parisians would glimpse the latest Chanel creations; ensuring stocks of Champagne never ran low, bolts of fabric were where Mademoiselle needed them; issuing and receiving invitations; making sure that used sketch books were replaced with fresh ones, pencils always sharpened; fresh flowers – camellias, Mademoiselle's favourite – placed throughout the atelier and apartment. Adèle had to ensure the chauffeur was always ready at a moment's notice, the chef and housekeeper were working in harmony behind the scenes at the Riviera house or in Paris, and she carried out personal shopping and shopping for the atelier.

And now almost all of it had gone. There were no meetings in which to take minutes, even the dreaded list of menial errands had dwindled to such a low level that these were now the highlight of Adèle's working day. And if there were correspondences or insurances to renew, it was a breath of fresh air rather than the norm. Her working day had always been long and fulfilling and now it was long and near-empty.

At midnight when Mademoiselle had not returned from her mysterious diary engagement and the housekeeper had retired to the servants' quarters, the shining silver Champagne bucket was delivered alongside a tray of six Champagne flutes.

'How many flutes will you need?' the waiter asked.

'I do not know,' Adèle said as she showed him in, leading him through to the empty sitting room. 'Perhaps best leave them all and I can ring if we need more.'

'Certainly, Mademoiselle. Shall I open it?'

'I think not actually,' Adèle said after a pause. She hated waste and if Mademoiselle chose not to return soon there would be hell to pay for flat Champagne.

'You're working late,' the waiter commented.

Adèle simply shrugged. She was at Mademoiselle's beck and call at all hours of the day as her role had drifted into something now indefinable. She would like to say it was the war that had done this and that she must do what was necessary but that didn't sit easily with her when she was in the middle of arranging an ice bucket of Champagne at a time when Parisians were struggling to find food and coal.

Adèle showed him out and waited another ten minutes before wondering if she should go to bed herself. It was her day off tomorrow. If there was no one to take her guest's coat and ring to the kitchens for titbits to eat Adèle would only hear about it in the morning.

She sat on the settee and waited. She was aware her position was privileged, that Mademoiselle gave her special treatment. Mademoiselle was a fierce advocate for women to know their own worth, instructing Adèle never to be held hostage emotionally or in terms of wealth.

In a rare moment of openness, Mademoiselle Chanel had sat one evening that cold winter in 1939 by the fire at her house in the South of France. Adèle had been invited to join her after a dinner party when the guests, including Pablo Picasso and Jean Cocteau, whose sketches adorned the walls around Mademoiselle's suite now, had departed.

Mademoiselle had studied Adèle wordlessly as she'd sat watching the flames dance in the fireplace. Adèle had been thinking how such a simple thing as wood for a fire was so easy to obtain for some and yet how hard it had always been for her mother to find. Adèle could remember being cold, even in the orphanage with the nuns. But under Mademoiselle's care Adèle had never once been cold, never once wanted for warm clothes or sustenance. 'You remind me a lot of me when I was young,' Mademoiselle had surprised Adèle by saying as the fire leapt in the grate.

Adèle had blinked and smiled at her employer. 'I cannot believe that,' she had replied.

'Why not?'

The glamour, the enterprise, the life she led . . . it didn't seem possible Mademoiselle could be anything like Adèle. But she continued. 'I was an orphan once too.'

Mademoiselle fitted a cigarette into an elegant ivory holder, pushed back the rolls of her dark hair as she dipped her head to light her cigarette from her gold lighter.

She snapped it closed. 'When you came to me and I asked about your education, you very honestly told me you had been educated with the nuns at the orphanage at St Nazaire.'

'I am not ashamed of my education,' Adèle admitted. 'I am not ashamed my mother died. I did not see the point in hiding it.'

'Quite right,' Mademoiselle admitted, inhaling on her cigarette and allowing the smoke to unfurl gently from her lips.

'I was telling the truth,' Adèle replied, 'about my experience working, when I said I had been apprenticed in the convent, helping Mother Superior with the administrative tasks.'

Mademoiselle smiled indulgently. 'Yes, I did not doubt it. It is why I hired you,' she said.

'Because of my experience in book-keeping, in administration?'

'Non, of course not. Because, as I said, you remind me of myself when I was young. No parents. No prospects.

No money. I clawed my way up with the only talents I had. You have done the same.'

She wondered if her employer had felt the same as her when she'd been young: frightened, alone, petrified of living the life her mother had led with a young child in a hovel that they could not afford. Perhaps it was a blessing that circumstances were as they had been then, instead of now when the war raged around them. What other horrors might have happened to them in a time of war? Thank God she didn't know anyone who'd gone to war. Thank God none of her loved ones were making decisions to kill or be killed.

'Do you know anyone fighting?' Adèle asked her employer.

'My nephew André is in the army,' she replied quietly. 'I do not think it will end well.'

'For André?'

'Or for France,' Chanel admitted. 'For any of us. But immediately, for all of those young men holding the Maginot line. They will all be arrested. They will all become prisoners of war.'

'What will we do, Mademoiselle?' Adèle asked. It had never occurred to her that France would capitulate. The war had only just begun.

'We will adapt, whichever way the tide turns, we will adapt. We always do.'

And now in the comfort of the Ritz Adèle was awoken by the sound of the door opening. She leapt from her position on the settee. She'd slipped off her shoes, curled her feet underneath herself and had rested her head on a cushion. Chanel did not like disorder and the last thing she would tolerate was Adèle looking shabby, the cushions crushed underneath her. Quickly she slipped her shoes back on, neatened her dark hair, adjusting the pins, and straightened down her dress. Before moving to greet Mademoiselle she plumped up the cushion that looked as if it had clearly been slept upon. The apartment must look pristine.

It was one o'clock in the morning and the ice in the bucket had almost melted.

'Good evening, Mademoiselle, how was your—' But she was rendered unable to say any more because behind Chanel was a tall, fair-haired man Adèle thought she might have recognised from previous social occasions over the last few years both in Paris and in the South of France. He was wearing a well-cut suit.

'Good evening, sir,' Adèle said to the good-looking man reaching out to take his coat. He was younger than Mademoiselle, Adèle thought. But certainly much older than Adèle. Over the past few years Mademoiselle had kept the most odd company. Artists, musicians, members of the political elite, British aristocrats. But even with the plethora of people coming and going from Mademoiselle's dining room, Adèle was sure she recognised this man.

His brown eyes watched her as she moved. She felt under direct scrutiny all of a sudden and self-conscious.

'Good evening. Adèle, is it?' he said in English in a distinctly clipped German accent.

Adèle stiffened. Germans were not supposed to be in the residential part of the hotel. How was he here? Why was he here? Presumably his charming smile and the donation of a few coins had won over a lowly sentry. 'Yes, sir,' Adèle returned in English, amused that this man clearly did not speak French. Mademoiselle and Adèle both spoke English, although Adèle's was not advanced. It had been some years since Adèle had the chance to practise it properly.

It made her smile when Mademoiselle turned to him, stroked his chest affectionately and said, 'Be a darling and open the Champagne.' And then to Adèle in snappier tones, 'It has been sent up I assume?'

'Yes, but the ice has melted. I'll send for more.'

But these were details that clearly didn't interest Mademoiselle as she waved her hand at Adèle dismissively and, with an adoring gaze that Adèle had hardly ever seen on her employer's face in the short years she had known her, followed the German man into the room.

Chapter 6

It was the distinct thud of the suite's front door closing that woke Adèle the next morning. She picked up her wristwatch from the little bedside table next to her metal bed and blinked.

It was earlier than Chanel usually woke. Through the high window in Adèle's room, sunlight was only just stretching its distant reach through the faint chink in the dark curtains.

Adèle did not usually have to rise for another hour but now she was awake she could not rest. Had Mademoiselle risen for the day and left already? Had any instructions been left for her? She hoped not. It was her day off, but she'd grown used to tidying the suite quickly and checking everything was as it should be. Adèle washed and dressed and then padded through the corridor to Chanel's rooms. Down the corridor, the door to the bedroom had been left slightly ajar. It was most unlike Mademoiselle to go to sleep with her door open. Through the gap in the door Adèle saw last night's pale silk dress casually thrown in a heap on the floor. And still asleep with a silk mask over her eyes was Mademoiselle.

The other side of the bed was unoccupied but the covers

were thrown back. It was clear to Adèle that whomever the German man was who had returned at one o'clock in the morning to drink Champagne, had only just that moment departed.

Adèle and the housekeeper Madame Basset ate breakfast at the table in the little staff side room. The décor was sparse, with a small round wooden table and chairs. The food had been brought up from the hotel kitchens. It was always the same, buttery croissants and preserves, plates of seasonal fresh fruit, hot coffee. Rationing had not reached the realms of the Ritz. The housekeeper was much older and when making Mademoiselle's bed that morning, if she suspected a gentleman had stayed the night, she said nothing to Adèle. It was not their place to gossip and they talked idly instead, both pointedly ignoring what had occurred.

'It's your day off today?' Madame Basset asked.

Adèle nodded, pouring them both fresh coffee from the silver pot.

'Any plans?'

They had been having this same discussion every time Adèle took her day off, which could change at a moment's notice whenever Mademoiselle decided Adèle was needed. But of course, with the atelier now only selling fragrance and the ability to travel now curtailed by the Nazis, Adèle knew she had less to do and was slowly becoming surplus to requirements.

Alongside this was the fact that, Adèle dared admit it, she didn't have any friends, which was becoming more of a concern as more free time appeared on her hands. Life with Mademoiselle Chanel had been frenetic. Prior to the war, Mademoiselle had travelled so frequently that Adèle had seen more of the world in her short time with Mademoiselle than she was ever likely to in the rest of her life. But such a transient way of living had made it impossible to make friends.

She'd had two good friends in the orphanage and when she'd stayed on to work with Mother Superior, her friends whom she'd grown up with had mostly married local boys and were now raising families. Adèle had been the oddity in wanting to earn her own money, wanting some freedom of her own choosing and, in turn, a life. But of course, a life was the one thing she hadn't achieved.

'No, no plans.' Adèle sighed. 'Just a long walk. Perhaps I shall explore parts of the city I am still not familiar with,' she said. 'Anywhere you would suggest?' she asked politely.

'There is a new exhibition and film on at the Palais Berlitz,' she replied.

'An exhibition? In wartime?'

'Life goes on,' Madame Basset suggested. 'And it's because of the war there's an exhibition being held. Apparently, it's scientific and explains a lot about why we are at war. You should go.'

Adèle moved through the ever-present crowd of soldiers as she walked towards the exhibition. It was only a few streets away from the Ritz and she passed the new German street signs in heavy black lettering; almost calligraphic in style. With very little else to do she may as well spend the morning wandering around the new exhibition, especially when it was so close. Heaven knew when another dose of culture might present itself. She turned into rue Louis-le-Grand and towards the exhibition hall. What she saw made her stop and stare. The long, draped sign hanging almost the length of the art-deco building simply said, 'Jews and France'.

Adèle blinked and thought that could not be right. Madame Basset had suggested the exhibition was scientific and that it would explain why the world was at war. This was, surely, something else entirely. Adèle frowned at the cartoonish, hideous face that had been drawn to illustrate a Jewish man. It was, in every sense, a caricature. Was it meant to be funny? Was it meant to put her off going in? What a strange thing to draw in the crowds. But crowds there were.

She queued patiently, curious that she was joining a long line to enter. Why were so many people here? Perhaps they were just as curious as she was. But as she queued, she felt uncomfortable, a rising sense of dread deep within her core, as if she was doing something wrong. Paris had a long-standing and large Jewish community, and yet this exhibition was to vilify it, surely? She couldn't think. Adèle knew about the Nuremberg Laws removing Jews from positions of power in government and eventually stopping them from becoming citizens in Germany but what was happening in France? Was this where things were leading?

Curiosity had her in its grip but she was determined to reserve judgement on how this French exhibition portrayed the Jewish community until she was inside. What was France now? France had already divided itself in two opposing directions. How did life differ in the unoccupied zone – the zone that had given in and allowed the Nazis to walk right in without any kind of fight – compared to here? Paris had fought. Paris had lost.

Inside the curved lobby were stained glass windows and a booth selling entrance tickets. Once she'd handed over a few francs for a ticket and politely declined the offer to purchase a catalogue – she did not have the funds for such a frippery – she moved into the main hall. Inside she saw a large sculpture of a man: hook nose, pointed features.

She'd once been forced to study a Shakespearean play as part of her literature lessons. She had tried so hard to understand old-fashioned English literature translated into French. She had hated almost all of the texts the nuns had taught and *The Merchant of Venice* was no exception. The treatment of Shylock the Jew had been cruel, unnecessary and the class had formed the general opinion that Shylock was as much a sinner as sinned against by those around him. But the physical description had been uncomplimentary, uninformed and just plain wrong. And that is what Adèle thought of now when she saw the sculpture that was holding a globe.

'The new France freeing herself from the Jewish grip,' Adèle said the title of the statue aloud and then shook her head. She shouldn't be shocked about this really, not here of all places. And yet, she was. It was so blatant.

'The globe represents world domination,' a woman said next to her.

'Yes, thank you,' Adèle said as politely as she could. 'I understood that.' The gathering of people around them nodded appreciatively at this knowledge. There were only one or two people who looked as uncomfortable as she and she barely looked at the placards, sculptures and photographs adorning the space.

Adèle moved on with the crowd and into the main auditorium and found herself a space waiting for the next showing of the film to start in a few minutes. Most of the club armchairs were taken and she was happy to stand at the back as the film started.

'In 1936 there were eight Jews in the president's council, thirty-three Jewish cabinet ministers and seventy Jews in French national radio. The war against the Jew in France will be won . . .'

Repulsed, she turned to leave.

And that's when she saw them: Mademoiselle and the German man from the night before, his hand on her back as the two laughed together, wandering through the auditorium in search of chairs.

Distinctly uncomfortable, Adèle looked away immediately for two reasons, the first that she didn't want to be seen here, the second that she hadn't wanted to think her employer would be here either. But it was too late as she heard Mademoiselle call her name.

Adèle forced a look of delight onto her face as they approached her. Mademoiselle was impeccable as usual, dressed in a burgundy red skirt suit and hat, her layers of long pearls draped around her neck. A few people turned to look, whispering, 'It's Coco Chanel.' The man accompanying her was even more handsome than he had looked yesterday, although admittedly he looked tired and Adèle blushed when she thought about the pile of clothes she had found discarded on the floor of Mademoiselle's bedroom, the sound of the suite door clicking into place as he left this morning.

It was the man who spoke first as the three greeted each other in the melee of people eagerly looking towards the next offensive sculpture or artwork. 'Mademoiselle . . . ?'

'Fabron,' Adèle clarified.

'Mademoiselle Fabron, how nice to see you again,' he said. 'We were not properly introduced yesterday. I am Baron von Dincklage.'

He leant forward, kissed both of her cheeks informally. She could feel remnants of his saliva and she resisted the overwhelming urge to wipe it with the sleeve of her coat.

'And what do you think of the exhibition, Adèle?' Mademoiselle asked.

'I'm not sure what to think, actually.' Adèle opted for honesty. 'I think I've either seen enough or nowhere near enough to understand the consensus.'

'But you understand the point though?' the baron asked. 'You understand what it's trying to convey?'

'I thought it might explain a few things, yes,' Adèle said vaguely. In truth she hadn't known what to expect but now she was inside she could see the horrid theme the exhibition was taking.

'Did you purchase a catalogue?' Mademoiselle asked.

Adèle admitted she had not had the funds to do so and Mademoiselle handed over hers. 'Please. I've read enough.'

Adèle thanked her employer, not quite sure what to make of her comment. As Mademoiselle and Dincklage talked briefly about where they would dine later, Adèle skimmed the opening page:

> *By presenting the Jew in his various manifestations, by showing by means of irrefutable and carefully chosen documents how deep the Jewish hold on all the activities of France was, by revealing the depth of the evil which was eating away at us, we wish to convince those of our fellow citizens who are still of sound mind and good judgement, of the urgency of seeing things as they are and then to act accordingly.*

Although the day was not cold Adèle felt chilled to her bones. 'Act accordingly?' she queried.

It was the baron who spoke. 'In supporting Nazi ideology,' he said simply.

Choosing her words carefully, Adèle said, 'There are those who do not support the ideology.'

Dincklage nodded. 'Resistance groups have been gathering with speed.'

'In hopes of doing what?' Adèle asked, genuinely interested.

'Helping the Allies,' Mademoiselle said as if Adèle was stupid, which Adèle was starting to feel might be the case.

'From within Occupied Paris?' Adèle asked.

'From everywhere,' Dincklage said with a smile. He clearly wasn't worried. 'But yes, there are people in Occupied Paris who are trying to thwart us.'

'And you think this exhibition will put a stop to that?' Adèle spoke out loud and was immediately reprimanded by Mademoiselle.

'Adèle!'

'My apologies,' she said quickly. 'I was merely thinking aloud.'

'Well don't,' her employer said.

'Perhaps,' Dincklage stepped in, 'this exhibition is more useful to bring the populace onside. To prevent any new resisters once they have walked these halls and seen the damaging effect the Jews have.'

Adèle drew in a small intake of breath and decided she wouldn't think aloud again. 'And what is it you do here in Paris, Baron?' she asked politely changing the subject. Part of her wasn't interested in what he did at all; the other half was concerned for her employer and how close she was growing to him.

'I am a diplomat,' he said enigmatically.

Adèle nodded. Her interest in this man and his false ideology waned. 'I will let you enjoy the rest of your day,' Adèle said and made to move on. Dincklage nodded and clipped his heels together in that way she'd seen so many German officials in uniform do over the past few months.

Mademoiselle barely glanced at Adèle. She only had eyes for the baron.

A few streets away from the hateful exhibition Adèle threw the exhibition programme into the nearest wastepaper bin, found a news seller in a kiosk and purchased a copy of *Le Figaro* newspaper. She thanked him and he tipped his cap to her before reaching into his top pocket, taking a piece of hard-looking bread from within and nibbling it. It was too easy to forget the struggles of severe rationing that had gripped Paris. Adèle wasn't subject to such things, tucked up as she was in the Ritz. She noticed the newspaper vendor's sallow skin and turned quickly, hoping she'd been quick enough to cover her pitying expression.

Flicking through the newspaper as she meandered

through Paris, Adèle saw something that made her stop in the street as she read. Behind her someone walked heavily into her, swore loudly, stepped around her and continued on their way, cursing as they walked. But continuing on her way wasn't something she could do after what she had just read. Those who weren't Jewish would have to have a certificate proving their non-Jew status. She folded the newspaper up, forcing the printed words out of sight. Would everything she read today make her feel sick? Adèle could not read on.

She toyed with the newspaper as she turned into Square Louvois. She sat on the grass near the fountain, listening to the comforting sound of the water splashing into the pool below and looked at the passing people, the hint of shabbiness already apparent in the frayed clothing some wore, the flap of a piece of shoe leather that the owner hadn't the money to have repaired.

Where would this end, if it would end at all? She thought of the exhibition, wondering if it would do what the baron had said; if it would educate the populace further. Or would it do what it had done to her? Would it make the people of Paris feel as if the Nazis were even more odious than they had thought them to be? How could they persecute so freely, so unchecked?

She watched a woman walking briskly through the square. The woman was well dressed, immaculate even, her hair bouncing healthily, her skin clear. It struck Adèle just then that already the signs of strict rationing were making themselves known in Paris, choosing its victims; its winners and its losers in this daily struggle for survival. The news seller looked hungry, while Adèle herself, like the passing woman, looked well fed, well dressed and thus stuck out.

Suddenly a smile appeared on the woman's face and she broke into a semi-run. In front of her a German soldier opened his arms to receive her, lifted her in the air, spun her around until her feet landed gently on the ground. And then he kissed her.

Adèle was entranced by this spectacle – entranced and, she realised, disgusted. Is this what was considered normal now? Is this what was considered survival: a French woman and a German lover? If anyone else in the park seemed interested in this, they did not show it. Not even a flicker of interest. But of course, that's what was happening in the room adjacent to hers inside the suite in the Ritz: a French woman and a German lover. She got up from the grass, dusted down her skirt and walked towards a rubbish bin, moving around a man who had annoyingly stopped in front of her, and promptly deposited the newspaper within.

'I said hello,' the man said to her with a laugh.

Already wearing a frown of anger, Adèle spun around to confront the man. If it was some kind of Nazi officer she was going to have to bite her tongue or risk some sort of punishment – although what kind that would be was anyone's guess.

'Oh,' she said, forcing the unattractive frown from her face. 'It's you.'

Doctor Dixon lifted his hand by way of greeting. 'Hi,' he said again. 'How are you?'

She nodded. 'I'm well. Thank you,' she said formally. 'And you?'

'Busy, but . . . I'm well.' A pause. 'Are you sure you're all right?'

'Of course,' she said, slowly brightening. She shook her head a little as if to shake away the anger that had risen. 'Of course.'

'OK,' he said uncertainly. 'You looked a bit . . .'

'A bit . . . ?'

'Angry,' he ventured uncertainly.

His honesty forced Adèle to smile. 'I was,' she said, also opting for honesty. 'But I'm not now.'

61

'Good.' He put his hand into his pocket. In the other he clutched a copy of the same newspaper she had just placed in the bin. He wore a suit and tie, his trilby hat covering his dark hair. 'What made you so angry?' he asked.

She gestured towards the newspaper. 'That,' she said. 'The story about the Jews and the certificates. I . . . I was shocked, I suppose and then that shock turned to anger.'

'It's unstoppable,' he said with a shrug that wasn't quite nonchalant enough to indicate he didn't care. Of course he cared. How could anyone not?

A woman moved towards them and Doctor Dixon watched her carefully then smiled as she deposited something in the bin and moved off. He pointed towards a bench. 'Shall we?'

She had nowhere else to be and so took him up on his offer. They were less conspicuous sitting and out of natural earshot of anyone who might take offence to their anti-Nazi talk.

'You sound resigned to it,' she said when they'd sat next to each other, close but not too close.

'I am. There's no way we can stop the big things,' he said. 'No way at all. Things like that . . .' He blew air out of his cheeks. 'It's impossible.'

'But it doesn't mean we can't get angry.'

'Of course not,' he said. 'But anger won't do you any good.'

Adèle sighed. 'I know,' she said feeling like a child who'd just been dressed down.

A German soldier walked past them, clearly taking in the sights. There were so many of them now.

Doctor Dixon had grown sombre and was trying to avoid looking at the soldier. 'It's all around us isn't it,' he said.

Adèle thought of the couple she'd seen embracing earlier. 'Yes. Yes it is.' And then: 'I just watched a couple kissing.' The moment she said it she regretted it.

He spluttered with laughter and then when he'd recovered looked at her with curiosity.

'I meant . . .' Adèle replied trying to squash down the laughter that she'd also let forth. 'I meant a German man and a French woman.'

Doctor Dixon couldn't hide the mirth from his face.

'That's what I meant,' Adèle clarified.

'See? It's unstoppable,' Doctor Dixon responded with a smile.

'The war? Or love? Because I don't think that woman was in love with that soldier. That was about something else entirely,' Adèle guessed and then wondered if what she had seen was, in fact, love or something else, something more fleeting, temporary. She had no experience of either.

'Both the war and love,' he said with meaning. 'Especially love. Once that train has left the station there's no stopping it.'

'You sound as if you speak from experience,' Adèle probed.

'Not really. But history speaks from experience. Think of all the great romances, Helen of Troy, Romeo and Juliet—'

'Napoléon and Josephine,' Adèle joined in which raised a smile from Doctor Dixon.

'Possibly them,' he said and the mirth was back on his face. 'But you see what I'm driving at. There are many things in this world that can't just be switched off like an electric light. War can be halted with the right words, the right actions. But love . . . love is unstoppable.'

Adèle watched the water falling in the fountain in front of them. The sound of it splashing was suddenly overwhelming. 'I think that's quite frightening,' she said.

'Do you?' he asked shifting his body on the bench to look at her more closely. 'Why do you think it's frightening?'

She thought before speaking. 'Love must be a feeling of being out of control. And I'm not sure I would like that . . . that total powerlessness. It makes me worried that it could make a person . . .' she thought for the right word '. . . vulnerable. It makes me feel I would be vulnerable,' she said quietly. She wished she'd not said it. She wished she'd not fallen into her own trap of thinking aloud. The hot blush creeping up her face was unbearable.

He continued looking at her. 'You would be,' he said. 'We're all vulnerable in love. You should be able to be totally and utterly lost in love, swept up in it. That's how it should be. That's the beauty of it.'

Adèle turned her gaze from the fountain towards Doctor Dixon and found he was still looking at her. She opened her mouth to say something, although what it was going to be, she didn't know. No man had ever spoken to her in this way. But even so it was wonderful to talk so freely with someone about real subjects. It was so hard to know who to trust, but Doctor Dixon was kind and genuine and unlike every other man she saw out on the street – not a member of the Occupying force.

As if only now realising he'd spoken so entirely unrestrainedly, Doctor Dixon stood suddenly. 'Will you excuse me?' he said, glancing at his watch although not really looking at it from what Adèle could tell. 'I have to go.'

She nodded. Really he'd saved her from saying something stupid but it didn't stop a resolute feeling of sadness. 'Of course.'

'May I . . . walk you somewhere on my way to the Metro?' he suggested.

'I'm walking in a different direction,' she said apologetically as she stood.

'That's a shame.' He sounded genuine. 'I was visiting a friend and I should really get back to the hospital now,' he explained although he didn't need to.

'Yes,' Adèle replied. 'I also have to . . .' She didn't know how to finish this sentence. 'Goodbye,' she said.

He extended his hand. 'Goodbye. It was nice to see you again.' She shook his hand, enjoying the feeling of his warm palm in hers once again. And then she let go. And so did he. He nodded, smiled, turned and walked away.

Adèle watched him for a moment, wanting to call out to him but for what reason she just couldn't voice. She could never call out to him – could never embarrass herself like that. She had embarrassed herself enough already.

'Goodbye.' It came out as a whisper. And then she watched him leave the square, cross the road and then he turned the corner and was gone.

A few days later, Adèle was at work. She had tried not to think about the handsome doctor, as she ran to and from the hotel and the atelier. It was as if she'd dreamt the encounter with him, dreamt their talk about love that had brought her far too close to revealing things about herself that she'd never told anyone. She had never been in love and thanks to her upbringing had hardly ever met any men. She'd thought in Paris there might be some opportunity to meet people, make more friends. But until recently the incessant travel had put paid to that.

In the atelier, she climbed the mirrored spiral staircase, sad to think of all those women who were now unemployed as a result of Mademoiselle closing her couture business. At the time it had felt like the right thing to do, and Chanel's words that wartime wasn't a time to be fashionable were applauded in Adèle's mind, if not in the minds of those who were now unemployed as a result at an already desperate time.

On the street, she noticed a woman leaving Elsa Schiaparelli's boutique opposite the Ritz in Place Vendôme. Mademoiselle hated the woman and she hated seeing her shop in such close proximity. Unlike the couture of Chanel, Schiaparelli was still open and thriving. People needed clothes, and nice ones when there was money to be had for getting them. She wondered if Mademoiselle ever regretted her decision to close. After all her talk of women needing to fight for survival, when it came to it Mademoiselle had simply sent her all-female staff packing. Other than Adèle, who felt keenly that she had been spared this fate. But for how long?

She looked towards the ceiling as she contemplated this but snapped back into position as the tell-tale click-clack of Mademoiselle's shoes could be heard as she ascended the mirrored staircase and walked along the corridor to the office where Adèle was now hurriedly feeding a new ribbon into the typewriter. She didn't want to be seen to be idle at a time when there was already very little to do.

'Adèle,' Mademoiselle barked in that way she did when she was ready to do battle. 'I am going to do something about getting my business back.'

'Mademoiselle?' Adèle questioned. Adèle had always known that the Parfums Chanel business wasn't entirely owned by Mademoiselle Chanel; that at its founding seventy per cent had been assigned to two Jewish brothers, the Wertheimers, when Chanel first decided to manufacture fragrance with her name on it. Mademoiselle had also made no secret of the fact she had felt swindled by the brothers, having given over far more of a share in the business than she felt she should have done. After twenty per cent had been assigned to the department store owner who had made the Wertheimer introduction, only ten per cent had been left to Mademoiselle; something she agreed to at the time but bitterly regretted now.

Despite the fact the ten per cent paid for such grandeur and riches, Mademoiselle had been muttering for years about how she would one day go about clawing back that which was hers. Adèle had opened many correspondences from the Wertheimers over the years and had taken dictation for letters from Mademoiselle in return. But her tone today was different.

'The Wertheimers are no longer here,' Mademoiselle said. 'They ran away long ago and left my business to turn to dust, the Chanel name to turn to dust.'

Adèle didn't point out that this wasn't quite true, that the Wertheimers, like so many other prominent Jewish families in France had escaped persecution, knowing what was coming for them, knowing what hatred was spilling out of Germany and reaching out across the rest of Europe. Adèle also could hardly point out that Mademoiselle had willingly closed part of her business for the duration of the war. Instead of speaking out and inciting anger in the woman who paid Adèle's salary, she simply agreed.

'Today, I will do something about it,' Mademoiselle said, clasping her hands together in something resembling excitement.

'Mademoiselle?' Adèle questioned.

'Type this,' she instructed. She paused, pursed her crimson-painted lips and then turned to face Adèle, reeling off a set of instructions in a letter addressed to the German authorities that shocked Adèle so much that she paused in her typing, hurrying to catch up with the words that flew from Mademoiselle's mouth.

'Parfums Chanel has been legally "abandoned" by its owners. I have an indisputable right of priority. The profits that I have received from my creations since the foundation of this business . . . are disproportionate . . .'

Mademoiselle Chanel continued in a tone of excited anger, practically spitting the words she dictated to Adèle. Adèle could hardly believe what she was hearing. Her heart thudded in her chest. Adèle was about to be complicit in . . . she didn't know what. Was this a crime? Was what

Chanel was asking the authorities for actually a crime? She was going to try to wrest back control of Parfums Chanel by force. In the letter, her employer was citing the Nuremberg Laws prohibiting Jews from owning businesses in order to ask the Nazis to hand over the remaining shares in the business to her.

Adèle finished typing, her fingers shaking.

'Read it back to me please,' Mademoiselle instructed when Adèle had finally finished catching up with the dictation. She had paused for too long as she'd tried to force the shock of the situation from her mind and focus on the task.

She did as she was told, her voice level and steady as if she remained entirely unaffected by the vitriol that had found its way onto the page from the mouth of her employer.

'I have only ever owned a part of my own business, Adèle,' Mademoiselle Chanel said, walking over and forcefully tapping the page that still sat on the typewriter. 'With the Wertheimers not here to fight me and with the help of the Nazis, I will own it entirely.'

Mademoiselle's insistence that her business be handed over to her in entirety, when she had only ever retained a small portion of it in exchange for business acumen, investment and resources from the Wertheimer brothers, didn't sit well with Adèle. But Adèle had diligently communicated everything her employer had asked for in the letters; never once changing a word although she'd winced while Mademoiselle had dictated her impassioned missive. This seemed underhand, surely, and dare she think it . . . opportunistic.

Perhaps, she thought trying to see it from both sides, Mademoiselle would calm herself once her initial assessment of the situation was proven to be out of kilter with what would eventually feel right. Perhaps she would pause, sleep on it, not act so quickly—

'Type it up a second time and take a copy of it to my lawyer's office.' Chanel cut into Adèle's hopeful thoughts. 'He too has fled,' Chanel tittered. 'But important messages have a way of finding him.'

'And do you wish me to log any official request regarding the business to the . . .' Adèle couldn't even bring herself to say Nazis, so she said, 'authorities to be filed appropriately? Do we know which location that particular—'

'No. I can handle that myself,' Mademoiselle Chanel said dismissively.

Relief swept over Adèle like a cooling glass of water on a stiflingly hot day that she would not have to enter a Nazi office and file the request. She did not want to be any more complicit than she already was.

As she walked through Paris to the lawyer's office in the seventh arrondissement she debated the copy of the letter she held in her hand. On the one hand she could understand that Mademoiselle felt as if she had already been conned out of her business – although she had entered into all agreements willingly when the Wertheimers had begun working with her – and that this was the only choice left open to her in order to wrest back control. Adèle had no true possessions other than those within her Chinese lacquered box, but if she had ever owned anything substantial and she'd felt conned out of it, how would she feel? The same as Mademoiselle felt probably.

She delivered her letter to the secretary who said the lawyer would receive it in due course. Who knew how letters were finding their way out of France? People in high places, Adèle assumed wondering about how the city of light had grown so divided. The difference between those who had, and those who didn't, those who collaborated and those who resisted was so obvious and growing even more so as the months passed.

She wondered what kind of man the lawyer was, what

his reaction might be as he found out what one of his clients intended to do. Would he condemn or condone? Adèle walked back in the direction from which she'd just come, towards rue Cambon, intending to return to the atelier until her working day drew to a close, but down the road a police van caught her eye. Then she heard the pleading, tearful cries of a woman who was being pulled and tugged aggressively by police officers. The street was not particularly busy but those who stopped and stared only did so for a moment before rushing onwards; forcing themselves to be blind to what was happening to this woman.

Adèle moved onwards.

'*S'il vous plaît*,' she heard the woman cry. 'Please.' Was she crying to Adèle, to the heavens or to the police officers forcing her towards the van? 'S'il vous plaît.'

Adèle slipped into a closed apartment building entrance-way, almost out of sight of the police and turned back to watch. The woman caught her eye as she was pushed into the van and her eyes widened pleadingly. 'Help. Help,' she cried and the direction of her gaze changed. She looked upwards, towards the building from where she had just been forcibly removed. Adèle followed the woman's gaze upward to the second-floor window and drew in a sharp intake of breath.

Adèle looked back at the woman whose eyes were boring into hers.

'Help,' the woman cried. 'Help!'

Adèle nodded at her. She could do nothing else. She had to let her know in any way she could that it would be all right, even if it would be anything but.

And then the woman was pushed roughly inside the van. The doors were slammed closed, the policemen climbed inside the front cab and then the van moved down the street.

After that, it was as if nothing had happened; nothing

at all. Pedestrians moved seamlessly about their business, as if they had been frozen in time and had simply thawed, commencing their day. No one looked at where the commotion had just taken place. They were staunchly looking anywhere else. No one had noticed Adèle, still standing in the doorway, deliberating what to do. No one, it seemed, had followed the woman's gaze to the upper window. And, more importantly, no one other than Adèle appeared to have noticed the child in the window, its cheek pressed against the glass, a look of tearful despair on its face.

Chapter 7

2018

Dressed in jeans and a short-sleeved sweatshirt Chloé left the apartment and decided to walk through the city to meet her friend for dinner. Paris at night was a thing of wonder. The streetlamps were bulbous, old-fashioned and held up in ornate metalwork, but best of all gave off an antique orange-yellow glow so at odds with the modern white lights slowly being installed in the streets at home. Although it occurred to Chloé that she didn't really consider her little flat home anymore. It was more a crash pad since her tenants had left and she'd moved back in with her tail between her legs, making it a base.

But of course, she was now in Paris, taking time to explore, to work, and to recover from the train wreck of her divorce. So why did she feel like she was floating aimlessly? She was having a gap year and it was a perfectly legitimate reason to be taking time out. But alongside it, her appetite had been whetted by what Etienne had said about Coco Chanel's involvement with the Nazis and, in turn, what that meant in relation to her own grandmother. Was there a way she could understand more while she was here in Paris? What was it Etienne had mentioned about files only recently surfacing?

Under the glow of the lamps she was on her way to meet her old university friend Henri at Les Bols de Jean restaurant. It had been his suggestion and Chloé was excited to hear that every dish was served inside an oversized toasted and buttered brioche bowl. Rob had hated restaurants like this. Why was he in her mind now?

She arrived before Henri, sat down and took in the simple slatted wooden tables lined against the long window. It was stark and achingly hip and she felt so old compared to most of the other patrons. The delicious smells emanating from the kitchen and the steaming dishes being carried past were too much and made her stomach groan in hunger. She ordered a glass of wine while waiting for Henri, who was always fashionably late. Nothing had changed in the best part of two decades since they'd first met.

Chloé hadn't seen Henri since his 'Leaving London' party a few years ago. They'd known each other since university where they'd both been placed in the same halls of residence and doing similar courses. And after they'd left university and found jobs easily back when jobs were easy to find, they'd seen each other socially off and on. But two years ago Henri had moved back to France and naturally gravitated towards the dizzying fashion heights of Paris. He'd never been fashionable per se but as he entered the restaurant, grinning widely at seeing her, she noticed he'd really upped his game in the sartorial stakes.

'Chloé,' he called. 'It's so good to see you.'

They kissed each other's cheeks and held each other at arm's length so each could appraise the other. 'And you. You look so good,' she said appreciatively.

'When working at Le Bon Marché, it's best to make the effort.' He sat, gestured confidently for the waiter and ordered a bottle of beer. He looked at her and smiled. 'You look great. Divorce suits you. I could not believe it when you said you were here. Tell me everything.'

Five years ago Chloé had been walking down the aisle in not quite a big white dress but certainly a well-fitted, medium-sized ivory lace number; assuming all the pieces of her life had finally fallen into place. Marrying just before her thirty-fifth birthday had given Chloé some level of hope that having children would naturally follow but, more than that, she had been in love. And that was such a feeling.

'It was only a pity that the man I walked down the aisle with hadn't quite felt the same way,' Chloé told Henri. 'Not in the end. Probably not even at the start.'

How Chloé hadn't seen their love wax and wane was beyond her.

'We were too wrapped up in our jobs, planning five-star holidays and it wasn't really *me*. It was a lovely ride to be taken on, but it just felt . . .'

'Superficial?' Henri suggested.

'Yes. Superficial. And then it eventually became apparent we had nothing in common.' Chloé tried to phrase the next bit delicately; that Rob had never been content with what he had, always striving for the next big thing. That was what had initially attracted her to him – his drive, passion, determination. But he'd hated how she loved nothing more than staying home, cooking a good meal and it being just them.

'Just us wasn't good enough,' she surmised. 'I wasn't good enough.'

Henri frowned and blew air out of his cheeks. 'That is not true.'

She shrugged. They had been different people who wanted different things. The pain of having nothing to talk about on their honeymoon, once the thrill of the wedding was over, should have raised alarm bells. Maybe it did. Maybe Chloé simply hadn't noticed, or had decided not to notice. And on it dragged for another two years because Chloé hadn't wanted to let it go. And Rob hadn't wanted to let it go but he hadn't wanted to fight either.

Just remembering the humiliation of how it all came crashing down made her close her eyes tightly to shut it all out. She'd felt duped, angry, but most of all humiliated; totally and utterly humiliated that it had ended the way it had; that it had ended at all.

She told Henri all of it, that it was only when they really weren't getting on that Rob suggested they start a family and then Chloé could have sat out the working week at a house in Oxfordshire he was toying with buying, while he planned to join her at the weekends. Only then had she really realised things had gone so irretrievably wrong. They'd had such divergent ideas about what marriage should be. And neither of them knew how to fix it. But she knew having children wasn't the answer. When a marriage was already in trouble, children were the last thing to bring into it. Children weren't a sticking plaster. She'd felt so lost and alone. There was nothing quite so awful as feeling alone in a marriage and Chloé had walked out, her tail between her legs, feeling humiliated, ashamed and a complete failure.

It had taken her a full three months before she'd been able to admit to any of her family what had happened. By which time Rob had casually dropped into a text message that he hoped she was moving on because he'd already moved on with someone else. The pain of that had stung the most – how quickly he'd been able to replace her. Chloé didn't want to know what his new girlfriend looked like. She didn't want to know what her name was either. The thought of him with someone else made her sick. But she couldn't have stayed. She just couldn't. Even so, she had loved him and she couldn't simply switch that off, even if he had turned out to be so incredibly wrong for her. One by one their mutual friends had turned away from Chloé, deciding weekends at Rob's new country house held more charm than wine and takeout at Chloé's old flat.

'Then they were not real friends,' Henri surmised.

'True,' Chloé said after a moment's thought. She remembered how work colleagues who'd attended the wedding had looked at Chloé with obvious pity more recently and all of it together was enough to convince her that a change was as good as a rest.

On the day the decree absolute came, she had expected to feel a sense of relief, not the sharp sense of pain. 'The moment I put down the pen after officially ridding myself of Rob, the ink not even dry, I waited for an epiphany that never came.' Chloé shrugged.

'And so I forced an epiphany. I needed a change. I needed to get away from everything and actually live the kind of life I'd always wanted – not the kind of life I felt I should live.' She earned decent money, she'd kept her own flat and when her tenants had given notice she'd slunk back there after she'd left Rob.

But she didn't want to live in her old flat. Not now. That was just going backwards, adding to the failure. Instead, she was going to live anywhere she wanted and do all those things she'd always put off because she'd been too busy living the kind of life she thought she should have lived rather than the kind of life she actually wanted to live.

'So now I'm here, working at a little boutique called Anouk in Saint Germain. My friend who owns it has just had a baby and so she's popping in and out, but she was finding it too hard to be in the shop full-time with a newborn. She just wanted a bit of help for a few months and so when she told me that, I volunteered to come over and help.'

'Are you enjoying it?' he asked.

'Yes, actually, I think I am. It's so different to what I'm used to doing at work. But I love the environment, the boutique; I love the people who shop there. Such a variety. And such an easy pace of life. I didn't realise I needed that.'

'All work and no play?' Henri suggested.

'I've done a few tourist things, obviously,' Chloé was quick to point out.

'Obviously,' he said. 'Eiffel Tower?' he questioned.

'Check,' Chloé replied.

'A bateau cruise of the Seine?'

'Done. Quite romantic really, dinner for one.'

He gave her a sympathetic smile. Although she made light of it, she didn't want to say it had made her heart tighten and had been a painful reminder that she was now divorced. The waiter returned with Henri's drink and handed them both menus, before reeling off the specials. They chatted about the queues for the Louvre and how it had put Chloé off. Henri admitted he'd not actually been inside the Louvre since a school trip when he was a child. 'Why are you going to the Louvre? Try something different. I'm more of a Musée d'Orsay fan,' he replied. 'Although I've not been there since before I left to go to England for university.'

'Well I've not done the Musée d'Orsay yet so I'll add it to the list,' Chloé said.

'You should.'

They ordered food and Chloé's stomach rumbled in readiness at the thoughts of the cheesy-sounding dish she'd ordered, while Henri opted for a light carpaccio dish, which made him sound more noble than he was seeing as the whole thing was about to be served inside a white bread bowl.

'Other than the lonely boat cruise, how are you finding things since finishing with Rob?' he asked.

'I suppose I'm finding it all right,' she said thoughtfully. 'It's just hard, I think. I thought we were supposed to be together. But if Rob and I had really been perfect for each other then it might hurt a whole lot more. Now I'm back being single, back to how it was before we met. Exactly the same old Chloé. Just a bit older. Hopefully a bit wiser.'

'You're not exactly the same. You're different. Good different. Don't forget it was you who started divorce proceedings. If you hadn't, nothing would have ever changed. And now you're in Paris,' he said with a mischievous smile.

'That's true,' Chloé said. 'Perhaps it's time to live a little.' She smiled and raised her glass to clink with Henri's as they both said, '*Salut*.'

They talked through old times, reminiscing through dinner until Henri asked, 'What are you doing after this?'

'Nothing. Might get cosy and read a book in bed.'

'Non,' he said. 'That is not very exciting. I've been invited to a late-night exhibition in the Marais and you are coming with me.'

Chloé weighed up how tired she was feeling versus the opportunity to go out with a friend she'd not seen in years.

'I thought you just said you were in Paris to live a little.' Henri's mischievous grin was back. 'So come and live.'

Chloé remembered why she adored the Marais. It just gave off a vibe of coolness with its gay bars, historic streets, cobblestone pavements and an abundance of art galleries. Like most buildings in Paris the exterior of this gallery belied what was inside. The ornate plasterwork pillars surrounding the door made Chloé think the inside would be Baroque on a grand Parisian scale but pushing the polished brass handle on the intricate wooden doors led Chloé and Henri into a wide, open space, the structural steel running overhead indicating the one large room had once been many smaller rooms in a previous guise. The light wasn't as bright as she'd usually seen in art galleries. Instead, it was muted, with flickering candles in tea light holders dotted around on the floor, across which waitresses carried silver trays laden with Champagne. Spotlights over each art placement meant potential buyers could see what they were investing in.

And it was the art on the walls that made Chloé's mouth drop open. She stared, wide-eyed. Henri took two Champagne flutes from a passing waitress and handed one to Chloé.

She looked pointedly at Henri. 'Henri.' She nodded in the direction of the nearest canvas. 'This is porn.'

'Pfft,' he said. 'Of course it is not porn. It is French,' he teased. 'It is very tasteful.'

Chloé wasn't easily shocked or particularly prudish but now she'd reclaimed her ability to speak, she was trying to suppress the nervous laugh that had leapt into her throat. She hid her surprise behind her Champagne flute. The exhibition was a series of photographs of various men and women in states of undress, their arms and legs in the most curious of positions.

'By tasteful, do you mean it's in black and white?' Chloé asked. 'Or is it because you're a man,' she said eagerly. 'A Frenchman, that you don't think this is a bit . . . dirty?'

'Be quiet,' he said. 'Or you will make me laugh.'

A man's voice sounded from behind them. 'Why are you going to laugh, Henri?'

Henri and Chloé turned, chastised, hoping the beginning part of her conversation about comparing this to pornography hadn't been overheard.

'Etienne,' Henri cried and strode forward, his hand outstretched. The two men shook hands and inside Chloé died a little bit. 'Chloé, this is Etienne Vaillancourt. He owns the gallery. Etienne, this is my friend Chloé James. We were at university together.'

'Bonsoir,' Etienne said, looking at Chloé. A smile drifted across his face in recognition. 'Hello again. I was not expecting to see you so soon.' Etienne held his hand out for Chloé, which she shook. His palm was cool from where he'd been holding his chilled Champagne glass.

'Likewise,' Chloé said. 'Henri brought me to look at . . . er . . .'

'Pornography?' Etienne said seriously. 'That is what you were saying, non?'

'No . . .' Chloé lied. 'No no. I wasn't saying that at all.'

'Forgive her. She's English.' Henri shrugged by way of explanation. 'How do you two know each other?'

'We met at an auction,' Etienne said, his eyes not leaving Chloé's. 'I almost spent a few thousand euros on a dog bed because of Chloé,' he said. But before either Henri or she had the chance to query this statement Etienne continued. 'Have you had a chance to look around yet?'

'Non,' Henri said. 'We've just arrived.'

'Then I'll leave you to it,' Etienne said. 'Take your time, enjoy and do not leave without saying goodbye.' Etienne nodded, collected an empty glass from a tall, white cloth-covered table and, having dusted off some canapé crumbs, moved off.

'Quickly, tell me how you know him?' Chloé asked.

Henri turned in conspiratorially. 'Friend of a friend of a friend. He invites me because once I arrived here drunk and spent a large sum of money on a sculpture. Now I am on the invitation list.'

'Was the sculpture naked by any chance?' Chloé asked with a raised eyebrow.

'Oh be quiet,' he said. 'What is this about a dog bed?'

'We met earlier,' Chloé said. 'At the Ritz auction.'

'I read in the paper that was happening this week. Did you buy anything?' he asked.

'No. Far too expensive.' She explained her reasons for going, about her grandmother and Chanel living in the Ritz as the two of them moved around the room, sipping their Champagne and casting curious glances at the art on the walls. 'And then he told me something that was a bit . . . I don't know. Anyway.'

'No, go on,' Henri prompted.

Chloé cast a quick look around them and then, quietly said, 'Did you know Coco Chanel was a Nazi agent in the war?'

Henri just looked at her as if she was kidding and then: 'Truly? An actual agent?'

'Yes, Etienne told me. And then of course I had to check because it seemed so . . . obscene.'

Henri straightened. 'It is obscene, yes. But why are you bothered by Etienne telling you this?'

'He seemed to be suggesting my grandmother was in some way involved.'

Another couple approached, extolling the virtues of the piece in front of them. Henri put his hand on Chloé's back and gently ushered her onwards. 'How does he know?'

'He doesn't,' Chloé said. 'I think he's assuming.'

'What do you think?' Henri asked.

'I don't know what to think. I know hardly anything about my gran's time working for Chanel during the war. She's always remained so tight-lipped about it that we weren't encouraged to press her. She made her role sound so insignificant that we were almost put off asking questions. But files have recently been released that cast Chanel in such an ugly light that it makes me wonder.'

'Makes you wonder if your gran was involved in some way?'

'Yes, exactly that, Henri. Exactly that. I just want to know more before I go storming back on the Eurostar to confront my gran.'

'Is that what you intend to do? Confront your grandmother?' A frown line appeared between his eyes.

'Maybe. Depends what I find out, I suppose.'

Henri nodded thoughtfully and Chloé found herself

staring absently at a picture of a couple locked in a naked embrace. When she realised what she was looking at she blinked, looked away embarrassed and glared at Henri. 'Christ, why have you brought me here?' She laughed and then drained her glass.

Henri was spared answering as his mobile rang and he excused himself, stepping away to take the call.

Chloé's eyes were drawn back to the canvas. She tilted her head to one side trying to work out what the couple in the picture were doing. 'It defies gravity,' she muttered and then felt a presence behind her.

She turned to find Etienne looking at the same artwork. A deep sense of anxiety passed over her that he was standing there watching her as she looked at a picture of a couple doing things that, in her opinion, should probably be kept a bit more private than this. She felt voyeuristic.

He handed her a fresh glass of Champagne and took a sip from his own, a small smile on his face. He was clearly waiting for her to speak.

'Does this stuff actually sell?' she asked to fill the awkward silence.

Etienne pointed to a red sticker placed in the bottom right corner of the piece, indicating it had been sold. 'Yes,' he said simply.

'Well, jolly good,' she replied.

Etienne laughed quietly and then said, 'When I gave you my card, I didn't think I would see you only hours later.'

'No, it's an accident. Honestly, I haven't even looked at the card you gave me. If I had . . .'

'You would not have come when Henri suggested it?'

'Oh well . . . I mean,' Chloé fumbled for an appropriate response.

'Because I upset you?'

'You didn't upset me,' Chloé said. 'You sort of stunned me more than anything. Shocked me.'

'I apologise again,' he said genuinely.

'It's OK. I've had a bit of time to think about it.'

'And . . . ?' he prompted.

'I'd like to know more about her.'

'Chanel or your grandmother?' He tipped his head to the side, awaiting her response.

'Chanel. My grandmother. Both,' Chloé said.

'OK then,' he said and nodded to smile at someone who had caught his eye.

'What do you mean, OK then?' she asked.

'Just that, OK then.' He shrugged, returning his gaze to her. 'I will help you.'

'Oh, I wasn't asking you to—'

'Do you know where you are going to look first?' he cut in.

'No. I haven't really had the chance to—'

'Because I do,' he said.

Chloé stared at him. 'Really?' This was only the second time she'd met Etienne and both times he had successfully managed to stun her.

'There are archives available,' he said.

'Hang on a second,' Chloé said. 'I . . .' Did she want to look in those? Did she want written confirmation that her grandmother was mixed up in Nazi activity? She swallowed hard.

'We don't know that my gran was in league with . . .' She couldn't even say it.

'Well, no. Not yet. And even if she was, remember even Chanel wasn't a Nazi until she became one.'

Even though the room was crowded, body heat emanating through the gallery, a wave of cold shivered across her skin.

'I'm sorry, what exactly are you trying to say?' Chloé said after having digested that strange sentence for a moment.

He glanced around, eager to defuse Chloé's ticking time

bomb. 'Nothing. I apologise. I must say goodbye to some guests. What are you doing tomorrow?'

'Working,' she said, dazed.

'I have upset you again?' he said perceptively.

She shook her head although wasn't quite sure she meant it.

'Where do you work?' he asked softly.

'Anouk in Saint Germain.'

He nodded, smiled and made to say something else but it was Chloé's turn to cut him off. 'It was nice to meet you again,' she said, extending her hand. He took it in his. His eyes penetrated hers and Chloé had to turn away, mutter a goodbye, let go of his hand. She bumped into Henri by the door.

'Are you leaving?' Henri asked.

'Yes. I'm tired,' she said truthfully. 'And I can't look at any more porn.'

Henri laughed, kissed her on the cheek twice to say goodbye. 'I'll call you. Let's do this again.'

'Maybe not *this*,' she suggested, gesturing to Etienne's gallery. 'And don't get drunk on free Champagne and buy any naked art,' she warned. 'Because I promise you I'm not coming to your apartment if you hang one of those on the wall,' she teased before walking out into the warm night air of Paris.

Chapter 8

Chloé was hanging up a beautiful vintage dress that had just arrived in the boutique, looking at how to arrange it with some of the necklaces and scarves. She'd only been here a few weeks but restraining herself from purchasing any more of the stock for her own wardrobe was proving difficult. She'd already bought two dresses and a pale pink cashmere jumper that it was too warm to wear now but come winter would be brought out and worn with glee. And then there was her trip to Kilo Shop where vintage clothes could be purchased by weight. She'd been particularly pleased with her beginner's luck purchase of a faux fur jacket and a pair of faded Levi's that had totalled a bargain.

She'd always seen the joy in vintage pieces, the beauty of something old being worn by someone new. The unexpected find of an heirloom piece that had broken free of its ties and made it out from family connections into the wider world; or a piece that had managed to escape the vagaries of the clothing recycling bins and had made it into a flea market to be purchased fifty or sixty years later by someone who wanted to give it a new lease of life. This was the theory Brigitte, Chloé's friend and owner of the boutique, subscribed to and so did Chloé. Although in her career as a visual merchandiser, Chloé had only ever handled factory-fresh items, never anything that held historical value or that posed a question in her mind about a garment's origin.

'Yes,' Brigitte said as she stepped forward to adjust the angle of a shirt tucked into a skirt. 'Beautiful. Just like that. And maybe—' She pointed to an amethyst pendant held on a delicate rope-like braid of silver. 'Shall we pair it with that? Oui, it's perfect,' Brigitte said as her little baby Fabien cried and she moved to pick him up, gently shushing him and consoling him while she instructed Chloé to find a delicate pair of heels with which to style the piece. 'Sorry, I am teaching you your own job,' Brigitte said, eyes wide with horror.

'I'm not offended,' Chloé soothed. 'I'm happy to be shown how you like things done. Besides, it's a foolish person who thinks they know better than everyone else and you know your customers better than I do. You know what catches their eye.'

'And makes them open their wallets,' Brigitte teased. 'Well, I will try to restrain myself. Sometimes the whole ensemble sets their eyes alight and it's too hard for them to resist purchasing it all,' Brigitte said with a wicked glint. 'As you know only too well.'

Chloé did know this only too well. 'Not me and not today,' she said. 'I've already bought enough.'

'You are already my best customer this month,' Brigitte teased.

The bell above the door rang, indicating someone had entered the shop. Brigitte turned to see if it was a regular customer and on realising it wasn't, mouthed to Chloé, 'I will just pop through and feed little one.'

Chloé nodded and turned to greet the shopper. She smiled politely but sighed inwardly. Etienne, off-duty in a white shirt and well-cut jeans, closed the door behind him and turned to give Chloé a sheepish smile.

After a few seconds it was Chloé who spoke first. 'Hello. Come to buy something or come to stress me out a bit more?'

He looked around and replied, 'Hmm, I do not know yet. I will think.'

Chloé felt a smile pull at the edges of her mouth as Etienne said, 'I am here to apologise. Yet again.'

'Apology accepted,' she replied, watching him as he glanced around the shop.

'Good. Thank you.' He turned and reached for the door handle.

'Er . . .' Chloé made her confusion at his sudden departure audible.

He looked back.

'Is that it?' Chloé asked.

'What do you mean?'

'You came all this way to say just a few words and now you're off?'

'Yes?' he said uncertainly. He was mocking her, teasing her. She was sure of it. But actually, she wasn't sure at all. 'Not going to insinuate anything about my family history?'

'Non,' he said and looked at her as if she was mad.

'Well, I must say I am disappointed.' Chloé folded her arms.

Etienne looked at her and smiled. 'I would invite you to join me for lunch, but I am worried I have offended you too deeply.'

Chloé thought and then leant over the counter a little to reinforce her point when she said, 'I can't work out if that's actually an invitation to lunch or not.'

'Yes. It is,' he said. 'Where do you normally dine near here?'

'I usually just run out, grab a salad and eat in the shop,' she said.

He looked as if he disapproved heartily, but said, 'Let's do that then,' and with that Chloé realised immediately that Etienne really had just come here to apologise and be gone. And now she'd strong-armed him into a lunch he didn't really want to have with her. Was it really this hard? Was communication between men and women so difficult that even planning to eat an innocent and impromptu meal with someone carried all this subtext and weight?

From the back room the sounds of baby Fabien crying for a few seconds rang through and Etienne looked curious.

'My friend Brigitte who owns the boutique,' Chloé explained. 'She's just had her baby and . . .' in a louder voice so Brigitte could hear '. . . refuses to stay at home with him.'

'I am bored. Babies sleep all the time,' Brigitte called from the back room.

Etienne smiled and called out a polite hello, which was returned.

'I will come back with lunch,' he said and left, casting Chloé a near-devastating smile as he turned past the window and down the street.

Chloé sat back and wondered what all this was in aid of. Was he really just sorry or was there an ulterior motive? But before she had time to analyse it too carefully Brigitte called out, 'Come in here at once and tell me who that was!'

It surprised Chloé and Brigitte that Etienne returned with three salads, fresh warm baguettes, a round gold-foiled soft pack of salted butter and bottled sparkling water for them all. It warmed Chloé that he had automatically bought one of everything for Brigitte too and the three of them sat at the counter and ate while Brigitte pushed baby Fabien back and forth in his pram with her foot. Not once did they discuss Chanel or Chloé's gran, but Etienne engaged Brigitte in conversation about the boutique, and the three of them talked about the upcoming elections and tennis.

Then Brigitte said she would need to get Fabien home. 'I am going to be a good new maman and I am going to go home and rest while little one sleeps.'

'Good,' Chloé agreed. 'Or there's little point me being here.'

'Yes, yes, I know. I will not even come in tomorrow,' Brigitte said.

'Tomorrow's Monday,' Chloé pointed out. 'We're not open on Mondays.'

Brigitte looked aghast. 'I do not even know what day of the week it is.'

After Brigitte left, Chloé cleared up from lunch while Etienne browsed the stock.

They fell into a comfortable conversation with Chloé asking about last night's exhibition. 'How many pictures did you sell?' she asked with a smile.

'Enough,' he said enigmatically.

'I'll admit,' Chloé said, 'I was surprised by . . . all of last night.'

'Go on,' he said.

She looked at this elegant, good-looking man and said, 'I was surprised you were at the gallery.'

'I own the gallery,' he said.

'Yes,' she replied. 'I know that now. I was still surprised. And I was astonished that you were exhibiting . . . the kind of thing you were exhibiting.'

'You didn't approve,' he said.

'It's not that.' She didn't want to sound like a killjoy. 'It's just not my cup of tea,' she said.

He laughed. 'It's not mine either. But I can see the beauty in it even if I don't want it adorning the walls of my apartment.'

'So it's about the money?' she dared.

'Most employment is about the money,' he replied.

'Touché, I suppose,' Chloé said and then offered to make them both coffee from the machine in the back.

'I bought you a present,' he said while she busied herself with the machine. 'But now I am worried it will offend you.'

'As long as it's not some of last night's art . . .' she said and Etienne laughed loudly.

When she returned with their coffee he reached into the leather satchel he'd brought with him, opened it and gave Chloé a bag embossed with the Galignani bookshop logo.

'I've always wanted to go there,' Chloé said running her finger over the name on the bag.

'You should,' he said and stood up as Chloé lifted out the book. 'It was the first English bookshop on the continent, apparently.'

But the book Etienne had purchased wasn't in English. It was in French and titled, *The People of Wartime Paris: Collaborators, Resisters, Survivors*.

'Oh,' she said uncertainly. This looked very dry. And then, recovering, 'Thank you. I'll . . . give it a go.'

'You are very welcome. It's a human history of what happened,' Etienne explained. 'No maps and battle plans. Just real life. How people existed. How people survived, how they co-existed with the Germans.'

Chloé opened the book and glanced inside, nodding her appreciation for the gift.

'You are not offended?' he checked, his confidence wavering.

'I'm not offended,' Chloé confirmed. 'It's very thoughtful of you to buy this for me.'

'I hoped,' he went on, 'that it would give you some idea as to what your grandmother lived through. And I'm not suggesting anything by it,' he was quick to say, holding up his hands. 'But you said she hadn't told you much about

90

living through the war in Paris. I hope this will give you some wider, general insight.'

'Thank you,' Chloé said again. She flicked through the book and while she did so, Etienne got up to look out the window at the wide alleyway dotted with hanging baskets and potted plants. Shoppers came and went in and out of boutiques.

She stopped reading and watched him. 'You mentioned you knew where to look, in regard to . . . specifics.'

He looked at her, waiting for more.

'I mean, if I wanted to look at public records. You mentioned new files?' she asked hopefully.

'Yes, I did. Are you sure you want to though? What if you find something you don't like?'

Chloé thought. 'I don't know how I'll feel until I . . . know,' she said simply. 'I think I just want to know what her involvement with Chanel was like if Chanel was a Nazi sympathiser.'

'She was a Nazi sympathiser,' Etienne said. 'And it went further than that. But as you say, it does not stand to reason that your grandmother was also one. Or if she was, she may not have been willing.'

She frowned.

It was clear he was choosing his next words carefully. 'From what I understand, I think Chanel chose to be a Nazi sympathiser in the way you change the football team you support depending on who is winning the game. But that is history being generous with its information.'

Chloé smiled wryly. 'I think I understand what you mean.'

She flicked through the rest of the book and then put it down. 'Etienne, can I ask why you're so interested in this? Why are you so interested in Chanel's part in the war? Is it really just the art side of things?'

He breathed in deeply, looked at his feet and then at her.

'Much like your grandmother, my grandmother was also a footnote in the history of Chanel.'

Chloé sat back. 'Really? In what way?'

'She was a seamstress,' he said simply.

'Go on,' Chloé prompted.

'She was a seamstress before the war broke out. Then when Chanel closed her boutiques, she was fired.'

Chloé nodded, expecting more but Etienne was no more forthcoming than that.

'I've read the book,' Etienne gestured to the new copy in Chloé's hands. 'But it was a couple of years ago now.'

'I take it Chanel gets a mention,' Chloé said but she was still wondering if Etienne had more to tell about his own family history.

'She does. You have to understand that she had a very chequered past. She was an orphan, a cabaret singer, had an affair with the Duke of Westminster, she was friends with Churchill and then she was the lover of a man named Baron von Dincklage who was a high-ranking Nazi official. She didn't keep it a secret. Why would she have done? The Nazis were winning. She showed him off proudly. There is more. Much more . . . and it was all happening during the war, at the same time your grandmother was under her roof.'

Chloé listened, growing more uncomfortable with this information the more she heard.

He returned to the counter, picked up his bag.

'Are you leaving?' Chloé asked.

'I must. I have an appointment. But I've very much enjoyed our lunch. Goodbye Chloé,' he said moving towards her. He bent to plant a gentle kiss on each cheek.

'Thank you for buying lunch. The next one is on me.'

'I hope the next occasion I see you I won't have to apologise for something,' he said as he opened the boutique door, its little bell tinkling overhead.

'No,' she replied. 'I think you're safe.'

When he'd gone, she looked at the book thoughtfully, wondering what her next move was. If she dipped into this, hopefully it would give her a wider understanding of what her grandmother's daily life might have been like during the Occupation. But for specifics? She wouldn't find the answers here. Instead, she needed to dig deeper.

Chloé opened a web browser on her phone, searched a combination of terms relating to 'files released', and used words such as 'resistance', 'war', 'Chanel', 'agent', and anything else she could think of that sounded appropriate. Eventually the internet provided something relevant among its hundreds of thousands of returned results.

Archives, uncatalogued, undigitised and newly found in no particular order – from what the article said, had been discovered by historians at a medieval castle to the east of Paris. Château de Vincennes, the armed forces archives, was open to the public and contained a mishmash of original documents relating to both the Gestapo and French Resistance that had only recently been unboxed by the busy historians working their way steadily through years and years worth of newly discovered documents.

Within were files relating to the entertainer and Resistance spy Josephine Baker, various Resistance fighters who had turned coat for the Nazis (Chloé would try to work that one out later) and Coco Chanel. And that was only a few documents highlighted from just half the collection that had been sorted. What was in the remaining half?

That night Chloé was only too happy to go home, put her feet up and read on the sofa by the deep yellow glow of the table lamp while the lights of Paris lit up below her balcony window and the sounds of pedestrians filled the air. There were so many things she wanted to do while in Paris and being a bit of a homebody had been one of the things Rob had most disliked about Chloé. It was because she kept reminding herself of this that she felt she should be up and out, doing something, finding an art class to join or a new bar to visit, perhaps a really gimmicky one that Rob would loathe.

But she not-so-secretly just loved downtime – not all the time but some of the time. So why did she feel guilty and that she should be doing something more interesting instead of reading a book in a cosy armchair? Who did she feel guilty on behalf of? It wasn't herself. And it was hardly Rob anymore.

While the morning had been busy stocktaking with Brigitte and changing the displays in the windows, the afternoon had been equally busy with regular customers coming in to see what was in stock, purchasing a few pieces each and chatting about baby Fabien, disappointed he'd returned home with his maman. The boutique had such a community feel to it that it made Chloé really glow with a newfound sense of happiness that she'd never experienced before. She'd only been here a short while but already staff from the other boutiques in the alley were waving to her as she walked home from work and a few of the regular customers recognised and greeted her too if they were out walking their dogs or stepping onto their small balconies for a cigarette or a coffee as the end of the working day approached.

She'd never had that sense of community anywhere, not when she'd lived with Rob in Islington, not when she'd been at her old job in central London. Colleagues came and went and Chloé had been one of the longest-serving employees. And then, packed on the tube to go home, she never saw the same face twice. Was it just the buzz of the change that made Chloé believe her old existence had been soulless? Or had her existence *actually been* soulless?

Added to all the new feelings swimming around her was

the oddity of Etienne coming to see her in the boutique. The strangeness of it wasn't lost on her. He'd made the effort to visit her at work to apologise, had made even more of an effort to buy lunch for the three of them, although it had felt a bit as if she'd prompted it, but he'd seemed to want to get to know her a bit more. He'd even purchased a book for her although he must have forgotten entirely when he'd arrived seeing as he had been preparing to leave the moment he'd apologised.

Or had he been? Had he been teasing her? It was so hard to tell. He was hard to work out. Why buy her the book? It was an odd present. Obviously he felt she was so unknowledgeable about his country during the war that she needed educating. Perhaps now wasn't the time to reveal to him that she was equally uneducated about her *own* country during the war. Maybe she should show less enthusiasm. The last thing she wanted was Etienne showing up with a book about what Britain had endured during the Second World War. Or maybe she did, she thought guiltily. After all, he was certainly attractive, well dressed, courteous and . . . nice. He was also sure of himself; a trait Chloé wasn't sure if she liked or not. There was confident; and then there was Etienne who held her gaze unashamedly when they spoke. He had insinuated they'd see each other again but hadn't said when and the more Chloé thought about that the more intrigued she became by Etienne Vaillancourt.

But there was a part of her that was smarting a little too much still. It felt too much of a risk to think about dating again so soon. There had been too much change in Chloé's life recently. Divorce, a new country, a new job. She couldn't add a new man into that mix or else her head would explode. And maybe Etienne didn't have that in mind at all? Maybe he just wanted to be friends. And Chloé didn't have enough of those in Paris to turn down the opportunity to make one. After all, she was hoping to stay here for at least a year.

She switched the radio on to the sultriest French café jazz she could find, threw open the Juliet balcony doors and indulged in cooking bouillabaisse for her supper. She couldn't resist springing around the kitchen, swaying to the music while she stirred to the upbeat sounds. She lifted the spoon out of the pot and watched the sauce thicken soupily. If she ate like this every night she was going to have to take up running again.

Looking down from the balcony, she saw the streetlights in their old-fashioned orbs glowing dimly, dusk settling into its stride. And only a couple of blocks away the Eiffel Tower eased in to the first of its nightly light shows, flashing in time to its own beat. It was impossible not to look. While the bouillabaisse thickened, Chloé poured herself a chilled glass of Sauvignon Blanc and padded across the small apartment, looking out the balcony to watch the trees below her – picture-perfect lush and green and rustling as a gentle breeze ran its way through the Parisian streets. A soft feeling of contentment made its way consciously into her mind and she sighed deeply, allowing her ribcage to open and close as she did so.

And then she turned, picked up the book Etienne had bought her and took it back to the kitchen so she could keep half an eye on her dinner. Flicking absentmindedly, she stopped in the centre pages where a series of black and white images lay. One included a picture of a sporting arena with contestants skating around it in the pre-war years. The caption said:

In July 1942, French police, acting under orders from the German authorities in Occupied Paris, used the vélodrome to hold thousands of Jews and other perse-cuted peoples in a mass, orchestrated arrest. The Jews

*were held at the vélodrome before they were moved
to a concentration camp in the Parisian suburbs and
then to the Auschwitz extermination camp. The inci-
dent became known as the 'Vel' d'Hiv' Roundup'. For
more information about the Vel' d'Hiv' roundup, see
page 87.*

Chloé turned directly to page 87 and felt the chill of fresh
horror as she read how the sports stadium, usually used
for cycling, had been turned into a holding pen for Jews
on their way to camps.

The Vel' d'Hiv' had a glass roof, which had been painted
dark blue to help avoid attracting bomber navigators. The
dark glass roof, combined with windows, which were bolted
shut for security, raised the temperature in the building.
The 13,152 people held there had only basic sanitary provi-
sions. Of the ten lavatories, five were closed because their
windows could have provided means of escape, and the
others were blocked. The arrested Jews were kept there for
five days with only water and food brought by volunteers
from the Quakers, the Red Cross and the few doctors and
nurses who were allowed entry.

Further down the page Chloé read that by late September
1940, a German census registered 150,000 Jews in Paris,
including 64,000 foreigners.

She leant back against the kitchen worksurface and
processed the information. How had Paris gone from a city
priding itself on its core principles after the revolution of
liberty, equality and fraternity to finding itself culpable of
holding over 13,000 Jewish people in a cramped stadium
with the windows screwed shut? It was unfathomable.

Chloé looked out the windows as the Eiffel Tower's light
show drew to a temporary close before it would sparkle again
an hour later. The world was a different place now. Thirteen
thousand people. It was a number almost incomprehensible.

But then, she realised, she'd always thought that about the Holocaust. That the exact figure killed in the atrocity could never be fully known. When she'd learnt at school that it was an estimated six million Jews that had perished in the Holocaust it was a figure utterly unworldly. One death is a tragedy, but six million felt like a statistic she couldn't get her head around. How can anyone imagine six million lives, six million individuals, robbed of their lives in such an inhumane way?

But then, of course, the Nazis never viewed the Jews as humans. Did Parisians know that thousands of Jews had been rounded up and housed inside the stadium? Did her grandmother know? Did Chanel know? And if so, what did they think?

Henri and Chloé had arranged to meet later in the week on their lunch breaks and after Chloé had told him about the book Etienne had thrust upon her, he told her he had a plan for where they could go.

Chloé could have laughed when she arrived at the address, realising the significance: 31 rue Cambon. 'Oh you've got to be joking,' she replied when she arrived a few minutes late to find Henri leaning nonchalantly back against the cream stone façade of the flagship Chanel store.

'What surprises me,' he said as the two of them kissed cheeks, 'is that this is where your grandmother worked and yet you've not been here once yet.'

She looked through the doors feeling like a tourist. 'Are we going in?'

'Of course.'

A security guard greeted them and opened the door to let them in. Chloé and Henri walked through the shop. It was modern, white, stark, almost sparse and looked nothing at all as it would have done when her grandmother had been here, of that Chloé was sure. All ornateness stripped from it, long ago presumably. It was so startlingly white and bright. Perhaps it did a lot to show off the jewels and accessories in their best light. She didn't even dare to reach out and look at any of the price tags. And then she walked through the wide building. In Etienne's gifted book it said the shop had originally just comprised 31 rue Cambon but that Chanel had expanded to encompass five adjacent buildings in the street. The cosmetic and fragrance section made Chloé's eyes widen in a level of excitement that caught her off guard.

'Oh dear,' Henri muttered as Chloé beelined towards it.

'The famous Chanel Number 5,' she said as she picked up an enormous tester bottle, turning it over in her hands and watching it as the overhead lights caught it and glinted through the amber liquid. She sprayed a little on her wrist and inhaled. 'Do you know, I've never owned any Chanel perfume before.'

'Would you like this one?' Henri asked. 'I'll buy it for you. As a present for all the birthdays I've missed.' He said it so casually as if he purchased expensive bottles of fragrance for women every day of the week.

Chloé shook her head, gave him a contented look. 'No thank you. I'd like to buy it for myself, if you're not too offended by my refusal.'

'Not at all,' he said as Chloé held out a thirty-ml eau de parfum to the shop assistant and pulled her credit card from her purse.

'You can buy a round of drinks next time we meet if you really want to spend your cash.'

'I will do just that.' And then he gave her a curious look. 'But see how easily you've just succumbed to the allure of Chanel. You've bought a bottle of perfume, fallen under her spell. And you've not even been in here ten minutes.'

'Oh don't be silly,' she chastised, recognising some truth to his words. If Chloé had fallen under a spell as Henri put it, within such a short amount of time, here among Chanel's legacy, she wondered how her grandmother had felt being here, and in the presence of the grande dame herself. It must have been mesmerising.

The woman behind the counter began to wrap up her perfume, as Henri told her, in excited tones, that Chloé's grandmother had worked with Chanel a long time ago, in this very building.

The assistant's eyes lit up with interest as she handed over the white gift bag adorned with black edging and ribbon. Chloé felt the rush of endorphins as she took the bag. How easy it was to get a high from simply shopping.

'Your grandmother worked with Chanel?' the shop assistant asked, giving Chloé her full attention. 'What was she like? What did your grandmother do?' Chloé hated admitting she didn't actually know the answers and gave the barest of detail because it was all she had.

'During the war?' the assistant echoed. 'Oh what a time.'

'Yes,' Chloé said. 'It must have been . . .'

'Would you like to see the famous mirrored staircase?' the assistant asked when it was clear Chloé had no insider information to bestow.

Pale carpet and a black handrail swept up the wide staircase with the outside wall bedecked in tall multi-faceted mirror segments that swirled round the turn of the stairs and went up, up, up.

Even with Chloé's limited knowledge of Coco Chanel, she had read about the mirrored staircase. How Chanel would sit at the top when she put on a fashion show, watching her audience's reaction to her latest collections while she herself remained out of sight. To see it for herself was something wonderful. How many times had Chloé's grandmother walked up and down this staircase as a matter of course, up, up to the atelier and the offices somewhere above? Being here, touching the handrail, triggered a real connection between her grandmother and this place then, and Chloé in the here and now.

Henri looked as impressed as Chloé felt. She turned to the assistant. 'I don't suppose there's any chance of seeing upstairs—'

'Non. I am so sorry. It's not allowed.'

'Not to worry.' Chloé sighed, not able to hide the disappointment from her voice.

'It was a good try.' Henri smiled as the two of them left 31 rue Cambon and exited into the Paris sunshine.

'You really do not know anything at all about your grandmother's past?' Henri asked as they both put their sunglasses on.

'No,' Chloé said. 'But I am determined to find out. Now I've been here, seen part of what my gran saw during her time here, I feel . . . a bit more connected. Does that make sense?'

'Sort of,' Henri said.

'Before coming to Paris I just accepted that there wasn't more to it than what she had told me. She would talk a lot about the orphanage and then her time in England but her time in Paris, with Coco Chanel in the middle of the war, is surely the most interesting of all of it and yet *that's* the time she won't speak of.'

'Perhaps it is only interesting to the casual observer,' Henri volunteered diplomatically.

'*Please,*' Chloé said. 'Do you believe that?'

He shrugged. 'Probably not, no.'

'I feel almost as if I need to rediscover her, the places she walked, the place she lived. Maybe it will help. Although help with *what* I'm not quite sure.'

She looked across Place Vendôme towards the Ritz.

'You want to go in?' Henri suggested, seeing where her gaze fell. 'See the place your grandmother actually lived?'

Chloé looked across at the Ritz. Almost as if she was

looking across at a Disney castle. 'Yes,' she said. 'Yes I do.' And then she looked down at her outfit of ripped skinny jeans and rock star band tee. She was wearing them with elegant black studded heels but still: 'Not dressed like this.'

Henri appraised her ensemble and replied rather judgementally with: 'Yes. Good point. Another day then?'

Chloé laughed at his abruptness and with half an eye on punishing him said, 'You could shout me a round of drinks in there?'

He groaned. 'Are you trying to bankrupt me?'

Chloé thought. 'Yes,' she said, smiling.

'Fine,' he said. 'If the hunt to find out more about how your grandmother spent the war involves drinking in the Ritz, that's not a bad way to spend an evening.'

'Exactly,' Chloé replied. 'I feel there's more to know. I just don't know what that is yet.'

Chapter 9

1941

Were the cries of help and the intense eye contact intended to beg Adèle to help the woman get free from the gendarmerie? Or were they intended for something else entirely? What had the woman wanted Adèle to do? She couldn't possibly want her to do anything about the child looking down from the window surely. There would be another adult within that apartment and they would be able to assist the child.

But what if there wasn't? What if that child was alone?

Adèle swallowed, her mouth suddenly dry. Would she be doing anything wrong if she went to look? She would just go and knock, explain that she had seen the child at the window and was worried about it. Given how concerned the woman being arrested had been for the child, Adèle felt she couldn't walk away without checking. Yes, that's what she would do.

She crossed the road purposefully and did not dither, did not hesitate as she entered the street door to the apartment block. If living with Mademoiselle Chanel had taught her anything it was that once a decision was made it was best to simply get on and do it rather than waste time worrying about it.

It was one of those perfect buildings that Adèle had always hoped to live in, with an ornate filigree entrance door that opened into a small courtyard before letting you into the main part of the apartment block. Adèle climbed up the wide staircase and ascended. Outside one of the doors to the apartments, two women were gossiping about the events that had just occurred. But on seeing Adèle, they stopped talking, stared at her and then averted their gazes pointedly. Disassociation, Adèle thought. So easy to do, so very hard to live with. If they wondered what Adèle was doing, they did not ask her.

Calculating which was the door to the apartment was not difficult. The door facing the street to the right of the staircase was still ajar from the scuffle but not only that, a middle-aged man was standing in front of it, peering in. On hearing her tread on the stairs he spun around quickly.

'Yes?' he asked her imperiously. 'What do you want? But he did not wait for an answer before saying, 'I'm the concierge. I get first look. Not you. Which apartment are you from? I don't recognise you.' He narrowed his eyes at her.

She ignored his latter question and dealt with the remark that had grated the most. 'First look?' she questioned.

'You can wait until I've finished. Then the rest of the block can take what's left.'

Adèle almost choked on the sudden intake of breath that she inhaled into her lungs. 'You cannot be serious? You're stealing from this apartment?'

He bristled. 'She was Jewish.' As if that explained everything Adèle needed to know. 'If she's innocent, they'll bring her back.'

'Innocent of what?' Adèle cried, horrified.

'She cannot be innocent of being Jewish, of course,' he reasoned.

'And so she's entirely done for,' Adèle pointed out and it took every part of her self-restraint not to reach out and smack the old man in the face for what he'd done, for she suspected entirely that the concierge had done the unthinkable and had informed the authorities that the woman in his apartment block was on the wrong side of the Reich, in whatever guise that may be. There was no time to think about what to do or to say next; Adèle simply opened her mouth and without caring who heard shouted at him. 'You are vile. You and everyone in this building, in this city, in the entirety of France who is complicit in this.'

She reached out and grabbed the man by the crook of his arm and dragged him roughly back from the doorway. He stumbled to the floor and cried out but she felt nothing, no remorse of any kind as she stepped round him, into the apartment and closed the door behind her. Her heart hammered inside her chest as a sensation of utter disbelief that she'd just spoken to someone like that – albeit deservedly – and had lashed out at another human planted itself slowly in her mind.

There was now even less time than she originally thought she had. She was sure when the concierge got up and dusted himself down the first thing he would do would be return to his apartment and telephone the authorities or the police, instructing them to return. How fast French citizens found themselves in line with the Reich was bewildering to Adèle. After pushing herself away from the closed door she moved fast through the apartment.

It was clear the people who lived here were not well off and later Adèle would recall the shabby rug faded in the sunlight of many Parisian summers, the long velvet curtains that didn't quite fit the window but that once may have been a deep rose colour, the whitewash paint that needed a fresh coat and the heavy antique furniture that even Adèle could see had once been the height of fashion and that said this family had been prosperous once.

Later Adèle would wonder if the woman had been arrested, ripped from her home, simply because she was Jewish. And if so, had she assumed that by hiding her child there would be a better chance of saving its life than taking the child with her? But she did not pause to consider this. Not then.

In the main bedroom was a bed with a tatty leather suitcase open on top. The woman must have been disturbed while packing to flee to safety, as the case was half full of her clothing. Next to it was a pile of small outfits suitable for a child. The officers arresting the woman clearly hadn't spied these or else they'd have hunted for the child surely? Or did they simply not care enough about leaving a child alone? She couldn't work it out.

Adèle moved from the bedroom and into the only other room that faced the front of the building. This room was smaller and had a little bed with a wooden tea set laid out neatly and ready to play with on the floor. And next to it, sitting with her thumb in her mouth, her back against the wall and her knees hunched up under her chin was a little girl who couldn't have been more than three years old.

'Oh God,' Adèle said quietly and then when the child looked up at her, tears in its eyes, Adèle smiled brightly, too brightly.

'Bonjour, little one.'

The girl looked at her, fear in her eyes. Had she understood that she had just witnessed her mother being dragged from the apartment? Had she heard her mother's screams? Of course she had and it didn't bear thinking about.

There was nothing she could ever do to make up for the loss of a mother. This much Adèle knew first-hand. What if it was temporary? Who knew what the gendarmerie would do with that poor woman?

She couldn't leave the child here to fend for herself. She just couldn't.

She glanced around the building. Her minutes were numbered. The concierge would be summoning help by now. She had dallied too long as it was. Although she couldn't imagine any of the residents would want to get involved. She needed an address book, anything, something, to give her a clue about the family who lived here.

Adèle ran back into the hallway and began ransacking the bureau. She gave no thought to the drawers she opened, simply pulling them out quickly in the hopes of finding something that would say who the owners of the apartment were. Exasperatedly, looking at every piece of paper for far too long, she found nothing and time was now against her. She went back into the little bedroom and walked towards the child. The child looked full of fear.

'What is your name?' Adèle asked, crouching down.

The little girl took her thumb from her mouth. 'Mélodie.'

'I'm going to look after you,' Adèle said without a single thought how she was actually going to achieve that.

The child nodded.

'Come with me,' she said hurriedly. What if someone stopped them? What if the police came back? 'Let's bring your favourite toy. Do you have one?'

The child nodded, grabbed a teddy bear from the bed and stood watching Adèle with a mix of duty at wishing to be obedient and knowledge that everything was not as it should be.

'Let's take some clothes as well shall we? We're going on an adventure.'

The child followed Adèle through to the main bedroom where Adèle emptied out the woman's clothes from the suitcase and filled it with those of the little girl. It broke her heart to do such a thing but she daren't show it for Mélodie's sake. She closed the suitcase and did up the clasps.

'All right. Let's go,' she said in that bright voice she had summoned along with courage from the depths of her being.

On the way out of the door, Adèle took the key that had been positioned safely in the lock and pocketed it. Then she stopped by the heavily ransacked bureau. It was her fault the house looked a mess but it would benefit no one to tidy now. No one was returning here. Before they left the apartment Adèle scribbled a note on a scrap of paper and then speared it onto a nail sticking out of the back of the door.

For both our sakes, I dare not tell you my name. I saw you in the street the day of your arrest. I took your child to safety. I did not know what else to do. I could not leave her. If it was not the right thing to do, please forgive me.

Chapter 10

At the bottom of the stairs the concierge was waiting, blocking the only route out. Two steps up, Adèle and Mélodie stopped. Adèle tipped her chin up, ready for whatever fight might be necessary. She'd never had cause to engage in any kind of violence until today; that had always been the reserve of some of the more wayward boys in the orphanage. But now, a child's life depended on it because who knew what might happen if Adèle allowed this man to prevent Mélodie from departing. Adèle's hand tightened protectively around the child's.

'What's in there?' the concierge challenged her.

'Nothing to concern you,' Adèle replied, her voice wavering. She must steel herself to be stronger, to be more convincing. 'Get out of my way,' she said louder than she'd intended.

The concierge tipped his head to one side, his gaze drifting from Adèle to Mélodie.

'You've taken their family silver and now the child?' he taunted.

'I've done no such thing,' Adèle snapped. 'I have clothes for the child and that is it. Now you will get out of my way or I will make you.'

'You will make me?' the middle-aged man said. 'How are you going to do that?'

Adèle had the height advantage from her position two steps higher than him. She let go of Mélodie's hand, thrust the suitcase into the man's chest and pushed hard to send him off balance. The man staggered back a few paces and into the wall behind him, shouting profanities at them as Adèle held tightly to the case, taking it with her. Quickly, she grabbed Mélodie's hand, pulling the small child with her and the two of them ran down the street.

Far behind them the police van was parked outside another apartment building. It didn't occur to Adèle that it was because the gendarmerie were presumably arresting another citizen. But the concierge, up and moving, staggered out of the doorway and into the street, shouting at anyone who would listen, 'That woman is a thief, stop her.'

Adèle did not stop. She did not stop for anything. Those in the immediate vicinity were too stunned by the man's shouting to help. By the time any of them had collected themselves in order to hinder her, Adèle had scooped Mélodie into her arms and run as fast as her cork heels would allow her.

Later, Adèle thought about the note she had left in the apartment. She replayed what she had written and everything she hadn't. In truth, she hadn't known what else to write. She knew what she had wanted to write, that she would watch the apartment for signs of the woman's return over the next few days so she could reunite her with her child. But of course, if someone else found and read the note, that laid Adèle open to being watched out for in turn and she couldn't risk that for the child's sake.

And then of course what would she do with the child now she had her? Adèle held the little girl in her arms and she was certain her limpness meant she was napping. Adèle stole a peek to confirm her suspicions were correct. She was obviously happy to be carried into slumber by a stranger or simply too exhausted to care. Such innocence, Adèle pondered, when trusting the kindness of strangers these days could lead to all sorts of terrors. But Adèle would do her very best to keep this child safe.

Eventually they sat on a park bench and when the little girl woke up Adèle hoped they looked like a mother and child, just out for a stroll. She was aware bringing the suitcase might now have been a mistake.

'Where is your papa?' Adèle asked.

'Gone.'

'Gone where?'

'To heaven to be with my grand-mère and grand-père.'

'Oh.' Adèle gave her a concerned look. 'I'm so sorry, little one. Do you have any other family? Uncles? Aunts?'

The child shook her head. 'Just Maman. I'm hungry.'

'Of course. Let's find you some food.'

Adèle picked up the suitcase and carried both it and the little girl. Adèle had always been adept at being by herself but as she hurried along the streets hoping to find a little café, she now felt alone and out of her depth.

Inside the eatery she fed the little girl a croque-monsieur with a very small slice of ham and cheese that barely coated the bread while Adèle just drank a bitter cup of what passed for coffee these days. She needed to think. Where could she take Mélodie? She could hardly take her back to the Ritz and her little box room. She would have to sneak her past the German sentries, the housekeeper, and Mademoiselle Chanel. There was no real way of explaining where this child had come from that wouldn't leave Adèle and the child exposed and in danger.

Adèle clutched Mélodie's hand.

'When will I see Maman? When will she come back?'

'Soon,' Adèle said as a hollow feeling entered her

stomach. She hated lying to anyone, but it felt kinder to lie to her given she was already so dreadfully frightened. And who knew? It might be the truth. Although the moment she thought it Adèle knew it could not be true and despair for the little girl hit her suddenly. She had to save this child. She had to find a way. But how? Who did she know who could help?

'Is our adventure over?' the little girl asked when she'd practically licked the plate clean and gulped down her glass of water.

'Non,' Adèle said as she desperately tried to work out what to do. And then, chastising herself that it had taken her until now, Adèle knew who might be able to help. With a voice braver than she felt, Adèle said, 'Our adventure is only just beginning.'

'Come in,' a man's voice commanded.

Adèle and Mélodie stood on the threshold. The man's head was down, his fountain pen working across a small stack of papers.

When he didn't look up, Adèle spoke. 'I need your help.'

Doctor Dixon's head shot up and he looked at her in stark surprise. 'What are you doing here?' he said, flummoxed. And then he looked as if he wanted to say something else, had thought better of it and stopped himself as his gaze drifted to the little girl and the small suitcase.

'Bonjour,' he said to Mélodie after a second or two.

'Bonjour,' she replied quietly, obediently.

He stood, sending his chair scraping back across the floor. 'Come in,' he said, gesturing to the two chairs in front of him. 'You want to close the door?'

Adèle nodded and shut it behind her. She stood awkwardly near the door. Now she was here a tinge of regret had entered her mind. What if he couldn't help? What if he wouldn't?

A flicker of a smile arrived at the corners of his mouth. 'How did you get past the front desk? They didn't call up and tell me you were here.'

'We just did. We simply walked past.'

'No one stopped you?'

'Non.' Adèle shrugged. It was the truth. She had just slipped seamlessly past the polite queue of people waiting to check in with the receptionist and had moved straight along the corridor to the elevator.

He gave a small laugh. 'All right then. How can I help, Mademoiselle Fabron?'

Adèle was surprised he remembered her name. 'It's delicate,' she started and then glanced down at Mélodie.

Seeming to understand, the doctor put a smile on his face and directed his attention to Mélodie. 'Are you hungry?'

Adèle interjected. 'She's just eaten.'

'Oui,' the little girl said. 'I am hungry.'

'But she just ate,' Adèle said disbelievingly.

The doctor laughed. 'In my experience children are always hungry. Even when they're not.' He directed his attention to Mélodie again. 'Would you like my last couple of pieces of brioche to nibble on while your . . .' he was grasping to work out the relationship between Adèle and Mélodie and instead opted for '. . . while we speak.'

Mélodie nodded and the doctor gave her a little paper parcel of food to nibble on. 'Here, some pencils and some paper to draw with as well if you like. I'm afraid I don't have any colouring pencils.' She took a seat and he pushed the items towards her.

Mélodie inched forward on her chair and reached for the paper parcel.

Adèle could see he was desperate to presume that she was Mélodie's mother. But instead of speaking, he waited patiently as Adèle and he moved away from the little girl, near the closed door as she quietly relayed the events that had brought her and the child together.

She watched his face change with every whispered sentence she uttered, how anger flashed in his eyes at the actions of the police, at the actions of the concierge and wide-eyed amazement at how Adèle had taken the child. As she spoke, brief moments of regret flashed through her mind. Had she done the right thing? In the heat of the moment it had certainly seemed so but now . . . hours later?

Doctor Dixon sighed and then rubbed his hand over his forehead. He seemed tired now she looked at him properly, as if the weight of the world lay on his shoulders.

'I'm sorry,' she said quietly when he didn't reply. 'I shouldn't have come. I didn't know who else to turn to. I don't know that many people in the city.' If anything that was a lie. She didn't know anyone at all other than those who worked for Mademoiselle Chanel and a few of the staff inside the Ritz and she could hardly trust any of them. 'And the woman's eyes,' Adèle said. 'She was begging me for help, I could see it.'

'And now you're asking for my help?' he asked quietly. He tipped his chin up. 'What makes you think I'll help you with a problem like this?' he whispered, so Mélodie couldn't hear.

'She's a child. Not a problem.'

'She's a child and a problem,' he replied.

They stared at each other until he acquiesced. 'What do you want me to do?'

'You know people. Rich people. You said so last time I was here.'

'Yes,' he said uncertainly.

'Trustworthy?'

He paused. 'Some.'

'Trustworthy with a Jewish child? I mean . . . they'd look after her willingly away from prying eyes?' she asked.

'Jesus Christ. What if the mother returns?' Doctor Dixon looked as horrified as he sounded.

'What if the mother doesn't return? Do you think the Germans will let her go?'

He shook his head and the two of them looked over to Mélodie who had eaten the brioche and had picked up the pencil, staring at the blank sheet of lined notepaper, clearly wondering what she should draw.

'We can't exactly put her back into an empty apartment, can we? I do think I know someone who could help,' he said.

'I thought you would.'

'Why did you think I would?'

Because in the park, by the fountain you talked to me about love; about life. Because I can tell you're kind.

'I saw inside your office,' she said truthfully. 'I saw what was inside your office last time. Or rather, I saw *who* was inside your office.'

His dark eyes trained on hers. 'So now you're going to blackmail me? Hold me hostage over it?'

'Of course not,' Adèle said sharply, her eyes wide and Mélodie's head turned to look at them both. They both smiled at her, placating her, and the little girl looked back to where she'd started drawing.

Adèle continued. 'That's not what I meant at all. I just thought you'd be able to help.'

'Saving a child. This is a lot of pressure to heap on a guy.'

'I know. But it's not really that different to what I think you've been doing already.'

'May as well be hanged for a sheep as a lamb,' he said.

She narrowed her eyes.

'Not an expression you have here?'

She shook her head and smiled as she thought it through. 'Not like that but I know what you mean.'

He tipped his head back and looked up at the ceiling, exhaling loudly.

'I'm sorry,' she said.

He sighed. 'Don't be. You did a good thing. You did the right thing. Not many would.'

'It's a shame I didn't know what to do afterwards.'

He looked at her warmly. 'You did. You knew what to do. You came here.'

She nodded. 'I couldn't find anything to indicate who the woman was so I don't know how I can reunite mother and daughter when all of this is over.'

'They won't bring her back you know,' he whispered. 'You know what they're doing to Jews don't you? They're arresting them, simply for existing. And I don't think she'll be coming back.'

Nausea made Adèle's stomach turn over violently. 'But where will they send her?'

'Detention camps have been springing up all over in the south. And I hear in other places across the continent. It's not just happening in Germany and France. It's happening all over. So far, I know a lot of men have been taken. And it was only a matter of time before they came for the women.' He glanced at Mélodie. 'And then the children.'

Adèle put her hand to her mouth for fear of throwing up.

'I'll find somewhere safe for her.' He looked over at the child. 'But it might take me a little while. I'm a doctor, my capabilities only stretch so far. Speaking of which . . .' He glanced at his watch. 'I need to hunt down some files before I forget. Can you take her back to your apartment tonight and I'll see what I can do?'

'Non,' Adèle said. 'I can't, I'm afraid.'

'Why on earth not?' he asked.

'I live with my employer,' she said. 'It's complicated.'

Doctor Dixon looked startled and then unimpressed.

116

'I live in the Ritz. I work for Mademoiselle Coco Chanel,' she said eventually.

He raised an eyebrow. 'What? You live in a hotel that's swarming with Nazis?'

'Yes,' she said sadly. 'Although so far I've had very little to do with them. Mademoiselle Chanel, however . . .' And Adèle left the sentence there, disloyalty flooding her.

He looked disbelieving and then furrowed his brows. 'Interesting,' he said slowly. 'All right.' He sighed exasperatedly again. 'Leave her here with me and I'll work quicker at sorting something out.'

'Thank you.' She reached out and clasped his hands in gratitude but he seemed not to immediately notice her gesture.

'You're welcome,' he replied as he eventually looked at where their hands met.

'How will I know she is safe?' Adèle asked withdrawing her hand.

He thought. 'Come back in a week. I'll have news for you. It's safer than telephoning. Who knows if anyone's listening on the line these days.'

Adèle walked over to Mélodie and crouched down next to the chair. 'Doctor Dixon is going to keep you safe,' she said. 'You can trust him. I trust him.' The little girl blinked and looked between the two adults. If the child understood she chose not to reply. Adèle kissed the top of the little girl's head and said goodbye before giving Doctor Dixon a grateful look and slipping out of his office, closing the door behind her.

Adèle spent the following week carrying out administrative tasks under Mademoiselle Chanel's watchful gaze and counting down the days until she was due back at the hospital to hear news from Doctor Dixon. The tension was killing her and she found herself on more than one occasion

117

sitting and typing, filing or logging order forms with her leg jittering up and down underneath the desk. She itched to telephone him but had restrained herself as per their agreement.

'What is wrong with you this week, Adèle?' Mademoiselle asked. 'You're not your normal self.'

'Nerves,' Adèle said.

'Why?' Mademoiselle asked.

'The case to reclaim your business,' Adèle said, grasping for a believable answer. Earlier that day a reply had come from the lawyer that Mademoiselle had practically ripped from Adèle's hands when she'd picked up the letter knife to slice open the expensive envelope. The news had not been good, but her employer had not said as much. She hadn't needed to. It had been evident from the grim expression on her face that all was not well in the bid to regain her business.

'Ah oui,' Mademoiselle nodded her head in agreement. 'It is good of you to worry for me, Adèle. Alas it does not look good. At the moment.' She spoke as if things may become easier with time, a concept Adèle was more than a little curious about.

'You know what the Wertheimer brothers have done, don't you, Adèle? They have illegally passed my business on to an Aryan individual so it is not classified as Jewish. They have simply handed it over to a friend, a man named Félix Amiot. He is not Jewish and so the business has been completely Aryanised. It is such a risk that they have taken with my business,' Mademoiselle spat. 'They have played a game, Adèle. But they won't win. I will find a way.'

'Really?' Adèle's mouth fell open. 'That is . . . unfortunate,' she said thoughtlessly. At the back of her mind Adèle thought it was an incredibly clever move.

Mademoiselle pursed her red-painted lips. Her nearly

black eyes flashed in anger. 'It is more than just unfortunate, Adèle!' Mademoiselle cried. 'It's wrong. It's vile. It's my business and they've just handed it over to some . . . man . . . and not to me.'

'Why though? Why not to you? If the business was in danger of being Aryanised to anyone who wanted it, why would they not let you have it?'

'Because they do not like me, Adèle. They want my name, but they don't want me. And what I think they want to do is return to it, when all of this is over, take back their part and continue just as we were before. Where I get hardly any of the money and they get almost everything!' she shouted.

'How?' Adèle dared. 'How can they just take it back if they've handed it over?'

'Because they've given it to a friend, that's why. And he will hand it over when they return like the dutiful little lap dog that he is and I will be cast back out again.'

Adèle knew from her years with Mademoiselle that her employer was hardly on the peripheries of poverty. She'd done very well from the arrangement that saw the Wertheimers of the Bourgeois company making Chanel a very rich woman. Adèle wasn't sure she was clever enough to quite understand the repercussions of this but from what she had seen, Chanel had been made very rich – the Wertheimers obviously even more rich – and that Chanel's business was thriving.

'Tonight I am away,' Mademoiselle cut into Adèle's thoughts. 'I will think about all of this and then we will attack in another way, I am sure of it. But for now, I have other things to worry about. Why does everything come at once?' Her employer threw her head back dramatically. 'I am negotiating for André to be freed from his prisoner of war camp.'

'Your nephew is to be freed?'

119

'Of course. You did not think he would languish in a German camp when my lover is a German official?'

'I . . . I did not know he could do that,' Adèle said pointlessly.

'Of course. He has managed to find a way.'

'A way? What sort of way?'

'All the questions.' Mademoiselle chastised, evading the topic. 'In the meantime, organise for my black dress with the white silk ribbon and long sleeves to be ready, as tomorrow I have dinner with Baron von Dincklage and some of his work associates.'

'What does the baron do?' Adèle dared to ask.

'Questions again, Adèle. Press attaché, intelligence . . . you know. That sort of thing,' Mademoiselle snapped.

There was something about the word 'intelligence' that made Adèle grow cold. Wasn't intelligence just a word for all sorts of other frightening things? She wasn't versed enough in the ever-increasing vileness of this war. Chanel obviously understood but there were ways and means of understanding and Adèle wasn't quite sure she approved of Mademoiselle's methods.

When Adèle finally managed to slip away it was only because Mademoiselle Chanel had left to enjoy an early dinner engagement with the baron. Adèle sent a message down to the kitchens that she would not need any supper that night. She didn't have time to wait for even the simplest of servants' dinners to be provided. It had already been over a week since she'd left Mélodie with Doctor Dixon and she'd promised to return before now, but the opportunity to slip away had never occurred before curfew fell. What if he thought she was never coming back? What if he thought she had simply abandoned Mélodie with him and was not interested enough in the little girl's fate to enquire again? If only she had managed to get away earlier.

She slipped out of the hotel, nodding politely to the German sentries always posted at the doors. They operated on rotation and she was growing used to them and they to her. It was almost normal now to see them, an ever-visible part of her day.

This time, at the hospital, she was unable to get past the reception desk undetected and after giving her name and waiting for the woman to connect via the switchboard to his office, the woman on duty gave Adèle permission to go up, giving her instructions on how to get there. Adèle politely listened and chose not to reveal that she knew the way to Doctor Dixon's office off by heart.

Adèle opened the door and walked inside. It hadn't occurred to her to knock given that she'd been told to go straight up. Inside the office was a woman dressed in civilian clothing, bending low over the doctor's desk as he filled in something for her. She straightened up and gave Adèle a look that suggested annoyance.

'Oh, my apologies,' Adèle said and backed out.

'No, come in. It's all right. Mademoiselle Vachon was just getting ready to go home,' the doctor said as he stood up and moved round his desk to sit in the guest chair. He gestured for Adèle to sit in the other of the two chairs.

Mademoiselle Vachon took the papers from Doctor Dixon's desk and walked out of the door barely acknowledging Adèle any further. She noticed Doctor Dixon didn't introduce either woman to the other.

'I'm so sorry,' Adèle repeated when she and the doctor were alone and seated.

'It's fine.' He got up, closed the door and returned to the seat. 'That's my secretary. I put my foot down about getting one but she was thrust upon me, so to speak and so now I just need to be even more careful than usual until I work out where her loyalties lie. Anyway, I have good news about Mélodie, Mademoiselle Fabron.'

121

Adèle interrupted him and spoke in hushed tones. 'Between us, we are attempting to save a Jewish child from the wrath of the Nazis. It is probably time to drop the formalities, don't you think? Please, call me Adèle.'

'Adèle,' he repeated with a hint of humour in his eyes that was quickly replaced with a serious look. 'I found a family willing to take Mélodie. They're on the outskirts of Paris. They're friends of friends. Trustworthy, which is the main thing. They say they'll look after her as long as necessary.'

Adèle breathed a sigh of relief, all the tension from the past few days seeping out of her body as she did so. 'Thank God. I am only sorry I didn't get a chance to say goodbye to her.'

'Probably for the best. These things move fast, if they move at all. You did a good thing, you know.'

'So did you. Thank you.'

He nodded, flashed that smile again. 'I didn't think you were coming back,' he confessed. 'When you didn't show after a week . . . I'm glad you did though.'

'I couldn't get away. I wanted so much to know she was safe. *Is* she safe, do you think? There, with them?'

'I think so,' he said simply. 'And what choice do we have? I approached someone I trust and this was the only option. I had to say yes. They were putting themselves at risk. So was I and I've already . . .' he hesitated '. . . got a lot going on.'

'I know,' she said. 'You are already putting yourself in the most awful danger if you're doing what it is I think you're doing.'

The doctor looked at her, tipped his chin up. 'I don't think we should dance around the facts anymore,' Doctor Dixon suggested. 'So I'm going to ask you outright. What is it you think you saw in my office?'

'I don't think I saw anything. I know exactly what it is that I saw.'

'And that is?' he asked.

'A British pilot.'

He leant back against the wall. 'So you did see.'

'Did you think I was lying?'

'I wasn't sure. I wasn't sure if you were chancing it the other day when you held me hostage.'

'Chancing it?' Adèle queried. 'And I did not hold you hostage.'

'Testing me then. Trying to see which side I was on because you guessed there was something amiss in here.'

'I would certainly call a stranded British pilot "amiss", yes. I am assuming he must have been stranded because Occupied Paris is a most unusual place to be at the moment for an Allied airman. But that is how I knew you were a good man.'

He looked down at his shoes, attempting to hide the fact he was smiling. 'You've got to try, right?'

'Yes,' Adèle agreed. 'You have to try. Where is he now?'

'I hope by now he's somewhere over the Pyrénées, on his way to Spain, Gibraltar and then back to England.'

'Where he will fly again and help the world defeat the Nazis, because of you?'

He waved his hand dismissively. 'And so many others. I'm just one tiny cog in this. I'm not the one actually taking them across a mountain range.'

'How many have you helped?' Adèle couldn't hold the awe from her voice.

'A few,' he said. 'He'd just arrived when you walked in. Shot down two days earlier. He'd been hiding, not sure what to do or where to go. He'd made an attempt to disguise his uniform but obviously not well enough if you clocked him at first glance. He was picked up by a friendly farmer out near Versailles who keeps a lookout for downed pilots. I didn't even know he was in here that day.'

'I assume the nurse who shouted not to enter is part of it, too? It seems an incredible risk for you both to take,' Adèle said.

The doctor shrugged. 'Yeah,' he said with a sideways smile. 'It is. They'll kill us if we're found out. Bullet between the eyes. I'm a good doctor but even I can't fix that one.'

Adèle smiled at his gallows humour and made to stand up. 'Well, Doctor Dixon, I promise not to put you in this position again.'

'Don't make promises you can't keep,' he joked.

'Another rule, Doctor Dixon?'

'Another rule.' He laughed. He looked at her for a moment, smiled and repeated her words from earlier as he stood up, 'And, Adèle, between us, we are attempting to save a Jewish child from the wrath of the Nazis. It is probably time to drop the formalities now, don't you think?'

She smiled, nodded. 'What is your first name then?'

'Theo,' he said as he extended his hand to shake hers. 'Nice to meet you, Adèle.'

Adèle laughed and shook his hand in return. 'Nice to meet you too, Theo.'

She held his gaze, considering that his eyes were so dark she could hardly tell where his pupils were. It was intoxicating. She smiled slowly. If she never saw him again then there would always be this, always be this connection between them; that they had done something great – had saved a child from whatever the Nazis had in store for her.

'Goodbye, Theo.'

As she turned reluctantly to leave he said, 'Wait.'

She turned back.

'Would you . . .' He paused searching her face for the answer to a question he hadn't yet asked. And then: 'Would you like to have dinner with me? This evening? Now?'

Adèle blinked and looked at him thoughtfully. She smiled shyly and her stomach grumbled, almost answering for her. 'Yes, actually. I would like that very much.'

*

They walked the few streets together to his apartment. This was a different part of Paris than Adèle was used to, quieter, a sense of refined gentility rather than ornately overblown like the Ritz. They were closer here to the pleasure garden of the Bois de Boulogne and the Longchamp racecourse. Adèle had only been through the leafy parkland of the Bois de Boulogne once on a day off before the war had started. It had been like stepping into a different world, one so far removed from Paris. She longed for that feeling again, to be far removed from Occupied Paris.

The apartment blocks were neatly jostled together, each building similar in style and architecture, sandstone in colour, tall windows, small balconies on every floor behind intricate-looking metal balustrades. When they climbed the wide staircase towards his front door in his apartment building Adèle felt as if a boundary had been crossed. Stepping foot in his apartment, Theo closing the front door behind them and giving her a wide smile, alleviated any concerns that she'd been a bit silly in venturing inside a man's apartment – a man she hardly knew. It was a distinctly masculine space with large dark furniture and small pot plants lining the windowsill of his sitting room. Dotted around the edge were bookshelves and as Theo said he'd fix them a drink, Adèle moved to look at what books the shelves contained. A lot were medical journals, well thumbed and stacked. A few books were in French and there were many works of American literature as well as a few English classics.

Adèle pulled out a plain white fabric book with gold lettering entitled *Peter Pan in Kensington Gardens* and looked through it. The illustrations were beautiful and although her English was good it wasn't good enough to read this at speed. She put it back on the shelf.

'That book is one of my favourites,' he said, returning with two glasses of wine and handing her one.

'I have never heard of it,' she confessed.

'It's probably an acquired taste,' he said. 'It's not the one with Wendy in it. That one's my absolute favourite but I don't have a copy here.'

Adèle gave him a look that indicated she had no idea who Wendy was.

His face came alive as he explained, 'It's the story of how Peter Pan came to be, well, Peter Pan. How he gets lost, doesn't grow up, stays in Kensington Gardens amongst the flora and fauna, looks after all the other lost children who inhabit an otherworldly space. You never read it?'

She shook her head. 'And it's one of your favourites?' Adèle said in disbelief. 'It sounds . . . strange.'

'It is strange. That's the point. I liked it because . . .' He looked as if he wasn't sure he should carry on.

'Go on,' Adèle encouraged him.

'I liked it because Peter plays all the children's games wrong. He doesn't understand a lot of what goes on around him and, well, that felt like me for a while.'

Adèle watched him with ever-growing interest. Who was this man who had helped her when she'd needed him to? 'That sounds incredibly sad.'

Theo looked at her and then looked away, almost nervously, vulnerably. 'I suppose it is really. But he makes friends, looks after the other children, falls in love with a girl. For a boy who professed he never wanted to grow up I think he did a pretty bad job of sticking to his guns.'

She thought about this for a moment and then worrying they were entering a conversation that was growing too deep said, 'It's very beautiful,' referring to the illustrations, which was true, even if the story sounded as if it wouldn't be to Adèle's taste.

'What do you think of the wine? Is it all right?' he asked, helping to change the subject even further. Perhaps Adèle should have been more enthusiastic about the book. A tinge of guilt shot through her.

She sipped it and it entered her system like a salve to a strange day. 'It's perfect. Thank you. It's delicious, actually.'

'I was saving it for a special occasion,' he admitted. 'But I think this is probably about as special as any occasion is going to get these days,' he confessed.

'What is it?'

'Château Margaux. I was given a case by a friend who fled before Paris fell. Worried their wine was going to be drunk by the Nazis. Told me if I didn't turn up and take a few bottles then they'd pour them into the gutters rather than see the Nazis drinking it.'

'I'm glad you saved some.'

'So am I.'

They clinked their glasses together and chorused, '*Santé*.'

Adèle wasn't an expert, nor did she drink much really but she let the red wine rest on her tongue, tantalising her taste buds as she sipped again.

'I wonder when we will be able to live normally, drink, dance, celebrate . . . live,' she echoed his thoughts of special occasions being out of reach these days.

He leant back against the wall as she continued looking at the bookshelves on and off. 'I don't know,' he said. 'I really don't know. I feel . . .' he started, 'as if I can live like this for a while, but I can't live like this forever. I can go on helping any airmen who get shot from the skies, and I can get up every day and go to work, and I can come home. But it's not a life, it's just an existence. And it's one that petrifies me. Do you know what I mean?' He turned and looked at her intently, his head resting on the wall.

'Yes,' she said quietly. 'I do. We are privileged,' Adèle said. 'We do not struggle. Our everyday existence has its advantages. But I have no friends here and am unlikely to make new ones at a time like this. And if I do, I would not know which side they were on, if they could be trusted, what I could and couldn't say in front of them.'

'I'm a new friend you can trust,' he said.

'Yes,' she said, looking up at him. 'I know that. I feel that you can be trusted. You have proven it. And I hope I have also.'

He nodded. 'You have. Either that or you've just ensnared me in an elaborate trap that leads me to my death.'

'No,' she cried, inching towards him. 'I would never do that. That is not the kind of person I am. Mélodie needed my help. I did not trick you.'

'I know. I'm joking,' he said hurriedly. 'I'm joking.'

Adèle allowed her heart rate to steady. 'I could not bear it if you thought I was one of them.'

'It really is the worst thing to be accused of these days, isn't it?' he said, sipping his wine.

'Yes,' she said in agreement. 'It really is. I could not imagine being one of them, being with one of them. They think their hateful cause is worth all of this. They are blind.'

Theo inhaled slowly, exhaled slowly. 'And to think it started by trying to make Germany a superior nation, to claw back all they'd lost after the first time they embroiled the world in a war. And now . . . God how did this happen?'

'I don't know,' she said and then so suddenly it shocked her, tears pricked the backs of her eyes and she humiliated herself by crying. Theo acknowledged her tears before she did as he pulled a folded cotton handkerchief from his trouser pocket.

'Here,' he said. Instead of handing it to her, he lifted it to her face and gently wiped her cheeks. 'I didn't mean to make you cry.'

She laughed to deflect her embarrassment as his hands brushed her face. 'It wasn't you. It was me. It was this.' She gestured to the world around her. 'I'm being silly.'

'No, you're not,' he said, still standing close. 'You're not being silly at all. Is this the first time you've cried over all of this?'

'Yes,' she said. 'I'm sorry.'

'Don't be. I'm not much of a crier,' he said, which made Adèle laugh. 'But I have been known to shout in anger into my closet once or twice.'

Adèle looked at him, taking the handkerchief he offered and continuing to dab at her eyes. 'What must your neighbours think?'

He laughed. 'There goes Doctor Dixon, saves lives by day and shouts for no reason every second Wednesday.'

Adèle laughed hard at that and so did he. 'Thank you for making me laugh,' she said.

'It's my pleasure,' he said as he reached up and brushed something off her face as if it was the most natural thing in the world.

'Sorry,' he said suddenly. 'I just . . . you had an eyelash.'

'It's fine,' she said, touching the place his fingertips had just been.

She wondered if he was as embarrassed as she had just been that he had done that. Although for her it was the embarrassment at how an invisible line of desire had shot from her cheek to every nerve ending in her body. She'd never felt anything like that before and she blinked in light-headed confusion.

'You're not on your own you know,' he said as if blustering his way out of a strange situation. 'We are all enduring this . . . hell. Some have it easier than others but this way of living is no one's first choice.'

'I know,' she admitted, trying to focus on the conversation in hand. 'I think the sad thing is that my life is still much the same as it was before the Nazis came.'

'It probably isn't,' he replied gently. 'If you really think about it.'

She paused before responding. The letters she was writing for Mademoiselle, the cause that she was having to pretend to adopt as her own in order to appease her mistress. This

129

wasn't what she should have been doing at all. And yet it was. Theo was right. She didn't want to think about that now. She had already ruined the night by crying once. She didn't want to do it again. She looked into his bookshelf again, picking out a volume she recognised. *Huckleberry Finn*. 'I have never read this either, I'm afraid.'

He glanced at it knowingly. 'I haven't read it in years. But I open it up every now and again, dip in, read a page or two and put it back on the shelf. It reminds me of home.'

'Do you get homesick?' she asked more directly than she'd intended.

'Sometimes. Do you?'

Adèle shook her head slowly as she thumbed through the pages of the book. She could feel him next to her, his warmth, his presence. 'No. I don't think I've ever felt homesick. I think it's a privilege to feel that. It means you have had a happy home to miss.'

He nodded. 'I suppose it does mean that.' He moved away from her over to the yellow settee, the back of which had faded through years of direct sunlight. Adèle moved away from the shelves and sat on the one opposite, not daring to sit next to him, suddenly nervous at how she might behave, sitting next to him.

'You didn't have a happy home?' he asked. 'Forgive me if this is a question you don't want to answer.'

'I did. For a time. Before I went to live in an orphanage, back when I had a loving mother. But we were poor. Very poor. And having no money can be a bar to real happiness.'

'I thought money couldn't buy happiness,' Theo suggested.

Adèle thought of Mademoiselle Chanel, rich beyond Adèle's wildest dreams but never truly quite happy. 'It doesn't,' she agreed. 'But it buys you the freedom to find happiness. Whether you find it or not . . .' She trailed off unsure whether it was up to the individual to find happiness or up to others to help. She didn't know and she thought about it for a few seconds before reasoning she didn't have the answer.

'How long were you in the orphanage for?' he asked as he sat back and sipped his wine.

'Long enough. From the age of ten to only a few years ago. I stayed on after my education came to a close and I worked there carrying out administrative tasks for Mother Superior. Book-keeping and ledgers, filing, helping with the day-to-day running, purchases for the children. It was becoming too much for Mother Superior in her ageing years.'

'A different life to the one you have now,' Theo suggested.

'Yes.' It was nice, having someone she liked being interested in her life before all this. It was refreshing.

'Do you enjoy it? Working for someone like . . . her? Chanel, I mean.'

'I don't hate it,' Adèle said. 'I am grateful, of course. I wanted to see so much of the world that I'd learnt about in books and magazines. And in such a short time, I have travelled the length and breadth of France when before I had never stepped foot outside of my seaside town until I made my way to Paris.'

'You're from the seaside? So am I,' he said. 'Maine. My father fished lobsters.'

'How wonderful. It sounds so free to be on the water every day. I didn't know my father. He left when I was very small.'

'I'm so sorry.'

'Don't be. You don't miss what you don't really remember.'

'I guess,' he said uncertainly.

The conversation moved on to the war and their place in it with Adèle confessing she didn't feel she had a place in it. 'It feels so wrong to live in such luxury at a time such as this. It feels so utterly surreal that arrests have begun, right under our noses, that so many people in the street did nothing about it; did nothing to help that woman.'

'What could you do?' he asked. 'Run over, grab her, pull her back from the clutches of the gendarmerie? If you'd attempted such a thing you'd have been arrested yourself, never to be seen again.'

'I know,' she reasoned sadly. 'But it is just too surreal that it's happening in our streets, endorsed by the authorities.'

'They're under the command of the Gestapo, of the Nazis. They can rebel. They can say no. But why would they? What would happen to them if they did? How can they?'

'Because it goes against everything we were ever taught as children about kindness to others.'

'All bets are off now,' he reasoned.

'So we keep our heads down?'

'Yes,' he said inching forward on the settee to enforce his point. 'But in the meantime we do whatever we can without bringing suspicion down on ourselves.'

'You've done a good thing smuggling a pilot home and rescuing a child. You've done two good things and I've only known you a short amount of time,' she said.

'You've done two good things as well,' he placated. 'You haven't ratted on me about the pilot and it was you who bravely went in and took that little girl out of harm's way. Who knows what would have happened to her if you hadn't stepped in.'

They were quiet for a few moments and then Adèle said quietly, 'Do you think they will take children to . . .' She daren't say it.

'Yes,' he said darkly. 'I think eventually they will. They'll come for everyone who doesn't fit with their vision of what their ideal world looks like.'

Adèle swallowed and put her wine glass on the dark mahogany coffee table between them.

'Do you think they'll let them all out, if they lose? Or even if they win?'

'No,' he said. 'I don't.'

'Oh,' Adèle said, her shoulders slumping. Tears threatened again and she swallowed the lump in her throat back into place. 'It's as if we live in a nightmare.'

'Imagine how it is for them. It'll only get worse,' he pointed out quietly.

'I cannot see how this can be allowed to happen,' she said, anger tingeing her voice.

'Too easily. Blame Hitler and then blame Marshal Pétain if you want to look closer to home. France has its own king collaborator.'

'What you and I helped do . . . is it what General de Gaulle meant when he broadcast on the radio?' Adèle asked.

'*Whatever happens the flame of French Resistance must not be extinguished and will not be extinguished,*' Theo quoted de Gaulle's radio broadcast made on the BBC from two years prior, the line seared into every freethinking French resident's immediate memory.

'Yes.' She nodded. 'The flame of French Resistance . . .' she repeated to herself.

'Be careful,' he warned. 'Don't go looking for it.'

'For what?' she asked.

'Trouble. Helping the Resistance,' he said. 'You've got to be committed, willing to die. Are you willing to die for it, Adèle?'

A thick layer of silence fell over them both as he directed his challenging gaze towards hers.

'Were you?' she asked.

'It's different for me,' he said, not letting go of her gaze. 'I didn't go looking for it. But I found it hard to say no when it found me.'

She said nothing and sipped her wine. She should probably

stop if she was to stay upright, given her stomach was so empty.

'Are you hungry?' he asked echoing her thoughts. 'I promised you dinner after all.'

'Yes.'

'I've not entertained in . . . forever. I can make chicken soup,' he suggested. 'I've got one piece of cold cooked chicken left over, and a ton of vegetables. I feel guilty that I've been gifted a lot of supplies for the hospital and medical staff and so I'm not yet down to my last piece of bread.'

'One piece of chicken,' she queried, looking at his smiling eyes and the thin tell-tale blood shots running through them, indicating his tiredness and ultimately his need for sustenance. 'You have it. I'm happy with just the vegetable soup.'

'No,' he protested. 'I can't do that.'

'I'm . . . vegetarian,' she lied, hoping she'd used the right word.

He frowned.

'I don't eat meat,' she clarified.

'Yes, I know what a vegetarian is. I just don't meet too many in these days when any kind of food is hard to come by.' He was still looking at her. She could see he didn't believe her but he turned and walked into the galley kitchen regardless. She moved to follow him, keep him company as he peeled vegetables, put water on to boil and began making a basic soup.

She offered to chop carrots and as they worked together, he topped up their wine. They moved around each other tentatively, quietly. To Adèle it seemed he was as nervous as she of bumping into each other in such a tight space. It struck Adèle that they could be any Parisian couple, enjoying each other's company, cooking together after a long day. Good wine, food, the four walls keeping them away from the harm that was all too readily befalling other citizens of Paris. It was too easy to want to escape from it all here, with him. Except they weren't a couple and this gesture – cooking together – took on an unexpectedly intimate nature. She'd never done this with anyone before, let alone a man. And the harm wasn't that far away. As if he'd read her mind he said suddenly, 'I'm right under their noses you know.'

'Who?' She was broken from her reverie so quickly that she almost sliced her finger with the knife.

'Careful,' he said glancing down at her hand, touching the indentation where the knife had scratched her hand but not broken the skin. She flushed at his touch but he didn't notice as he said, 'The Gestapo, I mean.'

'Really? Why?'

'It's rumoured they've offices out here in Neuilly, the senior Gestapo officials; that they've taken up residence in some of the more expensive properties left behind when citizens fled.'

'Have you seen them?' she asked in horror.

'I don't actually know for sure. When they pass you by and they don't wear uniforms, only plain clothes, how do you know exactly who you're dealing with?' he reasoned. 'There are an awful lot of men in brown coats though, when there weren't any before. So I guess that's a clue.'

Adèle thought about the baron, von Dincklage. Who was he really? What did he do? Somehow she sensed he wasn't just in intelligence, nor was he really a diplomat.

They ate dinner at a little wooden table pushed against the edge of the kitchen wall. Theo dusted off her chair and moved a lot of magazines and journals from the table in order for them to eat. It was clear he didn't entertain much and his movements endeared her to him.

They ate their soup with crusts of bread while she asked him questions about his family, how often he ate lobsters as his father caught them: 'Not as regularly as you might think.' He'd laughed. They talked about travel and where they wanted to visit when the war finished. After hearing his charming boyish tales of adventure and plenty of food in America, Adèle had decided to add the United States to her ever-growing list of places she wanted to see. Not only did she want to visit Maine, now he'd described it – a place she'd never even heard of until tonight – she wanted to see all of America. She wanted to see everything.

And his reply to her question of where he wanted to go: 'I suppose it depends on which side wins,' he said simply.

'Yes, of course.' And there was that hammer blow of finding the war creeping back into a conversation that they had managed, for half a blissful hour, to avoid the subject of entirely.

'And if Germany loses?' Adèle asked. 'Where would you go?'

'I honestly don't know,' he said. 'Depends what it's like around here . . . after. But I don't know if they will lose. They're so entrenched everywhere. It will take something akin to a miracle for them to lose.'

'Don't say that,' Adèle whispered. 'They have to lose. We can't believe this is it – that this is our way of life forever.'

'No,' he replied and they sat in companionable silence, drinking their wine while it lasted until he said, 'You know what we need?'

'The Nazis gone?' Adèle suggested with a smile.

'That too,' he replied. 'I was thinking more along the lines of music. You finished?' He looked at her empty bowl.

She nodded as she rose and he reached out, taking her hand and leading her from the kitchen.

'Are we going to leave the dishes there?' she asked, glancing back at the table. It went against everything she'd grown up doing.

'Sure,' he said dismissively. 'They'll keep.' She smiled at his easy nature, the way he took her hand so gently, so keenly that it felt so natural for him to do so, despite the fact it made her feel flushed. She obviously wasn't having the same effect on him or else he would stop, surely?

She'd tasted heavenly morsels since she'd worked with Mademoiselle Chanel but the simplicity and camaraderie of a home-cooked meal with Theo was something she knew she'd remember forever. 'Thank you,' she said as he let go of her hand and moved towards the gramophone. 'It was delicious.'

'Anytime,' he said, his back turned to her while he moved the large gold horn around in order to ready the machine for the music.

'Be careful,' she warned jokingly, gazing at what he was doing. 'I may just take you up on that.'

'Do,' he said. 'I wouldn't mind seeing more of you.' He selected a record, placed it on the gramophone and clicked the needle into place.

The tones of Edith Piaf sounded from the trumpet.

Theo walked forward and took Adèle's hand. 'Shall we?'

His touch on her hand was as commanding as when he'd been readying her arm to donate blood. He'd been methodical then and he was that too now but something else: leading but not overbearing. As they danced to the music his eyes twinkled with enjoyment. Was she misreading this? Was he actually having a good time? Adèle hoped so because for the first time in a long time she was having a wonderful evening; the kind of evening that couldn't be real amid all this; the kind of evening that was so simple, so humble but one she knew she'd remember forever.

He held her close as they moved and she couldn't help but breathe him in. She couldn't place the scent, just that of a man who'd been to work, been in a kitchen after a long day and who had cooked her a meal. She'd never danced with a man and she was silently glad he wasn't attempting to move her in any kind of certain set of moves, because she wouldn't know what to do, how to respond.

Dancing was not part of her repertoire. It had not been deemed essential learning at the orphanage. He was just swaying gently with her but as he led her in slow circles even this felt expert, as they grew closer still. In all its various ways, this week had been a week of firsts. Some things she never wanted to repeat. Others she most certainly did.

'Tell me how you came to work for Coco Chanel,' he asked as they danced. And with that she came back down to earth.

She told him how she'd come to the city to better herself, to put into practice everything she'd been taught in order to be a clerical assistant, about how she felt herself free of constraints after she'd left the Sisters of Mary Magdalene but restricted due to a lack of funds. Mademoiselle Chanel had given her a job, a roof over her head, three good meals a day and Adèle had never looked back.

'And now I feel such loyalty and appreciation for Mademoiselle Chanel,' Adèle confessed. 'Even when I do not agree with some of the things she does and sometimes even how she lives.' It was true. Even after Mademoiselle closed her boutique and made all her staff unemployed, Adèle hadn't wavered in her loyalty. Instead there was gratitude to her employer for keeping her on at a time when all the other women in the atelier had been fired. When some of the girls begged Adèle to say a good word, she had tried and had been reprimanded and she knew she could never utter a cross word to her employer. She knew she would live to regret it if she ever challenged her. She knew how lucky she was. There were times when a small comment here or there meant Adèle was never allowed to forget that.

When Edith Piaf finished singing, Theo changed the record for The Ink Spots. He turned the volume down a little when the needle fell gently into place.

'Don't tell anyone,' he said with a wicked look. 'If they

think rescuing British pilots and Jewish children is wrong, they'll blow a gasket if they find out I also listen to what they consider degenerate music.'

'I miss jazz,' Adèle said as Theo repositioned himself in front of her and took her hand in his again, placing one on her back. Was it her imagination or were they closer now than during the previous song?

'Truly?'

It took her a second or two to recover enough to answer. 'Yes. I used to listen to jazz as it sounded through the floorboards of Mother Superior's bedroom.'

Theo laughed loudly. 'Really?' His dark eyes crinkled at the sides.

It was Adèle's turn to laugh. 'Yes. I'll admit I was surprised the first time I heard her play it. And it took me quite some time to enjoy it. But then I learnt to long for her to put it on the gramophone each evening. She was starting to lose her hearing and so with each passing month the gramophone grew louder and louder. Until she admitted she could no longer hear it and it stopped. I miss it. I have never owned a gramophone of my own. I should like one, one day, wherever I end up.'

'Hard to get hold of right now,' he said.

'One day,' she replied.

'One day when all this is over . . . I'll buy you one,' he said, looking down at her.

She pulled back to look at him. 'Thank you. But I won't expect you to do that.'

'Why not?'

'Because I don't suppose we'll know each other when all of this is over.'

'Why on earth not?' He sounded incredulous.

'You will go your way and I will go mine. That's what always happens, isn't it? I had friends at home but we none of us write to each other now. I don't really know why.'

139

'That's sad,' he said looking genuinely puzzled by this. 'You should write to them. Rekindle the fire of friendship.'

'They'll probably have forgotten me. It's been a few years. They'll probably be confused to receive a letter from me.'

'Would you be surprised to receive one from them?' he probed.

'No I don't think I would,' she agreed.

'Well then. I doubt they've forgotten you,' he said with genuine warmth. 'And you've not forgotten them?'

She thought of her friends back in the seaside town of St Nazaire; the only other girls from the orphanage who had stayed until the end of their education without being adopted, perhaps because they had arrived at such a late age when childless women always seemed to want to adopt babies, toddlers. 'No. But they have their own lives and families. Although my friend Camille's husband may be a prisoner of war now. He was going into the army.'

Theo sighed. 'I pity all those guys who went to fight for their country, for wider freedom. And now . . .'

'They sit in a prison somewhere, suffering, waiting.'

He yawned suddenly and then tried too late to stifle it. 'I'm so sorry,' he said.

She stopped dancing and looked up at him. 'I should go,' she said softly.

He didn't argue; instead saying, 'Would you like me to escort you home?'

'No thank you,' she replied softly. 'I know my way back to the hotel and feel quite safe. Besides, you look like you need some sleep.'

'Thanks.' He laughed. 'I do. But I'm reluctant to say goodbye just yet.'

'Let's not say goodbye then,' she said. 'I will just slip away and leave you to rest.'

'All right,' he said, an intrigued look on his face and then more seriously: 'Can I see you again?'

'Yes,' Adèle replied immediately. 'I would like that.'

'So would I. In a couple of days? Meet me at the hospital one afternoon? If you can get away.'

'I can get away. I think.'

'You're a surprise,' he admitted. 'When you walked into the hospital asking to donate blood I had no idea we'd end up like this.'

'Like this . . . ?' she questioned.

There was a pause before he said, 'Becoming friends.'

'You're very easy to be friends with,' Adèle replied.

'So are you,' he said as he accompanied her to the door. 'And we have to be friends now anyway.'

'Have to?' she queried.

'Sure.' The laughter returned so easily to his eyes that it made Adèle smile automatically in return. 'After all,' he said, 'we've got too much dirt on each other now. Goodnight, Adèle.' He bent and kissed her on her cheek, lingering for the briefest of seconds. She blushed, smiled and saying goodnight in return, slipped from Theo's apartment.

Chapter 11

Chaotic scraps of torn brown paper and packing crates were scattered through the drawing room of the suite a few days later, covering the deep, lush Chinese rug. There was now only a blanket of torn paper as far as the eye could see. And in a time of war when everything was rationed, the paper was a luxury. But what it had been covering was even more exotic.

'What is it?' Adèle enquired as she began picking up the paper, folding the larger pieces that could be saved and reused. She looked as the two men carried the large square item over to the bare wall. The large gilt mirror had been taken down, propped in the far corner to make way for this new item.

And then they turned to hang it and what they were holding made Adèle gasp: a large canvas, around six feet tall and four feet wide depicted a scene that Adèle couldn't place. A woman, nearly naked but draped in a deep blue cloth was being dragged along by three men, one of whom looked Roman. He had a dagger raised, ready to strike the woman. It was not at all what Adèle had been expecting and she could barely speak as she took in the picture before her.

'Isn't it sublime?' Mademoiselle Chanel cried as she held her hands together.

'It's . . .' Adèle wasn't sure what it was. She took in the deep sweep of blue on the robe that had come away from the woman, exposing bare breasts. Adèle was struck by how stark, how lewd it was and how awful the subject matter was, a woman being led to her execution, flanked by three men.

Despite the fire warming the room, Adèle shivered as if someone had walked over her grave. She couldn't grasp her feelings towards the picture, only that it had stopped her, made her stare, think. 'It certainly fills the space well,' was all she could reply. 'Where has it come from?'

'It's a gift,' Mademoiselle said.

'From who?'

Mademoiselle gave Adèle a knowing look. 'An admirer.'

'A strange choice of gift,' Adèle volunteered.

'Why do you say that?' her employer snapped.

'The content of the picture is . . .'

'Beautiful,' Mademoiselle said as the two men straightened the picture, looked for approval from her and then when they'd been issued a sharp nod, let themselves out of the suite.

Adèle struggled to agree. The content was almost vile, a woman about to be executed by three men. Who would send this to someone? What kind of odd gift was this?

'After the war it is going to be worth a fortune,' Mademoiselle said knowingly and then Adèle knew why it was here. If this was a grand gesture, it was financially motivated.

Adèle was curious as to what kind of person would want to invest in art after the war, or who would have the means to do so; wouldn't there be other, better priorities? But she chose to keep quiet.

Mademoiselle spoke, cutting into Adèle's judgement and

growing curiosity about the provenance of the painting. 'I want you to write a list of items I will need for a trip and then to pack the trunks. I am going to Madrid.'

'Madrid?' Adèle queried, her head darting up to look at her employer. But her curious gaze was met with silence and so Adèle pulled out her notebook and pen and perched on the edge of the settee.

If Adèle expected an explanation as to why her employer was visiting neutral Spain during a time of war, it was not forthcoming.

'The weather is milder than Paris,' Mademoiselle explained and so I will need . . .' She reeled off a selection of outfits, jewels, hats and shoes and Adèle scribbled the list knowing she would have to go back to the apartment above the atelier so she could fetch many of the items Chanel requested. She would also need to collect the travelling trunks, which were stored in the attics and which had been put back after they'd returned from the South of France when the Nazis had arrived in Paris. She had not expected to have to retrieve trunks again quite so soon.

'Will you need me to go with you?' Adèle asked. She'd never been to Spain before and the idea of accompanying her employer, to see the architecture in such a beautiful city thrilled her. As did the idea of a neutral country where there weren't Nazi officers or German soldiers goose-stepping down the road. She shifted on the settee expectantly, hopefully.

'No.' Mademoiselle waved her hand.

Disappointment waved over Adèle. 'Are you travelling alone? Is it for business?' Mademoiselle had mentioned opening a boutique in Madrid, Adèle remembered from long ago, before the war broke out, or was it to do with the fragrance side of the business, the only side flourishing during wartime?

But Mademoiselle Chanel didn't fully answer the question when she replied, 'I will be travelling with a friend. Baron Louis de Vaufreland.'

Adèle nodded and for reasons unbeknownst to her, she wrote the name inside the notebook she was using. *Madrid. Baron Louis de Vaufreland.*

'Shall I arrange travel for you – hotels, trains and, of course travelling documents? When do you leave?'

'The day after tomorrow.'

Adèle dropped her pen, picked it up and rubbed at the blob of ink that had fallen onto the floor. The day after tomorrow. Adèle knew she would have her work cut out arranging travel so soon. How on earth could that be achieved in record time? She rubbed at the ink spot with the palm of her hand and into her head flew the tunes from The Ink Spots she and Theo had danced to close together; the meal they had cooked together, the conversation that flowed as easily as the wine they had drunk.

'And the travel arrangements and documents have been taken care of by Vaufreland's office,' Mademoiselle Chanel said and Adèle stopped thinking of Theo and paid closer attention.

'I see,' Adèle said. 'Then there is very little for me to actually do.'

'You should be pleased, Adèle,' Mademoiselle offered as she stood to admire the painting again, smiling to herself. 'I have given you enough to be getting on with today. And I've left a list of tasks for you to complete while I'm away. I will only be a few days at most.

'And then of course there is the dance tomorrow, which I will be attending before I go.'

'Dance?' Adèle baulked. 'Where?'

'In the ballroom here,' Mademoiselle said.

She really did live a different lifestyle to the rest of Paris. 'I wondered, Adèle, as a thank you for all your hard work, at such a trying time, if you would like to attend as my guest? I have a table, of course.'

Mademoiselle waited more patiently than usual for her assistant's reply but Adèle didn't know what to say.

'Really?' she ventured at last. 'Me? Who else will be there?' Adèle asked and it was Chanel's turn to baulk so Adèle hurried on. 'I mean, do you have room for me?'

'Yes, two spaces. I am not in the mood for bad company and so I shall not issue the invitation onwards. There will be myself and Baron von Dincklage, of course,' she said with a wistful expression. 'And Baron de Vaufreland. The two men are already familiar with each other. I should like to invite you also.'

Mademoiselle looked at Adèle, giving the younger woman her full attention as she adopted a motherly tone. 'Adèle, have you made any friends in the city? I have enough to be worrying about without worrying about you also.'

'Yes,' she said after just the briefest of hesitations. 'One.'

'One is better than none as long as they turn out to be a good friend,' Chanel mused. 'And what is she like?'

What harm could come from admitting she'd made a friend. 'It's a he actually.'

'A he?' Chanel questioned sounding neither impressed nor unimpressed. 'Is he kind? What does he expect from you?'

'I don't think he expects anything from me,' Adèle replied.

'Good. Don't let him own you.'

Adèle laughed but not unkindly. 'He's just a friend.'

Mademoiselle clicked her tongue against the roof of her mouth. 'These things always start that way. Bring him tomorrow. To the dance.'

Theo in a room full of Nazi officers? Absolutely not.

'I must meet him,' Mademoiselle demanded.

Adèle stared in horror. No. Theo and Mademoiselle Chanel could not meet. Must not meet. Not in a time such as this. 'Why?' she asked worriedly.

146

'To check he is good enough of course.'

'He's a doctor and I'm the daughter of peasants from St Nazaire. Were one of us to be unsuitable for the other, it would certainly be me who was lacking.'

'Adèle, do not put yourself down,' Mademoiselle Chanel retorted. 'How will you ever rise if you diminish your own qualities? There are plenty of people who will work hard to make you feel less than you are. Do not be responsible for doing that to yourself. Stand tall, stand strong, be proud of who you are. And most of all, be proud of the woman you are becoming.'

Adèle nodded mutely. A thin smile confirmed she understood her employer's meaning. How many times had she heard Mademoiselle enthuse about her background, her ability to have made something of herself through her own raw talent? Adèle wished she had a talent other than typing and book-keeping. She stood and waited for further instruction or further words of wisdom but Mademoiselle had turned back to look at her new painting, her delicate arms folded over her thin frame. 'You can go,' she said with a wave of her hand.

'Yes, Mademoiselle.'

The room was darker now the mirror had been removed from the wall, darker thanks to the muted tones of the painting. But not only that, the curiosity as to where the painting could possibly have come from cast a bleak spell over the suite, over Chanel; adding to the darkness that had already engulfed Paris.

Chapter 12

Dincklage arrived to escort Mademoiselle downstairs to the dance. Adèle was drinking a glass of water in the little room she and the housekeeper shared to eat their meals when she heard him arrive. She was wearing a dress Chanel had gifted her before the war, one she'd no longer had any use for. Adèle had also had no use for it until today. Usually, she went nowhere to warrant wearing such an outfit. But today, she put on the black satin dress with its thin straps and low back and paired it with a low block-heel shoe, curling her dark hair in rolls and using her good nylon stockings, the ones that looked more like the silk counterparts that she'd long since stopped being able to get hold of.

The day before, Adèle had telephoned Theo at work. If she'd stopped to think about it, it was a bold move to telephone him so soon after seeing him, but she'd never been in this position before, never really been friends with a man before and so wondered if it was really so very different to being friends with a woman. Chanel had almost commanded she bring Theo to the Ritz and, not wishing to disappoint, she had done so. She assumed telephoning him to ask him to the dance was not something the Nazis would be particularly interested in – should they be listening in to the telephone call.

'Doctor Dixon?' she had asked when she'd been connected to his office at the hospital. 'Would it be terribly forward of me to invite you to a dinner and dance at the Ritz?'

He'd laughed and she'd heard him pushing papers around his desk. The papers stopped moving. 'Are you joking?'

She'd known it wasn't the opulence he was referring to, more the fact they'd be surrounded by Nazis.

'No, I'm not joking,' she'd replied carefully, ever aware there may be eavesdroppers on the line. 'I've been invited as a guest and Mademoiselle Chanel has asked to meet you.'

'She wants to meet me? Why? Does she want to vet me?' He'd laughed. 'Check I'm good enough for you? Check my intentions are pure?'

Adèle had bit down on her rising embarrassment but had smiled regardless. There was something mysteriously seductive about not being able to see him on the other end of the line.

'Are they pure?' Adèle had dared.

'I don't know what you're talking about,' Theo had said, holding back laughter.

'Exactly,' Adèle had stated. 'We're just friends.'

A moment's silence at the end of the line and then: 'Sure. Just friends.'

She'd wished he was standing in front of her. She'd wanted to see his face, his expression. And he'd still not given her an answer.

'If you don't want to go,' she'd offered, 'it's perfectly all right.' She'd needed to offer him a way out. She pictured Theo – who was helping British pilots – standing in a room full of Nazis. The thought of it made her perspire. 'And of course, you might be on call,' she'd offered insistently, pointedly. 'In which case I'm sure we would all understand.'

But he hadn't taken the offer to decline. 'I want to come. If it means I get to dance with you again.'

There was a recklessness to Theo that excited and petrified Adèle. Half of her wished he'd said no, for his own safety. The other half of her was exultant he'd said yes. 'As you know, Doctor Dixon, I don't really dance.'

'Sure you do.'

'I sway,' she'd joked.

'I'm happy to sway with you,' he'd said. 'I'm happy to do anything with you. And I'm looking forward to seeing you again.'

'Are you?' She'd closed her eyes in happiness.

She loved the way he laughed so readily, so openly. 'Of course,' he replied.

And now, at dinner in the Ritz Salon Vendôme, a dining room so large it doubled as the ballroom – a room she had never set foot inside until tonight – she found herself on one side of Dincklage while Mademoiselle Chanel had her arm threaded through his on the other as they entered the salon. And there was a cold feeling of bitter regret creeping across her that she had invited Theo. This wasn't wise.

She often felt she occupied a halfway space between servant and . . . not friend exactly but she'd always been treated just that little bit better than most of Mademoiselle's other staff. Not that there were many left now.

They sat down, Dincklage pulling out a chair for his lover and then one for Adèle but there was no sign of Theo yet. Out of the corner of her eye she watched her employer with her German lover as they talked earnestly. Was this strange relationship dependent on how the war played out . . . which side won, which side lost?

Adèle hoped she hadn't made it too obvious she disapproved of Mademoiselle's relationship. Dincklage was a Nazi, Mademoiselle Chanel a French citizen. And it was wrong, this relationship. Adèle could see that. She wondered, not for the first time, if Mademoiselle could see it too, or if she even cared. Why was she doing it? Genuine love? Or for other reasons such as self-preservation? Or even a heady combination of both?

Nearby a photographer took a picture, the light bulb flash startling her. A waiter arrived to offer glasses of Champagne and Adèle sat back, accepting one gratefully. There must be an unending store in the cellars, she mused as she looked around, hoping Theo would appear. Would the Champagne reserves under the Ritz last the entire year? The entire war? How long would that be? And if it didn't last, the Nazis would probably just steal more from wherever they could. Incredible how they wanted their definition of a better world while they thieved and pillaged; and everyone they sought to conquer suffered rationing and poverty.

While waiting for Theo, Adèle looked around the ballroom. It was old-Paris-ornate with thick, plush carpet, recesses and alcoves with Roman-looking sculptures inset, circular tables and well-dressed, well-fed people milling together, laughing and drinking. Within these walls was another world *entirely*, compared to what was happening outside. Adèle looked at the light as it danced from the chandeliers to the crystal Champagne glasses on trays carried by waiters. It reflected all around, bouncing bright white shards from one shiny surface to another and she followed its rays glittering around the room until she saw him.

He was standing by the door, pulling at the collar of his formal shirt. He looked so very different, so very dapper in his black dinner suit, his thick dark hair swept over and held in place. Her breath caught in her throat. Like this, he looked so very American, so very different to the other men in this room who were mostly French waiters or blond Germans, the very model of Hitler's Aryan race. But not him. Not Theo.

Was it very wrong that her heart thudded so heavily and sounded so loudly in her ears, just because she had seen him? Or was it right? It was such a new feeling that she couldn't identify exactly what it was he was doing to her without even knowing it.

She saw Theo glance around the room and when it was clear he couldn't spot her she pushed her chair back a little in order to stand, looking at him hopefully. He caught her eye and didn't immediately move. Instead, a slow smile spread over his face on seeing her and after a beat he began to walk towards her and she towards him, their eyes on each other the whole time he moved through the crowds of uniformed officials.

They met in the middle of the crowded room, waiters pushing past them, jostling them closer towards each other.

She looked up at him, the difference in their heights marginalised with the court heels she was wearing. The light from the chandeliers made his brown eyes stand out in a way she'd not seen before.

'Hello,' she said, finding her voice.

'Hi,' he said simply. He breathed in and out. 'You look . . .' He shook his head and blinked a few times. 'Dazzling. I'm dazzled. I'll admit it.' And with that he smiled and was the Theo she was coming to know and like so very much it stunned her into silence again.

She blinked away his compliment without comment but knew she had to converse so forced herself to say something. 'Thank you for coming.'

'Believe me, it's my pleasure,' he said with meaning as he looked only at her. If Theo could see the array of Nazi uniforms around him, which of course he could, then he didn't acknowledge it.

'We should . . .' Adèle gestured towards the table where she'd departed without even a word. For once she led him and thoughtlessly took his hand to guide him to the table. The moment she'd clasped his hand it was as if it burned her, so acutely aware she'd done such a forward thing. But he made no comment, letting go discreetly as they arrived at the table.

'Doctor Theo Dixon.' Adèle made introductions in order to shield her embarrassment of having taken his hand even if Theo had made a point of not letting go until all eyes from the table were on them. 'This is Mademoiselle Chanel and Baron von Dincklage.'

Greetings were exchanged and Adèle fidgeted from embarrassment again, as Mademoiselle did not even try to mask the scrutiny to which she was subjecting Theo, who stepped forward politely.

'Mister Dixon,' Chanel said as she raised her hand for Theo to kiss.

A mix of horror and embarrassment sent heat to Adèle's cheeks. But she refrained from correcting her employer that Theo should be addressed as 'Doctor'.

'Mademoiselle Chanel,' Theo said, seeming not to notice or care. 'A real pleasure to meet you. Adèle speaks incredibly highly of you. Thank you for the invitation.'

She waved his thanks away dismissively and he turned to greet the baron. The two men conversed in light small talk about the changing weather as they seated themselves. Behind her, Adèle sensed a presence and she turned to see a man in uniform.

Instinctively, everyone at the table rose. 'Baron de Vaufreland,' Chanel enthused warmly. 'How good it is to see you again.'

Vaufreland, a thin-faced man with high cheekbones nodded to those at the table as greetings were given. Adèle felt the mood change as he said, 'Mademoiselle Chanel, may I have a word in private?'

Baron von Dincklage sat forward to cover the awkwardness that had suddenly befallen them. 'Doctor Dixon, tell me about your work at the hospital.'

Theo launched in readily, keeping a lid on his anger as to how there were now shortages of medicines and food for patients would soon become a real issue. Adèle watched him grow enthusiastic about his work, his passion for healing, his hopes for how the hospital would carry on under straitened circumstances even through the Occupation.

'I am happy to help with anything you need.' Dincklage inched forward on his chair. 'If you have shortages, if there's anything the hospital needs, say the word and I'll see what we can provide.'

'That's very generous of you,' Theo said.

'Not at all,' Mademoiselle Chanel's lover continued. 'We are running an Occupation. The health of our civilians is of prime import to the Reich. And we are grateful to the American doctors and nurses for staying on to help. It's important we know who our friends are. Who do you have in there at the moment? I take it most American patients have . . . moved on?' he suggested delicately.

Theo smiled, holding eye contact with Dincklage. 'We've run the whole gamut of events so far at the hospital, from its use primarily treating American expatriates to setting up a station towards the fighting from which to treat the war wounded, and now of course we fly under the International Red Cross flag. Getting busier by the day and . . . you're right . . . hardly any Americans to treat these days. Most went the moment they sensed the war inching here. We helped some nuns not so long ago. A meningitis outbreak in their orphanage. They didn't know what to do and so we did all we could, showed them how to do lumbar punctures and how to administer penicillin. We gave them a lot of penicillin and now supplies are hard to get. I had a lot of donations from wealthy expats so finance isn't the issue. It's supplies.' He stopped, reached slowly for his Champagne while watching for Dincklage's reaction to all of that.

His reaction was almost to ignore the plight. 'But you have not gone,' Dincklage replied with interest.

'I have a job to do,' Theo replied.

'And if America enters the war – what then?'

'You mean what will happen in general or what will happen to me?'

'Both,' Dincklage suggested.

Adèle watched the game of verbal tennis as the two men volleyed back and forth, neither quite sure what to make of the other.

Theo inhaled. 'I couldn't say. I reckon you'd know more than me about that.'

Adèle put her hand on Theo's leg to still him. It was a personal move but a necessary one. She could see him growing heated and that was a dangerous place to be with a member of the Occupying force.

'But in terms of me,' Theo said more calmly. 'I'll stay in Paris as long as I can. Because I'm with the Red Cross I won't be arrested if the US and Germany go to war. I hope.'

'Do you now?' Dincklage said with a smile on his face.

Theo replied with a look that Adèle took to be horror. 'I'm here to treat the injured. I'm not here to cause upset.' This was a mistake. Coming here tonight was a mistake. Dining with so many Nazi officers tonight was a mistake.

'You don't wish to cause upset to who?' Dincklage leant back in his chair thoughtfully.

Theo shrugged. 'To anyone.'

They dined on veal medallions and a strawberry tart with delicate, buttery pastry and endless supplies of ice-cold white wine. Adèle wanted to say it was almost as delicious as the wine she'd drunk at Theo's apartment but dare not admit out loud to the other guests she'd been inside his home. Although what was occurring openly between

Mademoiselle Chanel and Dincklage did not compare at all to the innocent dinner she'd enjoyed at Theo's, there was something about it that she wanted to keep private. It was so early, so fragile.

'I thought you said you didn't eat meat?' Theo whispered after she'd eaten her veal medallions. Alongside the guilt of eating so richly when the rest of France was starving, was the shame of having been caught in a lie.

'I fibbed. I didn't want you to share your chicken. You should have it. You work hard.'

'Hmm, I guessed you were lying,' he said giving her his full attention. 'But there was a part of me that wasn't sure and if I'd forced you into eating the chicken and you had actually turned out to be a vegetarian . . .' He made a face to illustrate the awkwardness that would have caused and then she masked a loud laugh and he chuckled into the napkin he lifted to his lips.

'Mister Dixon,' Mademoiselle Chanel interjected. 'Tell me how you and my assistant became . . . friends.'

Theo looked at Adèle warmly and smiled before looking at Mademoiselle. 'She came to donate blood.'

Mademoiselle looked stunned. 'Did you, Adèle? You did not say. That is a very . . . different thing to do.'

'It was on my day off a little while ago,' Adèle said simply. 'I hope that was all right?' She could have kicked herself. Why was she asking for belated permission to donate blood? Why would she ask such a thing? Adèle could do anything she wanted on her day off without seeking permission from her employer.

On the other side of the table, a mute Baron de Vaufreland watched Adèle and she shifted in her chair under his scrutiny. Prior to this they had shared a conversation about travel and he had questioned her intensely about her views, philosophies on what makes a great nation. Adèle had felt the conversation being steered in a direction she was not comfortable with and had excused herself to powder her nose. She had felt awful leaving Theo in the fray and hoped in her absence he had not said anything too challenging. And when she'd returned her napkin had been folded and placed over the back of her chair and Theo had given her a look that said he understood exactly why she'd fled to the lavatories.

'Give blood. Don't give blood. I don't mind what you do on your day off,' Mademoiselle said, looking as awkward as Adèle.

'Of course,' Adèle admitted quietly. She'd known that. Only her mouth had run away with her.

'Now, Mister Dixon,' Mademoiselle said, readying herself to stand up. 'Would you care to escort me around the dance floor?' Although it was posed as a question, Mademoiselle did not wait for a reply.

'It would be my pleasure.' Theo placed his napkin onto the table and stood, courteously pulling Mademoiselle Chanel's chair out for her and taking her hand as they moved to the dance floor to join other couples moving seamlessly.

Baron de Vaufreland excused himself from the table suddenly and walked towards a table of uniformed officials.

Alone with Mademoiselle's lover, Adèle smiled politely, wishing her plate had not been taken away so she could push the remaining crust from her strawberry tart around for something to do.

'Mademoiselle Fabron,' Dincklage said, holding his hand out for Adèle to take.

'Oh, of course,' she replied nerves gripping her so much that she stood with her napkin still on her lap, watching as it fell to the floor. Dincklage stooped to pick it up for her and placed it on the table.

She murmured, 'Thank you,' and looked over the dance floor to see her employer laughing at something Theo had said. The two of them looked fluid, easy as they moved, whereas she was gripped with nerves and a sense of unease that was climbing to its pinnacle.

It was Dincklage who started the conversation. 'We have not had a chance to speak since I saw you at the Jewish exhibition,' he prompted.

'No,' Adèle said as she tried to focus on which foot went where as they circled the dance floor. She wished he'd not mentioned that hateful place.

'What did you think of it?'

'I'm not sure I thought anything.' Adèle erred on the side of caution.

'You were not convinced of the Jewish problem?' he said and Adèle's teeth grated together. 'The exhibition did not convince you well enough?'

'I still think I don't know enough about it,' she said.

She instantly regretted it when Dincklage replied, 'Let me educate you,' and spoke his own opinions aloud. After a minute or so of this, Adèle was desperate to get away but she homed back in on what he was saying when he said, 'You should be in receipt of your certificate soon.'

'Certificate?' Adèle asked in bafflement at the sudden change in conversational direction.

'To prove you're not Jewish,' he said simply. 'Everyone needs to have a certificate to prove they aren't Jewish.' He said it so mundanely, so matter-of-fact, that he could have been telling her anything.

'Oh yes, I read about that.' With every passing week, every passing day there was something else the Nazis had carried out that scared Adèle half to death, and she wasn't even Jewish.

The music changed and she felt a touch on her elbow.

'May I cut in?' Theo asked with a grin and Dincklage bowed out gracefully, turning to look for Mademoiselle.

As the band struck up, the song Theo had played in his apartment sounded from the staged area.

Adèle's mouth dropped open and Theo smiled widely as he took her in his arms. 'Did you not realise it was her, that it was Edith Piaf on the stage?'

'No,' Adèle cried. 'I was concentrating on dancing. Edith Piaf is singing for us. I adore her.' A thrill went through her, swiftly replaced with the horrifying remembrance that she was not an expert dancer. It hadn't seemed to matter when she'd been dancing with the baron but with Theo she didn't want to look silly. But it didn't matter because he didn't touch her, didn't pull her towards him, but waited while she watched Edith Piaf sing for them.

When she looked back at him, her eyes were bright with the happy surprise and his eyes shone at her reaction.

And then he looked at her; really looked at her, taking her in. She hoped she looked, if not lovely, at least agreeable. Mademoiselle had made a point of making sure Adèle always looked her best. 'My staff are well dressed in public,' she'd pointed out and had taught Adèle that clothes should offer freedom, movement. Since Adèle had begun working for Coco Chanel, a perk had been access to excellent clothes – when the fabric was readily available – pre-war. It was imperative she looked the part of a capable assistant at a couture house, even if that couture house had temporarily closed its doors.

'You're wearing . . . a very nice dress,' Theo commented. It was unlike him to be nervous but now he suddenly sounded as if he was and that he didn't know what else to say.

Adèle smiled, looked away, around the room, anywhere but at him. 'Mademoiselle tells me,' she blundered on masking her embarrassment at the compliment, 'dress women in white or black at a ball: they are the only ones you see.' And while that may not have been quite true – Adèle wasn't aware of anyone looking at her especially – other than Theo, she did feel special, here in this strange place.

'She's right . . .' he said. He concentrated on her, his fingers touching her exposed shoulders before he moved his hands down her bare arms and then gently pulled her towards him. She murmured something incomprehensible at his touch. It was a noise rather than a word. And they began dancing, both of them finally noticing that they were conspicuous by standing in the middle of the dance floor and neither of them actually dancing.

Theo moved her expertly, pulling her gently close to him and she lost herself in the moment. The piano started, the band played and Piaf sang deep and throaty over the crowd. Nazi officers gathered women to their chests and moved them stiffly around the room. Were these women their wives, sweethearts from home, or were they French women who had chosen their new suitor carefully – compliant, wanting a man in power to take care of them at this time of sheer uncertainty? Adèle could not work it out from the simple conversations, some in French, some in English, some in German that whizzed past her ear as couples skirted round each other.

She never dined like this, dressed like this, experienced an evening such as this. On any other night, in any other year and without a war raging it would have almost been delightful.

She looked up at Theo as they danced and he smiled down at her, pulling her closer to him, his mouth near her hair as she lightly touched his back with one hand, her other clasped gently in his palm as they moved. He was right, he could dance and he moved her expertly in a way he'd not done the night they'd danced in his apartment. This was showier, more in keeping with the mood of the night.

Out of the corner of her eye she could see Mademoiselle and her lover back at the dining table huddled with Baron de Vaufreland. Presumably they were discussing tomorrow's trip to Madrid.

Jolting her out of her turbulent thoughts Theo spoke and

she looked away from the table and at him as he said, 'In such a short space of time you've blown me away, Adèle.'

In embarrassment she glanced away and as Edith Piaf came to the end of her song and those around them clapped, he stopped, put his hand gently under her chin, tipped her head slowly until she had no choice but to look into his eyes. She found she didn't want to look anywhere else.

'Why do you do that?' he asked now he had her full attention. 'Why do you always look away when I say something nice to you?'

'I don't know. I just do.'

'Don't,' he said. 'Because in a second I'm going to tell you how much I really like you, Adèle, and I'm going to need to know you've heard me.'

She inhaled sharply. 'Really?' she said and then her hand reached her mouth to cover it. It took every fibre of her not to look away in elated embarrassment.

'Yes.' Theo let go of her, tipped his head as if he was about to kiss her; thought better of it and instead whispered near her ear, 'We've a while before curfew. You want to get out of here?'

Adèle looked up at him, nodded, and as he held her hand, the two of them slipped from the ballroom.

Outside the Ritz they moved quietly, sedately past the milieu of Nazi officers loitering around the hotel and made their way south towards the Seine. Adèle's dress whipped around her legs as the Parisian breeze drifted up from the river that sliced the city in half. Paris was a city of two halves, divided by the river, divided by collaborators and resisters, divided by the poor and the rich. And then there were the women: choosing to throw themselves too easily into the Nazi way of life. And women who wouldn't, couldn't do that at any cost. How had this happened in such a short space of time? Paris was not Paris anymore.

'You notice the Nazis aren't paying attention to us,' Theo said. 'Dressed like this. We look elite. We look on their level.' It was true. Despite their finery, which would ordinarily have drawn attention, no one was looking at them in this part of town and she gripped his arm as the moon fell momentarily out of sight behind a cloud, taking with it the only light that ever shone on Paris at night since the blackout.

'Being like them is nothing to be proud of,' Adèle commented. 'Being in this dress, enjoying myself in there—' she gestured back to the hotel '—makes me feel dirty. The food we eat, the Champagne we drink. Don't you feel tainted in some way? I do.'

'Sure,' he agreed. 'But I don't actually think you were really enjoying yourself. And as for me, other than dancing with you, the rest of it's an act. I'm not really there, with them. I'm there with you. And I know what I'm doing in the background supplants one evening of eating veal and engaging in awkward conversation.'

'I suppose, yes,' she said as she noticed Theo's hand tightening into hers comfortingly as they walked.

'It's the strangest thing,' he continued. 'To have blown the dust off this dinner suit. It all feels like before the war, dressing for dinner and a dance. And that food. My God. I'll remember that meal until the day I die. For various reasons.' He grinned down at her.

'The Nazis being here . . . the sheer number of them. That's when the comparison to before ends,' Adèle suggested as they moved out of the way of another well-dressed couple moving around them, giggling, smoking as they walked to the end of the street and crossed into the Jardin des Tuileries. Perhaps these couples too had been to the dance and were escaping for fresh air in the open green park crisscrossed with pavements and an abundance of trees. On a walk such as this with Theo it was hard to forget there were other lives, moving so closely in the same city. Were other people torn between the two? Were others feeling as lost as she was at the moment?

Paris in blackout was still a strange and eerie sight. The city of light had gone dark. Adèle tripped over a raised paving stone and Theo grabbed at her elbow. 'You all right?'

She nodded in the darkness. As they stood for a moment she felt his hand leave hers and he put his dinner jacket around her bare shoulders.

'Thank you,' she said catching the intoxicating scent of his cologne on the fabric of his jacket. He really had made an effort tonight.

On the other side of the park, was the Louvre, barely visible in the blackout. She thought of all the artwork the Nazis probably had their eyes on before Occupation began, but which rumours abounded had been removed by the clever staff in 1939. The *Venus de Milo*, the *Mona Lisa* all gone. Hidden somewhere safe from the thoughtless pilfering of Hitler and his ilk. It made her smile. Pieces of art she'd studied from textbooks as a child were now, hopefully, saved for when all this was over.

Adèle told Theo about the enormous picture that had arrived in Mademoiselle Chanel's suite. 'I think of the artwork in there,' she said, gesturing towards the roof of the Louvre, 'taken and saved. And I think of how Mademoiselle's picture came to be here placed in her suite. Not everything can be saved.'

'You know where that's come from, don't you?' he said.

'Someone not as quick-thinking as the Louvre staff left it behind I suppose,' she said, shaking her head.

He nodded. 'In all likelihood it's from a Jewish family, a Jewish collector. Probably part of someone's life's work of collecting and now pieces of that collection have been stolen – with a small piece of it now in Chanel's possession.'

'Don't say that. It might not be that at all,' she said. 'But all the Jewish families have fled, I suppose. Those with money, connections, passports. And they've left their things behind.'

'It's just things though, I guess. Hopefully as many as possible have had the foresight to get the hell out of here in time,' Theo cut in. 'They've left behind their possessions and saved their skins. If that's what's happened.'

Adèle thought of Mélodie, of her mother being dragged away and arrested for nothing more than being a Jew, if the concierge was to be believed. Mélodie's mother had been in the process of packing and she had been too late.

As if reading her mind, Theo said, 'Some weren't lucky enough to leave in time before all the visa formalities prohibited them from going. But it's worse than that,' Theo said. 'I've heard so many other things.'

'Such as?'

Theo glanced around him to see if anyone was listening. 'On rue Faubourg, there's a Jewish-owned department store. Or rather, it was Jewish-owned and the man's had the whole thing taken from him. The building, all his stock, cash registers even. It's being staffed by Jews.'

Adèle furrowed her eyebrows. 'Staffed by Jews? I don't understand.'

'It's like a strange kind of prison camp,' Theo said. 'I don't know how true this is. It's just a rumour. It sounds unfathomable. But everything that's been taken from Jewish homes is going in there. It's essentially still a department store except it's Germans shopping there for dirt-cheap Jewish goods.'

'I thought the Nazis hated the Jews,' Adèle suggested. 'Why would they want to buy their items?'

'Because they're good quality items. You name it . . . it's on sale. Sheets, pots, pans, pianos, paintings.'

'Paintings?' Adèle said.

'The Germans are stealing everything they can get their hands on. Imagine being Jewish, being forced to live inside that shop and seeing possessions that you and your people have owned being sold to some field marshal in a braided suit. It beggars belief.'

Adèle considered the Wertheimers, fleeing to safety, taking no chances with their business. Theo's story of the department store didn't sound so outlandish. 'Mademoiselle has had me writing letters,' she said.

'Letters?'

'Her perfume business is owned by two Jewish brothers,' Adèle started, explaining how Mademoiselle was attempting to use the hideous Nuremberg Laws to wrest her business away from the brothers. 'To Aryanise her business, as she openly calls it.'

'Jesus,' Theo said.

'She's been corresponding with her lawyer and the authorities repeatedly and with each telephone call, each letter I open for her, her temper rises.'

'Why?'

'Because it looks as if there's nothing that can be done. She does not control her own business, the Wertheimers do and they are safely tucked up in America while their part of the business is owned by an Aryan, officially. She cannot stand it. When I take dictation from her, she becomes angrier and angrier until she no longer makes sense and I am not sure what I am meant to be writing down in the letters and what I am not supposed to be writing down. It's frenetic. Even Dincklage and his friends seem unable to help her.'

'God, really? Why not?'

'Because the man is Aryan so the business has been Aryanised, leaving her, legally, in the cold.'

'That's almost admirably clever,' Theo said. 'I'm impressed, let's put it that way.'

'Mademoiselle Chanel is not,' Adèle said and allowed a slip of a laugh to escape her lips. She regretted it immediately. She'd been so disloyal telling Theo all this, but it sat so wrongly with her it had felt as if she'd simply been relaying facts. But laughing – that's where disloyalty struck fiercely at her.

'Do you like her?' Theo asked suddenly.

'I owe her everything,' Adèle replied.

'That's not what I asked,' he prompted.

'Did you like her?' Adèle asked.

'Good deflection,' he commented wryly. 'We danced. She's . . . commanding. I think at one point she was leading me.'

'She has that effect,' Adèle said. 'I hope one day I can be like her.'

'Really?' he spluttered. His eyebrows raised and then dipped again.

'In part, yes,' Adèle said. She'd long since held this belief but now she thought about it, here and in this place at this time, did she really mean it all these years later? 'She keeps me gainfully employed and in a time of uncertainty, that is more than enough. I can eat; I have somewhere to sleep. I'm safe. I should be grateful. I am grateful.'

Theo nodded, passed no comment and Adèle wondered if this was a good sign or not. Had she said something ridiculous?

'You don't see yourself with her forever though, do you?' he asked intently.

Adèle paused. 'Not forever no.'

'So you could leave her?' he asked and then raced on. 'I know this kind of job is different than your standard office work. But you're not caught up in the glow from her, are you? You would leave, wouldn't you? If it all got too much . . . her and . . . them,' he finished, watching her intently and Adèle assumed he was referring to the Nazis.

Adèle stiffened a little. Was he calling into question her motives for remaining? Caught up in a glow? 'Yes, I'm sure I would if better employment presented itself. But it won't.

And so I won't. Not now. Not yet,' she said certainly. 'Not at this time. It's too risky to leave a job like that at a time like this.' She wished he'd not talked about this. They were standing by the Seine, in moonlight while the rest of Paris moved in darkness. They could be talking about anything else, anything else at all, and they were discussing this. 'It's . . . complicated.'

'How?'

'She saved me, really.'

'Is that the story she makes you believe or is that the story you repeatedly tell yourself?' Theo asked.

'Theo!' she cried. 'That's so impertinent.'

He laughed. 'It wasn't meant to be. All I'm saying is don't let her write your history for you. She gave you a job. You don't owe her anything.'

'I do,' Adèle said emphatically. 'Where would I be now if I weren't with her? I would be homeless, penniless in the middle of a war. I would be destitute and then who knows what measures I might have had to turn to. Instead of being on your arm like this, feeling lucky that I found someone like you at a time like this, I might be on the arm of any of those German officers back there – just as Mademoiselle is – simply so I could eat, simply so I could survive.'

'You don't mean that,' he said quietly. 'I know you don't mean that.'

'Don't I? Women who've known poverty at least once would do anything to avoid it a second time. Perhaps I can see why Mademoiselle does it. Perhaps I am no exception.'

He turned, leant his back against the low wall dividing them from the river and looked at her.

'Are you shocked?' she asked. 'Say something.'

He stared at her. 'You'd take a German lover?' he asked incredulously. 'Like Chanel has done so openly? You'd do that? I don't think a girl like you could do that.'

'Yes I would,' Adèle said. 'If I absolutely had to. If I was starving and homeless and that was the only way out. But it wouldn't be through choice.'

'There's always a choice,' he said, pushing himself away from the wall and turning away from her to look out across the river. He picked up a stray piece of stone from the crest of the wall and threw it absentmindedly into the river. Somewhere far below it broke the surface and the water swallowed it, taking it to its depths. 'Why are we even having this conversation?' he asked although his jaw was tense, all trace of humour removed from his face.

'I don't know.' She looked away. The evening had taken a turn for the worse. They'd been dancing. He'd told her he liked her. At one point she had laboured under the delicious misapprehension that he was going to kiss her. She was glad he hadn't, in the ballroom with so many onlookers. But now, by the river would have been the most perfect place to be kissed by Theo, bathed in moonlight. She changed the subject to try to claw back what little remained of the horrific evening. 'I can get away a bit earlier over the next few days if you still wanted to meet as you'd suggested?'

'Sure. I'd love that. How come?'

'She's taking a trip to Madrid.'

'Good for her,' he said not unkindly. 'And you're not needed on this trip?'

'No. She has no use for me there, I think. I am of more use here in the atelier. I have done what I need for the trip by helping her pack. I pack more often than not these days. I think she's slowly turning me into a lady's maid. But it keeps me employed so I don't grumble.'

'Much,' Theo teased.

Adèle laughed, relieved the evening with Theo wasn't a total loss. 'Much. But one day when this is all over I shall go back to being a clerical assistant all of the time again.'

'Which do you prefer?' he asked.

Adèle didn't need to think. 'I prefer being in the office, thank you very much. I do like clothes though, to an extent. Mademoiselle has taught me to appreciate them. How I can change my appearance by dressing well, the right hat, the right piece of jewellery. A belt here. But I don't love clothes. Not the way she does.'

'Why not?'

'There are more important things in this world. I think even she now believes that. I think she loves clothes but I have come to learn she loves money more. She's a survivor. She's turning me into a survivor.'

Theo looked across the Seine, a small smile on his face. 'I guess there are worse things to be,' he said quietly. 'We're all surviving now. Or at least attempting to. Why's she going to Madrid tomorrow?' he asked suddenly.

Adèle sighed, turned and listened to the water as it lapped unsteadily against the buttresses. 'I don't know.'

'You do,' he said.

Adèle turned and looked at him. 'Why do you want to know?' she asked.

He gave her his full attention. 'Why does it matter why I want to know? I'm just asking.'

'What would you do with the information – if I did know?' she challenged him.

'If it's useful information then why wouldn't we pass it on?' he said. 'Anything could be useful to ending this war. Anything and everything.'

'Why? She's only travelling to a neutral country.'

'In a time of war, Adèle. Is she going alone? Or with one of them?' he gestured back to the hotel where Nazi officers wined, dined, danced in splendour.

'One of them has just offered to help you at the hospital.' Heaven knew why she was suddenly defending Dincklage and his kind. She didn't even like him and certainly didn't trust him.

'Exactly. Why? Why would he do that? I think I'm flying too close to the wind. I shouldn't have come tonight. The last thing any of us need is the Nazis looking closely at me.'

'Why did you come then?' She raised her voice.

'I came for you,' he shouted back at her. 'I came to be with you. And we've been surrounded by them. You even danced with one.'

'I had to,' she said. 'It would have been rude to refuse.'

'You don't have to do anything you don't want to, Adèle. You don't realise that by now? Chanel doesn't have to either you know. She chooses to.'

'It's not that simple.'

'Don't play stupid, Adèle. She's running with the wolves right under your nose.'

She turned, looked at the river again. 'How dare you,' she whispered.

'Why won't you tell me what you know?'

'I don't know,' she said more forcefully. 'Honestly.'

'And you wouldn't tell me if you did know?' he prompted.

'Why do you say that?' Adèle asked.

'You need to work out where your loyalties rest,' he said.

'To you?' she asked.

'No,' he said horror-struck. 'That's not what I meant at all. To France and to those trying to do some good in this war. Or to those who'll have blood on their hands by the end of all of this. People like her.' He gestured in the direction of the hotel.

Adèle breathed in sharply. 'She won't have blood on her hands,' she said forcefully. 'She's not like that.'

'How do you know? Yes, Mademoiselle. No, Mademoiselle. But how well do you actually know the woman you're working for? The artwork that came from who knows where; the Nazi sweetheart; and she's trying to get her company back using a heinous law.'

'It's her company,' Adèle said.

'It's not though, is it?' he said quietly. 'You said so your-self.'

She turned to him. Part of her wanted to shout at him but the other part didn't know what she could shout, what words she could summon. How had this happened? Every part of her told her she should never have invited him this evening. She should have made something up, told Mademoiselle a fib as to why Theo couldn't attend. The entire evening had been a mistake from start to finish.

'We don't have long until curfew,' he said, flicking his wrist to look at his watch. 'I should walk you back.'

'There is no need,' she said stiffly.

She turned to walk away but he moved quickly, grabbed her hand. 'Wait,' he said. 'Don't leave like this.'

'Like what?' she replied, snatching her hand from his, removing his jacket from her shoulders and thrusting it out towards him. 'Like someone who is stupid?' She echoed his words. He reached out automatically and took his jacket from her and the two stood looking at each other, neither speaking until: 'I'm going to go now,' she said eventually.

'Adèle—' he placated. 'Don't. Can't I—' he started.

But she cut him off. 'No,' she said forcefully. 'You cannot do any more than you have already done.'

He didn't try to follow her, didn't call her name. She continued walking aimlessly, passing the hotel, not wishing to enter as she felt the painful prick of tears behind her eyes. She had a little time before curfew and so she knew where she would go while she walked off her anger, her upset. She changed direction automatically towards Mélodie's apartment, taking care not to slip on the cobbles in her silly shoes. If she was clever, discreet, she could slip in and check for any return of the little girl's mother – although she knew in her heart of hearts it would be fruitless. She wiped tears away from her face as she walked, praying that if she might find Mélodie's mother there and alleviate her pain with good news, then at least one woman would be happy in Paris tonight.

As she walked through the darkening streets, tears falling so freely down her face she wondered how tonight had gone so horribly wrong; that in the course of such a short time she had found and lost the only friend she'd made here and the only man she'd ever found herself falling for.

'Is everything ready, Adèle?' Mademoiselle Chanel asked early the next morning after having informed Adèle only twenty minutes earlier she would need to pack a dress suitable for a dinner engagement at the embassy.

'Yes, Mademoiselle.' *Yes, Mademoiselle. No, Mademoiselle.* Theo's cruel words from last night came back to haunt her, cutting her like a knife. And that hadn't even been the cruellest thing he'd said.

'The porters are on their way to take your luggage on ahead of you.'

'Good girl. I cannot tell you what a balm it is to have you here with me, throughout all of this. Sometimes,' she said, 'I feel that I have no one—' but her words were silenced as the door sounded and the porters came to collect Mademoiselle's travelling trunks.

'I'll only be a few days,' Chanel said as the porters arrived, collected the cases and left as swiftly as they'd come. 'If you need me urgently, you can reach me here.' She handed Adèle a piece of notepaper. 'It's Baron de Vaufreland's office here. They'll connect us. Adèle, if you hear anything back from the lawyers, get a message via his office immediately. I must know.'

'Of course,' Adèle agreed. 'Mademoiselle?' Adèle asked tentatively.

'Yes.'

Bravery crept over Adèle like a cloak. 'What is the dinner for at the French embassy in Madrid?'

'It's only a small, boring event,' Mademoiselle said dismissively. 'Nothing important. And it's not the French embassy,' she said, adjusting her strings of pearls. 'It's dinner at the British embassy, with Sir Samuel Hoare, the ambassador.'

Adèle opened the front door of the suite, accompanying her employer down the ornate, sweeping staircase as she made her way outside to the waiting motorcar. Why on earth was Mademoiselle travelling to Madrid with a Nazi officer, and then dining with the British ambassador?

As she watched Mademoiselle's chauffeur-driven car move along Place Vendôme and out of sight, she wondered if Theo was right. Would she have to make a difficult choice soon? Was she brave enough to take any kind of stand in this war? And what would she sacrifice in doing so?

Chapter 13

2018

Chloé's eyes were tired after reading the book Etienne had given her. She'd gone home from work, taken the paperback into the bath and then when she'd grown sleepy had curled up with it on the sofa while the lights of Paris flickered outside her window. The table lamp had cast its benevolent glow onto the pages of *The People of Wartime Paris: Collaborators, Resisters, Survivors*.

She'd just got to the bit where businesses were being Aryanised and after contorting her face in disgust, had put the book down as if by doing so she could undo the words written within. She'd taken a Metro ticket and placed it inside as a bookmark and gone to bed. That was at 2 a.m. this morning and Chloé was suffering for it. Thankfully she was working only a half-day today.

She dug around in her bag, found the business card Etienne had given her and assembled the percolator for the fine-ground coffee she'd bought from the local delicatessen. She eyed the book where she'd left it in the early hours of this morning but her eyes couldn't cope with any more reading today and so she threw open the balcony doors and sat on the little metal bistro chair, waiting for the coffee to percolate, listening as it hissed and steamed, smelling the deep aroma as it slowly dripped, forming enough to make a cup. She took out her phone and looked at Etienne's expensive stiff business card before deciding what to do.

As she typed, a message appeared, flashing up at the top of the screen. Her first instinct was to swipe it away but her gaze caught on the name of the sender: Rob. Chloé stopped typing and stared at the name of her ex-husband disbelievingly. She stared at it for so long the message timed out and vanished from the screen.

What did he want? She opened it to look. It didn't take her long to read through his short note: *Do you think we made a mistake?*

Chloé opened her mouth and exhaled in shock. Her whole body stiffened. He couldn't be serious.

He was online waiting for her to reply. He could see her status was online but she wasn't responding. Him doing this now . . . she didn't know how she felt. Before, she'd felt free. But now, seeing his message like this . . . there was only confusion. And then, perhaps because he'd got sick of waiting, Rob's status showed him suddenly offline.

Chloé's good mood was over. Why would he do this? They were divorced. There was no going back from that. She remembered sitting in the solicitor's office when she'd originally applied for divorce. She'd had no idea how it all worked, envisioning standing opposite him in a court and then deciding to forgive and forget the hurt they'd caused each other as their marriage spiralled downwards, both of them running across the courtroom and into each other's open arms. She'd never been through a divorce and didn't know anyone close to her who had. So she felt she had no one to ask, other than the solicitor who explained to her that it was a case of putting signatures on documents, that as long as they agreed financials in advance, there was no real need for any of the face-to-face pain or grand gestures across a mediation table.

She and Rob had agreed it needed to be done and that both of them would leave the marriage with exactly what they'd put into it, which did square the financial intricacies off relatively easily – especially given there were no children in the equation. It really was the end. They didn't have to speak to each other ever again. And back then Chloé had felt almost robbed of that opportunity. So why now? Why was he doing this now?

Rob making contact again made her feel as dumbstruck as the day the decree absolute had arrived, with the solicitor explaining in cold, hard terms, 'This legally concludes divorce proceedings and ends your marriage.'

Ends your marriage. Your marriage is over. Your marriage lasted less than five years. You are a failure. There was none of that buoyant relief Chloé had assumed there would be, none of that feeling of freedom. It was a feeling of loss, of everything they might have been if they'd tried just that little bit harder. Surely it would have been easier to try harder rather than go through six months of divorce proceedings.

There had been a time when she had been going back and forth from Rob's flat, removing all her items one hold-all at a time, procrastinating, drawing out the process, not because she wanted him back, but because ending things, leaving . . . it was all so final.

She put her phone down on the coffee table and stared at it warily as if it might burst into flames. She wished it would. She couldn't think straight; her mind flitting from memory to memory and when she thought about it in great detail, the unpleasant recollections of Rob far outweighed the contented ones. So it was the happier times she'd clung to throughout and this, ultimately, went some way to convincing her once again now that ending their marriage had been the only viable option.

She was taking hold of her own life. She was going to take some time out and just be. And she was not going to respond to Rob. Not yet anyway. She would collect herself first. And collecting herself started with broadening her horizons, making friends with people like Etienne. Because Etienne was quite probably not the kind of person she would normally have been friends with. But this was a different Chloé in a different city.

Chloé picked up her phone from the table in front of her and dropped him a quick message.

Thanks again for lunch yesterday. And for the book. I'm about a third of the way through. I'm enjoying it – if you can enjoy a book showing the horrors of war and how it affected people. I'll report back when I get to the sections about Chanel, she teased. It was a fib because she'd already flicked through and read a few bits here and there.

She hoped her Chanel reference came across as a bit of a friendly dig. She wanted to put a winking face emoji but couldn't quite work out what Etienne would think of that. She still had no clue how Etienne thought and operated. His sense of humour seemed to be unpredictable. He was unpredictable. Would he think that was lame? Quite probably. So she opted not to and instead followed the message up with: *I have a free half-day today. Any sightseeing recommendations?*

Now that did sound lame, but it was too late because she'd already hit send. She saved his number in her phone and as she was doing so a reply came in.

A new exhibition has opened at the Louvre. I am also not at work today.

Chloé thought about this for far too long. Was he suggesting they go together?

Isn't the Louvre horribly touristy? she replied. *Are you indulging my tourist fantasies?*

He didn't reply for what felt like ages. Oh no. Now she'd

embarked on a path of innuendo and he wasn't impressed. But this was a man whose latest gallery offering was of hundreds of images of nude couples. And then a reply arrived that made Chloé smile.

If your fantasy involves no queues . . . I know people who know people. Now does it sound better?

Chloé smiled to herself and went to get ready.

They met at the appointed time in the palatial Louvre courtyard in front of the glass pyramid that swept up in front of them. Etienne greeted her with a kiss on each cheek. She was wearing a long yellow summer dress and he cast his eyes over her so briefly she would have missed it if she hadn't been watching him equally closely.

'You look very nice,' he said. 'The boots are . . .' he laughed nervously as if fetching a finish to his sentence '. . . chic.'

'Thank you,' she replied self-consciously. She loved wearing dresses but today she'd paired her dress with a pair of studded black biker boots she'd bought in the shop. She really must stop buying all the stock but the boots had been in her size, and as a six and a half, nothing ever entered the shop in her size. It was fated.

Etienne dialled a number on his phone, speaking in rapid French.

'Are you trying to smuggle us in?' she asked as she caught his side of the conversation.

'Yes,' he replied, adjusting the zip near the collar of his sweater. She'd been expecting to see him in a suit and it was a refreshing change to find him in well-cut jeans and a casual navy sweater.

A well-dressed woman was walking in their direction. The woman was brunette with her hair in a chignon, a silk scarf tied delicately around her throat. She looked so typically French that it threw Chloé a bit. Did women her age

178

actually dress like this? Surely not. Chloé's mother wouldn't even dress like that. The woman looked a bit put out on seeing Chloé and so Chloé overcompensated with a wide smile that was only returned thinly.

The woman air-kissed Etienne while practically pawing him. He stepped back ever so slightly, an action neither woman missed. Awkwardly Chloé stepped back to give space to this complex situation. Her mind immediately ran wild as to what was going on here.

Etienne cleared his throat and introduced them. 'This is Cosette,' he said enigmatically and then reciprocated with only slightly more information when he said, 'This is Chloé, a friend.' The two women nodded and greeted each other politely but Chloé could see Cosette trying to work out if there was any hidden subtext behind the word 'friend'. Etienne was keeping up his appearance of a man of few words and continued to talk to Cosette in French. 'Thank you for this. I owe you.'

'You do,' Cosette said. 'I shall hold you to it. Coffee or drinks . . . maybe next week?' she suggested far too casually.

'Let me check my diary. I left it in the office.'

'Sure, sure,' she said leading them past the queues, unclipping a rope and ushering them behind it as they bypassed everyone patiently queuing in the shadow of the glass pyramid.

'Would you like a private tour?' Cosette asked. 'I could take my lunch hour early.'

'Oh, yes please,' Chloé gushed. Free entry and now a private tour; this day was getting better by the minute.

But Etienne cut in, 'Non. No thank you, I mean. I know exactly what I'm looking for.'

'You always do,' Cosette said and Chloé heard the sharpness bubble to the surface.

'Well, if that's all you need me for . . . ?' Cosette asked.

'It is. Thank you for getting us past all of them,' he said gesturing upstairs vaguely to where the queue of tourists snaked around the glass pyramid.

'Yes. Thank you so so much,' Chloé said, trying to retrieve the situation with some positive praise and aware she was overdoing it a little bit.

'My pleasure,' Cosette replied. 'Etienne, let me know about next week?' she asked but it was a vague suggestion now as if she already knew Etienne wouldn't reply.

'I will.'

Chloé's heart went out to the woman because there was clearly something unrequited going on here and when Cosette left Chloé said, 'What was that all about?'

'Nothing,' Etienne said. 'What do you mean?'

'She clearly has a bit of a thing for you.'

'Yes, I think she does,' he said matter-of-factly.

'Oh so you're not immune to the feelings of other people then?' Chloé laughed.

'What do you mean?' he repeated, his eyebrows furrowing together.

'Only that when you kept pushing me about my grandmother and Chanel and you kept dropping the word "Nazi" into every other sentence, I wondered if you realised I was getting upset. And now . . .' Chloé gestured to where Cosette was click-clacking down the corridor in her higher than high heels.

'I am not immune to the feelings of others,' Etienne said. 'I am not a robot and I have, after all, apologised unreservedly to you.'

'All right then . . . so you're just not interested in her? Because . . . dare I risk your wrath but you were a bit rude to her, I thought.'

He made a face. 'I'm not good at rejecting the advances of women.'

'I'm not sure that was an advance so to speak.'

'It was. It was one of many.'

'Oh,' Chloé responded and waited for more.

'She is one of my friend's past girlfriends,' he said. 'And dating friend's exes is quite simply something I am not into.'

'She seems quite into you. How good is this friend? Worth annoying?'

'No,' Etienne replied with an arched eyebrow. 'Now, are you quite finished analysing my love life?'

Chloé wasn't finished on this task by a long shot but she nodded politely and said, 'What are we here to look at then? Was your comment to Cosette that you were here for something specific just a brush-off or—'

'It was not a brush-off. I am here for something specific. Or rather, I want to show you something specific.'

'Is it a Chanel exhibition?' Chloé asked dryly.

Etienne laughed finally. 'No. It is better.'

When they arrived at the hall he wanted to show her there was, at first glance, nothing special about it. Two small rooms lined closely together with a jumble of assorted pictures of varying sizes in varying frames from varying times and places; no visible coherence, no actual curation that Chloé could obviously identify. Actually as loath as she was to think it, a Chanel exhibition might have been better.

Since working at the boutique, Chloé had been getting more and more interested in vintage fashion, whereas previously her work in fashion retail had only led her down the path of new, seasonal clothes. If it wasn't new, she hadn't been too interested. But now – aside from Chloé being so keen on vintage that she was spending all her hard-earned money buying it – she had been learning about every item's provenance and history. When customers brought items in to sell it was the history behind the garment that was often more intriguing than the item itself. Under her new and temporary leadership she'd been enjoying writing a potted history of each garment or accessory and attaching it to them. She appreciated the history more readily now and she tried as hard with this now.

Chloé zoned back in because Etienne was speaking and she'd missed the first half of his sentence.

'Sorry,' she said. 'Say that again.'

'I know,' he said, misunderstanding her meaning. 'I could hardly believe it myself when I heard the Louvre was doing this. In truth, I think they could have staged a much larger exhibition. France admits to its faults but rarely,' he said. 'And the theft of . . .' he gestured around the room '. . . all of this, is what you English call the tip of the iceberg. But nonetheless here is a small smattering of what the Nazis took from those who fled in a hurry.'

Chloé looked around the room with a renewed interest at hundreds of pieces of art from varying eras. 'You're joking,' she said. 'What's it doing here if it's all stolen?'

Etienne breathed in and out. 'It's complicated,' he started.

'Isn't it always,' Chloé suggested.

'Families that fled too quickly to sell anything or were rounded up and . . .'

'Sent to the gas chambers?' Chloé volunteered.

Etienne nodded, sweeping his hand around the room. 'This is mostly theirs.'

'And no one's been to collect it?' she asked and then shook her head and rephrased. 'You know what I mean . . . assuming people survived the Holocaust or descendants had a record of each item, couldn't they then come to claim it?'

'Yes,' Etienne said. 'Yes they could. This is only a fraction of what is left after those items that had proof of ownership were claimed. In essence, these are unclaimed.'

Chloé looked at the paintings slowly, moving away from Etienne. Under each was a short history of the piece, who it was believed the artist was if not obvious, and in which year it had been painted. But that was really as far as it went. Of course there was no written indication about ownership. If there were, each item wouldn't be here, would it? Chloé reasoned.

She shook her head slowly in a mix of horror and appreciation for the art. She could sense Etienne behind her looking at each item as she did.

'All of this . . .' he said. 'This is all that remains of our wartime indignities. I do not have an unhealthy obsession,' he said with a wry smile. 'But it's healthy to remind ourselves, sometimes, of what went before us and how lucky we are to be alive, not suffering such horrors. This is a visual reminder in a time when there aren't too many visual reminders left. France had suffered so much during the war that true collaborators and Nazi sympathisers were neatly . . .' He made a noise. 'Poof – forgotten, brushed aside. A past pushed under the carpet. France was encouraged to move on, to pick up the threads of anything that remained, to make the most of what was left. My interest lies mostly in the art side of things but everyone has their own piece of the puzzle they want explained, their own piece of the war that filters into their lives, trickles down the generations and makes them who they are.'

'Do you think so?' Chloé queried.

'Of course,' Etienne said. 'My interest lies here but my history doesn't,' he said as he glanced at a piece of art showing an eighteenth-century family grouped together, high hair and ruffled clothing. 'What about you?' He stepped back a pace to look fully at her.

Chloé glanced around the walls as if each stolen item held the answer. 'I suppose I never really thought about my family history as being French,' she revealed. 'I know that sounds silly because my grandmother is French but she lived in England for most of her adult life.'

'Did she? Why?' Etienne asked.

Chloé opened her mouth to speak. And then: 'Actually, I don't really know. She met someone she loved after the war and moved to be with them. I think.'

'I'm glad for her,' he said benignly. 'A rare outcome.'

'Love post-war?' Chloé questioned.

'Love at all,' he said with a shrug, which made Chloé look at him closely.

After a few seconds she took her gaze away from Etienne and turned to look at a portrait of a dark-haired woman, deep-set eyes and a faint smile on her lips. Had this been a portrait of someone's relative, commissioned to be painted out of love? Perhaps it would have hung in someone's sitting room, hallway or drawing room. Where did these pictures all come from? Which parts of Europe? Which castles and ordinary homes, which apartments or châteaux? Lost art. Lost loves. Lost lives. Everything just so lost.

'What did you think of it all?' he asked as they left the two small rooms and walked through the Louvre's white stone corridors.

'Sobering,' Chloé said. 'Like most things I've read so far, it's all just so sad and awful.'

'I'm glad you're enjoying the book.' He laughed. There was that slight flash of humour. It arrived unexpectedly.

'I'm not sure I'd say I'm enjoying it,' she said honestly. 'But it has made me want to dig deeper.'

'Has it?' he asked. He looked surprised.

'Yes. I discovered the location of the files you mentioned. They're at the army archives at Château de Vincennes just east of the city. Not far at all.'

'You want to go?' he asked.

'Yes, actually. If I book an appointment do you want to come with me?' The words were out of her mouth before she'd had the chance to think the invitation through. Was it weird to keep spending so much time with him?

'OK.'

'Oh. Great. Well, I'll book in and if it's a time you can't do then don't worry—'

'No, I'll come,' he enthused. 'I have an assistant at the gallery so I can leave quite easily.'

'Right. Great,' she said.

'Great,' Etienne repeated. He looked down at her, his smile still on his face, making his eyes just seem brighter, deeper when he smiled.

In front of them in a large gallery a throng of tourists had stopped, indicating a prized artwork had prompted them into pausing.

'The *Mona Lisa*,' Etienne said.

Chloé could barely see anything past the people gathered and milling in front of the picture.

'It's always like this,' he said resignedly.

'But isn't it good that there are so many people wanting to see a particular piece of art?' she replied. 'If art wasn't celebrated it wouldn't be popular and vice versa. Galleries would be dead. You wouldn't have a job.'

'I'm not complaining,' he said, looking at her curiously.

'Sorry,' she said, figuratively winding her neck in. It was a shame but she wasn't interested in the *Mona Lisa*. Instead, curiosity about her grandmother now rose higher on Chloé's priority list.

'You want to move on?' he suggested.

'Yes, please. If that's all right. It's much smaller in real life isn't it,' she said, glancing at da Vinci's masterpiece.

'Yes,' Etienne said. 'It is.' He placed his hand on her back, steering her gently through the crowd, through the galleries and out past the gift shop towards the exit.

The fresh air brought Chloé much-needed respite that she hadn't known until then that she'd needed.

'Thank you,' she said when she'd let the Parisian breeze gusting through the large white courtyard cool her. She was hungry and thirsty and as if Etienne could sense that, he looked at his watch.

'Lunch?' he suggested.

'Haven't you got anywhere else to be?' she said and then wished she'd not said it so sharply. She hadn't meant it sharply at all – she genuinely believed he must have somewhere far more interesting to be than here with her.

'No,' he replied. 'I mean, I could do my weekly food shop, or I could enjoy lunch with a new friend.' When Chloé looked confused he leant in conspiratorially. 'I mean you,' he clarified.

She laughed. 'Right. Sorry. My brain's all over the place.'

'Because of the exhibition?'

'Yes, and what it's made me think. And my head hurts a bit and I think I'd quite like a glass of water. And coffee. And a sandwich,' she said all in a rush.

'Come,' he said, taking them over to a street cart with a wide blue umbrella and buying them a bottle of water each. 'Here's this for now,' he said. Chloé thanked him, unscrewing the lid and gulping eagerly at her Evian. 'But I think we can do better than a sandwich,' he said conspiratorially.

Etienne hailed a taxi and took her to what he called his favourite way to eat lunch. In the Marais they entered a street food market hidden behind iron gates to the Marché des Enfants Rouges. Roast chickens, Moroccan food, stalls selling ripe cheeses and delicate morsels of charcuterie made Chloé's stomach rumble. The sight of all the deliciously tender fruit, thin slivers of salted fish and thick wedges of pale cheese brightened Chloé immeasurably. It was easy to be led by her stomach in a place such as this. Etienne clearly had his favourite vendors but he waited patiently, allowing her to be a tourist, languishing by different stalls and tasting tiny samples on cocktail sticks. At the third time Chloé muttered, 'Oh my word,' after the rush of a sample of bavette steak hit her taste buds, he laughed.

'Come on,' he said with mock impatience. 'I think I know what you'll like.'

They chose bags of small garlic-roasted chicken, cheeses and boxes of fresh salad and with their parcels of food and bottled water he led her, through the crowd of locals shopping for lunches and special food for dinner parties, a short distance away to the Rohan Garden. They sat on a bench that backed onto the high garden wall and ate, surrounded by lush plants and greenery. It was an incredibly romantic spot and if she'd been with a boyfriend it would have been dreamlike. It *was* dreamlike.

And when they'd sat, there was no preamble, they just opened their bags, laid the food out on their laps and tucked in.

'You're the perfect tour guide,' she said, licking a rivulet of oil from her lower lip as it broke free from its softly supple artichoke. He watched her carry out the action and then looked back to his own food with an almost confused look on his face.

He ripped a piece of ripe brie and ate it without ceremony, his eyebrows slowly knitting together in contemplation while he chewed.

Chloé leant over, and with a mock-challenging look tore a small chunk of cheese from his paper bag and popped it into her mouth.

'Hey, you have your own,' Etienne said putting his hands in a ring around his food and giving her a smile that suggested if she wanted to do it again he wouldn't stop her.

'What are you planning for the rest of the day?' she asked.

He looked at his watch. 'This was the only plan I had.'

'Now you have had a very late lunch, do you feel as if you might enjoy a research trip?'

'Isn't that what we've just done?' he replied.

'Another one,' she said. 'If we phone the Château de Vincennes and if they have space at a research desk, would you like to go and look at the archives?'

He smiled. 'Today?'

'It's a long shot but I have a day off. I don't want to waste it.'

'You have a taste for it now.'

'I do.' She shrugged. 'Why not? And only if they have space for us, of course. I am sure since the announcement, the files have been *very* popular with amateur historians everywhere.'

He laughed. 'All right, but Chloé,' he said. She loved how her name sounded when he said it, as traditionally French as her mother had always intended it to sound. 'Far be it from me to put you off, but what if you find something that you do not like? Have you considered that possibility?'

Chloé had considered this but: 'If I want to find out why my grandmother won't talk about the war. If she's not going to tell me, documents from the time containing reference to Chanel are probably the only place to look.'

They exited the Metro station, talking about their families, about her sister, about his two brothers, his parents, where they were raised. He'd always lived in Paris but had dreams of owning a little holiday home out in the Loire Valley.

'Fields of lavender as far as the eye can see,' he said. 'Making my own wine. Making my own cheese. Doing something creative. I sell other people's art but I am a frustrated artist. I used to work in art museums and then I wanted to sell it, make it more accessible, put it on people's walls, not just have it in museums. I have achieved one of my dreams but there's always something a little simpler to hanker after, I find.'

Chloé nodded. 'I understand this entirely.'

'What do you dream of doing?' he asked as they walked towards the château.

'Until I took this time out I genuinely had no time to dream of greater things. No yearning for something different. But I'm enjoying working in Brigitte's shop so much that I think my love of high street clothing has run its natural course. I love clothes. But I'm not sure I love fashion. Maybe making my own clothes, just for myself at first perhaps? And then seeing what I can do after that. I don't know if I want to run a shop though. I guess I still have to really think it all through. But that's what this year is for, to find out.'

He nodded in agreement.

The Château de Vincennes stood alone in the centre of the square, its cream turrets high and imposing. With the clear blue sky above them, the scene was picture-postcard-perfect. The two walked inside and stopped at the registration desk.

Etienne looked to his left at a long wooden sign on the wall and chuckled to himself as he read the list of names of manager and curator and others who worked in the building and what floors they could be found.

'What?' Chloé asked.

'So this is where he works now.'

'Who?'

'The museum world is very small,' he pointed out. He tapped the board with the list of names. 'I know the curator. Although I have not seen him in a long while.'

He spoke to the receptionist, 'Is it possible you could dial up and ask if Claude is free. If so, can you tell him Etienne Vaillancourt just wants to say a quick hello.'

Etienne's friend arrived wearing glasses and sporting a surprisingly sharp haircut for an academic. They greeted each other warmly and Etienne introduced Chloé to Claude.

189

'We wanted to look at the files you have recently found and digitised,' Etienne said after they'd finished catching up.

'Only half have been documented so far,' Claude confirmed. 'But I think it's the more interesting half. Have you booked a desk?'

They confirmed they had.

'That's most of the battle then,' Claude said. 'The other part of the battle is getting you a reader's ticket and logging your ID. All the research catalogued so far is on the system. I'll be in my office but you have my number. Call me if you get stuck and I will try to advise if you can't see what you're looking for. Actually, what are you looking for?'

'We aren't sure yet,' Etienne said, glancing at Chloé.

'OK. I'll set you up at a computer and desk. It's good to see you again, Etienne. Since I moved this side of the city I've been very slack at keeping up communication. Let's grab a drink over the coming weeks.'

'Definitely,' replied Etienne. The two men shook hands.

'Call me if you get stuck,' Claude said. 'Suggest some dates for a drink? I'll come into the city.'

Etienne confirmed he would and then he and Chloé sat at the desk and computer terminal they'd been assigned.

'Is there anyone in Paris you don't know?' she asked.

'Of course.' He laughed. 'I told you the museum and gallery world is very small,' Etienne said, 'and what makes it even smaller is that he is the friend I was telling you about.'

'Which one?'

'Cosette's ex-boyfriend.'

'Really?' she exclaimed.

'Now,' Etienne suggested. 'Do you think he would have been so accommodating to us if I'd been dating his ex-girlfriend?'

'No. No way,' Chloé said. 'So our lesson of the day is don't sleep with our friend's exes?' she replied, laughing.

'Exactly,' he said. 'Now, shall we start scrolling through the files at random or would you like to search for anything in particular?'

'I'm dreading this actually,' Chloé said. 'So maybe let's just start scrolling through what they've uploaded and stop when we find something interesting.'

They hovered their fingers over the mouse as they scrolled, the screen showing documents that looked as if they'd been uploaded in no particular order. They moved from one document to the next, one photo to the next, with odd annotations and file numbers scribbled in the corners.

'Coco Chanel's wartime files went missing for a long time,' Etienne said quietly.

'And ended up here?' Chloé asked.

'I think they were scattered. I think a lot of files were scattered. I think some have turned up here and some are elsewhere so even now we may not get the full picture.'

'Or maybe some were even destroyed?' Chloé suggested.

Etienne gave her a knowing glance. 'Or destroyed, yes.'

Internally Chloé wondered if any of the lost or destroyed files had contained any reference to her grandmother. And then she asked herself what it was exactly that she was hoping to find. Did she actually want to find anything incriminating here? Of course not. She just wanted some kind of answer to a long-burning question. What exactly had her grandmother Adèle done in the war?

'From what I can remember, your grandmother doesn't make an appearance in the book you know,' Etienne said. 'So I am unsure if you will find anything much here. If that's what you are worried about?'

'I am a bit worried, yes. But if there is anything here, linking my gran to the Nazis then it's evidence isn't it?'

'Evidence?' Etienne queried. 'If there is anything here, it is unlikely a woman like your grandmother would come

191

under much scrutiny. Coco Chanel, however, that is a different set of circumstances entirely.'

'I know. But you hear . . . things . . . don't you. Elderly people, who did things they shouldn't in the war, being punished now. I don't know what I'd do if anything happened to my gran, regardless of what kind of mess she'd got herself into in the war.'

Etienne nodded. 'I understand. So perhaps, if we see anything we don't like . . . we sit on it? Think about it for a while before we . . .'

'Before we . . . ?' Horror of exposing her grandmother as some kind of Nazi sympathiser made Chloé want to run far away from here.

'Nothing,' Etienne said. 'Let's just see what we find.'

They scrolled through the file relating to various Resistance fighters who had given their services to the Nazi cause. Chloé wanted to know how anyone could fight so strongly for one side before turning to the side of evil and then she found her answer as she and Etienne read that while one Resistance fighter had been held captive, his wife and children had been threatened by the Gestapo until he felt he had no choice but to help the enemy, if only to spare his family.

Chloé opened her bottle of water and took a sip, pondering this. Neither she nor Etienne said anything. There was nothing to say that wasn't obvious.

As Etienne scrolled on, Chloé said, 'I know why you wanted *me* to read the book but why did *you* read it?'

He twitched his mouth as if formulating the words inside his mouth without speaking them. 'My grandmother and your grandmother were . . . hmm . . . in the wrong place at the wrong time, perhaps?'

'Is that a question or a statement?' Chloé asked.

'I think it's a statement,' he said uncertainly. 'Yes, I think it's a statement. But I may not be correct. From what you've said your grandmother was a young woman, simply carrying out her job. So was mine.'

'When was your grandmother a seamstress with Chanel?' Chloé asked.

'Just before war broke out and Chanel closed her atelier. Chanel then stopped making clothes and focused mainly on perfume from what I can gather. And that left no place for women such as my grandmother.'

'What did she do during the war?' Chloé asked.

Etienne was silent, digesting how to answer.

'I mean,' Chloé prompted, 'did she manage to find a job as a seamstress after Chanel closed her atelier?'

'No,' he said simply. 'She did not. She joined the ranks of the many jobless at a time of awful change.'

'I'm so sorry,' Chloé said. 'Not an easy time for anyone,' she surmised.

'It was an easy time for some people,' Etienne chimed in and she knew who he meant.

They scrolled further on until Chloé jumped and grabbed at Etienne's hand. 'Go back,' she said.

It was the first reference to Coco Chanel. Notes taken from a letter, although which source was unclear. Chloé read the documents in French aloud:

'*She travelled with a senior Nazi to neutral Spain. In Madrid, she met the British ambassador. As did the senior Nazi.*'

Etienne and Chloé gave each other a look. 'Make of that what you will,' he said.

'*This forms part of a spy-recruitment mission. Chanel's dinner with the ambassador is speculated to be a cover for the main mission. Recovered Nazi files claim later similar missions form part of a wider plan to broker a peace deal with Britain, favourable to the Nazis, code-named Operation Model Hat.*'

Etienne clicked to turn the page on the screen.

Chloé read again. '*While Mademoiselle Chanel had been campaigning vocally to no avail to have her nephew released from a German prisoner of war camp, shortly after she returned from Madrid . . . her nephew was released.*'

'So she gave a cover story and in exchange they released her nephew from his prisoner of war camp,' she said.

Etienne looked less than impressed. They sat there for a long time, scrolling through more documents and photographs until they saw a picture of Hermann Göring dining on a huge platter of food in the Ritz. Chloé pulled a sickened face and scrolled on to the next file. Another image of the Ritz ballroom came into focus.

A ball appeared to be in full flow, couples in the background dancing, their images blurred as they swirled around the room. Some were in the forefront sat at tables – the same tables Hermann Göring had been dining at in the previous picture.

Etienne and Chloé both looked at the woman the photographer had focused on, her head half turned, her dark hair cut and curled near her chin, a cigarette in hand. 'Is that who I think that is?' Etienne said. The prominent chin was a giveaway.

But it wasn't that woman Chloé's attention was on now. It was the one sat on the other side of the table, a young woman wearing a long black satin dress with thin straps, sat straight and slightly nervous-looking, engaged in conversation with a Nazi officer, a woman whose youthful portrait she had seen many a time in family photographs.

Chloé wanted to throw up. She couldn't speak. Couldn't say a word. Couldn't tell Etienne. Couldn't do anything. Because here was a picture of her grandmother, dining with Nazis.

Chapter 14

1941

The porter knocked on the door to the suite so urgently Adèle thought it must be a matter of life or death.

'Letter for you,' he said and then turned and walked away down the corridor. There was a look in his eye that housed barely disguised disgust. Was she marked as a collaborator because she lived under the watchful eyes of Nazis? She was so insignificant in the grand scheme of things. She was just like him; she was staff. But it made no difference to the porter clearly. How quickly Paris had turned into a city of lies and distrust.

She looked at the letter, said good morning to the housekeeper who was already hard at work and crossed the corridor to her bedroom to read it undisturbed. There were no postage marks and the envelope so crisp that it must have been hand-delivered. There were only a few lines.

I'm so sorry.
Forgive me.
Theo
x

Adèle's first instinct was to smile. She knew her heart was in trouble. She held the letter close to her chest and then held it out, looking at his words again.

The argument they'd had by the Seine was still so fresh in her mind. The things he'd said to her. All night long she'd dwelled on it.

But he had apologised, asked for forgiveness. He could have just as easily forgotten about her, moved on, got on with saving lives in the hospital and smuggling downed pilots over the border.

For a man who'd professed he had been too close to Nazi attention yesterday, he'd braved delivering this to the hotel. He'd taken a risk even coming to the ball at the hotel yesterday. That he had done so when invited was the real idiocy. And if anything awful had've happened to him because of her, then that would have been her fault. He had said Chanel had been running with the wolves but Theo and she had come too close yesterday. Too close. That kind of thing must never happen again.

Adèle didn't tell him she was coming. She simply boarded the Metro and made her way to Neuilly. Inside the hospital she saw the nurse who'd instructed she and Theo not to enter the office all those weeks ago.

The nurse greeted Adèle and smiled at her knowingly as she introduced herself and asked for Doctor Dixon. Did the nurse know what Adèle had done for Mélodie? And did she in turn know that Adèle knew the kind-hearted nurse had been harbouring downed airmen?

The risks being taken in this building, Adèle mused as she walked the corridor alongside the nurse.

'How do you still have stockings?' the American nurse asked suddenly.

'I'm down to my last two pairs,' Adèle replied. 'Then

it's a case of painting a line on, I think. I've not worked out which would be best.'

'You could lower your hemline?' the nurse suggested kindly. 'I'm not sure that's too fashionable though, is it?'

'No, I don't think it is, sadly,' Adèle said. She could only imagine what Mademoiselle Chanel would have to say about that.

'You're not here for an appointment, are you?' the nurse asked.

'No. Theo . . . Doctor Dixon doesn't know I'm coming. We're . . . friends,' Adèle opted for something safe and true.

'Good,' the nurse said appraising Adèle as they walked. 'He could do with a . . . friend.' A flicker of a smile touched the corners of her mouth.

Adèle smiled as the nurse knocked on Theo's door. There was no answer. 'I take it it's safe to enter this time,' she said.

The nurse looked at her through narrowed eyes housing a flicker of recognition. 'This time, yes.' She opened the door, saw it was empty and closed it with a thoughtful expression on her face. 'I think I know where he'll be,' she said with a sad sigh.

Adèle looked up and down the corridor as they walked, checking they were alone. 'I know what you two are doing,' she whispered. 'And I want you to know I think it's terribly brave. A huge risk. But brave.'

The nurse stopped and glanced behind them. It took her a moment before answering. 'Thank you. Theo said you could be trusted.'

'He's right. I can be trusted.'

The door to another room opened and out stepped Theo's secretary – Mademoiselle Vachon. She glanced at the nurse, smiled tightly and stepped in the other direction, moving along the corridor at pace.

The nurse gave Adèle a look. 'It's a shame not all of us are trustworthy,' she said when the other woman was out of earshot. 'But for those of us that are, we have to do anything we can to stop them winning.'

Adèle didn't have the chance to reply because the nurse stopped outside a closed consulting room door. 'He's probably in here,' she said, knocking and then followed it up with: 'It's Nurse Carmichael.'

'Come in,' he said.

The two women entered. Theo glanced quickly at the nurse and then on seeing Adèle just behind her he smiled widely.

'I'll leave you to it,' the nurse said and then left the room, closing the door behind them.

Adèle stared at Theo in a mix of respect and horror. He was lying on a consulting couch, a tube in his arm that was conveying blood to a bottle. 'What are you doing?' she asked, although she knew.

'What does it look like?' he said, not unkindly. There was a grin working its way to the surface of his tired face.

'How often do you do this?' she asked, putting her bag on the counter along with her hat.

'As often as I need to,' he said. 'As often as I can manage without passing out.'

'Is it really that bad that you need to do this?' she asked perching on the edge of the couch.

He nodded. 'It will be when the Allied raids really kick it up a gear. They're been targeting train lines from what we can gather, trying to stop the tide of German troops being deployed as much as they can. And now factories are being taken over, Renault, Citroën . . . to help the German war effort. You wait . . . the Allies will be coming for the cities. It's only a matter of time. There'll be casualties,' he said. 'The factory workers who were making car parts are now making trucks for the Luftwaffe. The Allies need to fight back or else what hope is there? And when the bombs drop, which they inevitably will . . . I have to do everything in my power to save as many lives as I can. That starts here.' He gestured to the bottle slowly filling up.

She wanted to cut in, to tell him to stop, but he asked suddenly, 'You've got somewhere to go in a raid?'

'Yes,' she said slowly, hypnotised by the slow trickle of crimson liquid as it drained out of him and into the glass bottle. 'The Ritz has a shelter in the basement.' She thought of the practice runs they'd done down the grand staircases, carrying Mademoiselle's gas mask on a velvet cushion while she lugged her own in its box.

'Good.' He nodded. 'The Brits would have given anything to protect those factories but now they're in the hands of Hitler. And so those who fought so hard to protect them are probably going to blow the hell out of them. There are men and women inside working. Those who survive . . . those we can save . . . we'll run out of blood, Adèle. It's that simple. Even with the blood drives. Something so humble as a pint of blood really could be all they need.'

Adèle took off her jacket, rolled up the sleeve on one of her arms. 'I don't know if it will help but take some from me.'

'No. It's too soon.'

'I don't care,' she said. 'It's been long enough and I have nowhere to be today. If it makes me feel faint, I will stay here for a little longer. With you,' she added.

He sat up. She hoped her eyes conveyed the steely determination she felt.

He sighed and said quietly, 'Fine. But only this once. We're not doing this again.'

'We'll see about that,' she said. 'As long as you don't end up using this on the Occupying force,' she muttered.

He laughed as he disposed of the equipment he'd just been using, labelled the bottle of his blood and then rolled his shirtsleeve down. 'No chance.' A second later he said, 'Thank you.'

'You're welcome.' His attention was on the job in hand while she kept her eyes on him. Without realising it she was enjoying watching him move seamlessly, expertly as if . . .

'I'll confess I do this more than I should,' he said, reading her mind.

'I knew it,' Adèle replied.

'So I'm just going to . . .' He pulled a second consulting couch over, next to the one she was on. 'I'll be on this one while you lie there. OK?'

'Theo,' she chastised but reached out and touched his arm. The action stilled him and he looked slowly to the place where her hand rested. She could feel the heat emanating underneath his shirt. Unspoken between them was everything that had happened yesterday: dancing together, him holding her so wonderfully close, the moment she thought he'd been about to kiss her on a crowded dance floor and then caught himself and stopped, just in time. And then the argument.

But instead of mentioning any of that Adèle cowardly avoided the subject and said, 'It's fine for you but not for me to donate blood regularly?'

'I'm doing it perhaps too regularly,' he said. 'And I don't even have madeleines to give you this time.'

She pretended to get up. 'Oh forget it then,' she said. 'I'm only here for the madeleines.'

He laughed. 'Hold still,' he said and she watched him work as he readied the tubes and bottle, giving her arm a swipe with rubbing alcohol. 'Ready?'

She nodded and he inserted the needle. She winced a little and then waited for her body to forget it was in there. He sat next to her on the couch and then lay back and the two of them were side by side.

She looked into his eyes as they aligned with hers, next

to her, lying so intimately together. 'You got my note then,' he said after a few seconds.

'Yes,' she replied, her tongue suddenly twisted. She recovered enough to say, 'Thank you.'

'Don't thank me. I was a bastard. I'm so sorry.'

'So you said,' she replied with a raise of her eyebrows at his language.

He rose a little, looked towards the bottle to check on it as it filled and then lay back down again.

'I wasn't very nice either,' she offered.

'Don't,' he said. 'This war's making me the best version of myself. And the absolute worst. There's no defence for taking a woman on a romantic walk along the river and then shouting at her.'

'Romantic?' she queried.

He smiled, looked around her at the bottle again. 'It didn't occur to you that I wanted you out of that god-awful place so I could be alone with you? Clench your hand every now and again,' he said, giving her no time to reply. He sat back and she did as he'd asked.

'I enjoyed dancing with you,' she said. 'I enjoyed everything with you, but not as much as I would have done in . . . normal times.'

'No Nazis breathing down our necks while I held you,' he replied.

Adèle nodded, shifting on the consulting couch and attempting not to accidentally pull the tubing out of her arm in the process. Neither of them spoke for a minute and she was only aware they were just watching each other quietly, in a state of strange relaxation, their breathing slow, easily synching with each other's when a sharp rap sounded at the door and they both jolted. Theo's secretary entered without waiting to be invited in.

Her mouth dropped open when she saw the two of them side by side together, their bodies apart but it could be so easily misconstrued and obviously had, despite the blood being drained slowly from Adèle.

'What is it?' Theo asked.

Mademoiselle Vachon gathered her wits and then replied, 'Telephone call. It's someone called Madame Dupont. I couldn't find you so I told them you'd telephone them back if and when you were available.' She looked at Adèle in distaste.

Theo sat up, looked at his secretary and said, 'Thank you.' She didn't leave and he repeated it again, more pointedly and she left the room, banging the door closed behind her.

'I don't think she likes me,' Adèle offered with a faint smile. Theo moved round her and, with the bottle full, began removing the needle and packing away, labelling, discarding used apparatus.

'It's not you,' he said. 'It's everyone. She's a busybody,' he said.

'Oh I don't know,' Adèle said, holding the bandage in place he gave her. 'It just sounds like she's doing her job.'

'Maybe,' he said, glancing towards the closed door. He moved towards it, opened it and looked into the corridor, clearly checking if Mademoiselle Vachon was lingering, listening.

'If you don't trust her, get rid of her,' Adèle said and then realised it sounded very unfair to a fellow woman to just sack her at the drop of a hat.

'I can't,' Theo said. 'She's been appointed by my senior who got sick and tired of my paperwork being so slack. If I get rid of her now someone else will be thrust upon me. Better the devil you know, right?'

'I guess so,' Adèle offered as Theo lay back down next to her.

'You need to rest a while,' he said. 'We may as well rest here together, until we feel well enough to move again.'

'All right,' Adèle said, relishing the opportunity to spend time with him like this. 'But shouldn't you go and telephone that person back?' Adèle asked.

'Don't you start,' he said. 'What are you doing later?'

'Nothing much,' she said.

'Have dinner with me.'

Adèle tingled at the invitation.

'I can't promise you anything like last night's gourmet dining but I can promise good company, I hope. And categorically no shouting at you this time.'

She loved how one second he made every part of her feel alive and how the next he could command a laugh from her, even in a time such as this. 'I would like that very much.'

'You can't change the course of the war, one pint of blood at a time,' she said at his apartment later that evening.

'Yes, ma'am,' he replied.

'I mean it,' she said, pushing him playfully. 'You have to stop, Theo.' He'd been asleep on the settee when she'd knocked and he'd confessed as much to her. 'You can't go on draining yourself mentally and physically. You'll have nothing left to give when you really need it.'

'I know,' he sighed.

The corners of his mouth turned into a faint smile. 'But I can do whatever I can here to help thwart it – to save people; to help the Resistance.'

'I thought you were only helping downed pilots?' She looked up at him suddenly mid-way through unloading her string bag and he leant against the doorframe watching her actions. He watched as she lined up the ingredients that she'd queued for almost an hour to buy, ready to cook. She wanted to cook for him, wanted to look after him the way he was looking after so many others, the way he was literally draining himself drop by drop. She'd never cooked for anyone before. She'd hardly ever cooked before. That was at least one job she hadn't had to carry out in the orphanage or for Chanel.

'I was only helping downed pilots but there's more I can do.'

'Not if you can hardly stand at the end of the day because you're overdoing it,' she chastised. 'It'll get you killed. Or you'll kill yourself first,' she said pointing to his arm, where his shirtsleeves were rolled up casually, bruised evidence on display in the crooks of both arms.

He folded his arms as he settled in against the doorframe, although if he was attempting to hide the damage to both arms he'd failed. 'What are we cooking?'

She sighed, realising she wasn't going to get him to stop. She looked at what she'd brought. 'I don't know,' she said with thinly veiled exasperation. 'I don't know what to do with these. I don't actually know how to cook,' she admitted.

Theo's shoulders shook with laughter and Adèle's expression went slowly from annoyance at her own inadequacies to mirth as she watched him laugh and she couldn't help laughing with him. Eventually he pushed himself away from the frame and as the amusement fell away he looked at her with such intense interest in his eyes that she was forced to look away under his gaze. She fiddled with the empty net bag as a distraction as she acknowledged to herself how he made her joyful and nervous all at the same time.

'You're doing it again,' he said.

'Doing what?' she asked knowing exactly what she was doing. She forced herself to look back at him. 'I should be annoyed that you are laughing at me,' she said, jabbing at him gently in the chest.

'You should be,' he said. 'I'm not going to compliment you to have you look away again.' He smiled. 'Adèle Fabron, you can't cook. You can't dance. Your seduction technique is just plain awful. I don't know what the heck I'm going to do with you.'

'I do,' Adèle replied teasingly before purposefully changing tack. 'You will cook and I will pour the wine.'

'U-boat enclosures?' Adèle questioned over dinner. In the end he'd had her chopping and dicing the few potatoes she'd managed to buy and he'd boiled them, then fried them in the thinnest cut of butter, sprinkled a few herbs from a tin box on his window and chopped the rind of bacon on to fry. Then he'd let the chunk of ripe camembert cheese she'd bought melt gently on top. It was a simple supper but one of the most delicious she'd ever eaten. She would remember the taste of this forever. And the company she was dining with.

'Yes,' he said as he wolfed the last of his dinner. 'U-boat enclosures – holding pens. Along the coast, obviously.' He laughed at himself. 'I've told my contact I can do more to help. My French is perfect. I'm willing. I'm able. I need to do so much more,' he said.

'You're doing enough already, surely.'

'I'm not. Not at all.'

'What are you intending to do?' she asked, not under-standing at all what he was driving at.

'I've been asked to travel and it looks less suspicious if there's two of us.'

'Two?'

'A man and a woman. A couple. Less suspicious. Nurse Carmichael and I have volunteered.'

'What if you get stopped? What story will you give as to why you're travelling to a coastal town together?'

'We're travelling medics from a country with which Germany isn't at war. And we have permission. All the correct paperwork to move around for the Red Cross.'

Adèle filled her cheeks with air and then let it out slowly.

'Then you are already at risk of attracting attention before you've even left.'

'People are still travelling around the Occupied zone by rail, Adèle. Well, until they come to a part of track that the Resistance has blown up. Then all bets are off. But life goes on.'

'This isn't life. It's Occupation,' Adèle said.

'Exactly. And I want to try to help bring an end to it in whatever way I can.'

'Where on the coast?' she demanded.

He looked at her, toying with whether or not he should say and thus bringing her into the plan. He shifted in his seat, obviously deciding to risk it. 'St Nazaire.'

She sat back, wanting to tell him – not wanting to tell him. 'I know it. The orphanage I grew up in was near there. And before that, with my mother . . .' She trailed off.

Theo was respectfully silent for a moment and Adèle drifted back to a happier time, playing on the sawdust-covered floor with her doll. Funny how talk of St Nazaire had taken her to that particular memory instead of the many she'd had at the convent in more recent years. Outside Theo's apartment a door slammed and Adèle blinked herself back to the present.

'But isn't it in the new forbidden zone that's being created?' Adèle asked. 'I have seen in *Le Figaro* that Hitler's grand plan is to strengthen the Atlantic Wall all across France, all the way up into the Low Countries and beyond; to build a kind of Fortress Europe. How will you get in?'

'I have permission to travel,' he said tapping his chest pocket where the paperwork sat. 'The benefits of being a doctor from a neutral country.'

'What are you planning to do about the U-boat enclosures?' she asked.

'Reconnaissance. I need to take photos.'

'Dear God.'

'They're strengthening the submarine holding pens. Enlarging them, apparently. They want to know how many submarines it can hold. How many are in there now. That kind of thing.'

'They? To do what with the information?'

'To pass on to those who need it. Those who want to . . . blow it up I guess, or spy on the sub commanders? I don't know. I don't need to know,' he said pointedly.

'You're mad,' she whispered.

'What do I do, say no? Leave it to someone else? What if there is no one else? We all have to help. On paper I'm respectable. And I can talk my way out of anything,' he said, his dark eyes sparkling.

'You think that will be enough to stop the Gestapo killing you if they catch you in the act?'

'If I can do this,' he said. 'If I can pull this off, then I've allowed another man, another Resistance fighter – a proper one – to do something else equally important, if not more so somewhere else. This . . . turning up in a town posing as a couple, taking photographs of the U-boat pens . . . this could be the thing that swings the war.'

'You're American. It's not even your war,' she said.

'It will be though. You know that don't you. Eventually. What better time to help than when America hasn't declared war on Germany. Because you know they're going to. What better time to help than when I'm from a nation with which Germany is not at war?'

She sighed, sipped the last of her wine. Now, of all moments she understood why some people turned to drink in times of crisis. It steadied nerves, or exacerbated them, she didn't know which. 'When are you going?'

'Tomorrow morning.'

'Tomorrow morning?' she cried. 'Good God, it doesn't give me much time to pack. How long for?'

'Why are you packing? Christ, you're not coming.'

'Of course I'm coming,' she said.

'No—' He stood up. 'You're not.'

'I am,' she said, standing so she was almost eye-level with him. 'I know where I'm going. I know where we can go to view the U-boat enclosure without being seen. I think. And because it is where I am from, I am allowed to travel home. It will appear normal if I take a man home to meet those I grew up with. What doesn't look normal is if you travel to a town you've never been to before with no real reason to go and nowhere to stay and no idea where you can actually carry out this insane—'

But Adèle didn't get the chance to finish because Theo moved round the side of the small kitchen table and kissed her.

Every part of her caught light and after a second of fighting sheer desire with a sense of panic that she had almost no idea what she was doing, she reciprocated.

When he pulled back he looked as flushed as she felt.

'You're maddening,' he said and then lowered his lips to hers again.

'So are you,' she said, not fighting the desire to kiss him back.

He held her close, planting small delicate kisses on her mouth in between the words. 'I don't want to put you in danger. I don't need you to come along.'

She touched his face and kissed him again. 'Yes you do.'

'While the cat's away,' said Madame Basset, the housekeeper, on entering Mademoiselle Chanel's suite and noticing the small suitcase that Adèle was taking to the door.

Adèle clutched the handle so tight her knuckles turned white. Anger at herself that she'd left a few minutes later than planned and had been caught threaded its way through her. But she opted for brazen confession rather than denial.

'If I can take some time off, I'm taking it,' she said. 'You're not going to tell on me are you?' she challenged.

The housekeeper thought for a moment, then shook her head. 'Don't mind if I do the same in that case. I wanted to. I was worried you'd tell Marie Antoinette.' The housekeeper then looked abashed, obviously at letting slip her private nickname for their employer. 'Got a couple of days, may as well use them. Who knows when we'll get the chance to sneak away like this again. I'll go and visit my sister. Where are you going then?'

'A few days with my sweetheart,' Adèle confessed. It was mostly true. As she left, taking the back stairs and passing the sentries on the door, nodding at them politely, she thought through what she'd told Madame Basset.

The Adèle from before the war would never have thought about travelling overnight with a man she wasn't married to. The Adèle from before the war would not have thought of helping a Resistance network. Mademoiselle's ever-present mantras about being the best version of herself, the strongest version of herself, rang through her mind. Oh if Mademoiselle knew how she had interpreted that. Theo was right. War was bringing out the worst versions of people. And, Adèle thought with a smile, the best.

Chapter 15

On the steam train to St Nazaire, Adèle watched the thick clouds of smoke plume and whirl into the sky through the grimy window, streaks of black scarring the pane of glass. Boarding the train had been surprisingly easy, as Theo had suggested it would be, although it didn't stop Adèle's palms from sweating as she'd bought their tickets, talked to the French attendant and nodded politely to the German supervisor who'd asked to see their papers and asked the purpose of their visit. She reeled off her story as if she was a giddy schoolgirl, excited at the prospect of taking her sweetheart home to show him off. How easy the lies came to her and the story seemed to hold up.

The French ticket inspector nodded uninterestedly as they presented their tickets a few moments after boarding.

'It's easy to spot those who are pro-Vichy and those who aren't,' Adèle pointed out quietly to Theo. 'Those who take more of an interest than normal.'

'It is and it isn't,' he said. They were seated in a second-class carriage. The seats were padded and she made the most of the slight comfort for the hours that lay ahead. Theo nestled in beside her, turning to kiss her cheek gently and then whispered, 'We just need to be wary of everyone.

Let's not talk about it in here,' he said. His kiss was no less intoxicating now, all these hours later than when they'd embraced the night before.

Reading an old copy of *Marie Claire* Adèle felt him relax against her, his body pulling him towards sleep, his hat over his eyes. She smiled to herself, despite the danger – perhaps even because of the danger.

The night before it had taken every ounce of restraint they both had to prise themselves from each other before curfew came. The choice Adèle had undergone was a difficult one: to stay with him and wait until curfew lifted in the morning when she knew she would have given herself to him entirely, or to return to her room at the Ritz with moments to spare before the streets emptied of all but German patrols and to maintain some modesty and decorum.

Outside the smeared window Paris gave way discreetly to open countryside and the journey south until eventually she too let the train's rhythmic movement guide her gently towards sleep.

Adèle awoke hours later and found Theo had returned from the food car with what appeared to be stale baguettes and a runny sort of sugarless compote. 'Better than nothing,' he'd said while grumbling about rationing.

They disembarked through the smoky station, full of the rush of civilians and German soldiers bound for who-knew-where. Adèle gripped Theo's hand as they emerged into the darkening night skies.

At some point along the journey the blue light in the carriage had been switched on overhead and the blackout blind pulled down, which had made Adèle acutely aware how visible the train lines must be to attack. To help aid the close of the war, she and Theo could easily have been blown sky high at any point by an Allied raider with bombs to spare on a return journey. A chink of light from the cabin as it puffed and chugged its way through the darkening countryside and a stray bomb was all that was needed to end their lives. Anything to prohibit troop movements across occupied France.

And now they had something far more frightening to contemplate. She dreaded Theo's mad plan to photograph the submarine holding pens. The whole idea was dangerous, insane. But she had an idea how she could help, and she knew that being here, with him, was the right thing to do. She looked down at his sleeping face, listened to the voice in her head and knew she'd have gone with him anywhere.

Now they were actually near St Nazaire the reality of what they were doing was brought upon her. With most hotels taken over by the German naval workers she knew the only place they could slip out of view of prying eyes would be the convent and its adjacent orphanage. She'd worked that much out the moment she'd suggested she went with him. But as they walked through the outskirts of St Nazaire, outside the forbidden zone in blackout where the villages dotted the landscape, she started to regret what they were doing. Would she be welcome there after all this time? Would Theo?

She'd sent a telegram from the post boy in the Ritz the night before, ensuring she paid him then and there so it didn't appear on any bill sent to Mademoiselle Chanel's suite. But of course there'd been no time for Mother Superior to reply and now Adèle knocked on the medieval wooden doors, dark and studded. She clutched Theo's hand tighter.

It was the caretaker who opened the door and Adèle recognised him immediately. With the warm smile of Monsieur Robert all fears faded, for now, and they greeted each other with Adèle introducing Theo. The two men shook hands warmly.

'Mother Superior has said you'd be here. It's been the talk of the convent all day.'

This was exactly the kind of thing Adèle hadn't wanted but it had seemed better to announce her arrival than to expect a bed for each of them for two nights, without so much as an advance note.

'She's already retired to bed,' he said. 'But I'll take you to your rooms and then send up some supper. We've put two plates by.'

'The kindness of strangers,' Theo remarked enthusiastically. 'Thank you so much.'

'You're next to me,' Monsieur Robert told Theo. 'While you, Mademoiselle Fabron, are on the other side of the building in the rooms there, of course.'

Theo smiled at Adèle as the two were led through the winding stone passageways. 'Of course,' he whispered to her and winked knowingly.

It was all Adèle could do not to laugh. 'Doctor Dixon,' she whispered, out of earshot of Monsieur Robert. 'If you've been expecting me to fall into your arms at the midnight hour in a convent then you've been misleading yourself.'

He laughed loudly, coughing to cover it and nodded his apologies at the startling noise to the caretaker who had turned back to look sharply. They stopped at Adèle's door first and she said a chaste goodnight to Theo. She watched him follow Monsieur Robert to his part of the building where he'd sleep for the night and then she settled herself in the simple room until a novice knocked gently, quietly offered Adèle a bowl of bouillabaisse and reminded her where the facilities were. With that, Adèle was left alone to eat, contemplate and sleep.

During the night she dreamt not of being caught and arrested, but of Mélodie. The little girl she'd rescued and who was orphaned. She could have ended up somewhere like this. It wouldn't have been so bad. Perhaps Adèle should have taken her to an orphanage in Paris. She dreamt of the little girl now looked after in a family. That was better. Of course, that was better. How would she grow up? Where would she grow up? Would she remember how Adèle had rescued her? Would she remember how her mother had been arrested while she herself had been hidden?

Adèle woke with a start in the middle of the night, covered in perspiration. An owl in a tree outside was the only noise in the medieval building. Eventually, hoping wherever Mélodie ended up she was safe and happy, Adèle closed her eyes and groggily fell back asleep.

The next morning it had been the bells, as usual, that had awoken her, taking her back to another time when she thought she'd been settled and happy but it had transpired she'd been neither of these things. But over the past few years she'd missed the clanging wake-up, the call to steel herself for the day ahead. When she opened her eyes the first thing she saw was the large wooden cross on the white stone wall at the end of her bed. If she needed any reminder there was a God it was today of all days.

When she had washed and dressed in fresh clothes – nothing too eye-catching, a dark blue skirt suit and a white blouse from her little case – she glanced back at the cross thoughtfully. She dipped to her knees underneath it and constructed an impromptu prayer that whatever happened to them today, they would not be arrested and shot as spies or resisters, because surely the moment they left the convent and embarked on this plan they were both spies *and* resisters.

She stood, looked once again at the cross and while she fervently wanted to believe what would happen today lay in the hands of God, she knew that ultimately not getting caught was up to her and Theo.

They ate a breakfast of thin porridge and dried fruits at Mother Superior's table in the refectory. The woman looked as if she hadn't aged a day since Adèle had left under the silent promise to herself of a new and better life.

'You've come back to us,' Mother Superior had said warmly. 'And you bring this young man with you to meet us?'

'Yes,' Adèle replied, 'I wanted to bring him here, to you. To see my home town.'

Theo played along with Adèle's plan amicably. 'I wanted to see where Adèle grew up, and to take a little trip to the seaside, while we still could. I can't think of anything better.'

'We are only too pleased to house you,' Mother Superior replied. 'You will always have a safe place here with us.'

Did she know? Did she know that Adèle's return in the midst of war was not entirely innocent? 'A few of our young charges are with us still who I think you will remember. And Dominique has stayed on as a teacher,' Mother Superior continued.

Adèle chose to put her worries aside and clapped her hands together, genuinely happy to hear this and enthused that Dominique – one of the older children she'd known – had chosen this quiet life of contemplation, learning, educating others, staying put, being safe. In the end, that life had not been for Adèle but it comforted her to know that some things would always stay the same, here in the convent, even though the world around them all was falling away to dust.

In the schoolroom, Adèle stood by the open door, peering in, listening to Dominique as she taught matriculation. A warmth entered Adèle's heart. Although a few years younger than Adèle the two had grown up together in those final years. Adèle followed along in her head, arrived at the sum and slowly moved into the doorway. Still out of sight she watched the girls being taught as they scribbled furiously, eager to gain the teacher's praise by being the first to raise their hand into the air with the correct calculation.

There was no chance for glory as Dominique spotted Adèle, gasped and putting all respectability aside ran straight towards her, engulfing her in an embrace. 'You're here!' she said. 'I knew you'd come back to see us one day but I thought at least it would be when the war was over.'

'Who knows when that day will be,' Adèle said holding her old friend out at arm's length and admiring how she'd blossomed into a fine young woman. It hadn't really been that long.

'And you're getting married?' Dominique asked. 'That's why you've brought your man back to see us?'

'Oh, I, no, well, that is,' Adèle struggled for an answer. She'd never said she was getting married, but of course that was what everyone assumed.

'We thought that's why you'd come back,' Dominique said with her head to one side. 'Were we wrong?'

'No, you're right but we won't marry during the war.' Now Adèle had a chance to recover herself this story might work in their favour, especially given where she intended to take Theo this afternoon in order to capture the photographs he needed.

After a few minutes talking to her old friend and reminiscing as quickly as they could in front of the pupils, they made an agreement to talk over dinner where Dominique wanted to hear all her news. How could she tell them she'd moved from a life in a convent to living with Coco Chanel? Hers was a world so very far removed from this one.

'Do you want to see the two married friends you mentioned who lived nearby?' Theo said as the two of them walked around the large convent garden, past fruit trees no longer bearing fruit for the season.

She looked up at him. 'You have a good memory,' she said.

'I remember everything you say,' he replied, casting her a curious look. 'Why wouldn't I?'

She tightened her clasp around his hand but remained silent on that point. Instead she said, 'No. I don't think it's a wise idea. I think outside the convent we should be discreet. Get the photos you need this afternoon. Sleep here tonight and then go straight home. The more people who see us, question what we are doing here, the more my story might start to crumble. My nerves are shredding. How are you able to be so calm?'

'You don't think my nerves are shredding too?'

'You don't look as if they are,' she said seriously.

'Don't I? Adèle, you know what we're about to do . . . if we're caught . . . I can't tell you how awful it's going to be. They'll torture you, hurt you. Don't come with me,' he said. 'Just tell me where to go and . . . don't come with me.'

'We've already discussed this and I won that discussion remember?'

'I didn't realise discussions were for winning and losing,' he said wryly.

'They are with me,' she replied, making him smile.

'Worth remembering.' He lifted his eyes and looked around the garden. Their hands were still clasped together and he pulled her out of sight behind a tree. Gently he pushed her against it, kissed her, held her hips beneath his fingertips, the fabric of her skirt bunching gently under his grip, making Adèle moan softly into his mouth.

Devastatingly, he pulled away, removed his hands, breathing out an exasperated sigh.

'Doctor Dixon,' she teased when she caught her breath. 'We're in a convent.'

'Don't I know it. And relax,' he teased back. 'Kissing in

217

a convent garden isn't the biggest crime we're going to commit today, I'll tell you that much.' He glanced around, kissed her again and she closed her eyes, melding her body into his.

'You're a different person here,' Theo said pushing back a lock of her hair that had come loose during their desperate kiss. 'Away from her.'

Adèle didn't have to ask who he meant. She knew. She also knew what he was saying was true. She nodded, looking around her at the medieval building, its large stone pillars, the ruins in the garden she'd walked around almost all of her life. 'It's different. It's home. Or what I know of as home.'

'Then I'll have to change that.'

'And how are you going to do that?' she answered.

'Easy,' he said, his expression serious. 'I'll give you a new home. I promise when all of this is over that I will provide you with a new home. With me, if that's what you want?'

'Theo . . . don't.'

'Why ever not?'

'We haven't known each other very long. This . . . this war is making people say and do things they wouldn't in peacetime. Don't fall victim to making a promise you can't keep.'

'Why can't I keep it?' he said. 'I *thought* I was falling head over heels in love with you. But now I know it. I know I love you, Adèle. And if I can't tell you this, now, here, before we head out there to put our necks on the line then when can I tell you?'

She drew in a sharp breath at that but he continued. 'I know there's a lot I don't know. But I want to learn. I want to learn everything about you,' he finished.

If he'd expected her to tell him she loved him too she didn't know what to reply. This was dangerous. Falling in love in the middle of a war was dangerous. 'It's impossible, isn't it?'

'Why?' he asked.

'This war . . .' she said and knew she didn't need to complete the sentence.

'Then I'll make this promise for later on and not for now,' he bargained. 'If we get through today alive and if you still want me when the war is won or maybe even when the war is lost, heaven forbid, I, Theo Dixon, will marry you and give you a place you can call home until the end of our days. If that's what you want.'

Adèle's voice failed her. Instead, her throat tightened in a mix of shock and wonder. She loved him. She did. Although with nothing else to compare it to the feeling had snuck up on her so suddenly. She'd realised something was happening to her gradually. But it was watching him on the train that had finally sealed that feeling deep into her core. Of course she loved him. She'd have never agreed to help him in St Nazaire if she hadn't. She stifled a shocked laugh and nodded.

'Is that a yes?' he asked.

'I don't want to tempt fate,' she said pleadingly. 'So . . . it's a yes for when the war is over, if we survive all of this.'

He whooped for joy, causing a bird to flee from a nearby tree. Adèle laughed joyously and so did he. Had she really just been proposed to? Had she just agreed? 'I can take that,' he said, repeating her words. 'A yes for when the war is over.'

They held hands as they walked through the streets until they reached the checkpoint where German sentries were standing, looking nonchalant, as if people hardly ever came and went this way. But they both stood up straight and walked towards Theo and Adèle the moment they saw them. One, smoking a cigarette, threw it hastily away and blew out a cloud of smoke. Adèle gave her best smile and he smiled back in return, disappointed to discover after a moment's conversation on presenting papers that she and

Theo were engaged to be married. This made him look at Theo closer and his papers were examined for far too long. Adèle's heart thudded so loudly as she handed hers over too.

For all the times she'd seen German soldiers in Paris, greeting her as she came and went from the Ritz, there had never been call to be stopped for this long.

Espionage. She was engaging in espionage against the enemy force; two of which were standing in front of her, looking closely at the reason for justifying their travel to a forbidden zone – despite the fact hundreds and hundreds of people lived in St Nazaire and needed to travel in and out for work and to shop in the town.

'What is in the suitcase?' the second soldier asked Theo in very stilted French.

Adèle was sure she heard a frightened noise come from the back of her throat.

Theo shrugged. 'I've learnt in this war to always carry a decent first aid kit wherever I go,' he said in slow French for fear of confusing or angering the man. He tapped his small case. 'I'm a doctor but I'm of no use to anyone in an accident if I don't have medical equipment. In here's pills and bandages, all sorts of things to patch people up if they're hurt. You want me to open it up?'

'Yes,' the soldier replied immediately.

Adèle forced herself to be calm, still, so very still, giving nothing away.

Theo placed the case on the ground, bent down and unclipped the lid. The soldier who'd been smoking bent down. They couldn't see his expression, on the top of his round helmet, as he poked into the case and moved the items around one by one, examining them. Theo had been given a suitcase that housed a false bottom, inside of which was the camera. A spyhole had been pinpricked discreetly in the case and he simply had to click the numbers on his briefcase and the photographs would be captured. If you wanted to find it you had to know where to look for a catch to open it up and reveal the illegal item within.

The soldier stared at the contents for far too long and Adèle forced herself not to look at Theo, not to issue him a look of startled concern. Instead, hand shaking, she casually removed her hair clip, allowing her long locks of dark, waved hair to fall down. She shook it out, allowing it to bounce around her shoulders. Both soldiers looked up at her and she lowered her lashes provocatively, before innocently rearranging her hair and clipping it back into place.

The soldier stood, open-mouthed. And then he blinked himself out of his daze, gesturing to Theo that he could close the case. He raised the barrier to allow them entry.

When they were some way off and out of earshot of the soldiers, Theo turned to her and gestured to her hair. 'What was that about?'

'I just needed to do something with my hands. That seemed as good a movement as any.'

'They looked at you like they'd never seen a woman before. *I* looked at you like I'd never seen a woman before. Who knew a girl taking her hairpins out could be so dangerous. If we get arrested could you do that again?'

She nudged him in the ribs as they continued to walk into town, her near-miss experience haunting her. She wouldn't be rid of this anxiety until she was far away from St Nazaire. They'd timed their journey so that dusk was some way off. She hadn't been gone long enough to forget what it looked like, but she could see with fresh eyes the difference between this town and the grand heights of Paris. But the beaches – how she remembered the beaches on the occasions they'd been allowed to day-trip there with the nuns.

He'd been delivered the camera case early, before they'd left Paris with instructions how to use it and, importantly, information how someone would collect it from him on the return journey to Paris. Adèle found everything about this plan entirely worrying but it was this part that concerned her the most. What if this mysterious courier was delayed, didn't turn up or even worse . . . what if this was a trap and on the train there was a host of officials, or worse the Gestapo . . .

But she couldn't think about that now. No. Instead she and Theo did exactly what they'd planned to do all along. She briefed him of her plan to use the church as their viewing point as they strolled all too casually into town.

Outside the church door she didn't even stop, didn't even pause to take in the architecture and neither did Theo. They simply opened the heavy wooden door and slipped inside. It couldn't be so easy, surely? Although they still had the climb to the top. If the priest asked, Adèle would use the story she'd used all along that the two of them wanted to look at the church because Adèle intended to marry in the church near to where she'd grown up, one that was so familiar to her.

But there was no sign of the priest and so Adèle and Theo lifted the latch on the small door that hid the steps to the bell tower and began climbing. She'd not been up here since she was about fifteen, when the job had once fallen on her to attend to the ailing flag on Bastille Day celebrations. She knew where she was going and from what she remembered, at the top of the bell tower was the most phenomenal view of the Loire, the surrounding countryside, the beach and sea and, most importantly, the docks where there were now the ugly, heinous, gigantic concrete submarine enclosures where there hadn't been years ago. When she saw it, it was as vile as she'd imagined it would be in order to support such a hateful cause.

'Wow,' Theo said as he caught sight of it once they reached the freezing top. The biting winter wind whipped and lashed their faces and Adèle pulled her coat even closer around her as Theo positioned his suitcase on top of the stone wall. 'I wasn't expecting it to look like that,' he said, holding the case tightly with one hand so it didn't topple over the edge, giving them away. 'It's huge. That thing holds at least fourteen submarines. But what the hell else is all that concrete for? What have they got in there?'

Adèle had no idea. 'Places for all the men to sleep? And work? And eat? How many men does it take to make a fleet of submarines seaworthy?'

'Hundreds judging by the size of that place.'

'I don't want to think about it,' Adèle said, pulling her coat around her to ward against the wind and the fear that was now creeping up her flesh.

And then Theo remembered why he was there. Instinct took over and he snapped photographs over and over, taking a line-up of shots to encompass its exact position as well as the magnitude of the structure. 'That should do it,' he said. 'It's not as if I can do any more. Good thinking by the way, taking me up here.'

'This is what you get when you hire a local as a partner in your crime,' she said before they turned, descended the staircase and exited the church as quietly as they had entered.

If it had been deemed too easy, it's because it was. Far too easy. They walked hand in hand, Theo's other hand firmly gripping the suitcase. In a town of submarine commanders, shopkeepers and those undergoing strict rationing it was little surprise that a tall, handsome doctor and the well-dressed assistant to France's grande dame of fashion didn't go unnoticed as they walked the streets of St Nazaire. Trying to blend in, trying not to be noticed had done nothing for their cause. The odd glance askew here and there had not perturbed either of them. It was, of course, most unusual for there to be visitors whom no one recognised and this alone elicited unwanted attention.

They walked past a policeman who nodded at them and then as they returned his deference, nodding and walking past, the policeman paused.

'Stop,' he said. 'If you please.'

Adèle, petrified, gripped Theo's hand. She needed to talk, needed to say something but she simply froze, not facing the policeman, not daring to turn around for fear of showing the shock and concern on her face. Before if they were caught with the camera it would have been bad enough but now the roll of film would show what they'd been photographing.

'Bonjour,' Adèle eventually turned and said with a bright smile on her face. Too bright. Theo looked as if he was about to say something, but she stopped him with a quick squeeze of his hand.

'Papers please,' the policeman asked.

'Of course,' Adèle replied. There was nothing to hide. Their story held true. She was home in her place of birth; Theo was her sweetheart, come to visit her friends and what had once passed for her family in the convent. He was American, a country with which Germany was not at war. Not yet. They just had to get past this moment.

Adèle handed over her papers from her clasp bag and noticed her hand was shaking as she did so. It would be this sort of behaviour that gave them away, that gave Theo away. She hated herself, begged internally to pull herself together.

The policeman noticed her shaking hand and raised his eyes to look into Adèle's.

'You'll have to forgive her,' Theo said. 'I've just proposed. She's a little shaken up I think.'

Adèle smiled although she felt like doing anything but. 'Oui,' she said too loudly. 'He is right. We are engaged,' she said and pushed her hand to her mouth to prevent hysteria from erupting.

Theo pulled her towards him, kissing her in the street to stop her from talking. The policeman bristled at this inappropriate display of affection and then turned his attention to Theo. 'Your papers now,' he said without returning Adèle's.

'Of course,' Theo said and pulled them out of his coat pocket.

'What is your purpose in St Nazaire?' the man asked.

'Visiting my family, my friends,' Adèle replied.

'American,' the policeman said to Theo but it wasn't posed as a question. 'Once again America takes its time to enter the war, non?' The man dropped his arm to his side, still holding Theo's papers but looking at him curiously, contemptuously.

Theo adopted a tone of neutrality. 'We do. We don't tend to rush into anything that might be detrimental.'

'Pfft,' the policeman said. 'Just like the last time. Where are you staying while you are here?'

'We're staying with the Sisters of Mary Magdalene just out of town,' Theo explained.

The man's head snapped to look at them. 'You are? Why?'

'It is where I used to live as a child,' Adèle said. 'And where I used to work.'

The man stopped paying attention to Theo's papers and thrust them back at him, before unfurling Adèle's and taking a closer look.

'Adèle Fabron . . .' he said thoughtfully. 'And then, I think you were friends with my wife,' he said in a tone that sounded neither friendly nor unfriendly.

'Your wife?' Adèle couldn't help the bemusement creeping into her voice at this sudden information.

'Camille Joubair, or Houde as she was before we married.'

'Oh my word,' Adèle cried with genuine warmth at hearing her friend's name, quite forgetting the predicament she and Theo were in being questioned in this way. 'Yes, yes I do! How is Camille?'

'She is fine,' he said unenthusiastically. 'We have three children. She is busy and also late meeting me.' He looked over their shoulders. 'Ah, here she comes now.' He gestured down the street where Adèle's old friend Camille was walking slowly towards them carrying a basket of shopping in each hand. She moved at a sluggish pace further down the road. Adèle wanted to move towards her friend, run to her, greet her but the policeman showed no signs of moving towards his own wife and so they stood there, awkwardly awaiting Camille's lumbering arrival.

Adèle turned back to the policeman. 'I thought you were going into the army,' Adèle said conversationally. 'Camille wrote to me before the war and told me her husband was going to be a soldier.'

The policeman looked at her as if she had struck a nerve. 'I went into another kind of force instead,' he said. 'I wished to remain close to my wife without compromising my loyalty to France,' he said as if it was a well-rehearsed line.

'Of course,' Theo struck in, nobly saving Adèle from any further faux pas. 'Bravo.' It sounded genuine enough but Adèle knew that, like her, Theo would hold no truck with the man getting out of fighting for his country at a time when he could have been the most useful. Not here, like this, questioning people who might be enemies of the Nazis.

Adèle turned as Camille arrived. 'Camille,' she called. 'Do you remember me? Adèle. Adèle Fabron.'

Camille smiled with an exhausted kind of warmth. There was no energy behind the woman's eyes and she looked at least ten years older than her years. And heavier. Adèle wouldn't have recognised the woman. Camille didn't rush to kiss Adèle on the cheek and didn't look as if she would welcome Adèle doing so to her.

'Yes. I remember you. You look . . . wonderful. Whereas

I . . .' The woman shrugged, lifting her arms up and down.

Adèle didn't know what to say to that. She opted for safety. 'You are radiant,' she said spying her friend's very large baby bump. She must be ready to give birth any day and here she was lugging baskets of food shopping home. 'Here, let me take those,' Adèle said.

Camille simply put them on the ground and then rubbed the round bump on her already large stomach. 'Do you have children?' she asked dully.

'No, not yet.'

'But one day,' Theo cut in, continuing to play the part well.

Camille's husband spoke. 'They have just got engaged,' he said. 'They have returned for a variety of reasons I have, as yet, not been able to quite establish.'

The meaning of this remark wasn't lost on either Adèle or Theo but it was only Theo who let it show on his face.

'How long are you here for?' Camille asked.

'Not long, I'm afraid,' Adèle said.

'When will you be back?' the woman looked desperate.

'I think, when we get married.' Adèle spoke her lie too easily. She had no intention of coming here to marry Theo. She had no intention of coming here ever again.

'Then I wish you best wishes for the future and hope I will see you again soon, Adèle.' Camille looked Adèle up and down and then cast her gaze at Theo, not for the first time. 'You look like you have done very well for yourself,' she said to her old friend and then picked up her baskets. 'I am starting dinner soon,' she called to her husband as she moved slowly off. 'Do not be late. Goodbye, Adèle.'

The man reddened at having been spoken to in such a way in front of people, thrust Adèle and Theo's papers back at them and gave them a look that indicated he in no way trusted their motive for being there.

Adèle stood in stunned silence as the man moved off and

227

began loudly berating his wife as she struggled on with her baskets.

'Oh my goodness,' Theo said when they were alone. 'We need to keep moving in case he comes back.'

'I can't move,' Adèle said as Theo pulled her along.

'You have to.'

'It felt so different to when the soldiers stopped us. They seemed uninterested, vendetta-less. Camille's husband seemed to *want* us to have done something wrong,' she said.

He led her down an alley in between two shops whose awnings shielded the low sun. Theo pulled her towards him, holding her close.

'And of course,' Adèle continued. 'We had done something wrong. We had. Your camera. It's full of pictures now. We would die. We would be shot. I'm shaking,' she noticed, looking at her arms, feeling her breath jagged now.

'It's adrenalin,' he said.

She looked at him uncomprehendingly.

'It's a hormone. It's created when you most need it, essentially. It forces you to fight or it forces you to flee.'

'Or it forces you to shake like a leaf and do neither of those things,' Adèle said from the shaded darkness of the alley, her temporary sanctuary. Her mouth was dry and she'd never known a feeling quite like the one ravaging her now.

'That was too close,' Theo said. 'Twice in one day. What was he going to do, I wonder?'

'Arrest us? Take us to the Nazis?'

'I know. I don't know where that was all heading but I'm glad as hell that your friend arrived.'

'Me too.' Later, Adèle would analyse what it was that had brought Camille so low, so drab in life, so unhappy-looking, so unable to offer a real drop of friendliness after all these years, and would decide it was her situation in life, her marriage to that man, being pregnant for the fourth time while her country was occupied by Nazis. But for now, all Adèle wanted to do was return to the convent and forget about such a near-miss with the authorities.

'I couldn't tell which side he was on,' Theo said, while they waited for Adèle to recover. He rested his head on top of hers as he held her close.

'I rather think that is the point. No one is willing to admit they don't agree with the Nazi cause, especially here when the Nazis are gaining ground along the Atlantic Wall.'

'And elsewhere in the world,' Theo said. 'He was happy to hold us there and question us though. Are you all right to walk yet?'

'Yes,' Adèle replied. 'I think I have finally stopped shaking now.'

Chapter 16

In the evening they dined in the refectory, Adèle gossiping with her friends of old freely and easily while in the back of her mind she wondered about what would have happened to them if Camille's husband had pushed his concern about her and Theo further. Added to that was her anxiety about the task ahead: boarding a train with a camera full of forbidden photographs of the submarine holding pens. What if they got caught on the train? Her nerves were too much and reaching for her glass of water she knocked it over, spilling the liquid into the grain of the wood. She mopped it up with her napkin, but Mother Superior noticed.

She blinked the feeling of fear away and tried to engage herself in the conversations being had at the table. When someone mentioned Theo and Adèle's impending nuptials, it didn't feel quite like a lie anymore. And Theo engaged those around the table in easy conversation about how weddings were hard to plan in a time of war. 'Not enough material around for Adèle to have the kind of dress she deserves.' How could he be so calm, so articulate? He sounded so easy and genuine.

She tried not to think about tomorrow because who knew what tomorrow would bring, or the day after or the day after that? Her life in this war had changed so very much since meeting Theo and she wouldn't have changed a single second of it.

Saying goodbye was even harder this time around than it had been when Adèle had left for Paris only a few short years ago. This time might be the last time she'd see her friends and Mother Superior.

She made promises to herself that if she survived today she would write more often. Now she knew she hadn't been forgotten she really would make more of an effort not to shed her past life in quite the same manner that she'd done up until now.

The next morning Adèle and Theo boarded the train and both offered up a winning smile to the ticket inspector who showed little interest in them. The journey began and Theo placed the suitcase in the overhead net that housed very little in the way of other passengers' luggage. So as not to confuse things, Adèle placed her little suitcase awkwardly between her legs. In the garden of the convent, Theo had stuffed his few belongings into her suitcase as he'd been told he'd be relieved of the entire case. She hoped whatever was supposed to happen occurred quickly so they could get this ordeal over and done with. Full of nerves, she and Theo didn't speak on the train and he chewed at his lip as he stared out the window. Both of them glanced occasionally at any new passengers who got on at each station, wondering if they were the one they were waiting for. Even though she'd had a fitful night's sleep she couldn't bring herself to drift off, as much as the clacking of the train on the tracks made her want to. She needed to be alert. Although for what, she wasn't sure.

The journey took all day, the train painfully slower than their outbound journey had been. After exchanging nervous smiles and after Adèle had smoothed her skirt over her knees for what must be the tenth time in as many minutes,

Theo suggested he go to the restaurant cart to buy them some hot drinks to go with the brown parcels of cold cuts and cheese that Mother Superior had insisted they take with them. But Adèle shook her head. 'I'll go,' she whispered. 'I think you should stay here. Hasn't whoever it is been told to look out specifically for you?'

He agreed reluctantly, asking if she had enough money, which she did. She purchased two cups of what passed for coffee, agreeing to return the crockery when she was done.

When Adèle returned, carrying the cups of steaming black liquid, Theo was unwrapping the parcels of food for them but next to them a man had arrived and was sitting reading a copy of a newspaper.

She nodded in polite recognition as she sat and didn't dare speak from now on. Friend or foe? She had no idea. How did one tell? Theo obviously felt the same, thanking her for the ersatz coffee and drinking it in silence. She could do nothing but the same and not to appear suspicious ate the food from their parcel while her throat closed in tension and begged her not to force any more food into it. She had no choice but to eat if she wasn't going to draw attention to herself by pushing food away in a time of rationing.

When the train pulled into the station, the man folded his newspaper and deposited it next to Adèle. On the front of it, by the title of the paper, he'd drawn a French flag. Theo noticed it first and his eyes narrowed in contemplation, his mouth opening and then closing. And then the man issued them a small smile, wished them a safe journey, reached into the overhead net, took Theo's suitcase and then left the train, closing the door behind him.

'Oh my God,' Theo whispered to Adèle when he'd gone. There were thankfully few people in the carriage with them.

'How did he know you were the right person?' Adèle asked quietly.

'When you were in the restaurant car he asked me what the weather in New England might be like now.'

'What did you say?'

'I said what I'd been told to say by my contact. I replied, *It's always cold there this time of year.*'

'And then?' Adèle asked.

'And then nothing. He sat down. The next time he spoke again was just now when he took the case.'

Adèle exhaled, looked out the window but the man was long gone, taking the camera and the film onwards to wherever its final destination may be, to do whatever good it might help do in this hateful war. She turned away from the window, picking up the newspaper. On it the man had intricately drawn the French flag, fluttering in an illustrated breeze. Underneath, he'd written the words '*Liberté, égalité, fraternité*'.

One day, France would stand for all of these things again, Adèle thought. One day.

Chapter 17

With Mademoiselle Chanel not due to return from Madrid until the following morning, Theo asked Adèle if she wanted to come back to his apartment. The way he'd asked, shyly, was so different to the exuberant way he'd suggested marriage and a home.

She knew he wasn't asking her back for supper because they'd already eaten a basic meal on the train – what little of it Adèle had been able to eat. There was no part of her that needed to think this through. War forces people to make decisions they wouldn't ordinarily make in peacetime. She knew that. And this was one of those snap decisions, so easily made.

They hailed a velo taxi outside the station to save walking after such a long day of travel and climbed inside the crude open-sided structure, pulled by a man on a bicycle who said very little and that suited them fine. The cost was still as extortionate as a petrol taxi, which was non-existent in wartime. Theo negotiated down only a fraction in that typically confident American manner he had; solid bargaining laced with a kind smile and friendly face. They nestled in together so closely, Adèle's small suitcase across their laps as they wound their way through Paris darkened by blackout; only a few hours remained before the city closed down for curfew.

Theo ran them both a bath to wash off the inevitable grime of travel, using a slab of soap to create lather. While he set about the task, Adèle sat on the settee and breathed in and out deeply, only now aware of all the tension she'd been holding in her shoulders, the nervous headache that had throbbed away gently. She rubbed her temples as she moved her head around, listened to the creaks and groans from the bones in her neck. They could have been killed. Right now they could be in some nondescript office or even moved to a prison cell, held separately, being questioned or tortured for information.

But instead they were here, in Theo's apartment after having done something incredible for the Resistance. They were alive. And they were together.

He moved over to her in the sitting room. 'Bath's ready,' he said and looked at her uncertainly, silently questioning whether she wanted to bathe separately, privately.

She stood, kicked off her shoes, walked towards him and took his hand, leading him to the tub. They undressed each other slowly, inquisitively, each of them looking at the other, running their hands over each other's skin before they bathed together. She should have felt embarrassed but the soap suds covered her and him, for a while, and then when it didn't they were too far gone to care, entwining themselves naked within each other's arms in the warm bath water.

And then he carried her damp body to his bed, placing her down and allowing the sheets and the heat of desire to dry them while they made love for the first time. Every part of her came alive underneath his touch, streaks of silent electricity bolting through her, making her unaware she was bunching the sheet in one hand and grasping the firm skin of his back with the other. At some point during their lovemaking, she'd held him as close as she could and whispered in his ear for the first time, that she loved him, that she wanted him forever and that she would only ever love him.

Afterwards they fell asleep together, their fingers touching as she lay next to him, the sheets around them untucked. She must have been asleep for hours but it felt as if only five minutes had passed when the shrill clang of his alarm clock sounded. He brought his hand down on it and blinked himself awake, smiling groggily at her and then pulling her towards him. She went all too willingly and tucked her head against his chest, letting the stubble on his chin graze her forehead. She was in danger of going back to sleep and he nudged her awake with the magical words: 'Do you want some breakfast?'

She stretched like a cat and pulled the blankets around them. 'No, let's just sleep a little bit more.' She was normally such an early riser but today was different, or at least she felt different. She wanted to stay here all day.

'No,' he said, nudging her awake again. 'Up up up or I'll fall asleep with you.'

She sat up, glanced at the clock. 'There's a little bit of time. Just a small sleep.'

'There's no such thing as a small sleep. We'll still be here at noon if we don't get a move on.'

'I like being in your bed,' she said, stretching.

'I like you being in my bed,' he said as he kissed her, groaned at the obvious lust that fired between them and then forced himself to climb out of bed.

She looked at Theo as he moved around the room, disappeared into his small bathroom and then back towards her again. She watched the muscles on his arms and back work as he pulled on a starched shirt, the tautness of his skin sending her mind somewhere very unladylike.

'What time do you have to be back?' he asked as he pulled on his trousers.

She sighed. 'I've received the hint,' she said. 'I'm moving.'

He laughed. 'This won't be the last time you'll be in my bed,' he said.

'We'll see,' she replied. 'I can hardly sneak out with Mademoiselle returning from Madrid. Who knows when she'll travel again and usually I'm expected to accompany her. This time was clearly different.'

'Clearly,' he replied, fastening his belt.

She got out of bed, searching for her clothes in the bathroom where they'd discarded them last night.

'It's the strangest thing,' Theo said joining her, 'to think I'm helping smuggle pilots into Spain through the most treacherous conditions, all of us at risk of being shot for our individual small parts in it, so many of us work like dogs to get one man through the borders every now and again . . . and Coco Chanel and some German guy are just travelling there so damned easily, legitimately, just so they can . . . do what exactly?'

'She's at the British embassy,' Adèle said and then closed her eyes, feeling a stab of disloyalty.

Theo's hands paused as he shrugged on his shirt. 'The British embassy? You didn't tell me that. With a German?'

Adèle shrugged. 'I'm as confused as you.'

He sat on the edge of the settee, pulling his shoes on, lacing them up but his face was pure confusion.

'That has to be a cover story.'

'A cover story?' Adèle clarified. 'She's lying to me?'

'Maybe. Maybe not. It's so . . . odd.'

Adèle slipped her dress on over her head and began doing up the buttons. She glanced around. Her shoes had to be here somewhere.

'How deep in all of this is she?' he asked seriously.

Adèle shrugged. 'I wish I knew.' But really, she didn't want to know. Not at all.

*

'He's to be freed,' Chanel declared shortly after she returned from Madrid. 'André,' she confirmed her meaning to Adèle, walking towards her assistant in the sitting room of the suite, pulling her hands into hers and clasping them. 'It has been agreed. André is to be freed from his internment.'

Adèle smiled and shared her employer's enthusiasm, joyfully. Adèle did not need to ask whether all the other French soldiers who had been captured as prisoners of war would be freed. Of course they would not be. 'That is incredible news.'

'It is,' Chanel said, her dark curls bobbing on her head. 'He's had tuberculosis. He must be at home. If it is too late . . .' she said and let the sentence hang. What would she do if it was too late? What could she do? Nothing, surely.

Theo was obviously right in his assumption that Chanel was in deep as he'd put it with the Nazis.

'Mademoiselle, it is wonderful news but why have they freed him?'

'It is simple,' Chanel said proudly. 'I had something in my power and they had something in theirs. It was an exchange. Most things in life are an exchange, Adèle. Learn that now. You will not receive anything for free. Someone always wants something of you. And if you have it in your power to give it, and it gets you what you want in return . . . then I recommend you give it.'

Adèle nodded obediently. There was so much she wanted to ask, but couldn't. Instead she remained safe and silent.

The next morning Adèle awoke earlier than usual after a fretful night's sleep. How easily she'd been able to sleep next to Theo. Whereas now she had been alone as usual in bed and hadn't been able to. He was right. She was a different person when she wasn't with Mademoiselle Chanel. Here, in Paris, she was a person she was starting to dislike.

She was up before the sun, which wasn't unusual for December in Paris. Where was the sun shining now in the world, while it waited to cast its benevolent glow on Paris? Was it already on the Pyrénées? She thought of the downed pilot who'd been in Theo's office all those weeks ago, the glimpse she'd had of him, his uniform, the perilous journey he had been about to undertake, the dangerous work Theo was pairing with his medical work. And now of course, his work for the Resistance. They'd not discussed it in his apartment. She very much hoped it was a one-off and that it wasn't set to be a regular occurrence. Her nerves couldn't take it if she thought he was risking his life in even more dangerous ways than he had been so far.

She took the time as she brushed her hair and dressed in a camel-coloured skirt and thick red jersey to think about what it was she and Theo were to each other. It was new, it was heavenly and indulgent in wartime to have fallen in love. Being wrapped around him in bed had felt wonderful, decadent and everything she'd never felt before. And now he was at work and so was she, she craved him body and soul; a fact she found scandalous, fascinating and enjoyable. She knew the relationship needed nurturing, gently as all relationships should, but that choice seemed to have been taken away from them as the frenetic pace of the war had accidentally dictated the growing speed of their romance.

She watered the plants throughout the suite, relishing the chance to nurture life. The housekeeper was forgetting to do this task. There would be hell to pay when Mademoiselle discovered this. While she moved around the apartment with the small silver watering can, filling it from the bathroom, she let her mind take her far away from the suite in the Ritz and back to Theo. Even with nothing else to compare it to, she knew the feelings developing for Theo were real, visceral. The shock and concern she'd felt for him repeatedly donating his own blood, what he was doing behind the lines

239

for the Resistance. She cared. She really did. Hardened as she thought she'd been through life, she didn't know her heart was capable of this jumble of feelings, this mishmash of repeated anxiety for a man she'd only known a few short months. But what months they had been.

Perhaps with time together, precious time spent together when she could get out in the evenings, precious days when she could take a day off, they would learn more about each other. Although she felt she knew all she needed to about the kind of man Theo was. And then over it all there was a sprinkle of guilt . . . while others were dying for their country, while others were attempting such bravery, she knew there was more she could do. But for now she lived right under the noses of prominent Nazis and right under Mademoiselle Chanel's nose.

Time, that's what she needed. She just needed time. Time to work out what she could do, what greater role she could play even through the crushing anxiety she'd felt during the St Nazaire trip, time to fall in love, precious time spent with Theo before the war brought something even more awful their way, even more awful than the Nazis with their green uniforms and jackboots and eating their breakfast only a few floors below in the dining room. And as if she'd accidentally summoned it, news came to take the luxury of time away from her and Theo.

The porter brought up the silver trolley with the various breakfast dishes for Mademoiselle, complete with silver domed lids. She would only pick at her food at the best of times and then smoke a cigarette but breakfast arrived daily nonetheless. A camellia, her favourite flower, was presented in a crystal vase. And on the lower shelf among the pressed linen napkins and cutlery was a newspaper, as always. A thin affair given such paper shortages but the headline screamed at Adèle and it was all she could do not to scream in return.

'I know,' the porter whispered, glancing around to see if anyone could overhear.

Adèle stared at the headline and its accompanying subheading. The Japanese had bombed the US navy base of Pearl Harbor in the state of Hawaii, destroying the entire US Pacific fleet.

'You know what this means, don't you?' he asked joyfully.

Adèle blinked. She both knew and didn't know. It meant nothing. It meant everything.

'It means the Japanese have declared war on America,' he said. 'They'll have no choice but to declare war back. America is entering the war.'

Chapter 18

Mademoiselle Chanel read the newspaper with even more intensity than usual but Adèle couldn't read her expression, couldn't identify that slight flicker of her eyes as she read and reread the text on the front page of *Le Figaro*.

'Hmmm,' was all she said, followed by: 'Well.'

Adèle hovered with the notebook, diary and pen, her fingers toying nervously at the pen lid, screwing it on and unscrewing it repeatedly while waiting for her morning instructions. She knew she'd have to concentrate hard on the activities she'd be asked to complete at her employer's whim, alongside those she was usually expected to.

Adèle wanted to telephone Theo at the hospital, cry in fear that something awful would now happen to him – an American officially now in enemy territory, thanks to the morning's news. But what . . . ? What would happen to him? He'd said nothing would happen, given his position but was that wishful thinking?

'I went through the accounts and ledgers,' Adèle eventually said when Mademoiselle put down the newspaper and looked at her breakfast plate. She picked at her food and then discarded it. The waste. 'I've been updating the expenses. Are there any I should record from your trip?'

'No, it was all taken care of. My bill at the Ritz in Madrid has been settled on my behalf.'

'All of it?'

Mademoiselle nodded.

Perhaps today there would be no further instructions and tasks outside of the usual and Adèle braced herself to pull on her coat and go around to the atelier. 'I will dictate a letter of thanks to the ambassador for a wonderful dinner,' Mademoiselle said. 'It will have to be passed through Baron de Vaufreland's office. But we will do that later.' She glanced down at the newspaper headline again, an expression on her face that Adèle couldn't identify as much as she tried.

'What did you do while I was away?' Mademoiselle asked.

'I've been organising the atelier, I've introduced a better system of filing and I saw Doctor Dixon.' Only part of this was true and Adèle was forced to acknowledge that lying, when she needed to, was getting easier and easier.

'The American?' Mademoiselle asked, as if after a night spent dancing and dining with him not too long ago she had almost forgotten who he was.

'Yes.'

'Your . . . friendship has turned into something more serious?' Mademoiselle asked.

Flashbacks surged in Adèle's mind of lying naked in his arms, his proposal to her underneath the fruit trees in the convent garden. 'Yes, we're serious about each other.'

Mademoiselle nodded and then: 'Not now surely? What will he do? Now America is in the war?' She inched forward in her chair.

What could Adèle say? She could not tell her employer anything – not really. Adèle's lover was helping the Resistance; Chanel's lover was a Nazi. As if the divide between the two women wasn't great enough already.

'I believe he's going to stay and continue working here.

He always maintained he would; that he wouldn't need to leave when America entered the war. Although, I haven't had a chance to speak to him since . . .' She gestured to the newspaper.

'He's always believed they would enter then?' Mademoiselle asked.

'Yes,' Adèle was careful now.

Across the room the fire sputtered in the grate and Adèle moved forward to prod the logs with the poker. The cold December air penetrated the room and Mademoiselle pulled her silk robe closer around her. Making room in the fire, Adèle placed another log on and watched the timber spark and sputter before she returned to the dining table, standing near her employer.

Mademoiselle sighed, looked towards the fire, creased her forehead in consternation, her pencilled-in eyebrows knitting close together. 'How do you think all this will end, Adèle?'

'I don't know,' she replied thoughtfully. 'I want to believe it will end with good triumphing over evil.'

Mademoiselle looked away from the fire, reached towards her coffee cup and sipped her drink, wincing as it had obviously turned cold. 'It's not a fairy story, Adèle. Life is not a fairy story. You know that. I know that.'

'I'm not sure, actually,' Adèle offered after a moment's hesitation. 'I have suffered the death of my wonderful mother; I have lived in an orphanage; I was fed and clothed, given shelter, taught a skill and independence. I was lucky enough to be employed,' she said and she smiled ever so briefly at her employer. 'And you have taught me to be strong and not to wear my heart on my sleeve.'

'It's a habit that needed knocking out of you,' Mademoiselle cut in, her red lips thinned together, no hint of humour in her face or her voice.

'And so,' Adèle persevered, 'I know life is not a fairy

story and good does not always triumph over evil, but we have to pray it will, to try to believe it will and try to make the best of it if it doesn't. To hope. Don't you think?'

Mademoiselle's chin tipped up to look at Adèle, her dark eyes watching her closely, and then she gave a low, deep laugh. 'Life is not determined on hopes and prayers.'

'I know, but—'

'And which side is good and which is evil, Adèle? There is only you, Adèle. There is only you, making choices for you, doing whatever you can for you. No one else is going to look after you. No one else is going to help you when the worst happens. It is always . . . just . . . you.'

The fire crackled and Adèle didn't know how to answer that. She didn't believe that. She didn't believe it would only ever be just that. She wanted life, she wanted love, she wanted freedom. Mademoiselle had all of it, but as Adèle looked at her employer, surrounded by riches and with a few extra lines around her eyes than she'd had when the two had first met, it seemed as if she had none of that. Adèle wondered, not for the first time, if she was truly happy. She never seemed it, despite the riches, decadence, fine clothes, successful business and the apartments in the atelier and in the Ritz, the house in the south; even apparently to be in love and loved by an influential man who seemed only to have eyes for her, who protected her.

But to listen to her it sounded as if she was never quite able to move on from being the girl in the orphanage, the girl who'd clawed her way up, the girl who'd loved and lost and never adjusted to her new life; the girl who was always fighting against something or someone.

Perhaps the things Mademoiselle had wanted for so long had come too late in life for her to fully appreciate them. Or perhaps she'd built up a picture of what it would all be like – achieving everything she'd strived for – and that when she got it, what she perceived to be happiness, it

245

wasn't what she thought it would be. Loving, living, success and riches . . . were they things best discovered and held on to while young and happy, rather than this version of it? Adèle shivered, hoping not to find out the hard way.

'Be careful,' Mademoiselle suggested, her words slicing through Adèle's thoughts. She blushed in self-acknowledgement of the unkind thoughts she'd allowed to drift through her mind.

'About what?'

'About all of it. About him. The absolute last thing you need is a man planting a baby in you and abandoning you to the fates.'

Adèle breathed in sharply. 'That would not happen. He would not do that to me.' As a doctor he'd known how to be careful.

'If you say so. Don't make plans, will you?' Mademoiselle instructed.

'Plans?'

'For after the war. He's American. America has just declared war on Japan . . . and then of course they'll be forced to declare on Germany in due course. What do you think can happen between the two of you now? As of this morning, he's now their enemy.'

And before Adèle could speak again, Mademoiselle Chanel said, 'Be careful is what I am telling you. I can do no more. Now it's up to you.'

Later that afternoon, Adèle was tidying the atelier. How a thin layer of dust had accrued in her absence was beyond her. She'd not been gone that long but it was her job to keep things tidy while the dressmakers were absent. As she used the feather duster to reach into the far corners of the room Adèle wondered when they'd return. Would the same seamstresses be happy to come back years after Mademoiselle had fired them all? Or would they show her they didn't need her, and continue with whatever employment they'd found in the interim if it wasn't war work? They had never hidden from Adèle the fact they all called their employer the fire-breathing dragon.

For the second time, Adèle picked up the telephone and requested the operator connect her to the American Hospital. And then once connected, she asked to be put through to Doctor Theo Dixon. And for the second time he was unavailable. She slammed the receiver down in a rare fit of anger and despair. Where *was* he?

Trying to occupy her mind she tried focusing on the post that had arrived. There was nothing out of the ordinary, thick crested invitation cards proving that life really did go on even throughout a war. Dinner parties were being thrown with black market food and cellars full of wine that people had been lucky enough to stockpile.

She stacked the invitations, ready to run through them with Mademoiselle later that day and only once they'd been given the seal of approval was Adèle allowed to meticulously add the events to the precious diary.

Next came letters from the bank including statements and interest sheets that needed assessing and then filing. And then under it all, the discarded copy of the newspaper that Adèle had been allowed to take with her to the atelier once Mademoiselle had finished with it. The headline still screamed at her. This was it. War had been declared on America and America was responding. Each time she looked at it she hoped to read more, find something that would mean Theo would be fine, would escape any further attention. But as he was an American in Paris she knew that was wishful thinking. So many Americans had fled so early on, fearing this. She fervently wished she'd not invited him to that dinner and dance now. He'd have escaped attention a bit longer. She hoped he was easily forgotten to everyone other than to her.

Mademoiselle's heels sounded on the corridor towards the office and Adèle quickly discarded the newspaper and took up the bank statements, simply in order to look busy.

'Put that down and return to them later,' Mademoiselle commanded. 'There are things I need you to do. Letters you must take to be posted. We must make arrangements for André. Make sure he has everything he needs when he returns to my sister. We must make everything just so, arrange a private nurse . . .' Mademoiselle continued with a list of instructions that Adèle wrote into her ever-present notebook.

She had never had illusions of grandeur and as if she needed any reminder of her place in comparison to Mademoiselle's it was this. Mademoiselle Chanel's nephew was being freed because she was helping the Nazis – collaborating. Adèle tried to squash the inevitable feeling of sickness further down her body, hoping it would reach the floor and she could stamp it away.

She wanted to go to Theo. She wanted to know what he was thinking, what he was planning. An American in Paris, today of all days. The pain of not knowing what he was thinking right now was stabbing at her chest.

'Adèle?' Mademoiselle snapped. 'You are not paying attention. You are daydreaming of your American. You knew this day was coming. We all did. Do not pretend at silliness, at shock.' And then in a softer tone: 'He is a grown man. Whatever befalls him he must take it as a man does. Heaven knows we women take everything thrown at us.'

Chapter 19

Adèle telephoned and telephoned throughout the day but as she reached Theo's secretary Mademoiselle Vachon for the fifth time that afternoon – who informed her yet again that Theo was seeing patients, and that he'd telephone her back when he could – Adèle conceded defeat. Mademoiselle Chanel had taught her never to let a man be her everything but Theo had become Adèle's everything. She both loved this feeling and hated it, wavering now between annoyance with herself and happiness she'd found him – that they'd found each other, like this and at such a time. And this uncertainty was abetted already by the fact Theo was silently resisting the Nazis, putting himself in such danger.

When she closed up the office for the evening she didn't know whether to go directly to the hospital or to trust that the secretary was telling the truth and that Theo was safe, not responding to her calls because he was rushed off his feet, and not because she was lying for any reason. But at the back of Adèle's mind something simply niggled. She couldn't deny it. Theo didn't trust his secretary and now neither did she.

When Theo still hadn't telephoned back by the end of his shift Adèle had climbed into bed in her little servant's box room, mentally exhausted. Her eyes were wide with worried wakefulness and her body so full of nervous tension she got in and out of bed three or four times to adjust her pillow and tuck her blankets back into her small truckle bed. Eventually she climbed out, sat on the edge and stared at the dark skies through the small slanted window under the eaves. Where was he? Why hadn't he returned her telephone call?

The next day Mademoiselle was dining out with Dincklage and Baron de Vaufreland. They were expected at Le Meurice hotel together according to what Adèle had written into the diary and her notebook. Like the Ritz, Le Meurice hotel had been requisitioned to house and feed senior Nazis.

She had tried to telephone Theo only once today. She couldn't face the thought he might accuse her of hounding him. It occurred to her now with a white bolt of fear that they had gone to bed together and now he wasn't returning her calls. And she couldn't face the gossip from the nurses and Theo's secretary's scornful tone telling Adèle for the sixth time that Doctor Dixon was still unavailable. She told herself that was simply a coincidence and that he was too busy, too tired to call her back. And, knowing full well she was risking her sanity and her dignity, after Mademoiselle left, Adèle did something she really didn't want to have to do. She waited until the opportune moment, slipped out of the atelier, hoping her employer wouldn't know she'd left work an hour early, and escaped.

Escaped . . . why did it feel like that? Why did it feel as if her life was so controlled by Mademoiselle? Of course it was. But it had never bothered her before. She ate, she slept, she worked and it would have been that way on a permanent rotation if she hadn't met Theo. Why did Adèle feel like such a culprit for going to see him? She should be working; she knew she should. She should wait until her next day off. It was the right thing to do, the honest thing to do. But Adèle had to know where he was and if he was all right. Visions of him being arrested flashed into her mind, and she hurried on.

As she crossed the road she glimpsed someone she recognised. It was just a glimmer, just a flicker, the edge of a face, the bounce of the hair as the woman walked towards Le Meurice hotel. It took Adèle a moment to recollect the face of Theo's secretary as she walked towards the building. Of course, she might not be going there at all. She might just be heading towards the Jardin des Tuileries for a stroll. Adèle didn't want to waste time. She wanted to see Theo but she couldn't stop herself turning and heading in the wrong direction, following Mademoiselle Vachon. And to Adèle's horror, but not her surprise, she spoke to the sentries on the door of the hotel and waited while one of them went inside. Adèle had seen enough and not wanting to be discovered, should the woman turn while waiting, left in order to find Theo.

Adèle found Theo in the hospital corridor near his office, head down over a set of notes as he walked hurriedly. He was moving so fast he nearly crashed into her but stopped himself just in time, lifted his head, blinked at her briefly and then smiled widely.

Adèle returned his smile and then without caring who saw her, wrapped her arms around him. 'Oh thank God, you're fine.'

He pulled her close, crushing his notes in the process.

'I've seen the newspapers,' she said hurriedly. 'I've been telephoning you.'

'You have?' He stroked her hair, gently, soothingly. 'I didn't know that.'

'I've been leaving messages with your secretary and I think she's had enough so I stopped. I thought you would have telephoned me back by now.'

'I would if I'd known,' he said. 'Perhaps she's put the messages on my desk and I've not seen them yet. I'm so sorry.'

'I just saw her going into Le Meurice,' she said.

Theo frowned. 'Really?' He narrowed his eyes, clearly trying to work out why.

'I was worried,' Adèle confessed. 'America . . . you . . . them . . .' she said in a sentence that made perfect sense to her.

'It was always going to be that way. But don't worry,' he soothed. 'It's all settled. I've been hard at it, making sure we're untouchable here. We fly under the Red Cross flag. The Nazis can't touch us.'

'You're sure?' Adèle said.

'Yes. Honestly. This is the easy bit. Trust me.'

'What's the difficult bit?'

He gave a wry laugh. 'Everything yet to come. Now, listen,' he said, pulling her gently to one side as a porter came past pushing someone in a wheelchair. 'For the next couple of weeks I'm working flat out but I've got Christmas Day off. I take it you have?'

She nodded. Mademoiselle Chanel would be spending an extended time visiting her sister and her nephew, reunited at last after his temporary imprisonment in a POW camp.

'I can't promise turkey or goose with all the trimmings but I do have a few contacts who can get things on the black market and a couple of friendly farmers always seem to be in my medical debt so it's a case of seeing what turns up. So, I think what I'm asking is . . . do you want to spend Christmas with me?'

On Christmas Eve Adèle and Theo dined together, cele-brating *le réveillon de Noël* once they had settled the argument of which day they should celebrate Christmas. They had both won, deciding both Christmas Eve for Adèle and Christmas Day for Theo would be as joyous as possible. They enjoyed a small stuffed capon just big enough for the two of them and made it last both days with various vegetables and some gifted wine. Theo had proudly stuffed the capon himself and Adèle did not even want to know where it came from. Neither did she want to know where the wine came from. She didn't want to conjure up any more guilt than she normally felt for being able to dine so well while much of France was in poverty. On Christmas Eve they danced to jazz together, made love and then wrapped themselves up in his blankets drowsy in each other's arms. The next day they repeated the process.

'I almost forgot,' she said as she detached herself from him in a more lucid moment. 'I bought you a present.' She got up, pulled one of the blankets from the bed, wrapping it around herself as she left the bedroom. She returned clutching the parcel wrapped in brown paper and string.

'You know,' Theo said as she returned and sat on the bed, still wrapped in the scratchy blanket. 'I've seen every inch of you. But you truss yourself up in those covers to stroll around the apartment. Why?' he teased, pulling at the edges of her blanket.

She batted his arm away. 'A woman has to preserve some modesty,' she returned. 'Now be quiet and open your present.'

He took it from her, his fingers working the string open then pulling the brown paper away. She had reused a small scrap of paper she'd saved from the horrid painting that had arrived in Mademoiselle Chanel's suite months before. 'It's a copy of *Peter Pan*,' he declared as he sat up further, hunching over and looking through the book.

'It's second-hand, of course,' Adèle confessed. 'I went to the booksellers with their boxes set up all along the river by the Quai de la Tournelle. And I tried to get one in English for you, to remind you of home. But they only had this in French and so I thought you wouldn't mind. And . . .' she said rambling on, 'you said you had the one about him in a garden—'

'Kensington Gardens,' he reminded her.

'But not the one with Wendy in it. And this is the one with Wendy in it, so the bookseller told me.' Adèle struggled to keep the pride out of her voice at her find. 'And you said it was your favourite.'

Theo leant forward and kissed her, threatening to crush the book in the process. 'It is. I love it. I absolutely love it.'

He turned the book over in his hands, leafing through the pages and the delicate illustrations.

'The boy who never wanted to grow up,' he mused. 'I always wanted to be that boy. For a start, being able to fly. And then not having to grow up, it sounded wonderful. I wanted that to be me when I was young. I wish I could go back to being that boy. Not knowing all this awaited me here. The innocence of youth. It's precious. Once it's gone . . . it's gone forever. But now I've grown up, I can't wait to read it again. Maybe this time I'll see different things in it. Thank you,' he said, kissing her.

And then he slapped his head, laughing, which in turn made Adèle smile. 'What?' she asked. 'What's so funny?'

'So . . . now I feel stupid but . . . hold on.' He stood up, climbed out of bed. Unlike her he didn't feel the need to wrap a blanket around himself and she watched his athletic body as he walked confidently to the other side of his bedroom, retrieved a parcel and returned to her. He sat opposite her and tucked them both underneath his blankets, his small stove in the corner of the room pushed out only minimal heat and now Adèle wasn't nestled against him, her skin was cold with goose bumps.

'Why do you feel stupid?' she asked.

'You'll see.' He handed it to her and she undid the

gummed paper. She breathed in at the beautiful gold lettering on the deep green cloth-covered book. And then she laughed as she read the title. He'd bought her the same book, albeit in English.

'You said you hadn't read it,' he said, laughing. 'And so, I thought . . .'

'I love it. I love you,' she said, climbing onto her knees and wrapping her arms around him, kissing him gently as he returned her words of love. 'Thank you,' she said turning the pages and reading the inscription he'd written inside.

For Adèle, who taught me to fly.

Her fingers brushed over the words and she smiled. 'You have taught me to fly too,' she said and hoped he knew what she meant. She felt guilty she hadn't thought to write an inscription in the copy she'd bought him.

'We could always swap?' he suggested after a beat. 'Then you'll get to read it in French.'

'No,' she said hugging the book close to her. 'I want this one. I want the English one because it's the one you purchased for me. Now I will get to read your favourite childhood book.' It would bring her closer to him, although she didn't want to say something that silly out loud. But she didn't get the chance to say anything else at all as they kissed, made love and their presents to each other fell to the floor.

As 1941 slid darkly and despairingly into 1942, it seemed as if the war would never end – despite the Americans joining the Allies – as Hitler's reach moved effortlessly across Europe and Africa. And with the weather growing even colder Adèle fell easily into a routine, as happy as she and Theo could make it: work, visits to Theo's apartment on her day off each week or in the evenings when Mademoiselle was 'otherwise engaged' with her lover. But over it all hung the cloud of fear of something . . . just something that Adèle could not identify. She knew it would come. But in what form or guise she couldn't say.

If the darkness had shadowed 1941 it was nothing to the horrors that played out in the early months of '42, when the weather lifted so gently that Adèle and Theo had taken to sitting on his rooftop ledge, he with his cigarettes, she with a blanket. She nestled against him as a rooftop view of a Paris she hardly ever saw stretched out into the distance, the Seine and the west side of Paris to one side of them and the Bois de Boulogne gardens to the other. This side of Paris was bathed in the faintest glimmer of moonlight as it reached its silvery beam through the clouds when they passed overhead.

'What's that?' she queried as they looked over the Seine towards a star-shaped walled enclosure. 'I hardly ever ventured into this part of Paris before I met you.'

'Fort Mont-Valérien,' he said darkly.

'And that is?'

'It was once a home to hermits and then it became a fort in the war against the Prussians. But now it's use is for more nefarious means.'

'Such as?'

'It's where they put resisters.'

Adèle looked towards it thoughtfully. 'In order to do what?'

'Question them,' Theo replied. 'Torture them for information. And then when they're done . . .'

'When they're done torturing them . . . is that what you mean? Why have you stopped talking? What do they do when they have finished torturing them?'

Theo inhaled slowly, exhaled even slower. 'Sometimes when I sit on the roof here, forgetting the world and the total horror around me, when Paris is in darkness and silence I'm reminded all too soon of what's out there as I hear the bullets being fired at resisters inside Mont-Valérien.'

'They execute them – in there?'

He nodded.

'I don't know why but I just assumed they would not do that in Paris. That they would take them somewhere else. But it happens right there. I had no idea.'

She pulled her coat around her even closer to help compensate against the dark chill that had wrapped itself around her body.

She needed to change the subject. 'Do you get any word of Mélodie?' Adèle enquired tentatively, still looking at Mont-Valérien with disgust. She thought of the little girl often and what she might be going through. How long after an event such as that would a little child remember? How long before she'd forget her mother? When she was much older would Mélodie ever remember that day Adèle had retrieved her from . . . who knew what? She hoped not. She hoped Mélodie would never remember that.

'Not since the last time I told you, I'm afraid,' Theo replied. 'The family who have her, the Duponts, live in Provins. I have to assume she's still safe. To keep enquiring would draw attention from someone along the lines. They said they'd protect her and I have to believe them,' he said. 'Do you go to the apartment still?' he said suddenly. 'To see if there's any sign of the mother?'

'Yes,' Adèle admitted. 'Every now and again. Sometimes if I think the concierge is milling around I stay hidden and look from the street to see if there is movement at the windows. I only go inside if it looks safe to enter.'

'It's never safe,' he said. 'It's a huge risk.'

'I let myself in so quickly each time and am as quiet as a mouse. But there is never any sign of the mother. Nothing has ever changed. My note I left saying I had tried to help remains where I left it and the dust has settled. I don't even think the concierge dared to go in and steal after the things

I said to him. I don't think anything will change in that apartment, not while this war continues.' She sighed, her shoulders lifting and then dropping. 'But I will keep going there when I can. I just have to see. If there is an opportunity for a mother and her daughter to be together, it cannot be me who separates them.'

'It wasn't you who separated them,' Theo said emphatically. 'It was the war and so many hated offshoots of it. But it wasn't you, Adèle. You did a good thing. Please don't beat yourself up about it again.' His voice slowed as he looked down from the rooftop into the street below. Two men, their brown leather coats giving them away as Gestapo, were positioned across the street, looking up towards Theo's apartment window. If the men looked up a little higher, looked a little closer, they'd see Adèle and Theo on the roof. The darkness protected them, almost.

After a moment, when it was clear the men were not moving but intending to stay put and watch the comings and goings of Theo's apartment block, Adèle said in horror, 'Are they here for you? Are you being watched?'

She looked down to see if the men had noticed the flicker of the match as Theo struck it to light his tobacco. But they seemed not to have done.

Theo sighed. 'Yes. I'm afraid I *am* being watched.'

'Good God, why?' It was such a silly question and Theo's initial answer was to chuckle.

'After what we did in St Nazaire? Why do you think?'

'But they can't know . . . can they?'

'Maybe,' he offered. 'Maybe not. If they knew for certain about any of it, do you think I'd be up here with you or closeted away somewhere having all my fingernails removed or whatever it is they do?'

Adèle breathed in sharply. 'So why are they watching you?' she asked.

'To be sure, I suppose,' Theo said. 'This isn't the first time by the way.'

'No?' She turned sharply and looked at him.

'No. I've seen them. Outside the hospital. When I'm standing at the grocery store. I've stopped receiving black market food from the farmers now. Even the old man out at Dinas Farm, the one who risks his neck hiding Allied pilots has gone quiet. All the Gestapo need is one little offence and we all fall down like a house of cards.'

'Shouldn't we move back a bit? What if they look up?'

'Then they look up,' he said with a shrug. 'And they see two people in love. That's not a crime, last time I checked.'

Adèle didn't know what to say. Until then it had been one of those perfect nights.

'Why haven't you told me you suspected you were being followed?'

'I didn't want to worry you.'

'Well I am worried, Theo. I'm terribly worried.' And then a wave of fear crashed towards her. 'Theo, are you still . . . doing things you shouldn't?'

'Define shouldn't,' he said with a sideways smile.

'Don't joke,' she said. 'You know perfectly well what I mean.'

'I haven't done anything too outrageous,' he said vaguely. 'And if a pilot needs . . . relocating and I can help, then I'm not saying no.'

'But you're not using the hospital to harbour them, are you?'

'Adèle, I have nowhere else to put them sometimes. But no. More often than not they stay out of harm's way near where they fell and we organise for someone in the network to start moving them.'

She was nearly, but not quite, appeased. A knot of tension tied itself deep in her stomach. 'The day America entered the war,' Adèle started, 'I told you I saw your secretary, going into Le Meurice hotel.'

Theo nodded.

Adèle wondered how to phrase the next part and she dallied so long, Theo prompted, 'Is there any more to this story?'

'Not really,' Adèle confessed. 'But you know the Nazis have that building now. Does she have a German lover?'

He looked thoughtful. 'Maybe. I don't know. But . . . they're everywhere. And I don't know what she gets up to when she's not at work.'

'But you still don't trust her?' Adèle helped him along a bit.

'No,' he confessed. 'I guess I should give her the benefit of the doubt. I mean, I'm in love with you and you're forever going in and out of the Ritz and that place is rife with Nazis.' He nudged her delicately.

'That's different,' she said. 'As well you know.'

'Maybe,' he said as he looked over the rooftops. 'Maybe she just likes the company of really athletic blond men in uniform.'

'I don't,' Adèle said petulantly. 'I like athletic dark-haired men in doctor's coats.'

'Thank God,' he said, running a hand through his brown hair.

Adèle looked at her watch. 'It will be curfew soon. I should go.'

'Already? It always feels too soon. Are you angry with me? About . . . you know . . . about still helping the Resistance.'

'I'm not exactly happy,' she replied. 'Please, Theo.'

'Sweetheart,' he said, touching her face in a way that made Adèle's stomach unknot itself ever so gently.

'I know,' she replied, placating. She took a deep breath. 'And now I must walk past them.' She gestured to the men below. 'I will see you the same time next week?' she asked. 'On my next day off?'

'You bet,' he declared but the sound of his voice was drowned out by the sound of aircraft overhead. Paris was no stranger to bomber crews passing over, dropping bombs on the outskirts. The city in all its architectural glory was mercifully no target for the Allies who wanted to preserve the capital city for its French friends in the government when they returned from operating out of exile in London. But tonight the sound of planes was louder, and grew ever more loud as they had their target in their sites.

'You don't think . . . ?' Theo asked, standing, holding Adèle's hands and pulling her to her feet as they stood at the edge of the roof.

'No, of course not,' she replied. 'They wouldn't.'

But they did and in the distance explosion sounded after explosion as bombs fell from the sky and the horizon spread out into a blanket of red fire.

'What are they bombing?' Adèle cried as the drone of bomb after bomb obliterated everything in orange and hell.

Theo put his hands on his head in horror. 'It's the Renault factory. I need to go.'

'Where?' Adèle cried.

'The hospital. We'll take as many as we can and I need to help. I knew this would happen.'

'I'm coming with you,' she said as she scrambled from the rooftop to the door that led inside.

It took only a few minutes of running across the streets of Neuilly to reach the hospital and when she was there Adèle had no idea why she'd come. She wasn't a nurse. What could she do?

Theo kissed her quickly and then instructed her to help him remove bottles of blood from the blood bank. She acted as porter and guardian of the precious red vials, transporting her macabre hoard to doctors and nurses.

Nurse Carmichael arrived and the two of them ran through the corridors with trolleys of supplies. Doctors and nurses were moving swiftly in all directions.

She stood by the door of the ward watching in horror as French civilians were admitted, triaged so quickly it made Adèle's mind whir. For the most part these were ordinary people who had been swept up in the horror of a moonlight raid. She held an old man's hand, his face crinkled in pain as he told her in short, gasping sentences that the bombs had found their target and obliterated the factory. But not only that, the local residential area had also been hit, the RAF not quite finding their mark.

'Once the fire started, the flames, the smoke, the dust, they could not see. They dropped their bombs anyway. Hundreds. Hundreds of planes,' the man gasped. Adèle could not believe it could be so many but later she would find out it was true. The Germans were making thousands of lorries in that factory and the British wanted, needed it stopped. Adèle looked at a trail of blood on the floor as a trolley was wheeled past slowly carrying another victim, this one female and dead. There were no longer enough sheets left to cover the bodies. This one was so burned, Adèle had to look away, closing her eyes tight like a coward. Such casualty, such loss of life. The price being paid for this war was astronomical.

As night turned to morning and doctors and nurses were summoned and called back onto urgent duty, shifts changed but hardly anyone left. Theo came and went, looking tired and dishevelled but his face a picture of calm concentration. In the early hours of the morning, exhausted and feeling useless after helping the porters wheel patients where they needed to be triaged, Adèle leant against the doorframe of Theo's office. He wasn't in there. He wasn't anywhere she could see.

Nurse Carmichael moved down the corridor towards her and Adèle straightened, waiting to be given her next instruction as to what she could fetch and carry to which-ever ward needed it next.

The nurse waved her hand dismissively. 'Go home,' she encouraged. 'It's fine, honestly. You've been such a help. Thank you.'

'It's the very least I could do,' Adèle said. 'I wish I could have done more.'

The nurse leant against the other side of the doorframe, resting her tired body as Adèle resumed her position against hers for the same reason.

'Theo tells me you donated blood again,' Nurse Carmichael said, tapping her apron, looking for something.

Adèle nodded.

'Then you've helped more than you know.' She found what she was looking for and withdrew a cigarette and a small pack of matches. She offered one to Adèle, who shook her head politely.

'Theo's probably saved everyone in this building tonight, the amount of blood he's given,' Adèle replied.

'He's a good man,' the nurse said, replacing her matches once her cigarette was alight. She inhaled slowly. 'I know you know,' she said vaguely.

Adèle nodded, although what she knew was certainly up for debate. Was Theo keeping things from her – to spare her?

'I worry. Nowhere's safe anymore. Not that it ever really was,' Nurse Carmichael continued. 'But . . . recently . . .'

'He's being followed,' Adèle blurted. 'By—'

'You don't need to say it,' the nurse said. 'I know by who. I've seen them. I'm being followed too.'

'No!' Adèle pushed herself from the doorframe and looked at the nurse. 'Did you tell Theo?'

'No,' Nurse Carmichael said. 'I haven't had a chance. It only just started today.' She inhaled on her cigarette. 'Or maybe I only noticed it today,' she said thoughtfully. 'Did he tell you about his telephone call?' Nurse Carmichael asked.

Adèle shook her head.

'A click on the line where there shouldn't have been one, he said.' The nurse smiled grimly.

'Are your contacts . . .' Adèle grasped for a word, looked around the empty corridor just to be sure they were alone. 'Safe? To be trusted?'

'I'm beginning to wonder,' the nurse replied. 'I don't know who they are. I know I shouldn't feel like this but I don't think I want to do this anymore. It's too risky.' The nurse wiped her hand over her eyes. 'I don't want to even be in France anymore,' she said. 'If I can, I think I'm going to try to get home, back to Wisconsin.'

'I can understand that,' Adèle said as the woman's stoicism fell away to tears. Adèle pulled her into a hug, this woman she hardly knew who was risking being shot if she was caught – the same as Theo.

'Nurse Carmichael, what's your first name?' Adèle asked, still holding the woman.

'Margery,' she replied and pulled back to look at Adèle. She collected herself. 'Maybe I'm paranoid,' Margery said eventually, wiping tears from her eyes. Her make-up had streaked down her cheek and Adèle gave her a kind smile and wiped it with a clean handkerchief.

'Don't worry,' Adèle replied but it was a hollow encouragement. Because she realised the moment she'd said it that feeling paranoid when being followed by the Gestapo was very much justified when you're doing something you shouldn't.

From inside Theo's office Adèle telephoned the Ritz, leaving a message to be given to Mademoiselle for when she woke up, telling her what had happened and that she was going to stay at the hospital until curfew lifted in the morning.

She'd intended to sleep under Theo's desk. But, feeling restless, instead she searched the entire building in order to find him. She ventured into the basement hoping he was there as that's often where he said he'd hidden downed pilots safely. But he wasn't. She asked a porter to check in the men's room, which had embarrassed both of them. And then after one final check of the wards, she left as the sun came up and curfew had been lifted.

Instead of returning to the Ritz to wash and dress in fresh clothes and begin her duties she walked, bone-tired, to Theo's apartment. Perhaps he'd gone home to rest. She knew it was unlikely that he'd have left the hospital while people needed him but she had nowhere else to look.

At his apartment she had no shame in knocking for the building concierge, who took in the state of her with astonishment. She had no idea what she looked like but given his expression, she assumed she looked bedraggled and dusty after a night running through hospital corridors. She felt grubby, dirty. After much agonising persuasion he let her into Theo's apartment when there was no answer. He wasn't there.

Everything was exactly as it had been when they'd left to run to the hospital. There had been no sign of his return. Reluctantly and with many thanks, the concierge used his keys to lock Theo's apartment door behind them. The street door banged shut ominously behind her as she walked towards the Metro station and began her return to the Ritz, and to Mademoiselle Chanel.

Mademoiselle was nowhere to be seen when Adèle returned to wash and change. But Adèle's note, dictated to the manager and delivered on crisp headed hotel notepaper had clearly been read. It sat, devoid of its envelope, on Chanel's roll-top desk, among sketches, photographs and fragrance. Adèle hurried through the motions of washing and changing and ran across rue Cambon to the atelier. She wasn't late. But Mademoiselle scrutinised Adèle's face, at the bags whose colour matched her dark eyes.

'Was it very awful?' Mademoiselle asked.

Adèle nodded.

'Did you sleep at all?'

Adèle shook her head. 'No.'

'If you cannot work you are no use to me exhausted. Do whatever you consider urgent, and there is some filing to be done. And then go and sleep,' she said dismissively.

'Thank you, Mademoiselle,' Adèle replied, knowing that until she heard from Theo she would not be able to sleep.

'You have a lunch today,' Adèle said, remembering today's diary appointments. 'With Baron von Dincklage. At Angelique,' she said mentioning one of Mademoiselle's favourite places.

'It is cancelled,' she replied. 'They are all tied up with the events of last night,' she said.

'Yes, of course,' Adèle said, swallowing down a sudden rush of bile that rose to the back of her throat. Of course the Nazis that Mademoiselle had been meeting for lunch were busy. On one side of the war was Theo and his kind and on the other was Dincklage and his creed. It had always been so apparent to Adèle. But today, it felt even more pointed.

When Mademoiselle went to her office, Adèle picked up the telephone at her desk and asked the operator to connect her to the American Hospital. After an age waiting for the hospital operator to connect her to Theo's office, Adèle heard a connecting click and the dreaded tones of Theo's secretary.

'Where is he?' Adèle asked after she'd gone through the formalities of a hasty greeting. 'Please say you've seen him,' Adèle begged.

'Non,' Mademoiselle Vachon replied as if she had better places to be. 'He's gone,' she said. 'Arrested.'

'What?' Adèle exploded. Her stomach had suddenly weighted with lead. 'When? How?'

'During the early hours of this morning,' she said. 'The Gestapo came and took them all.'

'All? Who is all?'

'Two of the doctors and both of their secretaries who must have also been doing something against the Reich. And then a surprising number of nurses. The number they took quite shocked me.'

'Nurses? Who?'

'Many I don't know but a few I do. I believe you are acquainted with Nurse Carmichael?'

'Yes,' Adèle said faintly.

'She was one of them,' Mademoiselle Vachon said. 'Rounded up, taken.'

Adèle sank back into her chair, coiling the telephone cable around her finger until she threatened to cut off all circulation. 'Nurse Carmichael,' Adèle whispered. 'And Theo? You are certain he was taken?'

'Yes. The Gestapo came for all of them.'

Adèle began shaking with fear and cold. 'Where have they taken them?'

'I do not know.'

'You do,' Adèle accused. 'You did it. You had them arrested.'

'Don't be ridiculous.'

'I saw you,' Adèle accused. 'I saw you go into Le Meurice hotel. Why were you there?'

'It's no business of yours. And it isn't as if you can talk. Remind me, where do you live? And with whom? Göring is in your building, is he not? I'm surprised by now that you haven't come to agree with the many of us who know they are going to win the war. Which side do you want to be on?'

'How can you talk like that?' Adèle cried, horrified.

'If I can offer you any advice it is that you do not want to become any more involved than you already are. You cannot help them. They cannot help themselves. Nothing Doctor Dixon and Nurse Carmichael and all the others say now will get them out of the predicament they now find themselves in. They are too far in. And if I am honest, they should not have done it or they wouldn't have ended up being arrested. They are probably already dead. No good comes of resisting. The vast majority of us know this.'

The secretary put the receiver down, leaving Adèle staring at the telephone cord wound round her fingers. And then, it happened. An audible click on the telephone line where there shouldn't have been one.

There was absolutely no reasonable excuse for Adèle to be standing as near to the fort at Mont-Valérien as she did that day. She'd crossed the city and the gardens, had walked past the hospital, not daring to go in, and past Theo's apartment building, looking up from where the Gestapo had stood all those weeks ago and towards the rooftop where she and Theo had last been happy. And then, punishingly, she'd walked across the bridge over the Seine and towards Mont-Valérien, the star-shaped fort that now held what the Nazis considered to be traitors to the Reich.

She remembered Theo's words. That when he tried forgetting the world and the total horror, that he sat on his roof in the darkness and listened to the bullets being fired at resisters, reminding him what was out there.

She had cried, every single day since he had been arrested. So used was she to reining in her emotions, especially when she was with Mademoiselle, Adèle simply couldn't go on any longer like that. She had not expected to grieve so painfully. She had not expected to fall in love so hard. She had not expected him to be taken from her, snatched so cruelly and so swiftly by the Gestapo. He was a good man, had tried so hard to help fight a war, in any way he could and now he had paid the price. 'It wasn't even his war to fight,' Adèle cried into her pillow on so many occasions she had begun repeating it like a mantra of disbelief.

Mademoiselle had given Adèle a few days off on compassionate grounds. Trays of food went untouched and she did not bathe for days, crying over and over again that it wasn't Theo's war, it wasn't Theo's war.

The few days' leave had turned into a week and Mademoiselle was giving Adèle discreet space in which to mourn. But Adèle didn't want to mourn. And couldn't mourn either. *They are probably already dead.*

She knew this was true. From everything Theo had told her about how swiftly the Nazis executed resisters, once they had been tortured for information, she knew he would be dead by now. She had only the memories of their short but wonderful romance, the proposal under the fruit tree, Christmas Day, making love whenever they had the chance. And then on the night of the Renault factory bombing they hadn't even said goodbye. They didn't think they'd have to. That was the last time she'd seen him, running into the abyss of what would be his last few moments on earth before he was taken away.

And now, she was punishing herself, sitting on a bench at the end of the gardens, directly facing the stark brick walls of the fort. Was he in there now? Is that where they buried them when they'd killed them or did they remove them from that awful place, bury them somewhere else? Had Nurse Carmichael been in there, begging for her life? Had they all been in there, beaten and tortured; waiting for more brutality in the hope of a confession and then . . . execution? Had they been led out one after another for a firing squad? Or had they been lined up, stood all together. All this had happened, and she hadn't known. She hadn't even known.

When Theo had said he didn't trust his secretary, why hadn't Adèle pushed it then? Knowing what she knew about Theo and what he'd been doing. When they'd spoken on the rooftop, why had she let the conversation simply drift away from her? But would it have been too late? Hours later he'd been taken from her. And now, he'd gone. Her only friend in this city had become the only man she'd ever loved. And now he was dead.

She wished he'd stopped helping Allied pilots. She wished he hadn't volunteered to go to St Nazaire. She wished so much. And he was probably dead because he wouldn't give up any of his contacts. She knew he wouldn't. He'd rather be executed than do that. Before she knew what was happening, the bile that had threatened to come for weeks rose to her throat and she leant forward and put her head between her legs. But it was too late for everything and Adèle shocked herself and the few near pedestrians passing by the fort by throwing up the only full meal she'd eaten in weeks.

In bed that night, she took out her copy of *Peter Pan* gifted to her by Theo, ran her fingers mournfully over the inscription he'd written in the front of the book.

For Adèle, who taught me to fly.

And then by the light of the dim lamp she began reading. The English words fell through her mind unread, a mash of letters grouped together meaninglessly and slowly, as she readjusted her mind and tried harder, instead of stumbling over some of the more intricate English phrases she formed them into words and then sentences and although she knew it was silly, it made her feel closer to Theo. And the closer she felt, the more she cried. He'd gone as she'd known one day he would. But not like this; ripped from her so suddenly and without warning. Arrested and executed.

Chapter 20

1943

'Have you found anyone to replace your Doctor Dixon?' Mademoiselle Chanel asked a year later in 1943 as the two women sat looking over accounts ledgers for Mademoiselle's personal expenditure. The figure for the month was more than Adèle could fathom.

Adèle gulped down the image of Theo that she'd tried to put from her mind in order to be able to work unhindered. She couldn't hold her employer's gaze and looked away. 'Non.' She took a deep breath. It had been over a year since that night at the hospital. How could she? How could Adèle move on in such a way . . . hunt down a man the way she believed her employer did? She had known him six months. Such a short amount of time – but she had been in love with Theo. They had met through chance, as with most things in life. But would another Theo ever walk into her life again? She didn't want another Theo. She wanted him.

'You really loved him?' Mademoiselle asked.

'Yes,' Adèle said simply as if the weeks and months of grief had not been evident. Perhaps Mademoiselle had no longer wanted to see Adèle's grief and had decided it had all ended. Adèle could not put into words how she had felt about Theo. She would not corrupt his memory by talking about it with Mademoiselle.

'Did you ever find out where he was buried?' Mademoiselle asked.

'Non,' Adèle said through teeth that were cementing themselves together in her skull.

'The only time I met him, he struck me as a little bit hot-headed. Quick to jump but not to think before. Does that sound about right?' Mademoiselle probed insensitively.

'No,' Adèle whispered in strained tones. 'You're wrong. 'You're wrong.'

But without pausing to acknowledge what Adèle had said, Mademoiselle pushed on. 'Of course his position changed the moment America entered the war. He became both a liability and a person of interest.'

Adèle swallowed down tears that stung the back of her throat, the back of her eyes. 'To who?'

'Who do you think?' Mademoiselle Chanel said simply.

'He was a good man,' Adèle replied, trying not to snap. She wanted to be able to say so much more but it felt like a betrayal of his memory and so she kept quiet, her jaw aching for clamping her mouth shut so tightly.

'Perhaps he was too good of a man and that is why he met the end he did. They are an army of shadows, Adèle,' Mademoiselle told her young employee suddenly. 'Did you know that?'

'Who?' Adèle asked

'The Resistance,' she replied. She stood, reached for her cigarettes and lit one effortlessly. Although Adèle noticed as she replaced her lighter that Mademoiselle's hands were shaking. As if sensing Adèle watching her closely, she turned away.

'What should we worry about the Resistance for?' Adèle

asked casually, looking back down to the ledgers and shuffling through the invoices that required paying.

Mademoiselle Chanel inhaled on her cigarette and Adèle watched as plumes of smoke filled the air around her employer. 'Reprisals,' she said simply. 'Reprisals, Adèle. I hear things,' she said. 'Do you listen to Radio Londres?' she asked suddenly.

'Of course not,' Adèle said, sensing she was being lured into a trap. To be caught admitting listening to the Resistance radio being broadcast from London by the Free French did not bear thinking about. 'Do you?'

'No, but of course the Germans do. They listen for every snippet that may be of use. And so . . . the Resistance do things and I hear about it and it interests me.'

'What do they say?' Adèle's interest was piqued now.

'They say there will be reprisals for every collaborator. Did you know that?'

'No,' Adèle said thoughtfully. 'But it does not shock me. I can imagine after everything they've been trying to do for France, those who have acted against France will be punished. It makes sense to me.'

'Does it, Adèle? Does it make sense? Does any of this make sense to you?' she gestured around the ornate, gilded room as if the world was upside down, which Adèle knew it was. Good men were being executed by evil men in an evil war that should never have been started.

'Not really. Everybody is in the fight for survival, in their own way. Their own fight, perhaps.'

'Yes,' Mademoiselle said thoughtfully. 'Perhaps. Their own fight,' she said slowly.

Silence stilled the atelier and Adèle glanced at the clock. It was almost time to pack up for the evening, close the office, switch off the few electric lights brightening the corner in which Adèle worked. Mademoiselle walked towards the window, picking up a heavy gold ashtray as she moved. Slowly, determinedly, she stubbed out the end of the cigarette.

'Adèle, I need you to take down a letter for me before you go.'

Adèle pulled out her notebook, which contained every piece of dialogue of importance, every letter she'd been asked to dictate. She was coming to the end of this particular notebook and must ferret out a new one before she went back across Place Vendôme to her room.

'It is to my dear friend Winston Churchill,' Chanel said.

Adèle's mouth dropped open and she stared at her employer.

'Everybody is in the fight for survival,' Chanel reminded her. 'In their own way.'

Chapter 21

2018

'Two dry martinis please,' Henri asked the bartender.

'Are they all for you, or are you ordering for both of us?' Chloé teased. 'Both of us, of course. It's Bar Hemingway in the Ritz. You *have* to have a dry martini.' Perched on a stool in the small, dark and moody wood-panelled surroundings, Chloé watched the bartender mix both their drinks while she and Henri put the fashion world to rights. Having forgotten she was meeting Henri tonight until his text to remind her, she'd been obliged to buy something suitable to change into at Brigitte's boutique before dashing out of the shop door just after late closing. As a result she was wearing a handmade silk green dress that hugged in all the right places. The addition of a pair of cream sandals set it off nicely. 'Why must it be a dry martini?' she asked. 'Rumour has it that after Paris was liberated, Hemingway sat in here, celebrating and drank fifty-one of these one after the other. Although no one is quite sure of the number.'

'That's some celebration,' Chloé said.

Their cocktails arrived and they clinked glasses gently, careful not to spill any. Chloé sipped. 'Sweet and bitter all at the same time. That is actually the best martini I've ever had. I doubt I could sink fifty-one though.'

Henri shuddered. 'Maybe five?' he laughed. 'Then some dinner.'

Chloé laughed. 'Not a bad plan.'

They talked about the liberation of Paris, which Chloé confessed she didn't know quite enough about. 'But Etienne has given me a book so no doubt I'll get to that bit soon enough.'

Henri gave her a knowing look but said nothing, making Chloé uncomfortable.

'We're just friends,' she said.

'OK. So you haven't seen him recently? Not seeing him again?'

'I've seen you recently and I'm sure I'll see you again and *we're* just friends.'

'Hmm, point taken,' he said watching her carefully. She loved that she and Henri had always remained friends. It was an effortless friendship that had lasted a long time.

'We went to the Louvre and then to this lovely little food market the other day. And then we went to look at archives and . . .'

'Well well well,' Henri said. 'That's a lot of dates since I last saw you.'

'No no,' Chloé protested. 'It was all in one day and . . .' She trailed off. That *had* been a lot to fit in one day with one person. Now she was temporarily thrown from her conversation.

'And?' he nudged.

Chloé glanced around the bar, at the Hemingway memorabilia on the wall, the black and white photos, letters and notes slipped behind glass cases. She chose to focus on the main issue. 'I found something in the archives. About my gran. And I'm not really sure what to make of it.'

'Go on,' he said, looking inquisitive.

She told him about the photograph, Adèle in the ballroom, in discussion with Nazi officers.

Henri muttered a shocked sound that was neither English nor French. 'Have you asked her about it?'

'No,' Chloé said without hesitation.

'Maybe you should.'

'I think I need to get over the shock of it first,' Chloé said.

'What did Etienne say?'

'I didn't tell him.'

'Really?' Henri said. 'Why not?'

'I felt stupid. I felt as if I couldn't. This was my gran. In this very hotel. In a ballroom. With Nazis. I just . . .' She left the sentence unfinished. 'It's so damning.'

'It's not great,' Henri agreed. 'Do you have a copy of the photo?'

'No. I just left it there. On the screen. I didn't request a copy. I didn't snap a copy on my phone. I didn't do anything. I was too stunned. And then we scrolled on and I was desperate to see something else of her, desperate *not* to see something else of her. I have no idea what we looked at after that but there was nothing else relating to her in there. All I could see was that image of her, here, wining and dining and dancing with Nazis.'

'Oh don't say that,' Henri said. 'That's a strange kind of torture if you aren't even going to ask your gran about it.'

'I am going to.'

'Just not yet?' Henri said.

Chloé nodded. 'Just not yet.'

Henri paused before replying. 'So bringing you here today to the place your grandmother lived was perhaps not the best timing?'

Chloé smiled sadly and then shrugged. 'I don't know what to think of anything. Let's just enjoy our drinks and then let's snoop round the hotel.'

The next day in Brigitte's boutique, Chloé had to field questions from an overly interested Brigitte who wanted to know exactly how it was Chloé had two men running around the streets of Paris for her.

'It's not like that,' Chloé said with a laugh. 'Henri's a friend and Etienne's . . .' She wasn't sure what Etienne was. He'd called her a friend but were they actually friends? They were something but it was a very strange kind of friendship. 'Etienne's a bit prickly one moment and then quite funny the next. I can't really work him out.'

'I think he likes you,' Brigitte said.

Chloé scrunched her nose up as she thought. 'Perhaps he does like me. But not like that. I also think he's the kind of man who's got a point he wants to ram home and he's found a willing audience in me.'

'Ooof,' Brigitte said. 'Poor Etienne.'

'Poor Etienne? Hardly. He's a busy man, working, fielding attention from other women and spending his time socialising with me. Lucky Etienne I'd say.'

Brigitte sat back and rocked baby Fabien in her arms with a knowing smile on her face. 'You have told me all about the five martinis you drank. But . . .'

Chloé rubbed her head. 'Don't,' she protested. 'I can't think about those. The bill at the end sobered us up a bit though.'

'I can imagine,' Brigitte agreed. 'But you have not said, did you find any answers at the hotel.'

Chloé shook her head. 'It's been completely refurbished. It's totally unrecognisable. It didn't feel how I imagined it would. If anything, we should have snooped before we went to the bar. Leaving it until the end was anticlimactic. Even the suites were all booked out so we couldn't bribe anyone

278

to let us see where my gran used to sleep even if it does look different now.'

Brigitte nodded sympathetically.

There had been a moment, in the empty ballroom that Chloé and Henri had snuck into where she recognised the layout of tables scattered around the long room, recognised the place where her grandmother had been sitting in the photo, recognised the marble décor. But in truth it had done nothing for Chloé. Instead it had achieved the opposite effect. She'd known immediately there were no answers to be found in the hotel.

'You will have to find other methods to answer your questions,' Brigitte said sagely.

Chloé agreed and went to make them both a coffee before returning to unpack some of the latest items to be sold in the shop. Brigitte had already approved them, costed them up and informed the client how much they could expect when the item had been sold through the boutique. Chloé's job this afternoon was to steam and press the clothes gently and create a display. She also fancied changing the window around a bit and with the bright sunshine working its way into the shop she was hoping to replace the current stock of pastel clothes and accessories that were gracing the window. She asked Brigitte if she minded.

'Do what you like, Chloé. Pretend I am not here.'

'You're not actually *supposed* to be here, remember? You're supposed to be at home, feet up, sleeping while baby sleeps or whatever it is they recommend.'

'I know, I know. It's more fun here, with you,' Brigitte said. 'Talking about fashion and boys. It's like we are twenty again. Besides, I am going mad at home. I have even started to talk to my husband in a baby voice when he gets home from work. To save my sanity and my marriage it's best I am here, with Fabien and with you so I can work, gossip, breastfeed.'

'I'm just worried you'll tire yourself out. But you know yourself best . . .'

'I do. But thank you for your concern. It is not needed. When I begin talking to *you* in a baby voice too, you have permission to be concerned.'

Chloé laughed as she delicately pulled out one of the new items for steaming. She gasped when she saw it. It was a perfect vintage Chanel two-piece pink tweed skirt suit. 'This is timeless,' Chloé said. 'And beautiful.'

'Stop. If you buy anything else you will bankrupt yourself,' Brigitte suggested.

Chloé shook her head. 'Oh no, I won't buy this. It's not really my style, and also it's far too small for me. But it is incredibly elegant. The detail on the pocket, the round neck. Another time. Another place. Another me,' Chloé said wistfully. 'It's funny,' she said, pulling herself together. 'This pink suit looks so similar to the one worn by Jackie Onassis. All those famous photographs.'

'The JFK assassination,' Brigitte offered. 'That pink suit.'

'Yes,' Chloé said slowly. 'What a horrible link.' She shuddered involuntarily.

Brigitte chimed in. 'I only really know about the latter Chanel years. Her comeback, they called it. Post-war. Nothing before the war really. I'm familiar, but not enough to cost up a garment from back then. Before the war is almost antique now. It takes a specialist eye.'

'I'm not sure my grandmother would love to hear the word "antique" associated with the time of her youth.' Chloé laughed.

Brigitte laughed and continued, 'Early vintage Chanel is a rare find. People know the value. They hold on to their items. Keep them tucked away safely. What is it Coco Chanel said? Something about fashion was made to be worn forever? I can't remember. Something like that.'

Chloé felt the urge to look up online whatever quote

Brigitte was trying not to misquote and found it. '*I am against the absurdity of creating fashion that does not last . . . To me old clothes are like old friends . . . You take care of your clothes . . . you repair them.*'

Brigitte nodded. 'Yes, I like that idea.'

Brigitte moved into the back room and Chloé fell quiet as she tumbled into an online rabbit hole of Chanel quotes.

Some were very tight, aggressive, rude, brave. '*Look at those women working in the press who decide what is in fashion. They are fat, ugly and badly dressed.*'

While some were funny. '*An elegant woman should be able to do her groceries without making the housewives laugh. Those who laugh are always in the right.*'

Some were just plain bonkers, outlandish. '*I take refuge in . . . red, because it's the colour of blood and we have so much inside of us that we ought to show a little of it on the outside.*' In some of the more outlandish quotes attributed to Chanel, Chloé sensed the woman had been speaking only because she liked the sound of her own voice.

And other words just made perfect sense: '*It is not the dress who should wear the woman but the woman who should wear the dress.*'

Chloé liked that. She loved clothes but she only ever loved clothes that made her feel comfortable.

And then the last one Chloé read made her shiver. '*Our closest enemies are within us. Those of you who are young, remember that your character traits only teach us their lessons when it is too late.*'

When had Chanel said that? Perhaps she had been speaking in later life, thinking of the misdemeanours a younger version of herself was guilty of. Was she thinking about the war when she'd said that? Or had she been thinking about something else entirely?

With everything Chloé knew about Chanel's background

and how she'd dragged herself out of humble origins, from an orphanage to being a milliner and then to opening her own shops, creating her own perfume, growing her brand, her longevity, Chloé could see how easy it might have been to fall under the Chanel spell. It was so hard to tally up a couturier who worked hard, loved hard against the Nazi secret agent with a Nazi boyfriend and her willingness to run missions for them, although Chloé could, in part, see why she'd been so willing to do all that in order to free her nephew. Family was everything.

As if the universe was agreeing with her, the phone screen changed to show an incoming call from her gran. Chloé swiped to answer with genuine warmth, 'Gran!'

'Hello, darling,' Adèle's voice croaked in English. It was almost as if the French accent had been obliterated through all her years of living in England. Adèle often told her granddaughter that she was so used to speaking English every day of her life, having lived there for so long that she dreamt in English, and she'd always talked to Chloé and Ava in English when they were little that she'd simply carried on. Hearing her gran's voice was like a hug over the airwaves. The two chatted for a few minutes about how well Chloé was settling in Paris, how she was enjoying working in the boutique and if Chloé had made any friends.

'Gran, I'm not eighteen anymore and this isn't my first month at university.'

Adèle chuckled in the background. 'I know. I remember how you chastised me when I asked if the university had provided a lock for the inside of your bedroom door.'

Chloé laughed. 'I don't remember that. It's the sort of thing you'd have asked though.'

'Just because I worry,'

'Ah, Gran, you don't need to worry about me. I'm big enough to take care of myself. And in answer to your question, yes I've made some friends. Well, actually, only one new friend because I knew Henri – do you remember Henri? And Brigitte from before.'

'*Bonjour, la grand-mère de Chloé*,' Brigitte called loudly from the back room on hearing her name mentioned, which sparked a crying fit from baby Fabien.

'Ooo, a baby. How lovely,' Adèle said wistfully after she'd called a long-distance hello back to Brigitte. 'Yes, I remember them. So who is the new friend?'

'He's called Etienne,' Chloé said and then continued before Adèle could speculate. 'Last night Henri and I went to the Ritz for a few drinks,' Chloé admitted.

'The Ritz?' Adèle queried. 'Did you have fun?'

'We did. It's been refurbished since you lived there.'

'I should hope so too.' Adèle chuckled.

If ever there was a time to mention the photograph it was now. And yet . . . she couldn't. She just couldn't. 'And the other day we went to the Chanel shop on rue Cambon.'

There was silence at the end of the line until Chloé said, 'Gran?'

'Did you, my darling?' Adèle asked. 'And what did you think?'

'It's very . . . bright.'

'It wasn't in my day.'

'No I thought as much,' Chloé replied. 'They wouldn't let me see upstairs though, where the offices are. Where you worked. That's where designers work now but I thought it was worth a try,' she rambled, hoping Adèle would volunteer information.

'Oh,' Adèle said quietly. 'Do you know it's been such a long time since I thought about all that.'

'All that?' Chloé asked.

'That place. That time. Her. All of it.'

Her? Chloé waited for more and when Adèle didn't continue she said, 'I saw the staircase.'

'The staircase?'

'The mirrored staircase where Chanel used to sit at the top and watch her fashion shows.'

Adèle simply made a noise, followed by: 'There were no fashion shows during the war. She closed the atelier down for all that. Just me upstairs. And the shop girls downstairs selling accessories and fragrance. War was not a time for fashion, so she said. But it was still a time for expensive fragrance.'

There was no fast way to ask what she wanted to ask. And now she thought about it, she didn't want to ask it after all. Something was amiss. Something. Just quite what, Chloé didn't know. And she didn't know what question to ask to get there. In the background baby Fabien cried loudly and the bell above the door heralded the arrival of a customer.

'Gran,' Chloé said. 'I have to go; a customer's just come in. Can I call you back? Or better still, I've got a day off soon. I thought I might pop back after work one evening on the Eurostar.'

'That sounds lovely. Let me know when you are coming.'

After Chloé helped the customer choose a delicate silk scarf and wrapped up the purchase twenty minutes later and said goodbye, a calm descended on the shop. The contented snores of a freshly fed Fabien sounded from his pram and Brigitte had taken five minutes out to go and fetch them both fresh coffee. Now she had time to reflect while she pottered around the shop and listened out for Fabien, Chloé just couldn't work out what was lingering in her mind. Now she'd dug deeper into Chanel's life during the war years when her grandmother had lived with her . . . there was, in general, something very unusual about the whole situation. Chloé just didn't know what.

Chapter 22

1943

'To my Dear Winston,' the letter had begun. Adèle finished transcribing it into her notebook, praying that Mademoiselle, who was pacing the room, her arms folded tightly across her chest did not see Adèle's hands shaking as the remainder of the words filled the paper. She would type it up momentarily, but for now her own handwriting stared back at her.

'Read it back to me,' Mademoiselle commanded and Adèle did, her voice never once wavering although what she'd just read out . . . was it treason? It was something, certainly.

'Good. Type it up,' Mademoiselle ordered. 'And then you are finished for the evening. What will you do tonight?' she asked conversationally.

Adèle looked up from the typewriter. The ribbon needed changing. 'Nothing. The same as every evening. I will eat, read and then sleep. Ready for tomorrow.'

'Good. Your beauty sleep is important.' Mademoiselle touched her face, tracing down the outline of her high cheekbones careful not to dislodge or smudge the powder. 'It's important for all of us.'

'Yes, Mademoiselle,' Adèle agreed dutifully. Adèle hardly looked at her reflection these days. When day after day sunken eyes stared back at her, it had only served to add to the air of depression that had clung to her since Theo's arrest.

'Mademoiselle?' Adèle began. 'The night of the Renault factory raid. Doctors and nurses were rounded up, taken by the Gestapo. I wondered if you might know . . .'

Mademoiselle waited and Adèle continued, 'I wondered if you might have heard by now where they had been buried.'

Mademoiselle sucked air in through her teeth. 'No. I haven't heard anything. And it is best you don't enquire. Adèle, this isn't a game. War isn't a game. I am sure we have had that conversation more than once. When you have typed up the letter to Winston, give it to me. I will see it reaches its destination.'

'How will it get to him in England?'

Mademoiselle tapped the side of her nose knowingly. 'There are ways,' she said. 'At the start of the war I might have had to fight through hell and high water to get messages from France to the Prime Minister of England. But that was then,' Mademoiselle said. 'And this is now.'

Chapter 23

2018

It took Chloé a long time to decipher the details of what she was reading in Etienne's book.

'What on earth was Coco Chanel mixed up in?' Chloé asked herself after she'd read a particular passage three times and realised she was still none the wiser. She'd rested a bowl of freshly made, piping hot tartiflette on her lap as she tucked in to both it and the book. She'd spent the evening fully immersing herself in a collection of French cookery books she'd treated herself to. They were old, tattered, second, third, possibly fourth-hand but she'd found them when she'd taken herself down to the used booksellers by the Seine. She'd been determined her evening stroll would be productive and that part of broadening her horizons involved French cookery.

She'd made far too much food and while she dished up a portion, her phone dinged, signalling a new message. She tentatively reached for it. The messages from Rob had begun trickling into her phone again and so far Chloé had done her best to ignore them. Each one she read had triggered multiple feelings deep within. On the Quai, listening to the water of the Seine lap steadily against the concrete wall dividing her from the river, she had been looking at the upturned spines of the books held within the crates, thinking about nothing but the feel of a book, enjoying unearthing the magic held between the pages of the covers. While she'd been turning the pages Rob had been sending a quick succession of short, sharp sentences, urging her to respond, checking she was all right, wondering where she was. *I hear you live in Paris now. Is that true? Isn't that a bit of a sudden move?*

How could he? How dare he? She was moving on, without him, and he was doing the same without her. So why was he making contact? There was nothing left to be said, and yet she felt her heart tug a little in the direction of a man who had married her and then had sat back and idly watched their marriage disintegrate to dust. Was he trying to make amends? Did he want to try again? And more importantly, did she?

She didn't know. Perhaps it would be different this time, better? There was only one real way to know and that would be to try again. No, no, no. How had he done this to her? How had she done this to herself? He wasn't suggesting that. He was just messaging her. There had been no hint – or had there? Oh she had no idea. She had to stop tying herself up in knots. Replying now would be an incredibly bad move. But he seemed so interested in her, which was something he hadn't been when they'd jointly discovered their marriage was 'rocky' at best. She needed time to think and couldn't send any responses that even to her would seem rash. She couldn't go back down that path with Rob again. Could she?

She took a big spoonful of the sticky, gooey potato tartiflette while she worked out what to do. The reblochon cheese dribbled down her chin before she scooped it back up again. There were times when the pleasure of living alone and being able to eat unashamedly really came into its own.

She forced herself to focus on the book again, wondering

if this time it would make more sense. Chanel really had been weaving such a sordid web. Chloé reread the details of what the Nazis had code-named Operation Model Hat after the fact Chanel had been a milliner. It was the given code name for Chanel's brief . . . to do what exactly?

The Nazis had hoped Chanel would carry out another mission, this time to give Winston Churchill a message from senior German commanders who were prepared to betray Hitler and who wanted to bring an early end to the war.

This bit was clear enough. But what the book insinuated happened next had stumped Chloé. She looked at the ornate antique clock on the apartment wall. It wasn't late; just past 8 p.m. and so she risked a message to Etienne. Without any preamble she simply asked, *Did Chanel switch sides?*

A moment later Etienne simply typed a question mark. He really was a man of few words.

And then just as she was about to reply, the phone lit up with an incoming call from him.

'I don't understand your question,' he said just as simply without even a *bonjour* as a greeting.

'The book,' Chloé clarified, and then just made a frustrated noise.

'Which bit are you at?'

'The complicated bit.'

At the other end of the line, Etienne laughed. 'It's all complicated,' he offered.

'This bit's bonkers though. Hang on,' she said and retrieved the book. She summarised and at the end when she finally drew breath, Etienne spoke.

'Have you eaten dinner yet?' he asked.

She looked longingly at her barely touched tartiflette. 'Not yet,' she replied failing to see the significance of the question.

'Good,' he replied. 'Come to my apartment. I am in the middle of making beef bourguignon and I have made far too much for one person.'

Chloé wasn't sure what kind of invitation that was.

'Your silence means you have eaten?' he asked.

'Not quite, but . . .'

'Good. I will message you with my address,' he said. '*À bientôt.*'

'À bientôt,' Chloé said and then when the line went dead she laughed out loud as she put the remaining tartiflette in the fridge.

His apartment was in the Marais, close to his gallery. The ultra-sleek interior of the inside of his flat was completely at odds with the historic architecture of the outside. She should have expected this, given his gallery looked similar.

You blow hot and cold, is what she wanted to say to him when he buzzed her into his apartment but instead she said, 'So this is where you live.'

If she'd thought he looked off-duty when they'd met at the Louvre then this version of Etienne was even more pared-back. He was in ripped jeans, barefoot and wearing a black V-neck T-shirt. The whole ensemble had probably set him back a small fortune in order to look so casual.

'Come in,' he said, smiling. 'I realise now that my invite was more of an order. I'm sorry for that.'

'Don't be. I wouldn't have come if I hadn't wanted to,' Chloé said truthfully.

'Good. Wine?'

'Yes please.'

'Red, white?'

'I don't mind. Whatever you're drinking.'

'I'm cooking us beef bourguignon so I'm drinking red.'

'Naturally,' Chloé joked and was pleased to see it raised a smile from Etienne.

'You do like it? Beef bourguignon, I mean,' he asked with a genuine look of concern on his face.

'Yes thanks . . .' Her eyes trailed him as he moved further

into the apartment down a long marble-floored corridor and into a large, sleek kitchen. Brushed metal surfaces and neat, tidy countertops stared back at her. 'You live very tidily.'

He handed her a glass of wine and then confessed, 'I opened a drawer and pushed as much as I could inside just before you arrived.'

She laughed. 'You surprise me,' she said and sipped at her wine.

'Why?'

'I don't know,' she replied thoughtfully. 'You give this impression of being . . . untouchable, otherworldly almost. Far too perfect.'

'Far too perfect?' he said with an eyebrow raised. 'I'm not sure if I should be flattered or . . . offended.'

'I'm not sure either,' Chloé confessed.

He stood, watching her for a moment before he said, 'If I'm untouchable then you're too accessible.'

Chloé almost spluttered on her wine. 'I'm definitely offended by that comment,' she said with a tiny hint of a smile.

'Don't be,' he said. 'It's refreshing.'

'Really?'

He nodded. 'I can ask you anything and you will give me a straight answer. You always say exactly what you think.'

'Not always.'

'Just to me then?' he asked, tipping his head to one side.

Chloé looked at him. His dark eyes returned her gaze. His lips raised in a small start of a smile.

'Not just to you,' she said eventually. 'And there are things I think about you that I don't actually say.'

'I dread to think.' His lips parted and he looked as if he wanted to say something. Instead he sipped his wine and then he said it anyway. 'What kind of things do you think about me but don't actually say?'

She'd walked straight into that trap. Like the *Mona Lisa*

she'd glimpsed with him in the Louvre, it was best to remain enigmatic. 'Things,' she said and before he could question her further: 'What can I do to help with dinner?'

'It's all taken care of,' he said. He leant back against the countertop and suggested she sit on a bar stool. She congratulated herself for climbing on fairly elegantly but hoped dinner was soon. If not, and if she drank too much more wine she was going to have issues getting off the stool. She pushed her glass a little distance from reach across the brushed metal counter.

'I'm afraid you don't get out of that question that easily,' he said, moving towards her and leaning against the counter.

Chloé groaned audibly.

'There it is again,' he said. 'You hide nothing.'

'I'm an open book?' she suggested. 'Entirely readable?'

He shook his head. 'No,' he replied thoughtfully. 'Not entirely readable. Maybe it's bravado.'

'Bravado?'

'Yes. And you . . . what is that English phrase . . . you take the piss . . .' he teased. 'You make a joke. Is it to deflect me?'

'Deflect you?'

'And now you feel awkward so you're answering every question with another question.'

'Am I?'

He laughed but not unkindly. 'See? You cannot help it.'

'Oh shut up,' she teased, going back on her earlier promise to herself and reaching for her wine. Where was this conversation going? She wasn't sure if she was thrilled by it or annoyed. He laughed and sipped his wine and she noticed how he'd stepped closer towards her during their conversation; how close he now was. His Miele oven beeped and he stepped away from her.

'Doesn't it take hours to cook beef bourguignon?' she asked.

'Yes,' he said. 'I've been cooking it for hours.'

'And you're sure there's enough for two of us.'

'I always make too much. I freeze it and then I can have something delicious to eat another day that I haven't had to cook from scratch.'

She looked around his kitchen, at his dinner table, a simple candelabra on the table, candles lit, cutlery and crockery for two laid out and waiting. 'You live very well,' she said, spying a large lit Diptyque Baies candle on a sideboard.

'That was a gift,' he said following her gaze, 'from a girlfriend.'

'Because men don't buy candles?' she suggested.

He laughed. 'This man doesn't. I've owned it for a couple of years and tonight, because you were coming, it is the first time I've lit it.'

'A couple of years. Not from a recent girlfriend then.'

He laughed. 'Non. Let's eat,' he said as he carried over two plates of food.

She sat down and picked up her cutlery. 'Bon appetit.'

'Bon appetit,' he said. He fiddled with his phone and jazz music suddenly sounded on a speaker system.

Too perfect, she thought.

And then he cursed himself, apologised, got up to the counter, retrieved their wine glasses, then got up again and went back for the bottle. Not too perfect after all.

'That's an offensive amount of money,' Chloé said after Etienne had opened a second bottle of wine and presented a cheese course. That Etienne had even offered three varieties of cheese to finish their meal sent her thinking he was too picture-perfect again. She wished he'd given her warning there was more food coming; she'd stuffed herself on the main course and it was mopping up the wine deliciously.

'Why is it offensive?' he asked. He too was sitting back in his dining chair toying with the stem of his glass. Like

293

her he was ignoring the cheeseboard he'd just artfully assembled.

'You made *that* much money from pictures of couples . . . at it?'

'But why is it offensive?'

'I'm not sure,' she confessed. 'I think I'm just shocked and it's the first thing that entered my head.' And then: 'I'm in the wrong job.'

'Are you?'

'No, not really. I quite like what I do, actually. Although I don't really do that anymore. But I'm happy now,' she finished. 'Actually I'm *happier* now.'

'Then that is the main thing,' he said. 'Truly. Happiness is the main thing.'

'Yes, it is.' She nodded, agreeing. 'How long have you lived on your own?' she asked. The wine had made her brave.

'A long time,' he said, narrowing his eyes.

'Does no woman match up to the exacting standards of Etienne Vaillancourt?'

He blinked. 'Is that what you think of me?'

She didn't know how to reply. 'Sorry,' she said. 'That was a bit rude. I didn't mean to offend.'

He shrugged, leant forward and topped up both their wine glasses. 'I'm not offended,' he said eventually. 'Just curious. Honestly, is that what you think of me?'

'You seem to like things the way you like things. You have opinions and you're not afraid to voice them.'

'Excuse me . . . you are the same.'

'Yes, all right. I thought we were talking about you though.'

He laughed. 'Carry on,' he said. 'What else is wrong with me?'

'Oh God,' Chloé groaned. 'Why are we doing this?'

'Because I'm curious. I believe you are unbiased. You have nothing to win or lose by telling me this. Also, it's very rare a woman points out what is wrong with me while not actually breaking up with me.'

'Oh dear,' Chloé said and reached for her wine. 'Have you had bad experiences?' And feeling even braver, she teased, 'Do you get dumped a lot?'

He shrugged and then smiled. 'I wouldn't say a lot.'

'What would you say?' Chloé leant forward and placed her elbows on the table, analysing him.

'Do *you* get dumped a lot?' he asked her.

Chloé straightened up, fiddled with her wine glass, reached silently for a grape from the cheeseboard even though she didn't really want it.

Etienne looked as awkward as she did. 'Sorry,' he said genuinely. 'I thought we were playing a game. I didn't mean to upset you.'

'No,' Chloé said. 'It's a fair question. After all, I asked the same of you.' Chloé thought about how to phrase it, aware that she was sobering up steadily the more she thought about her most recent romantic encounter.

'I'm divorced,' she said, realising after she'd said it that it hadn't exactly answered his question. 'Quite recently divorced, I guess you could say.'

Etienne's gaze homed in on her. 'Really?' he asked.

She nodded, reached for another grape for something to do and then put it on the edge of her plate. She couldn't eat anything else. 'Yes. I suppose you could say it was mutual. We were just . . . wrong for each other. But the warning signs were there long before we got married. I just wasn't clever enough to see them.'

He nodded. 'That's often the way. My parents are divorced,' he said. 'They should have divorced long before. There was no real catalyst – it had just been a long time coming.'

Chloé nodded. 'Yes, that sounds like Rob and I.'

'Rob,' Etienne repeated. 'And it ended badly?'

'It ended in divorce, Etienne,' Chloé said with a half-smile. 'So yes, I'd say pretty badly.'

'You know what I mean,' Etienne clarified. 'Nastily?'

Chloé thought, shook her head. 'No. It ended the way it started, really. Without sparks or fireworks. I'm always grateful we didn't have children. Now we're divorced the tie between us is well and truly cut,' she said. And then she remembered the host of messages from Rob she had waiting for her to respond to on her phone. She shook them out of her mind. She didn't want to think about it, didn't want to talk about it.

'Then,' Etienne said, 'he is out of your life and you can start again.'

Chloé looked up from the forlorn grape sitting on the side of her plate and at him. 'Yes,' she said. It was a shame she wasn't as certain as she sounded.

'Do . . . you have a boyfriend now?' he asked slowly.

'No,' she replied. An air of quiet fell across the room.

'So tell me which is the bit of the book you did not understand?' Etienne said and Chloé was grateful he'd changed the subject.

'Hang on a sec,' she said. 'I brought it with me.' Chloé retrieved her bag from where she'd placed it by the bar stool.

She returned, found the page and opened it up. 'It's all this,' she said, gesturing to the text. 'Chanel's meant to be running this complex-sounding mission to get a letter into Churchill's hands, via the British ambassador in Madrid.' Chloé paused for breath. 'But instead, she hires her British friend Vera Lombardi to go with her, who at the time was living in Italy because she'd been accused of being a German spy.'

'So far so simple,' Etienne deadpanned.

'It really isn't,' Chloé said. 'But then there's a whole bunch of stuff I don't really understand about how the two women's accounts differ as to how Vera Lombardi came to be wrapped up in all of this, but to cut a long story short, when they arrive at the British embassy, presumably letter in hand and ready to push the stop button on the war, Vera Lombardi shouts from the rooftops that Chanel is a spy for the Axis and all hell breaks loose.'

Etienne laughed. 'I can see why you are confused. But no, all hell didn't break loose. Quite the opposite in fact. The British embassy didn't seem to take Lombardi seriously. There was no proof.'

'What happened to the letter?'

'That is a very good question,' Etienne said.

'Everything goes conveniently missing doesn't it?' Chloé offered.

Etienne shrugged. 'It does seem to.'

'What happened to Vera Lombardi?'

'She remained in Madrid, neither able to travel back to Britain or back to her home in Italy until eventually Churchill intervened and she went back to Italy in 1945.'

Chloé's brow furrowed. 'And what happened to Chanel? Surely this was it; this was a close friend betraying her, telling the world she was a Nazi spy. It's out in the open now. So what happened to her?'

'Nothing.'

Chloé stared at Etienne. 'Nothing at all?'

'No. With no actual proof to substantiate Lombardi's claim, she was able to play both sides against each other. Remember, she had been a close friend of Churchill. And she was sleeping with the enemy. How she managed to get out of this particular sticky situation is anyone's guess.'

'See, this is why I asked if she'd switched sides. She was helping Nazis who wanted to betray Hitler, who wanted to bring about an early end to the war. I'm not really sure I understand why.'

'At some point there were senior Nazis who knew the game was up. That with the Allies growing ever stronger and with the arrival of the Americans, the Nazis needed someone with close connections to Churchill. Someone they could use to begin negotiations. And of course, to save themselves from further harm when the Allies eventually got hold of them. Enter Chanel.'

'Seedy. But I suppose a good thing, if it had worked.'

'Which it did not. And so the war rumbled on into the next year and lives continued to be lost.'

Etienne topped up their wine glasses with the remainder of the bottle.

'I wonder if my gran knew any of this was happening. I mean, I always thought she was too much of an underling – although don't let her hear me say that – to play any great part in the rise and fall; or perhaps the rise and rise of Chanel. But she must have known about all of this.'

'Why would she?'

Chloé stalled before responding and then realised she had to tell Etienne. She wanted to tell him. 'I haven't been very honest with you. When we were in the archives, the picture showing the Nazis in the ballroom and the women in beautiful dresses, eating, drinking, dancing with them . . .'

'Yes?' he asked.

'My gran's in that picture.'

'What?' he spluttered.

'Sat at a table, deep in conversation.'

'Are you sure it's her?' he asked.

'Sadly, yes. Dining with Nazis,' Chloé tortured herself by saying aloud.

Etienne put his chin in his hand and watched Chloé, waiting for more of her thoughts. But she didn't know what to think. Not yet.

'Not many people knew what was happening behind the scenes,' Etienne said. Chloé appreciated that now he was playing devil's advocate again. 'And those who did mostly kept quiet.'

'Not Vera Lombardi,' Chloé said wryly.

Etienne laughed. 'No. Not her.' He looked at her sympathetically, as if understanding her plight, her confusion, her inability to get to the truth.

'After we were at the Château de Vincennes, I called my friend Claude.'

'The curator?'

He nodded. 'We met for drinks last night and caught up. He told me they'd found other things in the files relating to Chanel. Do you want to know what he said?'

'I don't know,' Chloé said, honestly. 'Will I *want* to hear them?'

'It depends. He told me, towards the end of the war Chanel went to Berlin.'

Chloé listened. 'OK.'

'Not once, but twice. Once with her lover and then once with a man who was much higher up. His name was Schellenberg. They went to meet with Heinrich Himmler, the leader of the SS and the main person responsible for the Holocaust. SS records show that a large sum of money was to be sent to Chanel at this time.'

A breath escaped Chloé. 'Oh my God. That's . . .'

'Awful,' Etienne said. 'It's all just awful.'

Chloé nodded. 'It really is. But why go? Twice? This is why I asked if she'd switched sides, if she was trying to help.'

'I think if she had been trying to help it was for her own gain, hence the money. And also, peace negotiations wouldn't have been the kind of peace the world actually saw after the war was won. It wouldn't have been Nazi surrender. It would have been peace on a different kind of scale, one that would have left a bad taste in the mouth, one that didn't see the Nuremberg war trials punish those who needed punishing, one that saw the Germans still wielding a level of power in some quarters. I don't think the world would have been ready for the kind of peace that came from anything Chanel was helping orchestrate. It would have been an imitation of peace.'

'That's horrible.' After a pause, Chloé said, 'I suppose it's a good thing Churchill never listened to Chanel then.'

'They were due to meet, Chanel and Churchill. But he didn't show up.'

Chloé inched to the edge of her seat. 'Churchill knew better?'

Etienne smiled. 'Something like that. He was apparently too tired from one of his trips to stop in and see his old friend Chanel.'

'Knew he was about to get played, probably,' Chloé said.

'I'm not sure history would ever say Churchill "got played",' Etienne teased.

'Exactly,' Chloé offered.

They sipped their wine. 'What a tangled life she led.'

Etienne smiled. 'And that's just the war years,' he said.

'Stop!' Chloé protested, a bubble of laughter rising to the surface. 'I can't take any more.'

A companionable silence drifted across them, settled in gently as Etienne sipped his wine and Chloé made a valiant attempt to nibble some of the cheese he'd made an effort to present.

'It is my turn to tell you that I haven't been particularly honest with you,' he surprised her by saying.

Chloé's head lifted. 'In what way?' she asked tentatively.

'My reasons for . . . disapproving of Chanel stem from so many directions.'

Chloé waited, the piece of brie she was about to eat now discarded on her plate alongside a small pile of grapes.

'My grandmother and my great-aunt were . . .' he paused '. . . victims of reprisals, because of their . . . The official term is collaboration.'

Chloé stopped breathing. 'Really?'

He nodded. 'I already told you my grandmother was a

seamstress for Chanel. And after she was fired, along with all the other seamstresses when war broke out, no one was hiring seamstresses. No one was hiring anyone, for any job really. It was dire at the start of the war and then by the end of the war it was . . . hell. That's how my grandmother described it. Food became scarcer and scarcer until the best meal my grandmother ate was an injured pigeon that they roasted. A street pigeon. The only way they could catch it was because its wing had somehow broken. Before, the sisters would have tried to help it, make it fly. But they were so hungry they cooked it. It was the only meat they'd managed to get in weeks and weeks. They had hung on for so long, just the two of them and their mother – my great-grand-mother. But the war had made her old before her time and she was already widowed. There was no money coming in, and even if there had been, there was no food to purchase. And so that's when the sisters made a decision. Life or death, survival or defeat.'

'What did they do?' Chloé asked almost breathlessly.

'They took up with enemy soldiers. There was no glamour attached to it; the men were not officers. They were just regular foot soldiers. And they gave them rations. My grand-mother was always very honest about what she'd had to do and why. It was a form of prostitution.'

'Good God,' Chloé said and then wished she hadn't. Sleeping with a man in exchange for things you need. Was that prostitution or desperation during a time of war? Or both? Chloé was grateful she'd never been placed in such a desperate situation. Who knew what she would have done in order to protect herself, her mother and Ava. But how would she have reacted if Ava had done the same thing? She couldn't know. She couldn't compare her own experiences of life to a time such as Occupation.

Etienne continued. 'My grandmother said that she did it because she needed to keep her sister and her mother alive and that if she'd been on her own she would have rather let death take her. She didn't love the soldier she took up with. And then her sister did the same thing and she didn't have the energy to fight her. They needed every little ration they could get hold of to share between the three of them. They played their part, did what they had to do and in exchange they were fed a little better . . . a few extra potatoes, a whole head of cauliflower fresh from a field rather than blackened with age.

'And so,' he continued. 'My anger for Chanel and people like her, people who played the game, the system, people who really got away with living so well, with escalating their position even higher than it had been in peacetime by immediately ingratiating themselves with the enemy, by not even trying to resist . . .' He trailed off, collected himself, started again. 'And Chanel had already been living so well that she hadn't even needed to do any of this. She chose to.

'And women such as my grandmother,' he continued. 'Their choice was either to starve or prostitute themselves; because by this point in the war they were the only options open to them. So I wonder, sometimes, if Chanel hadn't closed her atelier, if she'd chosen to continue – because there was no real reason to close; other designers in Paris continued on – whether my grandmother would have lived a very different life, had a very different war, all because of a job. Because what happened to her at the end of the war as a result of sleeping with the enemy . . .' He went quiet again.

'What happened to her?' Chloé prompted.

'She was punished. She and her sister together. Dragged into the streets, clothes ripped from their bodies to humiliate them, their heads shaved, swastikas drawn on them.'

'By who?' Chloé asked in horror.

'By their own neighbours. Sham trials, show trials. It was the age of reprisals.'

'That's one of the most awful things I've ever heard.'

302

'There is collaboration and there is collaboration,' he said, the anger rising in his voice. 'It takes all forms. They are called the same thing but the spectrum is wide. But to find out what my own grandmother had to endure and what she did to survive and then finding that the woman who had fired her had carried on with her life without a backward glance as to how those who'd been under her care had gone on trying to survive. And that Chanel hadn't even needed to live in such a way; hadn't actually needed to join their ilk. She was financially well off enough to keep out of it. For her it was choice. But for others they were stripped of their choice, their dignity. I'm bitter, I will admit to that,' he said. And then a moment later: 'Sorry . . . I am starting to rant.'

'It's fine,' Chloé said, reaching out to touch his hand. He looked down at it, his gaze soft. 'You're not ranting,' she said. 'You're angry.'

'All this time later. And I wasn't even there,' he said as if he was mad.

'I think I'd be angry too if I found out things about my gran that I didn't like,' Chloé said thoughtfully. 'I'm going home to see her and I'm scared to ask what she did or didn't do. I'm scared to know how she lived so well, how she survived the Occupation relatively unscathed. I'm scared to know what she went through. But ultimately, I *want* to know. Family history is there to be discovered.' She withdrew her hand from his and he looked surprised, as if it was the most normal thing in the world for her to have been touching his hand.

He recovered himself, nodded. 'It's such a shame *not* to know your family history when you actually have people who have lived it and can tell you. When they have passed away, and when there's no one left to ask, the stories die.'

Chloé agreed but at the front of her mind was how she could talk to her gran without upsetting her, how she could lead her mind back to that time and that place without it distressing her. She could only try. Would it bring her closer to her gran, or would it put distance between them?

As the jazz music came to the end of its run, Etienne picked up his phone to switch the album.

'It's late,' Chloé said softly, rising. 'I should go.'

Etienne stood. 'Can I phone for a taxi?'

'No, I'll grab the Metro. But thanks.'

Etienne nodded and stood while she gathered her things. 'Thank you for coming,' he said.

'Thank you for inviting me. And for the lovely dinner. It was heaven.'

'It's nice to have someone here, to share a meal with,' Etienne confessed. 'I can't remember the last time I did.'

'I'll have to return the favour. I make a pretty mean tartiflette.'

Etienne walked her to the door, holding it open for her. 'I would like that.'

'Goodnight, Etienne,' Chloé said as she turned away and started to descend the staircase.

'Goodnight. And, Chloé, will you message me when you've returned home so I know you are safe?'

Chloé looked up the stairs towards him and wondered if he'd become more attractive over the last few hours. She nodded. 'Sleep well, Etienne.'

Chapter 24

1943

'Did your trip go well?' Adèle asked as Mademoiselle Chanel entered the suite one evening. Adèle had not expected her back so soon and rushed to greet her, and to supervise the hotel staff as they brought her suitcases inside.

Mademoiselle chose not to reply and Adèle didn't push the matter. She knew this mood. It was clear everything had not gone as expected.

'I'll begin unpacking, Mademoiselle.' She gestured for the bellboys to take the luggage through to the bedroom. She unpacked her employer's delicate items, placing them on the silk padded hangers in the wardrobe, putting aside those that needed laundering. This had become a large part of her job now – organising laundry, being a general maid of all works. She'd been accepting of it at the start of the war when she'd been grateful for the employment. But as she picked up underclothes for laundering out of the trunk, Adèle wondered if it was all worth it now.

'Shall I call for some coffee?'

'Yes, Adèle.'

Adèle used the telephone to dial down to the kitchen

with her request. There was one cup when it arrived and she poured for her employer. There was no request forthcoming for Adèle to join Mademoiselle. And Adèle found she didn't actually want to. After listening to her dictate that letter to Churchill, Adèle now didn't know what to think, what to feel. She was torn. What kind of woman was Mademoiselle? She'd been a complete juxtaposition for the past few years. Hot, cold, kind, ruthless, gentle, abrasive.

Having Theo in her life for those brief months had placed a wonderfully bright light over the darkness of her days. But now the darkness was getting darker. Being here was getting worse. Adèle couldn't smile anymore, couldn't see the hope in anything. When would this war end? *Would* this war end? Ever? It had to at some point. And if Mademoiselle's letter hadn't been delivered . . . then would it just drag on and on, taking them all down with it? The Nazis would persevere until the dying end, not caring what happened to the citizens of Paris in the interim.

Adèle turned away. She was in danger of crying in front of Mademoiselle and that would not do at all. 'I have unpacked and—'

'You did not need to do it now. You could have done it tomorrow, Adèle. Besides,' she said with a tired sigh, 'I am travelling again soon so you will need to repack for me.'

'Again?' Adèle couldn't keep the shock from her voice.

Mademoiselle Chanel closed her eyes, tipped her head back. 'They want me to help end the war,' she said.

Adèle's mouth dropped open. Was this a good thing? The end of the war was a good thing surely?

'I can see what you are thinking, Adèle. We all have our part to play.'

Mademoiselle looked at the coffee table, ran her hand along it and then rubbed her fingers together to dispel the dust. 'Where is the housekeeper?'

'She'll be back tomorrow as usual. Perhaps she has missed a spot.'

'You're supposed to be keeping a watch on the running of my household while I'm gone,' Mademoiselle chastised.

'I apologise,' Adèle said. 'I did not notice anything amiss.'

'What have you been doing while I've been gone, Adèle? Presumably you've not had enough to fill your days?'

'I've taken to helping the women in the boutique some afternoons.'

'Why are you helping in the boutique?'

'I like to be useful. To help the shop girls. I have not had anyone to talk to in quite some time.'

'But that is not your job, Adèle.'

Adèle looked down.

'You may go.'

'Yes, Mademoiselle.' Never had she felt so lonely as she did now.

In the morning, after serving Mademoiselle Chanel her breakfast in bed, Adèle walked round to rue Cambon and entered the atelier, greeting the shop girls with as much warmth as she could muster and climbing the mirrored staircase to the office. She sat in the chair, adjusted her pencils, entering them mindlessly one by one into the sharpener and winding them through. She took out her new notebook from her bag and looked through the scant details of the work she'd carried out since she switched notebooks. She pulled out the old one from her top drawer, and the one before that. A complete record of every task she'd carried out for Mademoiselle Chanel. Simple words on a page, but not so simple as to be innocent.

Actually what these notebooks contained was salacious. The communication to the lawyers and the Nazis, attempting to Aryanise her business – to seize control of the business from the Wertheimers, the letters to and from people who

307

would only ever be classed enemies of the Allies, dictation of letters to and from Vera Lombardi, and then the letter to Churchill. And so much more, for years, to and from senior Nazis, the offers of assistance in exchange for the release of her nephew André. These notebooks were condemnation. Reprisals. Is that what would happen to them all?

Adèle had been part of it too, even in such a small way. She had dined at the Ritz that night with Mademoiselle and her Nazi friends. Was that considered collaboration? It was hardly considered resistance.

She had tried to help the resisters when she'd accompanied Theo to St Nazaire, but that had been because he had been planning to go. It wasn't because she had taken any initiative and had formed a plan. No. She had been useless in this war. Theo had been everything that was good and kind, and he had known it might bring about his demise. That it actually had, even after all their discussions about it, had destroyed Adèle. She knew that now. There was nothing she could do to bring him back. He was lost to her. Gone forever. She was a different person because of him and now she was different without him.

But there was something she could do that would make him proud of her, make her proud of herself. There was something she could do to help the war effort. And if she did, it would be the best thing she had ever done.

But it would also be the worst.

Chapter 25

It wasn't too far out of the city before she reached the farmland that Theo had described to her all those months ago. She had borrowed a precious bicycle from the Ritz and ridden out towards the farm near Versailles. It had surprised her, really, how close arable land was to France's capital. She had no access to a map, so rare in wartime, and so she only really had Theo's description of the farmer and his land as well as his general location to go on. With summer having settled in to Paris the day was stiflingly warm and she'd been cycling for so long, which didn't help. Adèle took off her jacket and draped it over the crook of her arm.

She looked at the name on the plaque: *Ferme Dinas*. This was it. This man, this farmer, was the last link between her and Theo. He knew how to get in touch with the Resistance. He was one of them. As Theo had been. Once she'd carried out this task, there was very little else she could do for the war. Even now, it felt like such a betrayal. But it had to be done. These notebooks contained so much to bring down a multitude of people. They contained evidence of so much of everything that was wrong with this world, so much hate, so much condemnation, so many wrongdoings: Mademoiselle's communications, comings and goings in wartime. Her letters, her connections, the missions she'd carried out for the Nazis. If these books fell into the wrong hands . . . which of course they were about to. But was it the wrong hands, or the right hands?

War isn't a game, Adèle.

By helping downed airmen, this farmer, like Theo, like Margery Carmichael and all the others who'd been arrested and been part of the regular execution of resisters, had risked so much, had risked their lives to help so many people. If she could do anything to help the fight for freedom, she would. And it started here. It started with handing these notebooks over to the Resistance. To help with the evidence they would need when the Allies eventually came, when the liberation of occupied Europe eventually started. Because it had to start soon. It just had to.

Adèle only had this one thing in her power and she would use it. The man looked towards her, taking off his cap and greeting her uncertainly. Adèle walked towards the farmer, raised her hand in greeting and said, 'Bonjour, Monsieur.'

It was now or never.

Chapter 26

2018

A few days later the Eurostar raced through the French countryside, leaving Chloé with plenty of time to relax into her evening on board. She'd already stockpiled a selection of nibbles from the on-board buffet and treated herself to a miniature bottle of Champagne. She felt Etienne would approve and she'd replied to an earlier message he'd sent wishing her a good trip with a picture of the Champagne flute brimming with the delicious pale straw-coloured bubbles.

They'd been texting more frequently since the dinner in his apartment, getting to know each other in a very low-pressured, slow way. They had no expectations from each other. They were talking, enjoying each other's company and then he'd surprised her by telling her something she'd said had reminded him of a joke and when the punch line came it was dirtier than she'd expected and it sent her interest in this handsome, often hard-to-read Frenchman off the chart.

She sipped her Champagne. This small-scale luxury wasn't quite in line with the traditional concept of a gap year but then Chloé was finding nothing about this new life fitted how she'd thought it would be. She was living, she was happy, she was giving herself permission to be herself, to enjoy herself, to flirt a little, to be silly when she wanted to be, to just be. She realised this was who she was and that she'd been hiding most of these traits when she'd been with Rob.

But through it all there was a nagging feeling of unfinished business with her ex-husband that Chloé needed to deal with. The messages hadn't stopped and, Chloé realised, nor were they going to if she didn't put a stop to them. How was she ever going to move on, with Rob in the background pulling the puppet strings?

Back when they'd been married, and even before they had got engaged, she would message Rob casually throughout the day just seeing how he was, sending him a funny picture or asking him what he fancied for dinner because she was passing a food shop on her way home from work and . . . nothing. No reply. Not for hours. Or even the same day. It had grated on her then and was one of the main reasons Chloé had known he wasn't the man for her. That she had gone on to marry him spoke volumes about the obviously desperate person she'd once been.

But not anymore. She wouldn't be that person again. It was no good thinking someone would change. You had to accept them for the way they were. And now she found herself comparing him to Etienne. She didn't want to change him. She liked him just the way he was. He surprised her, made her laugh. He wasn't a foregone conclusion. There were perfections and imperfections. There was more beneath the surface she wanted to get to know.

For the first time since the swathes of messages from Rob began and then picked up at a relentless pace, Chloé had not hair-triggered a reply, had not embroiled herself in a discussion with Rob that she might not have been able to get out of quickly enough. Instead she'd used the time to think. She liked the new version of herself, or maybe it was the old pre-Rob version that had just come to the fore to surprise her, the version of herself she'd suppressed during her marriage. Either way, this version of Chloé knew what she needed to do.

Hi, she messaged.

The screen flickered to show Rob was online, but not typing. Just waiting. Was he waiting hopefully, curiously, or with a smile on his face that he might have won, that his chase had paid off and his ex-wife was playing into his hands? He'd chased harder now than he'd ever done when they'd actually been married.

He'd never been malicious . . . just uninterested. Now Chloé had found a new life, a new situation, he wanted what he couldn't have. She knew that now. The interest in her wasn't real, or if it was real, it was temporary. It would wane. As it always had. And besides, wasn't he with someone now? While the first few messages from him could have been put down to idle curiosity, the ten or fifteen she'd received since then just smacked of pursuit. What was he doing messaging her, pursuing her when he was supposed to be with another woman? He would grow bored of Chloé again the way he had before, the way he'd clearly grown bored of whoever the poor woman was who he'd moved to Oxfordshire with. Or else why would he be messaging Chloé? Nothing would ever change. Rob would never change. Spurred on by this thought, she typed.

Rob, I'm not sure why you're messaging me. We're divorced.

She could see him typing, but she ploughed on regardless, not waiting for his message to hit her screen. She had to keep going.

I'm happy. If you aren't happy, then I'm really really sorry for you, genuinely. But it's too late for us. Please stop messaging me. Let's get on with our lives. Separately.

Don't you miss us? he asked.

The cursor blinked in the chat window as she stared at those four words.

She took a deep breath. *No. I'm sorry, Rob. I really don't.* And she meant it.

Are you sorry? he asked. *You don't sound it.*

Don't do this, she said. She thought about typing all the things she'd previously gone over with him when she'd presented him with the once-heinous idea of divorce. But what was the point? And why did she have to? She'd done her duty to her husband and now he wasn't her husband she didn't owe him anything else. He knew they were better off apart. And if he believed they were better together, then he'd obviously not been paying attention at all throughout their marriage. No, she was done. It was time to say goodbye. It was time to really move on. This last tie, it needed to be cut.

Bye Rob, she said. *Be happy. Have a good life.* It felt like such a final thing to say to someone who she'd shared the last few years with, who she'd slept next to, who she'd let into her life, her soul, but who hadn't reciprocated much in return. She wished she'd said it at the moment when she'd collected her last bag of possessions from his flat. Perhaps if she had, he wouldn't have been messaging her now that she'd moved to Paris and came across a bit more interesting than she had ever been previously. She'd never know now. Because she'd said goodbye, and even if he messaged her again, this time it was final.

Chloé had finally finished Etienne's book on the journey. And the first thing she did was message him and tell him. Then she lifted and dropped her shoulders, breathing deeply and encouraging relaxation as she put the book in her bag and looked out the window at the green countryside racing past. The end of things. The start of things.

Her phone beeped with another reply from Etienne, suggesting a date for their next dinner together. She smiled to herself. The feeling of liking him had crept up so gently but it had been cemented ever since that dinner, since they'd been messaging more frequently, sometimes into the early hours of the morning. He was interesting, intellectual, fun, caring and genuinely himself. It also didn't hurt that he was good-looking. Those dark eyes. She'd enjoyed herself with him and wished she'd stayed longer at dinner at his apartment, but didn't want to ruin anything that might blossom slowly between them.

However, she'd just dared to suggest plans to meet when she returned from London and he'd put forward a date. She'd promised him tartiflette and he'd promised to bring the wine. He asked which wine she preferred and when she'd said, *Anything, as long as it's drinkable,* he'd replied with the head-smacking emoji and a suggestion he take her to his friend's vineyard out in the countryside one weekend. He wanted to spend time with her and the fact he was making such an effort to befriend her and then . . . a little more, if she wasn't mistaken, was not lost on her. All she'd offered in return was the promise of cooking him tartiflette. But he wanted to keep seeing her. And she realised with a feeling of warmth as the Eurostar pulled into St Pancras station that she wanted to keep seeing him.

She'd spent the night in her own flat on arriving in London and other than a bit of dusting and flicking the heating and hot water back on for her short visit, Chloé didn't have too much to do. And then, on waking up, she'd switched everything back off again and locked up. She'd already lived so very sparsely but as she closed the front door on a flat with barely any furniture in it, there was a feeling of inevitability this time. Who knew when she'd be back again? Flying visits were easy to achieve but in terms of coming back and living here full-time, she knew she didn't really want to do that. She had somewhere to live and a job in Paris, although the reality that both were temporary should have been something to be fearful of, but it wasn't – not really. Not now.

What had changed in such a small space of time? Nothing. Everything. She realised now she was in charge of her own destiny. If she needed to find a new job in Paris when her time with Brigitte came to an end and a new apartment when the lease was up, then she would. She'd done it before and she would do it again. She was a freer Chloé than she'd been in previous years and she decided that if she really intended to stay away for at least a year she should do something about putting her own flat on the rental market.

'Gran, you've made it look gorgeous,' Chloé said when she entered her gran's front door in her warden-controlled flat the next morning.

'Thank you. I like it,' Adèle said, kissing Chloé on both cheeks.

Chloé looked her gran over. She did look well, still as slim as a whippet, her hair a dark shade of salt and pepper grey and set in an elegant wave, her eyes a lighter shade of brown. She looked happy, better than she had done with the responsibility of a four-bedroom house weighing on her shoulders.

'How are you coping on your own here, Gran?'

'I'm not on my own,' Adèle was quick to point out as she waved Chloé into the little sitting room. It was bright and airy with tall windows and French doors that entered onto a large communal garden. Chloé recognised all the important knick-knacks from her gran's old house that had been decanted neatly into this small space on a tall dresser.

316

Chloé's mum stepped in through the French doors and closed them behind her. 'I've just been doing a little bit of secret pruning,' she said, pulling off her gardening gloves, which Chloé noted she must have brought with her.

'Hi, Mum,' Chloé said, enveloping her in a hug.

Chloé's mum, always referring to herself as 'the wrong side of seventy', and pretending to deduct a year from her age every time Chloé got one year older, always looked elegant, fresh, putting Chloé to shame. She was tall with neatly bobbed hair that always looked glossy.

'Where's everything gone?' Chloé said. 'I packed up so many other things when I was last at yours, Gran.'

'Your mum and Ava took them to the charity shop for me. It was good of you to pack them for me but I'm not sure what on earth I was thinking. I couldn't bring everything. Your mum did try to tell me that. But I had a ruthless sort-out and said goodbye to many objects. It's hard to let go sometimes, don't you find?'

Chloé nodded. 'I suppose it is, yes.'

'Especially when you are on the next stage of your life,' Adèle finished.

'Oh here we go again,' Chloé's mum chirped and received a sharp look from Adèle.

Chloé laughed at the exchange. Adèle was certainly on the next stage of her life but was Chloé? Perhaps. It hadn't really occurred to her until just now. Everything had been temporary. Everything is always temporary, she reasoned. 'Nothing lasts forever,' she said quietly.

'Quite. Coffee?' Adèle asked. 'I drink decaffeinated now, I'm afraid, but I like to pretend it's got a kick to it. It's about as naughty as I get these days.'

'I'll pretend it's got a little kick to it as well,' Chloé suggested, as the three women walked towards the tiny kitchen.

Chloé's mum was shooed away from helping.

'I can do it,' Adèle said.

On the fridge was a photograph Chloé had taken when she'd been a child, stuck on with a magnet Ava had made at school. It was lovely to see the things her gran had held on to.

'Ava not coming?' Chloé asked.

'Tomorrow,' her mum replied. 'She has work today.'

'Oh right.' She was hoping for some support when she quizzed her gran as to what she'd done during the war. She wasn't quite sure she'd get it from her own mum. Chloé lifted the photo out from under the magnet. It was a picture of her granddad and her gran together during a family day out on the pebble beach in Brighton. It was wonky, as all photos Chloé had taken at that age had turned out to be when they'd come back from the chemist's after having been developed. It made Chloé smile to see her granddad again, although a younger version than when he'd passed away about a decade ago. In it, Adèle and her husband were looking at each other adoringly.

She clipped it back to the fridge, wordlessly, and opened the door taking out the milk to help. 'Shall I pour the milk?'

'I'm quite capable of making coffee, thank you. And shockingly, Chloé, I still make my own meals and get in and out of the shower without too much bother,' she said with a look of mock horror.

'Point taken, Gran, sorry,' Chloé said, holding her hands up in defeat. 'Have you made any nice friends?' she asked, wondering if Adèle would realise her own words from last week were being echoed back to her.

'I have. A lovely lady called Doris lives in the flat next door and there's a few young men who live down the corridor; both have invited me for tea. One even made me a cake to welcome me. One of your favourites. Victoria sponge. There's some left if you'd like a slice.'

Chloé nodded appreciatively. 'Young men?' she queried.

'Younger than me. Eighty-five.'

Chloé laughed. 'Practically cradle-snatching.'

'There'll be none of that,' Adèle said. 'Just friendship, that's all I need at my time of life.'

'Friendship's hard to find,' Chloé reasoned.

'You've made a nice man friend, I recall,' Adèle said.

'Hmm.' Chloé smiled knowingly as both her mum and her gran inched their heads forward in joint enquiry. 'Yes, I have. Etienne. He's . . .' Chloé trailed off. 'He's so many different things all at the same time.'

'Is he now?' her mum said.

'That sounds interesting,' Adèle remarked. 'Us French are always interesting,' she reasoned. 'Is he nice to you? Because that's the important thing.'

'Yes. Yes, he is.'

'And are you nice to him?' her mum asked.

'I hope so. I hope he thinks I'm nice. I think he thinks I'm nice.'

The women just watched Chloé and then her gran said, 'It's not always a lightning bolt that strikes. Sometimes it starts slowly. And, in my experience, that's the best way. Friends first. Then lovers.'

'Lovers? Crikey, Gran. We're definitely not there yet.'

'Well then,' Adèle said, rounding off the conversation. 'Shall we?' She gestured to the doorway and the two women entered the small sitting room where Adèle sat in her upright armchair and Chloé flopped onto the two-seater fabric settee. Chloé's mum picked up her car keys from the side, needing to run to the car to bring in some plants she'd potted up.

'Need a hand, Mum?' Chloé offered.

'No no, you stay and have a catch-up. They're only little pots.'

'It's always lovely to see you, Chloé,' Adèle said. 'You know that.'

'I know. I do miss you, Gran.' Chloé put her cake and coffee on the little table. There was a distinct absence of candles, magazines, books, paraphernalia. But photos in frames adorned every spare space. Perhaps holding on to mementoes and not holding on to pointless knick-knacks was a by-product of her childhood in the orphanage, and moving country, Chloé reasoned.

'You're very quiet,' Adèle said. 'Is something wrong?'

'No, I was just thinking about how you seem to be able to up sticks and move so easily, without a backward glance.'

'I wouldn't say without a backward glance,' Adèle said. 'I suppose I'm just used to moving. Possessions are just things, houses are just big possessions.'

'Maybe. But you don't miss your old home? It's where you lived with Granddad? It's where you raised Mum.'

Adèle shrugged. 'I was on my own there in the end. And I have my memories of all the happy times, your mum growing up there, you and your sister playing in the garden all those years later, your granddad sitting in front of the fire after a long day at work. Way back when. Thankfully old age hasn't taken those memories from me. I've been very lucky.'

'You're right, I suppose. You don't miss your neighbours?'

'They're only a mile down the road, Chloé. And I've had bigger moves than this in my lifetime.'

'That's true. You didn't miss it all when you left? Paris I mean. You didn't miss the people you left behind?'

'It was so long ago,' Adèle said. 'I was younger. Easy to get up and go when you're younger. You leave less behind.'

'That's quite philosophical, Gran.'

'It is, isn't it,' Adèle said with a smile as she bit into a piece of cake. 'And I didn't really have anyone to leave behind,' she said when she'd finished eating. 'By the time I left . . . the man I loved had . . . gone. He hadn't been there for what felt like a very, very long time. And of course, the Paris I arrived in, the Paris I fell in love with, was quickly occupied by the Nazis. So by the time I left when the war was over, it was a very different place entirely. It wanted to be as it was before and I could see it would get there eventually but . . .'

'But?' Chloé prompted when Adèle stopped talking and stared into her coffee cup.

'But I wanted no part in that. Paris after the war was a horrid place to be. It was horrid during and horrid after. I had no friends there, by the end. It was time to leave.'

'No friends? Gran, were you and Chanel friends?'

'Non. Not at the end. Not at the start either,' Adèle said quietly. 'And not in the middle.'

'Why not, if you don't mind my asking? You worked for her for ages.'

'Yes, five years give or take.'

'But not friends?'

'Non, she was my employer. That is it.'

'But you were so close to her. You lived with her.'

'Yes.'

'And so . . .' Chloé prompted but as a gateway to what she didn't really know.

Neither did Adèle. 'What is it you are trying to ask, Chloé?'

She took a deep breath and toyed with getting there gently. 'I went to the Chanel auction . . .' She started, telling Adèle how she'd met Etienne, how she'd wanted to buy something for Adèle from the Ritz auction, how she wondered whether Adèle would even want anything that would serve as a reminder of Paris in the war, how Chloé didn't know if it would be considered a happy time or otherwise because Adèle had never really talked about it – short of the odd factual detail here and there.

'And then, I think I quickly got carried away. I wanted to understand more about you and about Paris in the war and how you lived. Gran,' she said softly, 'you've always been so . . .' Chloé felt around for the right word '. . . so guarded about your life back then and I wanted to understand why. And because I'm lucky enough to have you in my life and I know if I don't ever ask you about it, there'll come a day when I'll regret that I didn't at least attempt to understand the things you lived through. Does that make sense?'

Adèle remained quiet, but a faint smile glimmered. 'Yes,' she said quietly. 'Yes it does.'

'I know you were orphaned,' Chloé said. 'I know that things were incredibly tough, which when I say it out loud must be a huge understatement. And in stark contrast to how you lived, I have an incredibly easy life. I have a lovely gran, mum, sister. I know I've been through a divorce but I think that's child's play compared to living through a war. And I'd like to know. I'd like to know where I come from. I'd like to know more about you.'

'Are you resisting saying the words *before it's too late*?' Adèle offered.

Chloé smiled. 'I would never.'

Adèle's shoulders lifted and then sagged in a sigh. 'All right,' she said. 'What can I tell you that you have not already deduced? It was a horrific time to be alive; Paris, in the war with the Nazis breathing down our necks. They were everywhere.'

'In the Ritz?' Chloé nudged.

'Especially in the Ritz,' Adèle said. 'They took over every grand building they could get their hands on. They were everywhere,' she repeated. 'Everywhere I looked, there they were. I got used to them and, at first, I didn't feel particularly threatened by them. Until . . .'

'Until?' Chloé asked. She didn't want her gran to stop now.

Adèle shrugged. 'Events moved at a pace I was unable to stop.'

'With Chanel?' Chloé prompted.

Adèle gave a wry laugh. 'I wasn't thinking of her, but yes . . . with her too.'

Chloé waited, letting Adèle drift back to another time. She really didn't want her gran to get upset. If it looked as if Adèle would find this too painful, Chloé was determined to clamp down on the conversation, let her gran keep her secrets.

Chloé's mum re-entered through the French doors, startling them both by coming in through a different door to the one she'd previously exited. She paid no attention to the duo inside the room, dusted her hands off and went back towards the car.

They sat quietly for a moment until Adèle said, 'The man I loved was . . . helping the Resistance and I helped him . . . once. I should have done more though. I could have done more. And I hated myself, long afterwards that I didn't do more. I lived right under their noses – that's what I always told myself as to why I could hardly do any more.'

'The Nazis?' Chloé said.

Adèle nodded. 'Yes, Göring was forever coming and going. And Dincklage, although not as senior as he made out, was very much present. I was too close to them. And she . . .'

'She? Chanel?'

'Yes, Mademoiselle was . . . oh I don't know what she was. I'm not sure even she knew. She was very strong and strong-willed. She knew what she wanted and she, like me, had fought a lot in order to get it. She was determined not to go back to poverty again. Everything she did was motivated simply by her own need to survive. I knew that then, and coming from similar backgrounds – our childhoods were spent in orphanages – I understood her need to survive, to evade poverty. I even shared this need. Only, by the end of the war, I could see we were so very different. That my need to survive did not match hers. That the way I wanted to survive was not the way she wanted to survive. I have thought often about this, and about her and how I'm not sure that I could have done what she'd done. I'm not sure I could have helped the Nazis in quite the way she did. I'm not sure I could have lived as she did. I'm not sure I could have taken a Nazi lover. But the heart wants what it wants and she'd known him long before the war began, which was a token I held on to throughout their relationship. And she stayed with him after the war too, you know.'

'I didn't know that.'

'Yes, it was love, I think. Or as close to love as either of them could get. There was nothing to lose, nothing to gain for either of them by being together when the war was over. Nobody held a gun to her head to make her be with him. Nobody held a gun to her head to make her do any of the things she did. She did it all because she wanted to do it all. And I didn't think it was right. It wasn't right,' Adèle said, sounding more determined.

'What's right for some people, isn't right for everyone,' Chloé reasoned.

'For a long time I didn't like any of it, but Paris in the war wasn't a time to be alive. It was a time to survive. But I think by the end of it all, I was angry for everything that had happened and I wanted to take matters into my own hands.'

'Matters?' Chloé looked up but Adèle was looking away again.

'Yes, matters. I wanted to punish her. To bring her down.'

Chloé could have sworn her heart had stopped beating. 'What do you mean?'

'I regret it now,' Adèle confessed. 'But I saw red. After I lost him . . . that changed everything. The war had been something far away to me. Even the Occupation felt far away although it was on our doorstep, in the hotel in which I was living. But after I lost him it felt as if the war had only then been brought to me. It became personal and I looked at everything through a veil of hate and anger. I became the kind of person I would not have wanted to be friends with. I am ashamed now of what I did.'

'What did you do?' Chloé asked slowly.

'I knew the Resistance was going to want evidence of collaboration. And I was right. After the war there were trials, death sentences, which were carried out. People were executed. Did you know that? Collaborators were executed, Chloé. This is what I meant by Paris not being a good place to live even after it had been liberated.'

Chloé nodded as Adèle continued. 'And if I had known this was going to happen, I would never, ever have considered putting her in such a path, for such treatment. But I tried to make sure all the evidence I had was placed in the hands of those who had said all the way through the war that they would punish collaborators when they had the chance. I took my notebooks – they contained everything, every note I'd taken, every letter she'd dictated, her plans to retrieve her business, her plans and dates and visits to embassies . . . and so much more through all the war years. So many wrongs. And I went out to hand it to someone who I knew could place it in the right hands, and then when the war ended, as I knew it eventually would with the Allies gaining strength, then Mademoiselle would be punished.'

Chloé's mum entered the room again, placing her car keys in her bag. She'd listened as she'd walked in and moved around the flat carrying out odd jobs. She gave Chloé a glance that said, *I've heard this story before.*

Chloé returned her mother's look with one of curiosity and Adèle resumed. 'As I said, I became the kind of person I would not have wanted to be friends with. But I could not do it. When I got there, when I saw the man, I could not hand the books over to him. I could not. I did not even know then that there would be executions but still I could not do it. Because what had she done really? She had not killed anybody; she had done what she felt she needed to do to survive. But if she was to suffer for her part in the war, then it would not be because of me. She gave me employment and a roof over my head when I needed it most. So I did not do it. I had some loyalty, and while we were not friends, we were not enemies either. And so I returned home from the farm, and I placed the notebooks back in the drawer from which I'd taken them and I did not think of them again for quite some time.'

'Oh, Gran,' Chloé said. She didn't know what else to say and she sensed her gran needed a glass of water. Chloé returned with a glass for each of them and handed one to Adèle.

'I hate myself for even having got so close to doing such a thing. Imagine how I would feel all these years later if I had handed those notebooks over, if they had arrested her and if they had executed her, because of me. Because with proof, I think that is what they would have done. I would not have forgiven myself. I was hurting. Paris was hurting. People were being arrested and executed for crimes that often did not warrant such a punishment. Some of course did, and others did not.

'And in the end Charles de Gaulle understood this and he commuted the death sentences of nearly a thousand men and women. A thousand, Chloé. A thousand people convicted and sentenced to death for collaboration.' Adèle was out of breath and Chloé knelt at her grandmother's feet to console her as the horrific fact hung in the short distance between them. 'But by that time almost a thousand people had already been executed. Such a figure, Chloé. Such a high number at a time when so many had already died in the war.'

Adèle breathed slowly, calming down. 'After the time I'd spent with her I'd come to loathe her, but I couldn't condemn her to death, because that's what might have happened. Women were dragged into the street, heads shaved, paraded. I am glad that in the end I was not the cause of anything like that. Not to her.'

'Gran. I don't know what to say.'

Adèle placed her hand on Chloé's hair and stroked it absentmindedly, reminding Chloé of times long ago when, as a child, she'd fallen over or had an all-out fight with Ava and needed consoling. But surely it was Adèle who needed consoling now. Chloé reached for her grandmother's hand and held it. And then Chloé did know what to say. 'Gran, what happened to Chanel when Paris was liberated? Did Paris let her forget what she'd done in the war?'

Adèle lifted her head. 'No, Chloé. Paris did not let her forget. Paris wanted blood and they wanted it from her.'

Chapter 27

August 1944

Once again Paris was covered in ash. Particles of grey dust flew through the air, landing on everything in the city. And so four years after the Parisian administration burned documents to stop the Germans finding them, now it was the Germans' turn to burn their collective catastrophe to dust, to stop the Allies finding . . . everything. As the fight for freedom ended in siege, the bureaucratic evidence of Occupation fell and landed all around her. In the volcanic heat of a Paris in summer, a Paris undergoing the fierce liberation, partisans fought in the streets to help the Allies as the city was stormed. The molten lava of the Reich was slowly rolling away.

The Resistance began uprising from the depths of their long-concealed hiding places, armed, battling the Germans in the fight for Paris. Young men from both sides were gunned down where they stood. Barricades appeared in the city, trucks and tanks captured and blown up. Adèle pulled on her coat. If there was anything she could do, now was the time to help. She had run until her feet had ached during the night of the Renault factory bombing while helping

Theo and Nurse Carmichael. She knew she could keep a level head in a time of crisis and she ran towards the front door of the suite. If she could dodge bullets long enough to reach the main fighters, perhaps she could help.

'Adèle!' Mademoiselle Chanel screamed her name.

'I have to help. We have to help.'

'No.' Mademoiselle pulled Adèle back into the suite. 'This is madness. If you go out there you will die.' She shook Adèle by her shoulders. 'You must stay here. That is an order.'

Outside in the Place Vendôme, bullets flew and in the distance was the sound of tanks being blown up; the Paris she knew and had come to love and then had come to hate was suffering.

'I need you,' Mademoiselle Chanel said clutching at Adèle's sleeve with her thin fingers, her red lacquered nails digging into Adèle's skin. 'Stay here and get ready for the worst.'

Mademoiselle looked frail, lost, and as frightened as Adèle. Adèle nodded. She could not abandon her employer now.

Outside, thousands of partisans fought on, so loudly, so justifiably violently. After so long, they were intent on driving the Nazis out of Paris and saving Paris from the inevitable destruction, the reprisal of the Nazis for having lost their stronghold. Which buildings would be taken in the fight, which would be blown up by a retreating German army, as punishment for fighting back? Adèle could only imagine. Perhaps the hotel itself would be destroyed and as Adèle held Mademoiselle's thin body, her wide eyes looking around as if the walls held the answer as to what they should do, Adèle wondered if the two of them might die in here, if the last thing they both heard would be the rumble of a bomb as it exploded in the foyer and up towards their rooms.

On this last stretch of the war, and for what Adèle thought must be for the first time ever, she believed Mademoiselle and she were suffering the twin feelings of loneliness and fear in unison. The Germans had left the hotel. Gone, fled. There was no one to protect Mademoiselle now.

As the week wore on and the bodies of Resistance fighters and soldiers piled up in the streets of the city of light, the sounds of fighting died away and the rumble of Allied trucks forced Adèle back towards the window. As the American tanks rolled through the city, Adèle cried tears of hope and left a stunned Mademoiselle's side. It was over. It was all, finally over. And then tears of hope, gratitude and joy became confused with tears of sadness for everything that had yet to be gained, and for everything that had been lost.

All the tears she'd held within her over the last few years fell down her face until she had no more tears left to shed. She went across the hallway into her room, pulled Theo's gift of *Peter Pan* out of her lacquered box and said his name, clutching it to her chest while she sat on the floor, her back against the metal bedstead. She whispered to him that it was all over, that she loved him, that she missed him and prayed that wherever his soul had gone after it had left his body, he was at peace.

And then her door flew open and Mademoiselle Chanel stood at the threshold, a determined look on her face. 'Quick. Up. We must move. Now.'

Adèle scrambled to her feet. 'What are we doing? Where are we going?'

'The game is up, Adèle.'

She looked old. How had Adèle not noticed that until now? The skin around her high cheekbones had sagged a little, her painted red lips thinning and her eyebrows drawn on too dark. Her eyes were wide, almost mad. 'Once again

330

we women are left alone,' Mademoiselle continued. 'They are all gone, long gone and we women remain, to pick up the pieces of this broken city and to fend for ourselves. We must be clever, Adèle. If we are to survive, we must be clever, always clever, always one step ahead.'

Adèle and Mademoiselle left the Ritz into a Paris celebrating the arrival of the Americans. 'It will not be long before the tide turns again and then where will we be? We will be in trouble. We must stop that before it begins.'

The two women hurried across to rue Cambon. Mademoiselle pulled the keys from her pocket to open the shop doors, fumbling with them as she inserted them into the lock. 'Quick, inside.'

'What are we doing?'

'We must be clever. I have a plan, Adèle. Free fragrance for every GI. We are going to give it away, to every American who wants it. It will be a thank you, for liberating us. Chanel Number 5 for everyone!'

And as the Americans heard and queued to meet the famous Coco Chanel, and told their friends, more GIs came until the queue stretched all the way down the end of rue Cambon. Adèle, exhausted from running to and from the stockrooms to pull new bottles of fragrance to hand out to grateful, polite Americans, stepped out of the shop to breathe in fresh air for the first time in hours. And she heard the queue of men begin chanting Mademoiselle's name over and over and over until she thought she would run mad from hearing it.

They love her, Adèle thought. They do not know her but they love her. It would protect her, that love, that much Adèle believed to be true. And in a way it was a relief. There was no part of what had passed that lay in Adèle's hands to rectify. She had no power and nor did she want it. Mademoiselle Chanel's head had always been high above the parapet but she had always avoided any bullets. And in a way, despite the glamour and the money, Adèle felt sorry for her employer now. The lengths she had to go to, for her own version of survival. Adèle could not do that. There were ways of survival, and this was not it.

At night, in the suite days later, the women sat in mute contemplation. Many of the days following the liberation had been spent in silent reflection. Adèle had learnt to sit still and think easily in the orphanage in the quiet space of Mother Superior's office and then again in Mademoiselle's employ. And it came in useful now as Adèle tried to work out what her next move would be. She could not stay here. She would not stay here. But where would she go? She could not stomach this life, this existence any longer. The luxury, the glamour, it came at a price for Mademoiselle Chanel. And it came at a price for Adèle. And she could pay that price no longer. She must reclaim what she could of herself and she must leave.

On the rare occasion Adèle dared to walk the streets of Paris a few days later, staying to the main streets and passing happy, chatty, often intoxicated American servicemen, she had seen on only one occasion something that struck fear into her in much the same way as when she'd seen little Mélodie's mother being arrested and bundled into the police van.

Women were being taken from their homes and dragged into the street by their neighbours. Adèle gazed in horror from the sidelines at two women, one of whom looked familiar to her – had one of them once been a seamstress before Mademoiselle closed the atelier? Both women, sisters perhaps because they looked so similar, were catcalled and accused of *collaboration horizontale*. They were pulled, unwillingly but their faces were resigned to their fate, to stand in front of a gathering of older men whose age had played a hand in them being able to escape the call-up.

In front of them was a desk, set up on the pavement and the men were talking animatedly, waiting, waiting. Adèle adjusted her shopping basket on her arm and stood in much the same state of mute shock as she had done when Mélodie's mother had pleaded for help. But these two sisters did not plead to any member of the crowd for help. It was as if they knew no one could help them. They were already condemned, but to what Adèle could not have said. Until the men addressed the women in such a way that made Adèle compare the women to something in a circus sideshow. That coupled with the ugly way in which the women were being bruised by the grappling hands around their arms, the pulling of their ears as if they were less than human. And then it struck Adèle. These local people *did* think the women were less than human.

A show trial. That's what this was. Adèle swallowed, her mouth dry as she watched the horror unfold as the men at the desk surprised her by acting so calmly, acting to all intents and purposes as lawyer, judge and jury, condemning the women to punishment, giving contemptuous looks at the women's protestations that they had taken up with German soldiers because they and their mother had been starving.

Oh my God. Adèle closed her eyes for a moment to close out the scene in front of her. This is what they were hauling these women into the street for? For having German soldier boyfriends?

The women were turned around from the table, dragged even harder than they had been before, towards a stage made of wooden crates.

Cries of: 'He's not here to protect you now.'

'Boches' whores.'

Adèle couldn't drown out the gleeful calls as the verdict was thrown out around them. This could have been her. So easily, this could have been her, falling in love with the wrong man. But she had fallen in love with what Paris would call the right man: an American, a doctor. And so she had escaped this fate. And what good had it done her? But so easily she could be one of those women up there. Any one of the women happily standing and catcalling; any one of those women could have fallen so easily towards loving the wrong man. And now they stood as prosecutor as the women were thrown roughly onto the stage, their hair yanked and cut with large scissors and thrown to the ground in clumps around them. And then a blade was pulled out and the first woman's stumpy hair shaved from her head, blood trickling from haphazard cuts made by inexperienced hands.

The women didn't fight back, which Adèle thought she would have done if it had been her. But these girls were accepting of it; accepting that afterwards they had to live here in their family home. The women had to endure the punishment in order to resume their lives. It was what their neighbours expected. They demanded a resolution, satisfaction, punishment for these girls' crimes. And so the women stood there, holding hands, jaws clenched, eyes cast down, ashamed.

And then what happened next made Adèle move forward and cry out in protest but her cries were drowned in the jeers of the crowd as the humiliation continued. The women's clothes were torn so fiercely from their bodies that only their ripped petticoats and undergarments were on display for all of Paris to see if it so wished. And despite the heat, the women shivered through fear at this orchestrated move. Another woman moved forward, using a lipstick tube to smear a swastika onto each of the girls' foreheads. And then their shame was further strengthened as they were dragged from the dais, paraded half naked through the middle of the road, held firmly by the gaggle of men. Traffic had already stopped to watch the grotesque parade of 'collaborators' and as the spectacle moved past her, Adèle found her hand grabbed and she was pulled into the throng.

Adèle's shout of 'What are you doing?' melted away into the crowd.

But the gleeful woman who'd attempted to scoop Adèle up into the carnival of horrors replied, 'Come on! Enjoy it!'

'What are you doing to them?' Adèle cried but it was rhetorical because she could see exactly what was being done to them.

'They have been accused of sleeping with German soldiers,' the woman who had pulled her along told her. As if Adèle was stupid, as if she hadn't just stood there and witnessed the reasons why.

'But look what you're doing to them,' Adèle said, her voice shaking with horror.

'Of course,' the woman said as she skipped into the throng. And then she turned back happily from the crowd of hundreds in which she moved. 'The reprisals have started,' she cried.

Chapter 28

September 1944

And then it happened. The unthinkable. Resistance fighters had been gathering momentum for weeks, unchecked, unstoppable. The forced show trials had been carried out all over the city as people were dragged from their homes. The rumours were rife, the accusations even more so.

And then Mademoiselle Chanel was arrested, accusations thrown at her by men claiming to be officials, about her role in the war, her relationship with a Nazi, accusing her of the newly punishable crime of collaboration.

'He's English,' Mademoiselle grasped desperately at a response that might save her. 'Dincklage is English. His family is English. A woman in my time of life cannot be expected to look at a man's passport,' she cried as they arrested her.

But it was no use. While his grandmother may have been English, he was a Nazi. The Resistance fighters continued their war the only way they knew how, by pulling her from her rooms, dragging her into the street. She'd seen it with her own eyes now, the head shaving that awaited *les collaborateurs horizontales* – horizontal collaborators. A phrase brandished against women who'd remained in France, done whatever they'd had to in order to survive – but never the men. Oh no. Never the men who'd collaborated willingly with the army, never the men who'd been complicit with the new regime, traded black market goods with the invading enemy. Never them.

But the women, women like Chanel who were paying the price for dalliances where dalliances shouldn't have been, a friendly pair of arms . . . a safety net in that long mountain fall towards despair and loneliness. Yes the women were the ones subject to the pent-up aggression of a nation brought to its knees and now desperate to recover. Parisians – sickened by the suffering they had felt, the Resistance they had been a part of, the arrests by the Gestapo they'd been subject to, the deportations to concentration camps their friends and family had endured, the executions of fellow Resistance fighters outside the city as the gunshots of firing squads rang through the air.

This was the moment they had been waiting for, the payoff. It was her turn. After all these years, when she had so very nearly got away with it, Coco Chanel was being arrested for everything she'd done in the war and everything she hadn't. There was only one real choice to make.

Adèle knew what Mademoiselle would do. She would go with them.

And then she would deny everything.

Chapter 29

2018

'She was actually arrested?' Another fact that had been conveniently forgotten or glossed over in history.

'Yes, she was arrested,' Adèle said. 'And after every hope I'd ever had that she would be, I bitterly regretted it when she finally was. I feared the worst. I feared her execution. I feared her being paraded through the streets with her head shaved. I had seen so much of this. And I did not think she, or anyone in that kind of predicament, deserved that punishment. It was Dincklage's wife, you know,' Adèle said suddenly, lifting her gaze to meet Chloé's. 'Or should I say, his ex-wife who gave Mademoiselle away, told the new authorities about her.'

Chloé's eyebrows rose. 'Hell hath no fury like a woman scorned.'

'Exactly,' Adèle agreed. She inhaled deeply.

Chloé's mum began assembling the ironing board in the corner of the sitting room, glancing at Adèle and Chloé from time to time. She'd clearly heard this story before and when the ironing board was set up she plugged the iron in and filled it with water, only half listening to Adèle as she continued.

'His ex-wife was half-Jewish,' Adèle said. 'But even so she was a collaborator, black market dealer and Nazi spy. It turned out Dincklage had been seeing her on and off throughout the war and of course she knew about his relationship with Chanel. He only divorced his wife to save his skin when it was no longer acceptable for a man of his prominent position to have a non-Aryan wife. But his ex-wife was arrested as part of the reprisals and then in exchange for her life she gave up everybody's names who she knew to be associated with the Nazis.'

Chloé shook her head. It was too easy to judge this behaviour by modern standards. Again, if forced, she had no idea what she would have done under such circumstances. She thanked her lucky stars that the world was a different place now and that she wasn't in such a position, forced between fight or flight.

'So if Chanel had been given up to the authorities ready to punish her, why wasn't she punished?' Chloé asked.

'Because, as ever, she was lucky. I was not present at her trial with the Free French Purge Committee. She, at least, received an official sort of trial, rather than street-side retribution. When the Nazis burned their files and began the hasty removal of any files they wanted to keep when fleeing Paris, Mademoiselle Chanel's files, believe it or not, became lost.'

'I can believe that actually,' Chloé replied. And then under her breath: 'It's all I seem to hear.'

Adèle continued. 'In the true fashion of how she simply floated through much of her life and always came out on top, they were lost. And so in her trial she denied every seemingly flimsy charge thrown at her. Charges were put together based on rumour and hearsay.

'Amazingly, they had no documented knowledge of her

numerous trips to Madrid and Berlin, and they didn't know about the mission she had planned to deliver a letter to Churchill from senior Nazis. They accused her of being a Nazi spy but they had no actual evidence. She pre-empted them, said if her name had been found on any official Nazi document then it was without her consent or knowledge. She was incredibly clever like that and could talk her way out of any situation. And on the rare occasion she couldn't talk her way out of it, then she would talk down to someone, belittle them until they were too scared to push further. It was a trait I hated but it saved her life. She was clever. And of course, by this point the British authorities were involved but it worked in her favour that she had, once upon a time, been the Duke of Westminster's lover and a good friend to Winston Churchill.'

'So what happened?' Chloé inched forward, hooked.

'She was released with no further charges.'

'None at all?'

Adèle shook her head. 'Imagine if I had handed my notebooks over. In that moment, when she returned to her apartment, I was amazed to see her. And I was relieved that it was not because of me that she was arrested, that the Free French Purge Committee had nothing with which to condemn her death. I came so close to being a disgusting human, to inform on someone to whom I owed so much. I do not think I could have lived with myself if I had been responsible for her downfall . . . her death.'

Silence descended in the room.

Adèle sipped her drink. 'When Mademoiselle returned from her short trial, I was packing my bags. I was ready to leave. I assumed when she was arrested that I would never see her again. I had mixed feelings about that. But she was returned in such a state of shock and fear and confused happiness that she had been freed. And then a man arrived at the door shortly afterwards, handed her a note, told her to leave Paris immediately in case evidence was found or witnesses came forward, because then she would not be able to talk her way out of it again. There were many who could have given her up, who might have given evidence against her.'

'And what happened after that?' Chloé couldn't help but ask.

'She did not need telling twice. She left,' Adèle said with a faint smile. 'She left. We packed hastily and within a matter of hours she was gone and I walked round to the atelier, found the notebooks left exactly where I'd put them in the drawer. And I burned them there and then in the log fire.

'She went to Switzerland in self-imposed exile. She did not return until the 1950s after France had been officially encouraged to halt the reprisals, forget its collaborative history and, on a more positive note, encouraged to move on with the new decade, its new life. It was, as de Gaulle decreed, the only way France could heal: if it forgave and if it forgot.'

Chloé sat back and exhaled. 'And in all those years the official evidence never came to light?'

'Apparently not. I did hear that her Nazi contact Schellenberg, who took her to Berlin in the war and who had escaped punishment, was living in poverty and was unwell. He was threatening to publish his memoirs in order to raise money. And she paid for his medical bills and gave him a financial stipend. She bought her way out of any further . . . unsavouriness, any exposure in print and when his memoirs were published, strangely enough, there was no mention of her and the missions she'd run for him.'

Chloé processed this in wide-eyed wonder. 'And what about her lover, Baron von Dincklage? Did he never give her away?'

'Never. Quite the opposite. This is why in the end I think their relationship *was* genuine. Odd, but genuine. Because he too went to Switzerland and lived with her for years. I do not know how as a senior Nazi he didn't hang for his part in it all. He wasn't senior enough – let's just say that shall we? Despite the fact there were rumours he ran a spy ring that reported directly to Goebbels. I'm glad that I didn't know that at the time.'

Chloé exhaled.

'He was loyal to her for a while, in Switzerland,' Adèle continued. 'She didn't make the right decisions in love from what I witnessed. And she refused to give him up. Even after the war when France's eyes were on her Nazi collaboration. But the course of true love never did run smooth and after everything they had been through I believe the excitement of living so close to the edge in the war years could never be replicated in the relative quiet of a safe and unexciting exile in Switzerland. And so eventually, he left her.'

'I feel quite sorry for her in a way,' Chloé said after thinking about it for a moment. 'I think.'

It was Adèle's turn to lift her eyebrows but it wasn't lost on Chloé that she made no comment either way.

Chloé steered the subject back on course. 'And then she returned to Paris, presumably, given how well her fashion empire took off?'

'Yes, with the assistance of none other than the Wertheimer brothers. The very same men she had tried to swindle so horrifically out of their side of the Chanel business. They continued on when she returned to Paris in 1954, can you believe?'

'I knew about her trying to use the Nuremberg Laws,' Chloé said. 'And I knew she was livid because she'd failed. I read there was a complicated settlement in which she got handed more shares, more money from them after the war.'

'Yes,' Adèle said. 'But they knew the company would only grow and grow. And so despite everything she had tried to do, they continued to expand the Chanel business.'

Chloé looked away, stared through the French doors and out into the garden. 'My goodness,' she said absentmindedly.

'They still own Chanel today, the Wertheimer family, I mean,' Adèle said, drawing Chloé's attention back.

Chloé smiled, thinking about that. 'Good,' she said simply.

Adèle smiled. 'Yes, I thought so too. I read that files have been discovered in Paris,' she said simply. 'Only some have been released.'

'I've seen them,' Chloé confessed.

'Have you?' Adèle said, the shock in her voice evident.

Chloé nodded. 'I saw a photograph of people dancing and dining in the Ritz ballroom,' she said. 'I'm sure one of the young women in the photo was you.' She hated herself for having said it. The photograph felt a moot point now, redundant. Her grandmother in that ballroom back then with Nazis. It meant nothing – Chloé understood that now. She winced, waiting for the reply.

'It might have been me,' Adèle admitted. 'I was there. With them. Once. The Nazis loved to document everything they ever did with a photograph. There were always photographers trailing them around. They thought they'd be able to look back over the course of the war with victorious eyes. I only went once down to the ballroom and I hated every second of it. Perhaps not every second. I did get to dance with someone. He was the only one in that room who was not horrific,' she said. 'I . . . well . . . it was a long time ago.'

Chloé didn't get the chance to question who Adèle was referring to as her grandmother continued, circling back to Chanel. 'But it was all so long ago. After she died, the tale of what Chanel did in the war and how she had behaved . . . faded to dust. What is that English phrase? Today's news is tomorrow's chip paper. Your grandfather liked that phrase.'

Chloé smiled wistfully, remembering her lovely grandfather. How he'd had his favourite chair by the fire that looked out into the garden, how he and Chloé would read together. Nature books – they'd been her favourite back then before he'd passed away. And if the weather was fine they'd walk into the large garden and talk about the leaves, blossoms, the foxes that came to feed and the robins that seemed to stay longer each year. Funny how she'd forgotten all that until now.

She was brought back to the here and now as Adèle continued, 'I read the news reports, which took up a fraction of a newspaper page. Then I put the newspaper in the recycling bin, and I tried to forget. But she died long ago and remains . . .' Adèle grasped for the word '. . . untouchable. A legend. An icon. And despite everything she was, I think I would not want it to be any other way.'

'You don't sound so sure,' Chloé offered.

Adèle chuckled. 'I'm not.'

After a few seconds of contemplating this, something struck Chloé. 'Why didn't you go to Switzerland with Chanel where you knew you'd have been safe? Why did you come to England?'

Adèle gave a grim look. 'My journey with Mademoiselle Chanel came to an end. The damage had been done. Perhaps I had joined her during the worst time. Perhaps I had joined her during the best time. I will never know. But then, I knew enough to know I could not go with her. I had grown up. I may still have been young but I was not as naïve as I was when I had first arrived in Paris. I don't know why it took me so long. I don't know why it took for her to leave for Switzerland, for me to acknowledge I was not bound to her; that it was time I found somewhere else to be, someone else to work for. And I knew whatever happened next to me, that it wouldn't be the same as it had been with her. There would be ups and there would be downs but nothing would be quite like that time – Paris in the war with Mademoiselle Chanel, keeping her secrets. I hoped that my next adventure would not be like that.'

Adèle lifted and dropped her shoulders. She was tiring; Chloé could see that. 'I knew I couldn't stay in Paris anymore either. There was too much that haunted me about Paris, the moment the excitement of Liberation ended and the show trials and retributions began. I thought about the man I'd lost all the time. I thought about Mademoiselle Chanel all the time. I thought about the war and what it had done. I thought about all the children who were taken and killed in the Holocaust, all the parents parted from their children, and then when the news about the horrors of Belsen and Auschwitz and the rest of the grotesque extermination camps started filtering through, I felt even more horror at how a small cog can help turn a big wheel and how Chanel's part in it was so small but at the other end of such small acts were those camps, and all the men fighting on and being killed in the air and on the ground and at sea.

'I thought of how the man I had been engaged to marry had been arrested. At how Nurse Carmichael – a good woman – had been arrested and all because they had tried to stop the wheel from turning in its awful, unstoppable direction. How I had not done anything to stop it. How I had been useless. And then when I could have had Chanel arrested and punished, I didn't. Because . . . I just hadn't seen the point in causing any more harm to any more humans. What humans were doing to each other in the Forties was beyond me. I couldn't be a part in that after the fighting had ended. No, I knew I had to leave, start again where this collective horror didn't haunt me daily.'

She raised her head and looked at Chloé with a thin smile. 'Or perhaps, where it would haunt me just a little bit less.'

Chapter 30

1944

Mademoiselle Chanel had gone. She had closed up the atelier once again, her life in France paused for God knew how long. And nearly six years after Adèle had stood outside the boutique on rue Cambon, peering inside, clutching her suitcase and wondering if she might find a job inside, a different, older Adèle had now turned her back to it, suitcase in hand, lacquered box under her arm, housing her few precious possessions and walking away.

She didn't know where her feet would take her. She only knew it was time to go, time to find – if not a new adventure then at least a sanctuary, a new one. She could not go back to the orphanage; she could not be in Paris. She was only reminded of the horror of the past few years, the love she had shared. She saw him everywhere, and nowhere. She needed somewhere new, unblemished by these years. She would remember him forever, but she did not want to do that here.

There had been no promise to write to Mademoiselle, and none had been forthcoming from her in return, eager as she was to depart while she was still able. Adèle was part of a life Mademoiselle Chanel now wanted to forget and as Adèle walked away, eager to put distance between herself and rue Cambon and the Ritz only a short stroll away, she was also eager to forget the pain that had been caused by being here. And to remember the love she had shared with Theo, which now felt so long ago.

The pieces of her life had been inadvertently compartmentalised. Her childhood home in St Nazaire and then the orphanage, Paris and Mademoiselle Chanel. Whatever happened next, wherever she went next, what would that hold for her? St Nazaire wasn't home. She had to make a new home. But first there were things she needed to do, two final places she needed to visit, in order to know she had tried her best.

Someone else was living in Theo's apartment now. It had been so long since he'd gone and an apartment in such a part of town would never have stood empty for long, despite so many people having been deported or arrested. The world moved on. People moved on. Soon Paris would be a place of wonder once again. But not yet. Not today.

Over the last two and a half years since he had been executed along with the other medical staff, Adèle had tried to stay away. Visiting his apartment, looking up at his empty window had only ever brought her the pain in her chest she knew to be heartache. It had never made her feel closer to him, despite the fact she'd always thought it would. But it never did. Today however, inside, there was movement at the window. She could barely see all the way up, staring as she did on the few occasions she had found the courage to come past.

It occurred to her that she didn't know what had happened to his possessions. Had the concierge ransacked his items as the concierge in Mélodie's apartment block had intended to do? Had they been packed up and sold on?

She wished she'd come to collect his things, or at least something to remember him by. All she had were the memories of that precious time together and the copy of *Peter Pan* he'd given her, tucked safely inside her lacquered box, the clasp closed against the world. She didn't want to think about what had happened to his belongings, his childhood books. The thought of them having been thrown away stabbed her like a knife to her chest.

As the new tenant came and went from view, passing the window on their way from room to room she could see it wasn't Theo. She'd known it wouldn't be. But this one last time, she'd just had to be sure, before she left Paris forever. Because she knew once she left she was never coming back.

Adèle turned away and glanced towards the Eiffel Tower, the swastika gone; the Nazis having risen so high and now fallen so low. She walked in the direction of the other apartment she wanted to visit. Adèle had gone every few weeks to see if there had been any movement at the windows, any sign of Mélodie's family returning. But there never had been so much as a flutter of a curtain and she hadn't dared enter again after Theo's warning that it was too dangerous. Instead she had watched from the street, choosing different times of the day so as to vary her routine in the hope of catching the little girl's mother coming or going.

This was Adèle's last chance to check. She was not expecting any news but she had to at least know – one last time before she left Paris and the situation fell truly out of her hands – that she had done everything she could to see that Mélodie's mother hadn't returned, wondering where her child had gone.

With the Nazis gone and Paris trying its best to heal – in its own way, Adèle risked entering the apartment block. She climbed the stairs ready to face the same situation as every other time she'd checked. The apartment would be empty, no sign of Mélodie's mother. Except this time there was movement behind the door, a shuffling noise, the sound of things being shifted. She dare not place her stolen key in the lock for fear of frightening the person inside.

Adèle smiled, her heart rate picking up to reflect her excitement that this time she would be wrong, so happily wrong and that Mélodie's mother had been freed, had returned; that her fate was not to perish in a camp at the hands of the Nazis. And if this wonderful event was what had happened, then all Adèle had to do was find the Madame Dupont out in the medieval town of Provins who had taken the little girl and return Mélodie where she belonged. But before Adèle had the opportunity to knock on the door, it opened and a woman appeared.

A polite, tentative smile broke out on the woman's face. 'Yes?' she asked.

Adèle's hopes for Mélodie and her mother faded away. This was not the woman who had been bundled into a police van back in 1941. This was a different woman entirely, and past her – inside the hallway– a man holding a paintbrush looked at her with the same air of polite curiosity. Dust sheets, paint canisters abounded where once there had been bulky old-fashioned furniture.

'This is hard to find these days.' The woman gestured to the paint that Adèle was looking at. Adèle just nodded, unable to find her voice. All her hopes for Mélodie had just crashed down around her.

'Can I help you?' the woman prompted. 'Do you live in the block?' she said as if trying to help Adèle explain her presence at the front door. 'It's so nice to meet new neighbours. You're the third today. Which apartment are you in?'

The question encouraged Adèle to lift her eyes from the stark hallway and meet the woman's gaze, answer her question.

'No, I'm not from this block,' Adèle said finally. 'I knew the woman who lived here, sort of. I stopped by because . . . I wondered if she had returned.'

'I'm afraid not,' the woman said, not enquiring from where the previous tenant would have returned. She knew. 'I was told they . . .' she grasped for the right word '. . . went away a while ago. And, I'm sorry,' she said kindly. 'I believe none of them returned from . . .' She didn't say it. No one wanted to say it.

'But there was a note,' the man cut in, still holding his paintbrush.

Adèle thought of the note she had left, pinned to the back of the door. 'Yes, I left it,' she murmured dejectedly but neither the man nor the woman heard her as they began rustling around behind the door.

The man cut in. 'I don't know if it makes sense to you? It was written on the wall. We whitewashed over it yesterday but we copied it down onto this scrap of paper in case anyone came for it.'

'A note stuck to the wall?' There was no note stuck to the wall when Adèle had last been inside to check on the apartment. She had stuck hers onto the back of the door.

'No,' the man replied. 'Not a note stuck to the wall, a note written on the actual wall itself. The walls were in a state anyway so we needed to whitewash them, but the scribble on the wall helped force our hand in the decision to repaint, freshen things up a bit.

'Here,' he said, stepping forward and handing it to her. 'We copied it down. Does it mean anything to you?'

She held the note, glanced at it briefly but the words jumbled around on the page, in her head, making no sense as the woman continued talking. Adèle wished she'd stop, just for a moment so she could understand what she was looking at.

'The concierge had been in,' the woman said, 'cleared a

350

lot of the family's possessions when he knew we were taking the tenancy. Perhaps . . . a week or two ago. We could ask him if there was a note on the door, if you're worried about it?'

'No. It's fine,' Adèle said. 'I don't think it will do any good now.'

'Does it mean anything to you?' the man said. 'The note that was scribbled on the wall?' he said looking at the paper she held on which he'd copied it. 'Is it meant for you?'

Adèle read the words. And then she understood what she was looking at. And then she smiled. 'Yes,' she said. 'It's meant for me.'

Chapter 31

1945

Without being able to get hold of a map, Adèle had acclimatised herself to the streets of post-war London by riding the bus most days across different parts of the city, listening to the sounds, taking in what remained of the sights of a battered London still recovering from having lost so much to the Blitz. The city was scarred. The world was scarred. And when Adèle picked up a copy of *The Times* and sat in the park one Monday, she read that in Asia the battle for freedom continued. She folded the paper over, left it on the bench for someone else to read and then she stood up and walked around, taking in the beauty of Kensington Gardens.

This is where Peter Pan had been in the book Theo had owned. This is where he'd played with the fairies, watched the other children, wanting to be like them. She felt she knew every inch of Kensington Gardens now. She'd been here so often over the past few weeks. The red-brick façade of Kensington Palace, the statue of Queen Victoria just outside. And further along, the grandiose ornately Gothic Albert Memorial. The carvings were overwhelmingly detailed and Adèle had come here on many occasions, each time seeing something different. She'd stood for such a long time staring up, trying to work out what kind of book the statue of Prince Albert was holding.

And then she'd stumbled across it, the statue of Peter Pan and she had put her hand to her mouth to stop the laugh escaping. The bronze statue was tucked in a corner. A small boy, a musical pipe to his lips, standing on top of a rock, surrounded by smaller statues of characters from the book. She'd read the edition of *Peter Pan*, which Theo had given her, so many times until she could now recite passages from it. But standing here, by the statue of the boy from Theo's favourite book, she'd kept her hand to her mouth the entire time she'd stood there in awe of such an intricate and oddly touching statue. The boy who never wanted to grow up. The boy who could fly.

Adèle had put her plans to move to another part of France on hold, had applied for a passport and then a visa to travel to England. The paperwork was mind-numbing but ever adept at helping Mademoiselle Chanel run her business despite the excessively complicated government bureaucracy and ever-changing Nazi laws, Adèle had approached the visa application with tenacity, turning up for appointments early. And then she had received it at the boarding house where she'd taken up temporary residence, working in a little shop below by day; and at night sleeping the exhausted sleep as if she'd never slept the entire time the war had been raging.

And now, all these weeks later, in Kensington Gardens by the statue of Peter Pan she unfolded the letter once again and reread the precious words from the note that had been transcribed from the wall, written out by the new tenants of Mélodie's apartment and handed to her two years after it had been hastily, desperately written.

I hope you still come here to check from time to time like you say you do. Please forgive me. I had to leave.

They came for everyone. I couldn't find you. If I make it out of here alive and if I make it through the rest of the war and after all of this is over, I'll be waiting by the statue of Peter Pan in Kensington Gardens on the first Saturday of every month at noon. I will wait for you. I will wait forever.

It wasn't signed. But she knew. It had taken all her powers not to cry with relief while standing in the hallway of what had once been Mélodie's apartment. She had thanked the couple, politely wished them well in their new apartment and then she had left, the note held in her shaking hands. And then when she had made it into the street Adèle had collapsed against a lamppost and shaken with relief and shock. She had grieved for him and never once in all that time had it occurred to her that he might still be alive. His secretary had been so adamant when she'd told Adèle that Theo had been rounded up by the Gestapo. And there was only ever one outcome when that happened. The Gestapo didn't let people go.

But none of that had happened to him and for the next few months while applying for a visa to England and booking a boat passage she had dared to hope that if he had escaped safely after writing the note, that he had lived through whatever the remainder of the war in Europe had thrown at him.

And now, sat on a bench near the statue of Peter Pan in Kensington Gardens, far too early, she watched the comings and goings of children as they played round the statue, of nannies as they ushered children away in time for luncheon. Had he made it out alive after writing that note? And if so, how long had Theo been coming here? Where had he gone straight after he'd escaped? Had he gone to war? It occurred to her that he might have joined up, might have joined the medical corps or might be fighting in Asia where the war still raged on relentlessly. His note from so long ago had

354

contained a hastily thought-up plan as he desperately escaped from Paris. And in the harsh realities of a world still gone wrong, might not work now. If he didn't come, what then? Should she hope? Should she dare to hope?

As the minutes moved towards noon Adèle sat up straight and breathed in and out, in and out so deeply she could feel the expansion and contractions in her lungs. And then noon came and went and at five minutes past midday she slumped. He wasn't coming. Not this month. But maybe next month, or maybe the one after that. And if he didn't come at all over the next few months or years? Then she would continue to come here on the first Saturday of every month until he did.

Adèle rose, straightened her jacket, her hat, fiddled with the clasp of her bag; her fingers nervously in want of something to do. In amongst the natural comings and goings of children, parents and nannies there was one child rounding the corner and skipping towards the statue. She had long hair, two plaits and was alone, ahead of her people, knowing the way as if she'd been here a hundred times or more. When she arrived at the statue, she pulled a skipping rope with wooden handles from her coat pocket and began to leap and skip.

She stopped opposite Adèle and looked up at her, their gazes meeting. It took Adèle to the count of four seconds to realise who she was looking at and she stepped towards the little girl, who was so much older now than when Adèle had last seen her. The little girl must have been nearly six now, so much taller, of course, coming up to Adèle's stomach. But even so, Adèle crouched down, smiled and looked into Mélodie's eyes.

And then, behind her, there was Theo, looking exactly as he had done the last time she'd seen him before he'd exited her life so abruptly the night of the Renault factory bombing. Theo, after all this time. His gaze was directed towards the ground, his eyes lifted gently to check on

Mélodie. And then he stopped walking, his gaze lifted fully to meet Adèle's as she stood up from her crouched position. His mouth opened but no words came out. The look on his face said everything: that he'd never expected her to be there, never expected her to have found his note, never expected her to make the crossing, never expected her to be standing by the statue of Peter Pan in Kensington Gardens on the first Saturday of the month.

And then in a clear mix of shock, surprise and relief, he laughed. And so did Adèle as tears of joy clouded her vision. One hand flew to her mouth and Mélodie's little hand entered the other. Mélodie's voice that now only contained a hint of a French accent said, 'You came,' as Theo ran towards them both.

The lump in Adèle's throat almost prevented her from speaking. 'I did,' Adèle replied. 'And so did you.' But even she couldn't hear the words she'd said.

'How are you here?' Theo asked as he stood in front of her. He reached up to touch her face.

'I'm here because I'm meant to be. I think,' she said as the lump in her throat choked her words. 'I'm here because I went one last time to Mélodie's apartment.' She was aware of the little girl's hand holding hers tightly, her face turned up to look at the adults. 'One last time. Just to be completely sure.'

Theo nodded, understanding, the smile present on his face, his eyes looking into hers for the first time since 1942 when everything was different and waves of fear had crashed towards them hourly. Now it was just them, a bombed-out city that was foreign to all three of them and the statue of Peter Pan in Kensington Gardens.

A little boy looked at Mélodie shyly and she asked Theo, 'Can I go and play for a little bit?' On hearing his affirmative reply she ran off happily, holding her skipping rope out for him to play with.

'Theo,' she cried. 'I'm so sorry it took me so long to find out where you'd gone,' Adèle said.

His hands traced her cheek, her jaw, touching her, remembering her.

'I've missed you so much,' she said as his fingers brushed her face.

'Me too,' he said. 'I'm so sorry I left like that. I couldn't find you in the hospital. It was chaos and then my Resistance contact was standing in front of me in the corridor, risking his life to run across Paris to tell me the cell had been compromised, that the Gestapo were coming for me. I had no idea the others would be taken too. Their names were never associated with the Resistance. Only mine. My contact Michel practically dragged me out of the hospital.

'I saw them take her, Margery Carmichael. My only consolation is that she didn't go quietly. She clawed at them, spat at them. I tried to get to her. But they were all being bundled into vans and Michel pulled me back, pushed me out of the doors and into the night. I didn't know how they'd known to arrest her, or the rest of them. But now I do. Now I've had nothing but long days, just Mélodie and I in a little apartment, her asleep by seven o'clock and I have time to think. And I think I know how they were all arrested,' he said. 'My secretary – Mademoiselle Vachon. I can never prove it. Nor do I want to,' he finished.

Adèle hung her head sadly, thinking of the kindness of Nurse Carmichael and listening how Theo fought through the Red Cross to find out the fate of the medical staff. How they'd not been registered as prisoners of war, how they hadn't been picked up from any prison when the Allies crept across Europe, liberating the continent piece by piece. How they were most certainly dead, buried without ceremony, vanished.

'I needed to tell you where I was going,' he said. 'And Michel, my Resistance contact, pleaded with me not to. So

I didn't go back to my apartment. That really would have been suicide. Even in the blur of it all I could see that. And I could hardly go to the Ritz with all those Nazis and leave a message for you. You told me you went to Mélodie's to check from time to time and it was the only safe place to leave a note for you where the Gestapo wouldn't think to look for me. Michel picked the lock for me and I prayed you'd find the words I scrawled on the wall.'

Adèle found that at some point during his speech his warm, firm hand was holding hers. She'd missed the touch of him, the feel of him. She'd missed him more than she'd allowed herself to. She'd grieved for the man standing in front of her and she'd cried so many times and now she cried again. She couldn't stop herself.

'Don't cry,' he said softly. 'I'm here. You're here. Mélodie's here. We did it. We got out. Alive. Don't cry.' He wiped her tears with his hand.

'How did you get Mélodie here?' she asked.

'It wasn't easy,' he said, taking the opportunity to guide her to a bench where they sat side by side. Her eyes looked into his but every few seconds he broke off to keep a check on Mélodie, who was holding one end of the skipping rope, the little boy holding the other and a third child had joined them, skipping over the centre swing of the rope.

'Madame Dupont had suggested she couldn't have Mélodie any longer.'

'You didn't tell me that,' Adèle said.

'I didn't want to worry you. I thought I could fix it. She'd already told me she feared her neighbours had worked out she wasn't a member of their family. The Duponts lived in fear that if they were informed on they'd be responsible for sending a small child God knew where.'

Adèle shuddered. She remembered the tell-tale feeling of heat creeping up her face, followed by throwing up, when she'd learnt last year in the newspapers exactly what the

Nazis were doing with people they deemed degenerate. So many of them, wiped from the earth. She looked towards Mélodie. So small, so innocent, an orphan. But alive and laughing with other children.

'She was spared because of you,' Adèle said, still looking at the little girl.

'It was because of you,' Theo said emphatically. 'You'd risked so much that night you took her. Then it was my turn. I couldn't leave her. I just couldn't do it.'

'Michel telephoned the Duponts, organised everything and then the three of us left together along with a contact of his who was in charge of getting all those downed airmen across the border. It was hell, taking a child on that route. I carried her most of the way.'

Adèle's heart could have burst for this man; the man she'd loved back then, the man she'd never stopped loving. She leant forward and without hesitation kissed Theo, pressing her mouth to his, feeling him kiss her in return. He was alive and he was here and it was more than she could ever have hoped for.

Eventually Adèle pulled back to look at him. She looked at all the frown lines that she could have sworn weren't there when she'd last seen him. What he had been through taking a small child on an escape route. He held her hand, touched the ring finger for which he'd never managed to purchase an engagement ring. 'I thought I'd lost you forever,' she said. 'I thought you were dead.'

'I'm sorry,' he said.

Adèle shook her head. 'Don't be. It wasn't your fault. And we cannot change the past.'

He pulled Adèle closer to him as the two looked on at Mélodie laughing and running with the other children. 'No. We can only change the future.'

Chapter 32

2018

Chloé stared at her grandmother for what felt like a very long time and then her gaze switched to her mother. Slowly, the pieces of a puzzle she hadn't even realised needed completing, fell into place. 'The little girl rescued was you,' Chloé said to her mum.

Her mum nodded, walked towards her daughter and sat next to her on the settee. 'Yes.'

Chloé stared again.

'But you always knew I was adopted,' Mélodie replied to a question Chloé hadn't asked. 'We've never made a secret of it.'

'You've always been so . . . blasé about it,' Chloé said. 'It was never a secret but you never mentioned France, the war, any of it; only that you were a toddler and, like most children who were adopted at that time, your mother couldn't keep you anymore. It seemed simple enough to me but it's not. It's not simple at all. It's so complicated and awful. I had no idea you both went through all of that. And Granddad too.'

'I don't remember any of it,' Mélodie said. 'It's a past

I'm aware of, but I was only a child. And Adèle became my mother and Theo . . . he became my dad and both were everything to me.'

'God rest his soul,' Adèle said with a smile and glanced up at a picture on the shelf of a late-middle-aged Theo. In it he was standing outside his village GP practice on his last day before he embarked on a long and happy retirement.

But long before that, he'd been a young man, carrying a child out through a Resistance escape network and to safety in England.

Adèle brought Chloé back from her thoughts. 'Everyone did something during the war. Every family has a war history. This is ours,' she said in a matter-of-fact voice. 'Your grandfather was a good man, the best of men. He proposed again not long after we were reunited in London. I found a job as a typist, he had already found a job as a doctor in a London hospital, and Mélodie went to a local school. After a very lengthy process that part of me regretted ever having entered into – I wished we could have just pretended she was ours from the start; I was petrified she'd be taken away from us – we adopted her. Your mum always knew that she was adopted.'

Mélodie nodded as Adèle continued. 'It was when Mélodie was much older we told her the finer details. I always thought the terrible thing is that she could not remember her parents. Nothing at all. I always wondered if she wanted to find out more about her family. But she always maintained she didn't want to.'

'And I meant it,' Mélodie said with a warm smile to Adèle. 'I had a home, loving parents and I knew that whoever they were, my birth parents would have been good people and they would have perished in a camp. And if I did have any other distant relatives, I didn't want to return to live with people I didn't know.'

Adèle smiled at her adopted daughter. 'Whether or not

she went looking was for her to decide and I always told her I'd support her if she wanted to try to find other members of her family, maybe aunts or uncles, if they had survived. But Hitler's sweep of the Jews was so brutal, so brutal. It was always her right to find out their fate if she wanted to. But I am glad she saw herself as mine, as Theo's. Theo and I never minded that we were not blessed with more children. We had Mélodie. As if it was fate. As if it was meant to be. And I was spared accusations of not being her real mother when there were the inevitable teenage arguments, the staying out too late, the panic I displayed when one of her boyfriends arrived to pick her up on a motorcycle. I still remember the heart palpitations I had,' Adèle said, touching her chest and giving Mélodie a knowing look.

Mélodie laughed.

Adèle looked wistfully at her adopted daughter. 'She felt like ours. She became ours. And we were hers.'

Mélodie nodded, walked towards Adèle and planted a kiss on her mother's head.

After her strange and informative afternoon where family history had been shared in a way that had never happened in her presence before, Chloé made her way into central London to meet her sister after she'd finished work for the day. On the train journey over she thought of all the times she'd sat with her gran, going through old photographs, listening avidly to her while she reminisced. But of course it had always been of happier times. Never once had she told her the story of how her mother had been adopted. Never once had she spoken about her history with Chanel and never once about how her granddad had almost been executed by the Gestapo.

Bringing back such memories had been hard for Adèle – Chloé could see that. And there was a huge part of her that regretted asking. But an even bigger part of her that had been so glad she had asked; that she'd had her eyes opened to a part of her own family history of which she'd had no clue.

When Chloé walked into the bar, she saw Ava was already sat on a bar stool at a tall table with a bottle of prosecco in a Champagne bucket.

The women hugged and Chloé hopped onto the other chair as Ava said, 'I took the liberty of pouring a glass and drinking half of it before you arrived. Just to check it was OK, obviously.'

'Obviously.' Chloé laughed as she reached for the bottle and poured herself a healthy measure. 'I need this,' Chloé said as she leant forward and the two clinked glasses. 'Cheers. It's been quite a day.'

'I thought it might be. Did you manage to prise any information out of Gran about her past?' Ava asked.

Chloé laughed a strange, strangulated laugh. 'Oh, Ava, you have no idea,' she said before launching in and telling her sister what she'd found out.

'What?' Ava spluttered when Chloé had finished talking. 'Why have neither Mum nor Gran ever told us this?'

Chloé shrugged. 'Mum didn't seem to think the finer points of her adoption were a big deal, can you believe, and I think Gran wanted to forget.'

'We're even more French than we thought we were,' Ava said thoughtfully after processing everything Chloé had told her.

'And Jewish,' Chloé offered, 'I guess. Even though Mum has always made a point of being agnostic and raising us that way, making our own decisions about religion.'

'Mum's never investigated, dare I say it, her real family?' Ava asked dubiously. 'Never once wanted to know?'

'She says not. Too painful to have the truth about what happened to parents she doesn't remember laid out on a document in black and white, I suppose, if such a document exists. Did the Nazis leave a paper trail when they . . .' Chloé looked into her glass. 'You know.'

'I know,' Ava said. 'I guess I can see why the past is best forgotten – in some instances.'

The women were quiet, thoughtful for a moment, each lost in their own conclusion to a mystery they had neither of them known about.

'Gran says you're stopping by tomorrow,' Chloé said.

'Yes. They're having a tea party in the main lounge. Shame you're not here for that.'

'I'd have loved that. But I've got to get back to work. Brigitte told me to stay here for a while if I needed. But she's in and out of the boutique all the time with a baby in her arms and I can't expect her to do that when I'm being paid to carry the load. She's not even supposed to be at work. I'll be back and forth from Paris to here though so you haven't managed to get rid of me quite yet. Although I'm putting my flat up for rent again and I may even sell it, so I might need to stay with you when I'm going back and forth.'

'Deep joy,' Ava joked. 'In all seriousness, I'm glad you're moving on.'

Moving on. That was exactly what she was doing. Chloé looked at her watch. 'Speaking of which, I have a train to catch. I should run.'

They climbed off their bar stools. Then Ava leant in to hug her sister goodbye. And with her overnight bag in hand, Chloé ran for the tube to take her to the Eurostar and back to Paris.

On the train home, dashing through the Kentish countryside and into the darkness of the tunnel, she thought of returning to Paris, the shop, her little rented flat in the shadow of the Eiffel Tower. And to Etienne. She thought of how much she did actually like him. She had no idea she'd feel this way, that she'd really want to get to know a man like Etienne. He was a juxtaposition, with his pristine suits and casual sweaters, his expensive art gallery and his love for eating market food out of brown paper bags on park benches. He was so different to any man she'd dated before. He messaged when he said he would, was genuinely interested in spending time with her. He was clever, fun, kind, unpredictable, serious, funny. And it turned out she loved that.

At the station, Chloé lugged her overnight bag through the concourse, exited the Eurostar area and dug around inside her wallet to pull out her Metro ticket. She found it and looked up, into the smiling and somewhat nervous-looking face of . . .

'Etienne! What are you doing here?' He was holding a bunch of delicate pale pink roses and giving her a smile so abundant in sincerity that Chloé didn't know what to say.

Eventually she opted for: 'How did you know I'd be here?' *What if he's here for someone else?* Chloé thought and then turned instantly cold.

'You told me you were returning on the Eurostar tonight,' he said.

A stunned Chloé shook her head in disbelief. 'I didn't say what time my ticket was booked though.'

'I know. I have been here . . .' he looked at his watch '. . . quite some time,' he confessed. 'Actually, I have tried to be smooth but I have been here for well over two hours. I was worried you might get an earlier train and then miss my romantic gesture entirely. Are the roses a cliché?' he asked.

'Yes. But I love that,' Chloé said, stepping forward. 'They're perfect. I can't believe you came to meet me at the station.'

'It's not too much?' he asked. 'I wasn't sure.'

She liked this slightly uncertain, vulnerable side of Etienne. She liked it so much she could have kissed him. But was it too soon? What if it was too soon? But he was here, doing this. She'd been so used to no romantic gestures whatsoever from Rob that it was going to take her a long time to shift her mindset, to really understand that there were good men who showed up in stations with flowers. She looked around at the passengers, commuters, people rushing to and from different parts of their busy lives. But she was standing still, here, just for a moment on a busy concourse of Gare du Nord station, with a man she really liked who had been at the station for 'quite some time', holding a bunch of delicate flowers.

Was it fate? Was it fate that she'd met Etienne that day in the auction house? Was it meant to be? Was any of it fate? If so, this part wasn't. Him being here and her deciding what came next. Although she sensed with Etienne what came next would be up to them together.

'This is the most romantic thing anyone's ever done for me,' she said.

'Really?' he said, the relief evident in his voice. 'Thank God. After the first hour I started to rethink this strategy. But not enough to leave.'

'The first hour? How did you kill the time?' Chloé asked.

'I thought about seeing you and I have paced back and forward looking at the arrivals board. And I have drunk a lot of coffee.'

'Really?' What came next wasn't fate. She inched closer towards him and he towards her. And then he dipped his head and gently brushed his lips against hers before kissing her so deeply she could feel the gaze of passers-by trying not to look.

'I couldn't taste coffee,' she whispered when they pulled apart.

He laughed and so did she.

'There has been a lot of coffee. A lot of pacing. A lot of worrying if the flowers are wilting, a lot of worrying you would think this was the most embarrassing thing anyone had ever done to you.'

'And there was me thinking you were so smooth,' Chloé confessed. 'This—' she gestured to him, the roses, the station '—*is* actually smooth. We're so different.' She laughed.

'I don't think we're that different. All I know is that I am very attracted to you and I like spending time with you. And I like you very, very much.'

'Really?' she asked in a small voice, knowing she felt the same way. 'Etienne,' she said. 'I can't work you out.'

'Do you need to work me out?'

'Yes. And no.'

'We have plenty of time to try to work each other out . . . if that is what you want,' he said.

'I do. But we do things so differently,' Chloé suggested.

'Such as?'

'I forget to bring gifts when people invite me for dinner. I forgot to bring one to yours the other night.'

'Yes,' he said, looking thoughtful and then smiling, 'I know. You are a heathen, Chloé.'

She laughed. 'Is that so? I also drink white wine with red meat on occasion. What do you say to that?'

He moved in closer. 'I suspected as much. That is like a knife to my heart. I do not know how I am going to cope with this news. You are right. We are totally, utterly wrong for each other. I should just leave right now.'

He pretended to pull away and she dragged him back towards her.

'Oh no you don't,' she said as they enveloped each other, the flowers held by his side, almost forgotten. 'I'm in the middle of telling you how wrong I am for you. You could at least do me the courtesy of staying put and listening.'

He adopted a mock-serious expression. 'This is a ridiculous

act of self-sabotage and I will not be put off. But if you insist,' he said. 'What else do you have, Chloé? Do your very worst. What else do you want to tell me that will put me off you? Because I think I am too far gone for that.'

She tried to stop laughing, grasped around for something to tease him with. 'I secretly bought that awful antique dog bed in the Ritz auction and I put it in your name. They're delivering it to your apartment tomorrow.'

He moved closer, his lips only a fraction away from hers. He laughed. 'Thank God,' he murmured, 'because I actually really, really wanted it,' and kissed her again.

Epilogue

January 11th 1971

Coco Chanel, Dead in Paris

Yesterday, Gabrielle (Coco) Chanel, one of the finest couturiers of the twentieth century, died in her apartment in the Ritz Paris. She was eighty-seven years old.

Onset with a sudden illness after working to prepare for her latest collection, she took to her bed in the hotel and died, alone, later that night. Her body was discovered by her maid.

The creator of the Little Black Dress had lived in the Ritz in Paris since the 1930s, with a brief hiatus after the Second World War, where she resided in self-imposed exile in Lausanne, Switzerland.

Unmarried and childless, the designer returned to the Ritz in 1954 and gave the remaining years of her life to regenerating her fashion empire.

A full obituary will follow in tomorrow's edition.

Gabrielle (Coco) Chanel: 1883–1971

Adèle folded the newspaper over and held it in her hands for a long time, staring absentmindedly at it before placing it on the coffee table for her husband to read later. She wondered what he would think.

Tomorrow's fish and chip paper. She could hear his words already. All those people who had been pulled into Mademoiselle's life, all those people who had exited it. None had stayed the course. None had lasted.

Everyone seemed to leave her. What would Adèle's life have been like if she had stayed, even one moment longer?

If she had not been strong enough to leave when she knew she had to, if she had accompanied her employer to Switzerland, she would not have found Theo and Mélodie. She would not have grown into the woman she had become. She looked over at her adopted daughter, lounging on the settee, long legs draped over the arm of it, eyes fixed on a book. Mélodie raised her eyes to her mother inquisitively. It was unlike Adèle to sit still for so long.

Over twenty-five years after they were reunited, Mélodie felt more hers now than she'd ever done. More theirs, she thought, hers and Theo's.

The front door banged open and Theo entered with his usual exuberance after a long day at work.

'Did you hear?' he asked. His face held no expression.

Adèle lifted the newspaper from the table and pointed to the article.

'Eighty-seven years old,' he pointed out. 'Is it mad I thought she was actually going to outlive us all?'

Adèle looked back at the article and then at Theo.

'I think in a way,' Adèle said, 'she probably still has.'

Author Note

While Adèle is entirely fictional, the background story of Coco Chanel is not.

In most biographies of her life, Chanel's war years are glossed over; a piece of history forgotten or brushed away. How she lived in the Second World War is divisive and controversial. To some, she's abhorrent. To others, she's a trailblazer, who drew herself up from humble beginnings and paved her own path in life and in fashion. Either way, she's an icon.

Like most of the forgotten pieces of history I often find myself writing about, I was on my usual accidental foray into the recesses of history when I discovered an article professing that Coco Chanel had been a Nazi agent. I confess I blinked a few times in shock as this was news to me and I'm no stranger to history, especially when the Second World War is concerned. But this historical fact had passed me by. How?

And so I clicked and I read, and I read more and I found more articles and I simply couldn't believe what I was reading from different sources. It had always been suggested, very quietly, that Chanel had been aligned with the Nazis. She had, after all, been arrested after the Liberation of Paris and questioned about her suspected Nazi activities. But with no concrete proof the story fizzled out into forgotten history.

But in 2011 documented proof came to light thanks to the work of an ex-US Foreign Service Officer, Hal Vaughan, who I credit here openly. His book *Sleeping with the Enemy: Coco*

Chanel's Secret War formed the basis for the majority of Chanel's plotline in *The Dressmaker's Secret*. If you're spurred to read further, it makes for incredibly interesting reading.

Accidentally stumbling across research is a writer's dream and luckily for Hal Vaughan he discovered many of the missing files that Etienne and Chloé discuss in the novel. And that is why Chanel's real story of her war years only came to light in 2011 on publication of his book. His me-ticulous research led him to missing files scattered across Europe. Pulling one thread led to the unravelling of Chanel's history. After the war, papers had been spread about Europe liberally, perhaps to protect, perhaps to keep them safe out of the reach of various govern-ments . . . just in case they were needed again. Whatever the reason, I'm not sure we'll find out just yet.

And so, thanks to Vaughan's thorough research, I place Coco Chanel in the Ritz and in Madrid and Berlin at the height of the Nazi Occupation of Paris, with senior Nazis, carrying out missions, because this is where she was. The only location I place her where there is no documented evidence of her having been is the Jewish exhibition at the start of *The Dressmaker's Secret*. The documents where she tries to Aryanise her business make for sobering reading and where she is quoted, more often than not, I have tried to use her words where there is evidence she spoke them or wrote them.

There are numerous videos and documentaries available on YouTube where Chanel is happily and loudly anti-Semitic and many of her friends when interviewed outed her as such. But in the novel I have chosen to keep her opinions to herself on many aspects of Nazi ideology. There is a fine line between fictionalising a life and sensationalising one. I hope I haven't crossed that line. But I do hope I've told a story of a largely forgotten piece of the past in the way I usually try to: with real history, a sweeping romance and a huge element of intrigue.

Further reading

Sleeping with the Enemy: Coco Chanel's Secret War, Hal Vaughan, Vintage edition, 2012 (first published 2011)

Coco Chanel: The Legend and the Life, Justine Picardie, HarperCollins, 2010

Les Parisiennes: How the Women of Paris Lived, Loved and Died in the 1940s, Anne Sebba, Weidenfeld & Nicolson, 2016

Americans in Paris: Life and Death under Nazi Occupation 1940–1944, Charles Glass, HarperPress, 2010

Little Book of Chanel, Emma Baxter-Wright, Welbeck, 2020

The World According to Coco: The Wit and Wisdom of Coco Chanel, Jean-Christophe Napias and Patrick Mauriès, Thames & Hudson Ltd, 2020

Doctor to the Resistance: The Heroic True Story of an American Surgeon and his Family in Occupied Paris, Hal Vaughan, Potomac Books, 2004

Acknowledgements

Thanks firstly to my two editors, Rachel Faulkner-Willcocks for brilliantly helping cement the ideas and first structural thoughts for *The Dressmaker's Secret*. Likewise, big thanks to the wonderful Cara Chimirri for taking hold of the manuscript for the second stage of edits and bringing it across the finishing line. And to all the team at Avon for fighting the good fight in marketing and publicity, design, proofreading and all the other things that go on behind the scenes. Thanks also to Helena Newton, the last line of defence, for her ever-forensic copy-editing skills.

Huge thanks, as always, to my agent Becky Ritchie who is a font of wisdom and sage dispenser of advice. My books and I couldn't be in a safer pair of hands.

Steve, Emily, Alice, Luke, Cassie, Mum and Dad. Thanks for being you, being supportive, being there and being brilliant.

Thank you to Sue Lovett, my first reader who has an impressively keen eye for detail and an ability to drill right to the heart of a scene, that never fails to astound me.

To the Write Clubbers: Peter, Nic, Tracy, Sue, Karen and Snoopy, big thanks for the sound advice and monthly meet-ups. Likewise, I've found a huge source of support with fellow authors in the Savvy Writers' Snug, the Romantic Novelists' Association and the two Marks at The Bestseller Experiment Podcast and the BXP Team.

Finally, the biggest thanks of all to you, the reader, for

buying a copy of *The Dressmaker's Secret* or borrowing one from the library. Even though this is my fourth book, it still feels new and fresh and I love nothing more than receiving emails or social media chats with pictures of my books in various languages in readers' hands. What a feeling! If you are one of the lovely readers who's got in touch to say hello, left a review on Amazon to help steer other readers towards one of my books (you have no idea how valuable that is) or posted a pic on Instagram or other social media channels . . . then I give you the biggest and most genuine thanks possible. Find me online and say hello.

Lorna xx

www.lornacookauthor.com
Facebook: /LornaCookWriter
Instagram: /LornaCookAuthor
Twitter: /LornaCookAuthor

Don't miss Lorna Cook's
#1 bestselling debut

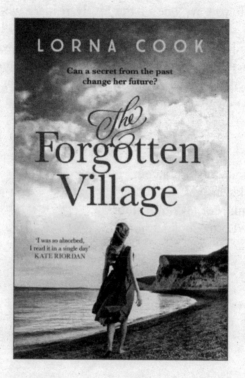

1943. The world is at war, and the villagers of Tyneham must leave their homes behind.

2018. A wartime photograph prompts a visitor to Tyneham to unravel the terrible truth behind one woman's disappearance . . .

Available now

Can one promise change the fate of two women decades apart?

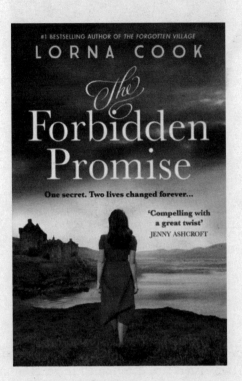

1940. When Constance sees a spitfire crash into her family's loch, she makes a vow that could cost her everything.

2020. Kate discovers Invermoray House has a dark secret, and she can't leave until Constance's mystery is solved.

Available now

A world at war. One woman will risk everything. Another will uncover her story.

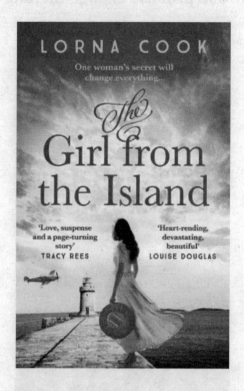

1940: When the island of Guernsey is invaded by the Nazis, two sisters are determined to rebel in any way they can.

2016: Two generations later, Lucy returns to Guernsey after the death of a distant cousin. As she prepares the old family house for sale, Lucy discovers a box of handwritten notes, one word standing out: *resistance*.

A timeless story of love and bravery. Fans of Fiona Valpy and Kate Quinn will be absolutely gripped from the very first page.

Available now.